IN THE HEAT OF THE NIGHT

"Is it all right if I get under the blanket with you?"

Since it hardly made sense to turn him away now, Josie lifted the buffalo spread and guided Daniel between the sheets. Warming himself, Daniel snuggled close to her, making her all too aware that he wore nothing but a pair of woolen drawers. Josie had prepared herself against an attack by the Indian, not an attack on her senses by this man. But it felt good to have him lying next to her again, to be safe and snug in his arms.

"That's better," Daniel said, slipping his arms around her back and waist. "There's nothing like body heat to take the chill out of a fellah." He kissed the braid at her temple. "Your hair is so soft. I can't get enough of it, the way it feels or the way it looks. The red in it reminds me of the sun breaking through a storm cloud. It's such a beautiful, coppery chestnut, it doesn't seem real."

His words were like liquid tremors pouring down Josie's spine, saturating her entire body with a nameless, heated desire. . . .

Books by Sharon Ihle

MAGGIE'S WISH

UNTAMED

Published by Zebra Books

UNTAMED

Sharon Ihle

Zebra Books
Kensington Publishing Corp.
http://www.zebrabooks.com

ZEBRA BOOKS are published by

Kensington Publishing Corp.
850 Third Avenue
New York, NY 10022

Copyright © 1999 by Sharon Ihle

Zebra and the Z logo Reg. U.S. Pat. & TM Off.

First Printing: September, 1999
10   9   8   7   6   5   4   3   2   1

Printed in the United States of America

ACKNOWLEDGMENTS

Special thanks to my invaluable Montana resources: the Saint Labre Indian Mission in Ashland, the Miles City Chamber of Commerce, and the Lame Deer Northern Cheyenne Tribal Headquarters.

PART ONE

I am as free as Nature first made man,
Ere the base laws of servitude began,
When wild in woods the noble savage ran.
—*The Conquest of Granada*
John Dryden

Chapter One

It wasn't as if she'd been caught with her drawers down around her ankles.

True, her skirts were mussed and her hem was raised high enough for an indecent glimpse of her knees. She wasn't exactly sure how the buttons of her blouse had popped open or why the pink ribbon that normally held her chemise together had slipped its bow, exposing most of her left breast, but it was true, sordid as it might be, all too true.

Still, it wasn't as if Josephine Baum had allowed a neighboring rancher's son to mount her and ride her as if she were a wild pony. Fornication led to babies and that led to nothing but backbreaking work and skin so raw it bled. Proof of that lay in the years and years Josie had been caring for her frail mother and her babies, not to mention tending the house in her place. When her mother had passed on some six months before during the stillbirth of what would have been her sixteenth son, Josie swore that she would never allow any man to put her in

the position of raising his endless leavings or risk dying giving
birth to one of them.

Of course, that didn't mean she wasn't curious about the
physical process itself. A gal didn't grow up surrounded by
men of all ages without giving some thought to their little
spigots and all the importance attached to them. She also wondered a great deal about her own God-givens, especially in
relation to the way they fit with that of a male. She didn't,
however, plan to learn about that final puzzlement firsthand.
Josie intended to hang on to her virginity until her dying day.

In the meantime she didn't see the harm in finding out all
she could about sex—short of committing the hurdy-gurdy, as
she and her brothers referred to the act. That was why she'd
invited poor Henry to step into the barn. Unfortunately, he'd
barely gotten the chance to kiss her and fondle her breasts a
little before her stepfather happened across them in the hayloft.
She expected Peter Baum to be shocked and perhaps a little
angry, of course, but never in her wildest dreams could Josie
have imagined his extreme reaction at finding her in such a
state.

She had long suffered her overly zealous stepfather's belief
that sparing the rod spoiled the child. She also knew why her
fourteen stepbrothers tasted their father's switch with far more
frequency than she did—Baum wasn't about to risk serious
injury to the only female and therefore slave in a house filled
with men of all ages.

Or so she had thought.

When Peter stumbled across Josie and Henry ''in the damning heat of rut,'' as he put it, he fired a load of buckshot at
poor Henry's backside as he ran off, then turned his self-
righteous wrath and hickory switch on Josie. The beating she
received was unmerciful, leaving welts across her back, bottom,
and thighs, along with more than a couple of patches of broken
skin. Brutal, yes, but not so bad as to break her, spiritually or
physically.

What happened less than ten minutes after the beating, however, was nearly Josie's undoing.

Taking no more care than he would have given a sack of potatoes, Peter flung her into the back of the supply wagon, then drove to Miles City. Instead of taking his usual route and skirting the saloons and unseemly businesses along the way, he drove straight toward them, pulling up at a place called Lola's Saloon and Pleasure Palace.

After that shocking turn, Josie's stepfather dragged her out of the wagon and tossed her through the front door of Lola's, shouting loudly enough for everyone in the county to hear that she was a fornicating Jezebel who belonged among her own kind. Washing his hands of her, Peter Baum then returned to the wagon and took off for his ranch with never a look back.

It took a minute for Josie to realize that she'd been turned out by her own family, shunned. When that shock wore off, she saw that several erring sisters who worked at the pleasure house had gathered around to have a look and a giggle at her expense. A few actually offered condolences, but Josie took little comfort in the gestures. At that point, her pride stung a whole lot more than her backside. It wasn't until Lola herself came to Josie's aid that she finally saw her ultimate humiliation for what it really was—freedom. A chance to make something of herself, on her own.

But for the toss of God's coin, she'd have been born male— a four letter word that meant *free*. Now it looked as if Peter Baum had accidentally righted that fateful coin by forcing her to find her own way in the world. Hell, she might even try cattle ranching, a lofty dream for a gal alone, but one that had sparkled in her mind like a distant star since she was knee-high to a steer.

As for the matter of obtaining that goal while her good name lay in tatters, Josie could only hope and pray for the sympathy of others. Besides, how could working in a whorehouse harm her reputation any more than it had already suffered at the hands of her no-account bastard of a stepfather?

Chapter Two

Northern Cheyenne Reservation

To Daniel McCord's way of thinking, a man wasn't much of a man if he couldn't admit his mistakes and then take the necessary steps to correct them. Rectifying his father's poor judgment was what Daniel had in mind some seven years before when he first set out to find his mother, whom he hadn't seen since he was six years old. He'd located her people, the Northern Cheyenne Indians, only to learn that she'd died during the tribe's bold escape from the hated reservation in Oklahoma, where they'd been forced to live.

Five years after that futile escape, the government finally sent down an executive order proclaiming a quarter million acres of their former homelands in southeastern Montana as property of the Northern Cheyenne tribe. An army scout at the time, Daniel was offered the head job at the new Tongue River Agency. Still trying to right his father's wrong, he accepted the assignment. Back then he also thought it would be a good idea to rehabilitate and educate his Cheyenne brother-in-law,

Long Belly, with thoughts of turning him into an accomplished representative of his people.

Now Daniel wished to hell that he'd never returned to his mother's tribe or tried to help them out. If he hadn't, he wouldn't know the frustration of having reservation lands stolen by the very same government that had allotted them, and wouldn't have watched helplessly as the Cheyenne's deep sense of honesty made them easy prey for dishonest whites. Even Daniel's own Irish fur-trader father, Michael, shamelessly defrauded the Indians, this despite the fact that his only son was the product of his short-lived liaison with a Cheyenne woman.

Daniel supposed his father's culpability in helping to eradicate the buffalo was the driving force behind his decision to help rehabilitate the tribe. He'd even tried to convince Michael to join him in that effort, but all he got for his efforts was a lot of name-calling and curses. The old man took off for Canada shortly after that, and Daniel hadn't seen hide nor hair of him since.

His problems today were of the opposite kind. Not only was Long Belly grateful for the efforts on behalf of the Cheyenne nation, he was slowly driving Daniel out of his mind with his mulish determination to repay what he saw as an eternal debt—the fact that thanks to Daniel's efforts, his tribe might become self-sufficient again through cattle ranching.

What Long Belly and the others didn't know was that Daniel not only hated the sight, smell, and thought of cattle, he didn't know any more about raising them than the Indians did. Now, thanks to his stupid plan, a spooky heifer, and his inability to get those damned cattle to follow his orders, Daniel had a broken leg, which pretty much left him helpless. Long Belly, smelling yet another way to repay the Cheyenne debt, insisted on living with him in order to tend his needs—a situation that left Daniel completely at his brother-in-law's mercy.

For the past four days, thank God, the crazy Indian had been gone, off on yet another insane search for the last surviving buffalo. Although no one had seen a live bison in the Territories for better than two years now, this thickheaded issue of his mother's half sister insisted that a lone bull still roamed the surrounding hills. If that were true, Daniel would be a happy man at last—free of the guilt and obligation he felt thanks to the fact that he and his father had been right in the thick of the last few buffalo hunts.

But it couldn't be true, which meant that Long Belly's plan was sheer fantasy. The buffalo were gone, they weren't coming back, and yet the stubborn Indian was set on the task and couldn't be dissuaded. Although Daniel would much rather have him working on his English lessons, at least Long Belly's fruitless quest gave Daniel a few days of peace and quiet now and then.

Today wasn't one of those days.

As much as Daniel normally enjoyed his solitude, there was a certain value in having someone around during his long recuperation period. Since he needed both of his hands to grip his crude wooden crutches, he couldn't hunt, cook, or even empty his own damn slop pail, which was full. All of that would just have to wait for Long Belly's return. Daniel couldn't.

After a slow and painful trip out of the cabin and down the stairs, he no longer had the time or the inclination to make the journey down to where the privy sat. The temperature had dropped dramatically from what it was a day or two ago and the wind had kicked up, chilling Daniel through to the marrow of his aching shinbone. The cold felt good after the unusually warm spring and blistering hot days of summer, but the frigid air made the urge to urinate unbearable.

In a big hurry now, Daniel dragged himself across the fifteen feet of dirt separating the house from a scraggly pine, propped his crutches against the tree, and quickly opened his trousers. The first rush of water had barely hit the ground before he realized that he wasn't alone. Someone or something was behind him.

Unable to stop the torrent, Daniel whirled around in mid-stream, spraying the legs of his buckskin trousers and bare feet, and came face-to-face with Long Belly.

The Cheyenne stood in the clearing like a great apparition,

his feet spread apart, the flaps of his great buffalo robe raised high, swept out along his sides like the wings of an eagle. Long Belly quickly glanced from Daniel's surprised expression, to his still unbuttoned trousers, and finally to his wet feet.

Then he smiled and said, "So, my brother—is it your plan to attract a mother for your sons this way, or is this how you wash your feet in my absence?"

Daniel adjusted his clothing, then grabbed his crutches, waving one of them at Long Belly as if it were a bludgeon. "I ought to beat you to a pile of dumpling dust for putting a scare on me that way. Now I've got to wash out these pants, which means I'm also going to have to cut up another pair to make room for this damn fool splint."

Long Belly's playful expression sobered. "I have been rude and do not deserve your friendship. What can I do to bring peace to your mind again. A gift, perhaps?"

"No, dammit." Daniel shoved the crutches into his armpits and started for the cabin. "No gifts and no favors—unless you've got a big fat steak in your pocket. I'm sick to death of salt pork and dried-up beans."

Long Belly surprised him by reaching into the folds of his buffalo robe and producing a fat rabbit. "How is this? He should make a tasty pot of stew for us to share."

"A rabbit, huh?" Daniel laughed from over his shoulder as he made his way inside the house. "I thought for sure you'd be bringing us back some buffalo steaks. What happened? Did your elusive ghost bison fade away again with the fog?"

"These eyes have yet to see a buffalo." If Daniel had offended him, Long Belly's tone did not betray those feelings. "But I know the great one is out there waiting for me. He is clever and hides from all white men and Indians, but he is no ghost. I saw this beast in a dream."

There was no dissuading the man when it came to his dreams. Daniel ignored the comment and made his way to the bed. By now his shinbone was pounding like a war drum. Daniel rolled onto his back and propped the broken leg up on the good one.

Long Belly wandered throughout cabin sniffing the air.

"What happened in here during my absence? Did something crawl under your bed and die?"

Daniel couldn't detect an unusually foul odor, but then he'd been stuck inside so long, even the stench of a dead skunk would have grown on him by now. If he'd had two good legs under him, he probably would have taken out the garbage sooner and cleaned up after himself a little better. And that gave him a pretty good idea where the odor might be coming from.

"Maybe if you'd stayed here and dumped the slop pail instead going off chasing ghosts, your delicate nose wouldn't be so damned offended."

"I do *not* chase ghosts." Long Belly swung the rabbit onto the table, then headed for the pungent pail. "We owe you much, but this preparing of the food and tending to your wastes is woman's work, not fit for a great warrior."

He stopped just short of raising the bucket off the floor. Then he turned to Daniel, a sudden thought shining in his dark eyes. "Perhaps I should make you a gift of my sister, Owl Face. She would make a fine mother to your sons and an obedient wife."

"Oh, no, you don't."

It wasn't that Daniel hadn't thought of marrying again, but having one Cheyenne wife had been nearly enough to send him back to the isolation of a mountain man's way of life. Although he'd found some pleasure in Tangle Hair's company during the short time they were together, and the union had produced a pair of beautiful twin sons, living with the woman had been an even bigger trial for Daniel than having her arrogant Cheyenne brother as a roommate. When a burst appendix claimed Tangle Hair's life less than two years after the birth of the boys, Daniel's grief had been tempered by an almost equal sense of relief.

If marrying again had an attraction, it was the chance for his sons to come live with him again. Due to their tender years and the fact that Daniel's job took him away from the ranch for extended periods, the twins had been living with their mother's family on the reservation since her death. Although he visited the boys regularly, Daniel missed them and couldn't wait until they were old enough to join him again. Still, it wasn't worth the risk of marrying Owl Face or anyone from her tribe. Cheyenne women were strongly opinionated and so highly regarded by the tribe, it seemed as if they, and not the chiefs, ran the camps. On more than one occasion, Daniel had seen a man chased from his own lodge by his club-wielding wife or her mother. Sometimes by both. Once Tangle Hair had even gone after him with a cooking pot simply because he'd complained about her stew. Daniel's mother had been even worse, according to his father.

Glaring at Long Belly, making sure he understood, he said, "I'd just as soon marry a grizzly as another of your sisters."

The Cheyenne nodded solemnly. "I remember your troubles with Tangle Hair and understand why you do not wish to accept Owl Face as your wife. Perhaps you would be more pleased if I found a white woman for you this time, someone from your father's people?"

Daniel burst out laughing. "That's one hell of a fine idea, brother. I'm sure that any self-respecting white woman would beg you for the chance to come live with a half-breed like me and his two motherless sons, especially in the middle of an Indian Reservation. Yessir, you'd probably have to beat them off with a war club."

Again he laughed, sure that Long Belly would see the folly of such an idea and join in. He didn't. Instead the Cheyenne took a long, hard look at Daniel, then flashed a stoical smile and headed out the door, slop pail in hand.

"Long Belly?" Daniel called after him. "I'm kidding, you know. You do know that, right?"

No response save the whistle of the wind.

"Long Belly? When I'm ready for another wife, I'll round her up myself, dammit." Daniel cocked his ear toward the silence. "You hear me, Long Belly?"

Sharon Ihle

* * *

Seventy miles north and two days later, Josie finished folding the laundry for the night and headed for the kitchen to make a sandwich for herself before the evening crowd began to arrive. As she made her way down the stairs, she pondered her situation and the likelihood that it would change for the worse once Lola got back from burying her mother in Denver.

It wasn't exactly Josie's idea of freedom, this business of scrubbing the soiled sheets and bedclothes of fancy women and their customers. Then again, it wasn't as insufferable as taking endless orders from an overbearing stepfather or cleaning up the dirty diapers of his progeny. In addition, she'd managed to learn a few more things about the goings-on between men and women, up to and including a peek at a couple in the throes of the hurdy-gurdy. Enough of a glimpse, anyway, to convince Josie that staying a virgin was the correct choice.

Best of all, no one at Lola's seemed to think she ought to step into the kitchen and fix them some grub. If she never again had to face a slab of raw beef or crack another egg over a sizzling skillet, Josie figured it'd still be too soon.

The problems would begin when Lola returned and insisted that she move into one of the upstairs bedrooms to start earning her keep in earnest. Josie had hoped that day wouldn't come before she was good and ready to light out on her own—a day that would be long in coming if she didn't find some financial backing or a partner, and soon. She'd been at the pleasure palace just short of two weeks now, time enough to earn her keep and a few toiletries, but precious little else. So far the upstairs ladies had been good about lending her the essentials, especially Sissy, a dark-skinned girl of undetermined origins who had lent her a clean dress and a frilly, if slightly immodest, nightgown. Nice, but Josie would just as soon have had a tough pair of denims and a thick flannel shirt. What she needed even more than clothing was money.

Fretting over ways of getting her hands on some cash without dirtying them in the bargain, she made her way down the stairs and turned on the landing to head for the kitchen. About that same time the front door to the pleasure palace suddenly banged open and in strode a wild Indian.

The savage was wrapped in a great buffalo robe and wore a bright red scarf around his throat. His shiny black hair hung down across his chest in braids, and a pair of eagle feathers flopped about from their anchor at the back of his head. Light from Lola's gaudy red chandelier reflected bloody beams across his high cheekbones, painting his cinnamon skin with eerie stripes of glittering war paint.

Terror-struck as memories of her family's fateful journey out West washed over her, Josie froze on the bottom step of the staircase, one white-knuckled hand clasped to the balustrade, the other fisted and shoved into her mouth. Everything seemed to stand still or move at one-tenth its normal speed. Time, the way the Indian moved, even his words, which sounded as if they were spoken through a tunnel of mud, all came to her with agonizing slowness.

"I come to buy a woman," said the savage, slapping a few coins on the counter. "I am told you sell them."

Marabelle Pickle, an aging whore who was Lola's first in command during her absence, looked up at her visitor in surprise, not with the terror Josie felt.

"That's right, injun," she said saucily. "But we ain't allowed to do no business with your kind. You'd best skedaddle on out of here."

After the Indian tossed a couple more coins on the counter, he whipped an axe out of his robe and buried it in the desk top. Marabelle shrieked as the weapon *cracked* into the cheap pine. When she looked up at the savage again, the proper terror shone in her eyes as she said, "C-course, if you insist . . ."

"I do." The Indian glanced around the room, which was deserted except for Josie, and settled his gaze on her. "Why does this woman have a spotted face? Is she sick?"

Marabelle giggled a little. "She's the healthiest one here. Them's just freckles, injun. I reckon your kind don't get freckles."

"Freckles?" After another long look at Josie, he turned back to Marabelle and said, "I will take her. Is this the right price?"

The worn-out whore didn't even count the coins. She nodded rapidly, then turned to Josie and said, "Take him up to room number three, and don't give him or me no argument about it."

Josie opened her mouth in protest. She wanted to scream, to gasp, to holler, to do *something,* but she couldn't speak or even think straight. In fact, she could hardly breathe. She felt as if she were a child of three again, a terrified mute watching the Indians approach the wagon train, hiding silently as they attacked and brutally murdered her father and brother.

The Indian in the whorehouse glanced at her again. "Tell this spotted-face woman that I want her to come to me now. I will take her with me."

"Take her with you?" Although Marabelle pretty much hated the sight of Josie and often complained that she wasn't doing her share around the place, especially upstairs, she came to her defense. "You can't take that girl out of here. We got plenty a nice rooms upstairs for you to do your business in."

"My business with you is finished. I have paid for the spotted-face woman, and now I will take her with me." He pulled the axe out of the desk and brandished it at Marabelle. "Yes?"

She nodded. "Yessir, whatever you say."

Josie screamed. At least in her mind she did. Her mouth was a perfect circle, but nothing came out of it, not even as the big brute started for her. The three-year-old child inside her trembled as he drew near, but she could do nothing to stop him as he picked her up and slung her over his shoulder. As he turned to walk away, he paused in mid-stride, his attention diverted by something at the top of the stairs.

Sissy's voice floated down from above, as calm as always, a perfect monotone. "What do you figure on doing with her?"

"I have bought this woman. She is mine."

Footfalls sounded on the stairs, and the next thing Josie knew, her only friend in the world was standing right beside her. She twisted her neck and angled her head, straining to get a glimpse of Sissy. She held the awkward pose long enough to see the Indian reach out with his free hand and touch Sissy's great tumbleweed of dark brown hair. Then Josie collapsed face first against the back of his pungent robe.

"How much for this one?" the Indian asked.

Marabelle sputtered a moment before saying, "Ah . . . that one ain't for sale."

The Indian turned so quickly that Josie's face whisked across the buffalo fur as if she were a human broom, kicking up particles of dirt that smelled like old socks.

"I will have her, too. How much?" the savage repeated as he strode over to the desk.

"The usual, Marabelle," said Sissy, joining them. "It will be easier for her if I'm there, too."

Upside down as she was, Josie couldn't actually see her friend, but she took some comfort in the sight of Sissy's purple satin slippers.

Marabelle grumbled a little, but didn't argue. "Suit yourself, but Lola ain't gonna like it one bit. This one'll cost you five bucks, injun."

As the Indian counted out more coins, Sissy's purple slippers turned and started for the stairs.

The savage stopped her in mid-stride. "We go now."

"Go?" The slippers hesitated, then turned. "What's he mean by that, Marabelle?"

"He says he don't want no room here, that you got to go with him somewheres."

A giddy sense of relief swept through Josie as those satin shoes strolled back within spitting distance.

"Where are we going?" Sissy wanted to know.

"To a lodge in the mountains. Come, we must go now."

This time when the Indian turned around and started for the door, Josie's head swung out and connected with the edge of the desk. Her captor didn't stop or slow down, even though surely he realized what he'd done. She rubbed the lump at the back of her head and glanced at the floor again, hoping against all hope to find the purple slippers following her out the door.

All Josie saw was the spot she'd missed while moping the floor this morning, a palm-sized area of dust that seemed to represent her chances of living through the night as the captive of a crazed Indian.

It had been foolish to think for one minute that the dark-skinned prostitute would follow her and the savage. Just because Sissy was the only one in the entire place with the exception of Lola who'd shown Josie a moment's kindness, it didn't mean that she would also risk her life in the name of friendship. After all, lending a nightgown was hardly on the same level as following a crazed hostile to his lair. But that didn't stop Josie from hoping for the impossible.

As the savage slipped out the door and into the night, he paused, apparently waiting for his second purchase to join him. After several moments passed and she still hadn't appeared, the Indian continued on his way.

Sissy wasn't coming. Josie knew that now. She was alone, at the mercy of a brutal savage, the kind of man who'd killed most of her family, then terrorized her mother so badly that the poor woman was never the same again. Sick enough of mind anyway to wed the tyrannical Peter Baum and let him run her into the ground.

As she thought about her mother and the despair that had never left her eyes until the day she died, Josie suddenly found the courage to fight for her freedom. And with it, she found her voice.

Kicking her legs against her captor's grip and beating her fists on his back as hard as she could, she screamed, "Let me go, you no-account, murdering savage! You let me go this instant, or I swear—"

The savage abruptly released her. He dropped her so fast, in fact, that Josie didn't have a chance to react or to break her fall.

She hit the ground head-first, and then she screamed no more.

Chapter Three

When Josie finally came around, she didn't know where she was or what had happened to her. It was dark, suffocatingly so beneath an old blanket that stank of sour horse sweat. Despite the smelly covering, she was cold and clammy all over, and her head hurt. The frigid floor felt as if it were moving beneath her, floating. Something *thumped* against her right ear, followed immediately by the muffled trickle of water. She was on a boat of some kind. Then she remembered the vicious savage who'd dragged her out of the pleasure palace. Her future suddenly looked grim, as bleak as her stepfather's soul.

Gripped with fear, Josie slowly inched her head up in hopes of catching a furtive glimpse of her captor. A rough hand immediately shoved her back down against the floor.

"Don't move," came Sissy's voice in a harsh whisper. "It'll go better for us if he thinks we're sleeping."

"Oh, praise God, you *did* follow me." It was a struggle, but Josie managed to keep from shouting with joy as she realized that her only friend in the world was lying right beside her. "I was afraid that you'd changed your mind, and that I'd be belly up and half rotted before anyone came looking for me."

"I didn't exactly come looking for you." Sissy snuggled closer, sharing her body heat. "That Indian came back for me when I ran upstairs to get us a couple of dressing gowns for later."

"Dressing gowns?" In her horror, Josie forgot to whisper. "What the hell do we want with them?"

"Hush up. As long as the boat is moving, I figure it's best that we ain't. Once this fellah gets us where he aims to take us is damn well soon enough to have to put up with him."

Josie grumbled under her breath. "I'm not putting up with anything else from that savage. I'll kill myself first."

"I don't see that we got much choice. We're somewheres out in the middle of the Tongue River. I cain't swim. Can you?"

An excellent point. Josie thought back to the fierce-looking Indian and the axe he'd buried in the desk. She shuddered, and not from the cold.

"You put up with that savage if you want to," she whispered, "but if the posse hasn't caught up with us by the time this boat stops, I'm making an escape."

"What posse?" Sissy uttered a muted snort. "We ain't got a prayer of having the law riding out after us, princess."

"B-but we've been kidnapped, taken against our will by a wild Indian. The law *has* to come looking for us."

"There isn't a man alive, much less one with a badge pinned to his shirt, that's gonna risk his neck chasing after a couple of whores who went missing in the night. You might as well get that idea right out of your head."

Without pausing to think how her words might affect Sissy, Josie blurted out, "But I'm not a whore. They at least have to come looking for me, don't they?"

Sissy took her time before answering. When she did, there wasn't a hint of mirth in her tone. "You work in a whorehouse, princess, remember? As far as everyone but you is concerned, you're just another bitch who can be bought, beaten, raped, or even killed. No one gives a damn what happens to you now. I'm not even sure that I do."

The words stung, but they also echoed in Josie's mind throughout the long boat ride. Once they were on dry land again, the savage made sure she couldn't escape by binding her hands and flinging her fork-legged across the bony back of a mule. He then led the pack animal, with Sissy mounted behind him on his horse, on a miserable trek through the mountains. If there was any hope of escaping from this nightmare, it would have to be after they reached their destination. Josie also realized by then that she would have to come up with a plan on her own. The law wouldn't be coming to her rescue and Sissy couldn't be counted on either.

Josie didn't know yet how she would regain her freedom, but she did know one thing—she hadn't escaped a life of bondage on the Baum farm, not to mention life as a prostitute, just to become the slave of a bloodthirsty Indian. She would be free again at the first opportunity—even if it meant hanging herself.

At the cabin, Daniel woke up with a start. Either he'd been dreaming or he'd heard the sound of his horse trumpeting the return of his companions—Long Belly's mount and a pack mule. Against Daniel's express wishes, the animals and the stubborn Cheyenne had disappeared the morning after they'd returned from the buffalo hunt. Long Belly wouldn't tell him where he was going, but Daniel doubted that he was off on yet another pointless search for a phantom bison. It was far more likely that the fool had gone after an even more elusive quarry— a white woman willing to accompany him to a remote mountain cabin so she could care for the even bigger fool who shared his ancestry. Irritated as he was by the fact that he'd been left to fend for himself again, Daniel had to chuckle at the thought of his brother-in-law actually finding such a woman.

He glanced out the window, figuring he still had a couple hours left before sundown, then began to coax his useless body toward the edge of the bed. Chores that had once taken only a few minutes now took hours or even days. If he didn't drag

himself out to the barn now and take care of the animals for
the night, Daniel knew he'd be warming up his supper in the
dark. A handicap he didn't need considering he could barely
manage in full daylight.

He'd just heaved his splinted leg over the side of the mattress,
and was sitting there sweating from both pain and exertion,
when Daniel heard the rumble of footsteps on the porch. Too
many footsteps to signify the return of one misguided Indian.
Cursing the fact that the awkward position he'd gotten into
made it impossible to reach his rifle, he grabbed the only weapon
at hand—the Bowie knife he always wore strapped to his waist.
About that same time the door swung open. Brandishing his
knife, Daniel twisted around and saw that Long Belly stood on
the threshold, framed by the sun.

"I have returned," said the man he called brother. "I bring
with me the gift I promised."

With that startling announcement, he gave a tug and pulled
someone into the cabin with him. It took a moment for Daniel's
vision to adjust to the blinding afternoon sunlight, but when it
did, he nearly fell off the bed in surprise.

Not only did Long Belly have a white woman with him, she
was dressed in a demure gown of lemon-yellow calico. Her
russet-colored hair, sparkling with a coppery sheen where the
sun kissed it, was twisted into a long braid that hung down
over her shoulder. She was in the prime of life, not at all used
up, and even more surprising, she wasn't what Daniel would
call hard to look at. Mercy. How the hell had Long Belly
convinced such a woman to accompany him onto an Indian
Reservation?

Almost the minute he asked himself that question, the Cheyenne dragged her further into the room. Daniel saw then that
the lady's hands were clasped at her waist, tied together at the
wrists by a thick ribbon of red satin. She was Long Belly's
prisoner. What had the damn fool done—kidnapped a farmer's
wife?

"Go to my brother, Daniel-Two-Skins," said Long Belly,
giving the woman a shove. She stumbled and nearly fell over

the pile of discarded clothing Daniel had shed yesterday. "Let him look upon your spotted face."

The woman squared her shoulders, as proud as any Cheyenne chief, and approached the foot of the bed. Too shocked to say anything yet, Daniel looked her over, noting that her eyes were a lustrous brown, the same shade as the agate hanging from the rawhide strip he wore around his neck. Even without the sun to highlight it, her hair was a rich shade of mahogany he'd never seen before, and her ivory skin was sprinkled with freckles. He also noticed that her expression wasn't nearly as enchanting as her features. Her jaw was set with hatred and a certain helpless terror pinched her mouth.

Daniel smiled, trying to ease the poor woman's anxiety.

Her expression remained unchanged.

"Hello," he murmured softly. "The Cheyenne call me Daniel-Two-Skins because I'm a half-breed, but I'm known in the Territories as Daniel McCord. What's your name?"

"Josic Baum." She glared at him with those beautiful agate-hard eyes. "That's the name of the woman the posse will be looking for when they come gunning for you and this savage."

Alarmed, Daniel shifted his gaze to Long Belly. "What did you do? Raise her up from another man's trap?"

"I am no a thief. I bought her as my gift to you."

"Bought me?" The woman shot a wary glance at Long Belly, then turned her wrath on Daniel. "That's just not true. He kidnapped me, knocked me senseless, then dragged me up here against my will. If someone doesn't take me back to Miles City this minute, the law will come gunning for the both of you, no questions asked."

Daniel shot Long Belly a serious, inquisitive look, all the prompting the man needed to defend himself.

"She lies. I bought this spotted-face woman from the House-That-Sells-Women. My coins were accepted. This female and her friend belong to us now."

"Her friend?" Daniel sat up a little straighter, straining his aching leg. "You bought two women?"

"There is another," Long Belly admitted. "She is a dark

female with the hair of a buffalo. She is in the barn tending to the horses.''

When the logic behind this hit him, it was all Daniel could do to keep from laughing out loud. Near as he could figure, Long Belly had gone to a whorehouse with the understanding that he could buy women there as slaves rather than for a few moments of pleasure. How he'd gotten away with such a brazen scheme was beyond Daniel, but he was, in a way, impressed.

''I'm sure you meant well, but I'm afraid you've made a big mistake. These women''—Daniel glanced at Josie, thinking she didn't fit his idea of a prostitute in the least—''can be bought all right, but it's just for a few hours or maybe the night. They sell their sexual favors, not themselves. Do you understand?''

As Long Belly pondered this custom, the woman beside him found her tongue again.

''We tried to tell him that back at Lola's, but he wouldn't listen. He attacked the place with an axe and scared us all half to death. You've got to make him take us back.''

''You will hold your tongue and do as you are told,'' said Long Belly.

She turned to him, shoulders trembling, and shrank back a few steps.

''You will tend to Daniel-Two-Skins now,'' Long Belly went on to say. ''As you can see, he needs much help. I will go see what is keeping your friend in the barn.''

With that he turned on his moccasined heel and stalked out of the cabin.

Josie followed his departure until the savage closed the door behind him. Then she breathed a tiny sigh of relief. At least her captor hadn't claimed her for his own. Not that knowing she ''belonged'' to the loathsome heap of man lying on the bed made her feel a whole lot better about her predicament.

She thought this Daniel-Two-Skins might be a mountain man of sorts, given the scraggly beginnings of a beard and unruly, shoulder-length hair. Both were as black as coal, tangled and unkempt, looking as if he'd used the blade of a dull axe to groom himself—if he ever did. Although it wasn't much reassurance, his startling Irish-blue eyes did seem to prove the fact that he was at least half white. What little she could see of his skin through the hair and buckskin clothing was darker than her own, a warm nutmeg.

Josie glanced up to see that he was staring at her, watching her with those bright, curious eyes as she studied him. It made her feel as if he might be imagining all the wicked things he wanted her to do to his odious body throughout the night. Nervous under the man's unrelenting stare and evil thoughts, Josie turned her attention to the cabin itself.

Lethargy and a modest loft hung over the large one-room dwelling, making it feel much smaller than it was, more like a trap than a home. It was a shambles of a place, with two wobbly-looking chairs, a floor that was more dirt than wood, a mound of unwashed kettles and plates, and a vast assortment of boots and articles of men's clothing scattered from one end of the floor to the other. The air smelled vaguely of wood smoke and stale urine. Not so unlike the atmosphere at Lola's Pleasure Palace.

"Josie?" Daniel said, startling her. "Don't be afraid of me or Long Belly. Neither of us means you harm."

This comment in no way relieved her fears. She knew firsthand how cruel and vicious Indians could be, and as far as she could tell, the savage who'd kidnapped her was no different from any other. If this man was, as he claimed, a half brother to the savage, Josie doubted that he was much more civilized.

She speared him with the most vicious gaze she could manage. "I'll see you both hang for this if you don't make that Indian take us back to Miles City soon."

"Long Belly will take you back all right, but not until tomorrow." He sighed heavily. "In the meantime, I'd sure appreciate it if you'd help me lift my leg back onto the bed. It's killing me."

Josie rather hoped that it would. She didn't move.

Daniel stared back at her, impressed by her gumption, misguided though it might have been. While he did mean to make sure that she and her friend were returned to their people, he didn't see any harm in making use of her services until then, especially since Long Belly had already paid for at least that much. In fact, it could be argued that she owed him a little of her time.

"If this is the best you can do," he said softly. "I might as well turn you over to Long Belly for the night. You're not a hell of a lot of use to me."

Her eyes flared and Josie lost her obstinate stance. "I'm not a nurse," she said, sounding much less defiant. "I don't know the first thing about broken legs and such."

"You don't have to," Daniel assured her. "Just get on over here and help me lift it onto the bed."

She moved grudgingly, but finally reached the edge of the mattress and held out her bound wrists.

"How am I supposed to help you with my hands tied?"

Daniel leaned up long enough to remove the binding, a satin sash that looked as if it had come from a fine dressing gown. He caught himself wondering if it was a gown she wore when plying her trade, then imagined her nude beneath the slick satin.

"Now what?" she asked.

Suddenly more interested in her than his injury, Daniel collapsed against his pillow and grinned. "I'll leave that up to you."

Apparently missing the innuendo, she got down on her knees, took his injured limb into her hands as if she were hefting a sack of sugar, and then flung it onto the mattress.

Daniel yowled in pain. "Damn it all, woman! Can't you see that leg is broken?"

"I told you I wasn't a nurse, didn't I?"

Beads of sweat were rolling down his brow, his teeth clenched against the pain, when the cabin door opened. Long Belly came into the room with a second woman following along behind him.

"Ah, brother," he said, kicking the door shut. "See how dutifully my gift tends you? I have chosen well, have I not?"

Daniel grumbled under his breath, in too much agony to risk speaking yet.

"This is my woman," Long Belly announced, dragging her up to the foot of the bed. "She is called Sissy."

Daniel looked her over, his grimace fading as he made out her unusual features. "She's a little different, even for you."

With a sudden grin, Long Belly patted Sissy's full head of tight curls. "She wears the great mane of a buffalo, and so may carry within her its spirit. I am thinking of taking her to my people in a few days and making a gift of her. I will call her Buffalo Hair."

The newly christened "Buffalo Hair" turned to him with a frown, but said nothing.

"What is your tribe, Buffalo Hair? I do not recognize it in you."

She gave him a blank look in return.

"Who are your people?"

Daniel laughed, then clarified the situation for Long Belly. "Africans, I would say, along with a little something else. Am I right, darling?"

The dark-skinned prostitute turned her frown on Daniel. "My mother whored same as me," she said in a monotone. "She didn't rightly know who or what that little something else was, and neither do I."

Long Belly scratched his head. "Africans? Who are these people? Where do they roam?"

"If you'd paid more attention to the lessons I've been trying to teach you," said Daniel, "then you'd know where Africa is. It's a whole different continent. Your woman's people are not from around these parts."

"Africa?" Long Belly looked her over again, then shrugged. "She is here now, she will be called Buffalo Hair, and she will do as I say."

"Good. Then send her to the stove." Daniel patted his growling belly. "I'm so hungry, I swear I can feel the weight falling off of me as I lay here. I could really go for some nice fluffy biscuits, a little gravy to dump over them, and . . . what kind of grub do we have left in the smokehouse, Long Belly?''

''A barrel of pork,'' he said, ''a couple of hams, and an elk roast.''

Daniel licked his lips and moaned. ''It all sounds good to me. Why don't we let the women decide, since they're the ones who have to cook it?''

The dark-skinned whore shook her fluffy head. ''I've been trained to do only one thing, and it ain't fixing grub. I don't know any more about frying pans than I do about having tea out of fine china.''

Josie, who'd been happy to listen, not join this conversation, watched as Long Belly and Daniel both turned to her expectantly. Savages or not, this was one area in which she couldn't be persuaded by Satan himself. She'd starve herself to death before becoming the galley slave of these two. Careful to avoid both men's eyes, she set out for one of the two chairs at the small table. Thanks to the long ride astride the back of a mule, her thighs were bruised and her bottom felt as if she'd taken a beating, but she managed to hobble across the room without drawing comment from either man. Taking care with her tender bottom, she eased onto the sturdiest chair, then stared out the window at the barn and the sparse forest beyond. She shivered against the cold, mildly longing for the smelly horse blanket.

''I wouldn't bother with getting too comfortable, Josie.'' Daniel was the first to address her. ''While Long Belly is out getting supplies, you and your friend ought to be stoking up that fire. You're going to need a nice hot stove to bake up a decent batch of biscuits.''

Purging herself of as much fear as possible, Josie swallowed the truth as if it were a dose of salts and lied through her teeth. ''I won't be baking up biscuits or anything else. I don't know how to cook.''

She didn't dare turn around to see how this information was received, but she could hear plenty of grumbling going on behind her. Plainly, this news not only astonished them, but didn't set well with the fellas either.

"You sure know how to go about finding me a woman," said Daniel at last. "Yessir, you really know how to pick 'em."

Josie looked up in time to see the savage shoot both her and Sissy a murderous glance. "I cannot understand women who do not cook," he muttered. "Perhaps we can teach them."

"In one night?" Josie said impulsively.

To that Sissy added, "Too bad you didn't buy Lola's cook while you were there, red man."

Long Belly considered all this, then said, "I will cook our supper tonight. Tomorrow will be soon enough for these lazy females to learn chores they should already know."

Daniel shook his head. "You're taking those women back to Miles City first thing in the morning—make no mistake about it, Long Belly."

"That is not possible." The savage pointed out the window. "Have you looked at the skies? The leaves of the cottonwood fill the river, and even the horses at the mission school have grown many thick hairs since the last moon. A big storm approaches."

"Are you sure?"

As the savage assured his brother of what he'd seen, Josie's spirits fell. She'd noticed the changes in the weather, but had hoped somehow to be rescued long before now. If an Indian who knew his way around these parts couldn't get down the mountain, how would she ever get away from these beasts and their filthy cabin? As she considered her increasingly perilous situation and ways of making good her escape, Sissy came over and fell into the seat across from her. The savage headed for the stove, grumbling to himself as he stuffed chunks of wood into it. And Daniel drifted off to sleep, snoring intermittently as his brother wrestled with the frying pan over a hot burner.

Supper that night turned out to be a throat-puckering combination of rusty salt pork and canned beans cooked up by the savage. This was accompanied by a lump of hardtack that was so dried out and old, it didn't even soften when Josie dunked it in her coffee. After the meal was finished, both she and Sissy begged off the mountain of dishes by claiming exhaustion, which in no way was an exaggeration thanks to the all-night journey to this godforsaken place. Josie's eyes felt as if they'd been rolled in cornmeal, and her bruised legs could barely hold her upright.

It was as she was contemplating a place in which to sleep that the savage approached with yet another demand—a chore Josie had no intention of taking on.

"You may wait until morning to clean dishes," he said magnanimously. "But tonight you must dump my brother's slop pail before you can rest. It is there in the cabinet by his bed."

Josie gagged at the thought. "Do it yourself," she said recklessly.

This enraged the savage. "You will do as you are told, and you will do it now."

Josie backed against the door, afraid that she'd pressed her luck with the Indian one time too many, but then Sissy surprised her by stepping between her and the furious man.

"I don't mind no slop jars," she said. "I'll take care of it."

Even though Sissy had already started for the cabinet, the savage still looked as if he might come after Josie and do her bodily harm. Just as she reached behind her and began fumbling with the latch on the door, Daniel spoke up, diverting the Indian's attention.

"Yessir, Brother," he said with a laugh. "Picking this woman for me was a mighty fine idea. Why, she's turned out to be what I would call the perfect gift. Mercy."

The savage kept one evil eye on Josie, but a smile tugged the corner of his mouth as he said to Daniel, "Perhaps if I beat this perfect gift of yours, she will be even more perfect."

"Perhaps," Daniel agreed, drawing a gasp from Josie. "But I'm too tired to listen to her caterwauling tonight. Beat her in the morning, if you must. For now, I think we could all use a little sleep."

Josie wasn't sure if her punishment had been delayed or if she'd earned a complete reprieve, but she was relieved when Long Belly went along with the suggestion. After Sissy returned with the empty slop pail, the savage chased her up the slender ladder that led to the loft—his lair, Josie assumed—then returned to the main room with one final order for the night.

"You," he said, pointing to Josie and then the bed, "will join my brother now."

"I can sleep in the chair just fine," she answered, not feeling nearly as brave as she sounded.

"In this, you will obey."

Faster than she thought any human could move, the savage was on her. Gripping Josie by the arm, he dragged her to the edge of Daniel's bed. "You will warm my brother and you will do it now."

"If she'd rather not," Daniel said. "I don't care where she sleeps."

That reprieve lasted only a moment. Still hanging on to her, Long Belly objected violently. "This she is trained for, is she not?"

With a shrug, Daniel had to agree. "From what I've seen of her, I would say it's probably the only thing she is trained for."

"Do you deny that you long for this female beside you?"

Daniel eyed her with a look that gave Josie a case of goose flesh. "It'd sure beat the living hell out of getting cow-kicked."

"Then it is settled. I have paid for this woman's services," said the savage. "And in this, she will submit."

With that he flung Josie onto the bed beside Daniel. Then he blew out the lantern and added one last order in the darkness.

"Call me, my brother, if this perfect gift does not use her training in ways that please you. I would be happy to beat her tonight if she fails in this."

Chapter Four

The following morning when Daniel awakened, his first thought was the same thought he'd had for at least three weeks running—why bother to wake up at all? He was sick of lying in bed, sick and tired of the stink of the sheet beneath him, and sick to death of his own useless body. He'd had other injuries in the past, including bullet and arrow wounds, but never had he been so completely debilitated, so helpless and utterly useless.

Mostly Daniel hated being confined by these four log walls. As a man who'd always lived in the out of doors—in a hastily erected lean-to, tipi, tent, or more often than not, right out under the stars on his bedroll—being stuck inside was giving him a powerful case of the jimjams.

He shifted his hips, seeking fresh mattress lumps to squash with his worthless body, and connected with something soft, a surprisingly warm object he initially mistook for his down pillow. Then he remembered the woman, Long Belly's perfect gift. He glanced her way, pleased to see that her expression was free of the hatred he'd seen yesterday.

Daniel shifted a little, testing the depth of Josie's slumber.

She didn't move so much as an eyelash. Thanks, no doubt, to
the arduous and sudden trek she'd been forced to make, she
was dead to the world. Rolling slightly onto his right side for
a better view of his unexpected bedmate, Daniel studied her a
little closer. The rigid lodgepole she'd been when she first
stretched out beside him last night was gone, in its place an
agreeable, lithesome willow. He wondered which tree she
would resemble when she awoke to find him staring at her.
The odds heavily favored the pine.

Not that Daniel blamed the woman for her obvious distress.
It hadn't been her idea to come here, that much was sure. Still,
he found her defiant nature a little puzzling. He would have
expected someone in her line of work to be more like her friend
Sissy, resigned to the situation. Josie, on the other hand, was
a study in contradictions, chief of which was her surprising
modesty. The woman had actually slept in all her clothes, right
down to her shoes.

How could a prostitute be too shy to discard even a scrap
of her clothing? If indeed she'd been worried about unwanted
advances, the chemise beneath her gown would certainly have
"protected" her just as well—another oddity. Why did she
feel she needed protection from an invalid when any man off
the street could have her for a price? It wasn't as if he'd given
her the idea that he planned on going where he clearly wasn't
wanted. Daniel was not the kind of man who condoned or used
force on women, and he hadn't given Josie any indication
otherwise. Yet when he'd reached for her last night, she'd
threatened to kill him. He simply couldn't make sense of her.

She stirred then, touching his upper thigh, unconsciously
testing Daniel's control. After the death threat, he hadn't sought
her comfort again, and now he had to wonder why he'd been
so generous. Surely not because of the broken leg. A woman
in her line of work would know plenty of ways to ease a man's
needs, several of which wouldn't disturb his injury in the least.
Just thinking about a couple of those ways, not to mention how
good it felt to have her warm body snuggled against his, made
him think that maybe he'd been a damn fool to let her off so

easily. From the few murmured grunts and groans he'd heard in the loft before drifting off, he had an idea that Long Belly hadn't been nearly so thoughtful of the dark-skinned whore who shared his bedroll.

With a breathy little sigh, Josie rolled into Daniel, brushing her cheek against his mouth as she threw her arm across his chest. She was so close to him now that he could feel the warm puffs of her breath against his face, count each auburn hair in her long curly lashes as they swept back and forth along the crests of her cheekbones. She looked ridiculously young and innocent. A whore playing the part of a maiden. So pure, so artful, so damned defiant. What was it about this wanton that made him think he ought to protect rather than ravish her?

Josie stretched and yawned then, an indication that she would awaken soon. Her lips were parted now, inviting and teasing, making him feel like a bigger fool than ever. And as horny as a penned-up jackrabbit. Without another thought, Daniel impulsively took her into his arms and smothered her mouth with his.

The kiss was heaven for about twenty seconds.

He'd barely tasted the sweetness of Josie's lush lips or had a chance to marvel over their velvety texture before her big brown eyes flew open. A moment later the lodgepole pine attacked, reaching out with fingernails that gouged his face like splintered branches.

"Hey!" he shouted, pushing her away. "What the hell is wrong with you?"

When she looked up and saw the scratches near Daniel's right eye, Josie was at once pleased and frightened—gratified to see that she'd drawn blood, but nervous about the knife he kept close at hand. She quickly rolled to the edge of the bed, then fell to the floor in a heap.

Peeking over the edge of the mattress, she made a halfhearted apology. "Sorry, but you startled me. I didn't know where I was or who you were."

That much was, in part, the truth. Josie had been dreaming of her brief tryst with Henry in the Baum barn, remembering how his lips had felt against hers and how she'd wondered where his inquisitive hands would light next, when she'd suddenly realized that the face rubbing against hers wasn't soft and smooth like Henry's, but more like kissing a bramble bush. By the time she opened her eyes, her memory had returned and she knew exactly where she was and who was assaulting her.

Daniel grumbled a little, but grudgingly accepted her apology. "I didn't mean to scare you. I figured a woman like you'd be used to waking up with a strange man in her bed."

Even though Josie had yet to explain that she was not a prostitute, the statement startled her. How could she be so easily mistaken for such a woman? The thought was unsettling. Worse, it titillated her somehow, made her feel sexy and desirable. A little shudder of pleasure coursed through her at the wicked thought.

"I, ah, have to . . . relieve myself." She thought of the odoriferous slop jar, praying to God there was some other way. "Do you have a privy?"

"It's out back," Daniel said. "Turn right at the door and head straight down the incline. You can't miss it."

As Josie climbed to her feet, arms still hugged tightly to her waist, he added, "I think you'll find it's plenty nippy out there. You'd better take my coat. It's the light buckskin one hanging by the door."

The last thing she wanted was to be in this man's debt, but as Josie skittered across the room and reached for the heavy, wool-lined garment, she could have kissed Daniel for the offer, stubbly cheeks and all. After slipping on the huge jacket, staggering under its weight, she headed to the door.

"Oh, one other thing," said Daniel, stopping her in her tracks. "If winter's coming on us as fast as Long Belly says it is, I'd be on the lookout for bears."

Josie turned to look at him. "Bears?"

Daniel nodded. "They'll be getting ready to dig in now, gorging themselves with anything and everything that gets in their way. That includes a tasty little morsel like you."

For a brief moment, Josie considered using the slop jar. Then her senses returned. "What do I do if a bear comes after me?"

"Just make a lot of noise as you walk. Bears are usually more afraid of us than we are of them." He paused to consider this, then narrowed his eyes and offered another suggestion. "Then again, that might not be true of a grizzly about ready to go into hibernation. Do you know how to use a gun?"

Although she'd never actually fired a pistol before, Josie had watched her brothers at target practice on several occasions, always with great envy. Figuring this was qualification enough, she nodded. "Of course."

Eyes still narrow, as if doubting her answer or even pondering the wisdom of arming her, Daniel finally said, "I keep a Peacemaker up on the shelf by the whiskey. Be careful getting it down—it's loaded."

After Josie reached the stove and the shelf above it, she slid her fingers along the edge of the sooty plank until she felt the cold steel barrel of the gun. Gingerly taking the weapon by the grip, she removed it and once again started for the door.

"Don't shoot right at a bear if you see one," Daniel warned as she headed outside. "There's nothing meaner than a wounded grizzly. Fire over its head if you need to use the gun. The noise alone ought to scare it off."

For some reason, this advice didn't make Josie feel any safer as she headed out into the gray, frigid morning. Holding the Colt between both hands, she waved it continually in front of herself yelling, "Shoo! Shoo!" as she hurried down the small incline to the squat log outhouse.

After Josie finished in the privy, a tiny building that was surprisingly clean and in some ways smelled a whole lot better than the cabin, she paused to lean against the trunk of a ponderosa pine that was located between the outhouse, the barn, and the house. Although she'd seen no sign of bears, she kept a tight grip on the gun as she drew in a long, frigid breath. Less afraid and more relaxed now, Josie gave herself a quiet moment to reflect on her situation.

A light snow had fallen during the night, dusting the ground more than covering it. She'd broken through this thin crust as she walked, leaving behind footprints that stood out like the markings on a pinto pony. Soon, she thought, all traces of her march to the privy would be obliterated. Dark clouds were building overhead, threatening an even more substantial storm. If he didn't know anything else, she had to concede that Long Belly did seem to know how to predict the weather.

Relatively warm inside the heavy coat, Josie hugged it even closer to her body, determined to stay in the out of doors for as long as she could. This was where she belonged, where she'd always belonged, with the wind to her back and all her senses alive. At the Baum farm, her stepbrothers had been expected from an early age to labor in the fields, mend fences, and tend the livestock. They laughed at her whenever she begged to go along with them, telling her how lucky she was to be safe and warm doing inside chores instead of breaking her back with them on the range. They'd even said that she was crazy in the head to be coveting their work in place of the comfort of kitchen and hearth. It seemed to Josie that if tending the home was such a darn enviable task, at least one of the boys would have begged on occasion to swap places with her. Of course, that had never happened.

Her only outings had been monthly visits to church along with semi-regular attendance at school. She was ashamed to admit the reason she'd been so adamant about getting her education was not so much for what she might learn, but for the chance to get out of the kitchen. She loved those few hours away from the monotonous drudgery of housework, in particular the ride to and from the little schoolhouse atop Duke, an old plow horse whose mixed origins gave him a high-stepping gait that didn't quite match his cumbersome body. With the exception of such days, life on the Baum farm had hardly been worth living. She'd been caged there as surely as the livestock in the barn, as much a captive as she was now. Was this all her life would ever amount to? she wondered. Escaping from one trap only to land in another?

Of the three cages she'd been penned in so far—the Baum

home, the pleasure palace, and now this stifling cabin—Josie honestly couldn't say for sure which was the worst. She couldn't imagine going back to either of the first two. And yet how would she ever survive in this cabin among these dreadful savages, especially if the weather turned so bad there was no hope of escaping until spring?

Behind her, the cabin door suddenly opened, then closed with a thud.

When she turned, Josie saw that Long Belly was headed her way. He was fully dressed right down to his buffalo robe, and he carried a large buckskin satchel, the same parfleche he'd toted when he kidnapped her. She glanced from him to the gun still tightly clutched between her palms, and saw in the weapon a possible means of escape, the impending storm be damned. Swallowing the lump in her throat, she turned as he approached and brandished the weapon.

"Take me back to Miles City this instant," Josie demanded, her voice quivering with fear. "Or at least down to the mission by the river. If you don't, I swear I'll shoot you where you stand."

Without so much as a glance at the gun, Long Belly simply said, "You are very clever. Perhaps in the future I should call you Foolish Woman Who Plans to Kill Her Only Guide." He brushed past her then, adding, "Water boils on the stove. Wash my brother and see to his needs. He is in much pain this morning."

With that, the savage continued on to the barn.

Feeling angry and impotent, Josie abruptly wheeled around after him and raised the gun above his head. Intending to fire a warning shot as Daniel had suggested in case of bears, she squeezed the trigger. It moved a scant quarter of an inch, but the pistol didn't fire. She tugged on the trigger again, using all her strength. As before, nothing happened. By then the savage had disappeared into the bowels of the barn, leaving Josie with nothing to do but follow his directions.

Feeling trapped and helpless again, she returned to the cabin and stepped into the comparatively warm room. Still wearing

Daniel's coat, she trudged over to the shelf and slid the useless pistol back in its place. A fire was roaring inside the stove, and a pot of coffee and kettle of water were perched on top of the greasy stove. Pausing there a moment, she warmed her frozen hands.

"See any bears?" asked Daniel, still lying in his bed.

"No," she muttered. "It's a good thing, too, because that gun of yours doesn't work."

"You tried to fire it?"

Caught, she gulped. "Ah—yes, I thought I saw something moving in the trees."

"There's nothing wrong with that gun. Are you sure you had it fully cocked?"

She turned to him at last. "Cocked?"

"Did you pull the hammer all the way back before you fired?"

Josie wasn't at all certain what or where this hammer could be. She only remembered seeing her brothers pull back on the trigger—again, and again, and again.

She shrugged out of Daniel's coat, hanging it back on the correct antler as she said, "I only know how to pull the trigger. It didn't work."

Daniel laughed. "My gun isn't a revolver. I guess I should have mentioned that. How's the coffee doing?"

"I don't know," she said, more concerned with her immediate problem. "I saw your brother going into the barn with his bag. He looked as if he might be taking a trip. Is he planning to take us back to Miles City today?"

Daniel pushed up to a sitting position, propping himself there by a pair of fur-covered pillows. Then he patted the mattress beside him. "Come sit with me a minute, Josie. There's a few things I ought to explain."

Although the last thing she wanted to do was get near this man, she figured Daniel was her best chance at freedom. She joined him at the edge of the bed, but did not sit down.

"I'm not your enemy," he said quietly. "And though it may not seem that way, neither is Long Belly. It was his idea to

bring you gals up here, not mine, but he honestly thought he
was doing a good thing. I want you to know that if I'd had
any idea what he intended to do when he left here that day,
I'd have done everything I could to stop him."

Josie could detect nothing but sincerity in his tone or expression. Sensing an ally, she pleaded her cause. "Then don't you
think you ought to do everything you can to make him take us
back?"

"I would if I could." He slowly shook his head and grinned,
amused by some private thought. "As the Indian agent at this
Reservation, it's undoubtedly my duty to see you ladies safely
back to Miles City, but since I went and busted my leg, there
isn't much I can do for now."

At this news, the fact that Daniel McCord was actually in
charge of the savage who'd kidnapped her, Josie stomped her
foot against the dirty floor, raising a cloud of dust.

"I had no idea you were an authority out here. A man in
your position should have no problem forcing that savage to
take us back where we belong. There's a storm brewing that
could keep us here for weeks."

Daniel smiled then with compassion and even the hint of
understanding, an expression that gave her a glimmer of hope.

"As an Indian agent, my job is to see to the needs of the
Cheyenne, not cater to the whims of white folks who'd just as
soon see every last Indian dead."

"If I have a wish to see that Indian dead, it's only because
he kidnapped me. I hardly think returning me to Miles City
can be thought of as catering to a whim."

"Sorry, but he doesn't think of it as kidnapping. I'll try to
talk to him about this again when he gets back, but don't get
your hopes up. Long Belly is one stubborn Indian. Once he
gets something stuck in his head, you pretty much need a stick
of dynamite to get it out. Right now his head is full of buffalo
that talk to him when he sleeps."

The Cheyenne was not only a savage, but crazy? Josie
thought with horror.

"I know what you must be thinking," Daniel went on to

say, "but there's no arguing with this or any Cheyenne when it comes to his dreams. Now that Long Belly has found your friend, a woman who he believes is full up with the spirit of the buffalo, he's more convinced than ever that he'll find that damned bull."

Josie was not impressed or interested in any quest except her own—freedom. "That savage can believe in the spirit of a three-headed goat for all I care. I just want him to take me back to Miles City, and to do it this minute."

From the loft above, Sissy's voice filtered down. "Sorry, princess, but that ain't gonna happen."

Moments later, Josie's only friend in the world inched her way down the ladder. Instead of her low-slung blouse and scarlet skirt, she was wearing a long jacket with matching leggings, both of beaded buckskin.

"This Long Belly fellah," Sissy said when she was on level footing, "has taken it in his head that the buffalo he's looking for will come to me. We're going out looking for it this morning before the weather gets too bad."

"But he can't go off chasing buffalo—everyone knows they're all dead." Desperate, Josie clasped her hands together. "Please, please, talk to him, Sissy. Tell him you're just a plain ole whore, that you don't have anyone's spirit inside you, and that you can't possibly find a stinking buffalo that isn't even alive. Then maybe you can talk him into taking us back to Lola's."

"Sorry, princess, but we ain't got a chance of getting off this mountain until that injun is damn good and ready to take us back down—which he ain't."

With that, she went over to the stove, poured a cup of coffee, and headed out the door. Josie was hot on her heels.

"Sissy, wait," she said, joining her on the porch. "You have to help me."

"Help you do what?"

"Survive, I guess. You can't just leave me here with that . . . that man. We should be figuring a way out of here."

Sissy looked her over, up one side and down the other. "You

don't look no worse for the wear. If you lived through last night, you can get through anything.''

''He expects me to bathe him.'' She shuddered at the thought. ''And God knows what else.''

Sissy shrugged. ''Then do it.''

''B-but I'm not a . . .'' Too late, Josie bit her tongue.

''You're a whore now, ain't you?''

Josie shook her head.

''You telling me you spent the night in that man's bed and he didn't jump you?''

''That's right. I wouldn't let him.''

Sissy snickered. ''He must be a whole lot sicker than I thought.''

''I don't see anything funny about this. If anyone around here so much as touches me, I'll kill him.''

''Relax, princess,'' Sissy said with a shrug. ''It's only your body. Give the man what he wants without a fight, and it'll go a whole lot better for you.''

Not only was Josie less than encouraged by this advice, it made her mad enough to chew nails. ''That's easy for you to say after all the men you've bedded—you probably even like what they do to you.''

Sissy's dark eyes were usually flat and expressionless. Now they turned hard and mean. ''I ain't never found a speck of pleasure in any man's arms. They take what they want, and I let 'em have it. You'll be better off if you do the same.''

''How can you say that to me? I thought you were my friend.''

''Friend?'' Sissy laughed, a bitter, hollow sound. ''You got to be a friend to have one, princess.'' That said, she stepped off the porch and started for the barn.

Josie stood there in the cold for a time, not pondering Sissy's words as much as hating them. Hating her. Part of that hatred, she had to admit, was pure jealousy over the fact that Sissy was riding off on an adventure, leaving her behind to tend hearth and home. Of course she didn't feel a drop of envy over Sissy's escort, but with that exception, Josie would rather have been on the trail with a savage than trapped in that pigsty of a cabin with his half-breed brother, who expected her to wait on him hand and foot. At least on horseback, there was always some chance of escape. As for Sissy's remarks about friendship, Josie wasn't at all sure how to take them. She'd never had a close friend before and wasn't quite sure of the boundaries. In any case, she was too cold to think about that or anything except getting her frosty backside into the cabin before she froze to death.

Resigned to her fate, if not happy about it, Josie watched the pair disappear into the forest, then dragged herself back to the confines of her cage. The minute she stepped into the room, she noticed the water in the kettle was simmering, ready for her to go to work. So was Daniel.

"If you've got nothing better to do with that pot of hot water," he called from across the room. "I could stand a little washing up."

Josie glanced at him, thinking there wasn't enough water in all Montana Territory to accomplish the feat, then hefted the kettle off the stove and carried it to the side of the bed.

"Where do you keep the soap and rags?" she asked.

Daniel scratched his head, giving her the impression that such items were foreign to him.

"If you'll take a look in my possibles bag over by the corner," he finally said. "I believe you'll find some flannel scraps or maybe a couple of socks that would do the trick. I'm not sure about soap. I bought a pound or so a couple of years back, but I can't recall whatever came of it."

Sighing heavily, Josie made her way to the corner where she found a dark leather pouch. After opening the outside flap, she spread the bag wide and peered into the depths. It contained an assortment of bullets, knives, beads, and packs of what were probably sugar or salt, but none of the rags appeared to be clean enough to touch, much less for use in bathing. Reaching gingerly into the pouch, Josie plucked out the cleanest dirty sock she could find, then returned to the bed.

With fourteen brothers of all ages in her keeping, it wasn't as if she'd never seen or bathed a masculine body. Thinking of the chore that way, as something she'd done a thousand times before, Josie made quick work of removing Daniel's clothing down to his drawers and assisted when necessary as he bathed himself.

She was studying his broad chest as he patted it dry, taking in the fact that his smooth nutmeg skin was devoid of hair, and thinking how refreshing a sight it was after having lived among the apelike Baum boys, when Daniel asked a question that made her choke with surprise.

"Will you help me get these drawers off so I can clean the rest of me?"

"Ah . . . no." She fought a blush but felt her cheeks grow warm anyway. "I'd rather not."

"No?" His bright eyes grew huge, incredulous. "After all the bare-ass naked men you've seen? Am I that damned hard for you to look at?"

Since she'd been thinking how much better Daniel looked without his clothes, and that nothing about him from his sculpted thighs to his well-muscled shoulders reminded her in the least of her brothers, Josie's blush deepened. To save herself from further embarrassment, she almost blurted out then and there that she wasn't a whore and didn't go around looking at strange men's naked bodies. But then it occurred to her that he might think of her innocence as some kind of prize—and that she'd then find herself in yet another kind of trap.

Handling the situation in the only way she could think of, Josie said, "This isn't a brothel and I'm not on duty. Just think of me as a kidnapped woman who's helping an injured man out of the goodness of her heart."

Daniel stared at her for a long, uncomfortable moment. Then he gave a short nod and said, "Fair enough. Can I talk your good little heart into loosening that splint and taking a look at my leg? I've been laid up for about three weeks now and should be pretty well healed, but it feels like it's getting worse."

Since Josie had set more than her share of broken bones and

felt she knew quite a lot about the healing process, this struck her as odd. "Who set the bone for you?"

"Long Belly, but I don't think that's the problem. That cow kicked a gouge out of my shin when she broke my leg, and right there is where it feels as if I met the business end of a branding iron. Might be a little infected."

Josie had hardly begun unwrapping the bindings that held the splint together before she knew without a doubt that Daniel had made a correct diagnosis. Blood and infected matter had seeped through the bandages, and she also picked up a slight whiff of decay.

"I'm going to have to clean this out," she said when she got down to the angry wound. "I'll be as careful as I can, but it's probably going to hurt some."

Daniel nodded, expecting this. "Whiskey's on the shelf above the stove along with anything else you might need. Would you be good enough to bring me the bottle? I think I'd like to get started on it before you get started on that leg."

After that, Daniel didn't say another word. He took a few deep pulls on the whiskey, then lay back on his pillow and closed his eyes. By the time Josie had finished cleaning the wound and covered it with a warm poultice she'd made of flour, salt, and water, he was sound asleep. Or passed out. She didn't know which.

It was as she was returning the whiskey and other supplies to the shelf above the stove that Josie came across the gun she'd been unable to fire earlier that morning. Determined to learn how to use the weapon should a threatening occasion arise, she took it with her to the table by the cabin's only window. Dropping onto one of the chairs there, she began a search for the hammer Daniel told her about.

When she found the little lever that he must have been referring to, Josie pulled it back, pleased to see that at the same time, the trigger jumped to the center of the finger guard. Now it all made sense. Once the gun was cocked, all she had to do was pull the trigger to fire a bullet.

Only trouble was, Josie didn't know how to go about

"uncocking" the thing without shooting at something. She certainly couldn't fire the gun inside the cabin. If she went outside, Daniel would surely hear the explosion and wake up, probably mad. Touching the trigger seemed out of the question, which left only one other way she could think of to make the gun safe again. Since she'd pulled the hammer in order to make the gun functional, Josie reasoned, all she had to do was put the lever back in its original place to disable the weapon.

Following this rationale, she pushed the hammer forward. It wouldn't budge. Understanding that the hammer was connected to the trigger somehow, she decided to hold it in place with her thumb, while lightly pulling against the trigger. The hammer began to move forward and then, without warning, slipped out from under her thumb.

Much to Josie's surprise and horror, the Colt went off in her hand.

Chapter Five

Relatively pain-free for the first time in weeks, Daniel dozed peacefully with images of Josie's long auburn hair swirling around in his mind like ribbons of silk. Although she still had her tresses braided, and even then they were mussed, he had no trouble picturing what her hair must look like when she unwound and brushed it for the night. He boldly went on to imagine those luxurious locks pouring through his fingers, figuring they would feel like spring rain sliding between blades of sweet new grass. She would be kitten-soft to touch, he thought, recent memories egging him on, with just a dash of wildcat tossed in to make bedding her all the more interesting.

Mercy.

Daniel then found himself wondering what, short of paying her himself, he had to do in order to convince Josie she ought to share her favors with him. In fact, he was getting good and worked up over the idea, enjoying the surge of blood to his nether regions and trying to remember how long it'd been since he'd last felt such a rush of desire, when something hot and sharp, like a knife blade fresh from the fire, suddenly parted his hair. In the next moment he heard the sound of gunfire.

Bolting to a sitting position despite the pain in his leg, Daniel reached up and grabbed the top of his head. When his fingers came away sticky with his own blood, he could hardly believe his eyes.

Then he spotted Josie sitting at the table, his Peacemaker still smoking in her hand. "You shot me—you goddamn shot me!"

"Oh, my God—no!" Josie dropped the gun onto the table as if it were a rock, then leapt out of the chair and hurried to the side of the bed. "Where are you hurt?"

When she tried to lean over him, Daniel reared back out of her reach. "Get away—I'm shot in the head."

Still unable to believe that she'd put a bullet in him, Daniel fingered his scalp. By then blood was flowing freely over his forehead, a gory little river that turned into a waterfall at the tip of his nose, then trickled down onto his bare chest and below. As he stared at the crimson puddle pooling in his navel, trying to make sense of it all, Josie crawled onto the mattress beside him.

"Don't be such a baby," she said, talking to him as if he were a child. "Let me take a look at the damage."

Daniel couldn't get the image of the smoking gun out of his mind. "Why should I? You just tried to *kill* me."

"No, I didn't—honest. I was just trying to find that hammer thing you told me about."

"Your search was successful. Now leave me the hell alone."

"I said I'm sorry, didn't I?"

Daniel was looking for a contrite expression to go along with the words, some sense that she meant what she said, but it was as obvious as hell that it wouldn't be forthcoming from this defiant female. To the contrary, she seemed downright pissed that he wouldn't just let her rip into his scalp.

Hands on hips, Josie said, "If you don't let me see how badly you've been shot, you might just sit there and bleed to death. If that's what you want, it's fine by me. I'm going out for a little air."

"No, wait." Half-afraid she might be right, Daniel grudgingly agreed to an examination. "Go ahead and look, but dammit all, this time be careful. I've had just about all a man can take for one day."

"Baby," she muttered as she hunched over his head.

Daniel might have come up with a snappy reply, but by then, Josie's full breasts were rubbing against his shoulder as she worked, making him all too aware that they were unbound, free of the corset he'd heard white women wore beneath their clothing. Aware of a sudden and surprisingly urgent response in his groin, Daniel strategically draped his hands across his lap as Josie parted his hair—this time with her fingers.

"Ugh," she said, grimacing as she peered at the wound. "What a damned mess."

"How bad is it?" he asked. "Did you blow some of my brains out?"

"No, you fool. It's just a little messy, a scratch that's hardly worth sewing up."

"How can you be so sure?" Daniel recalled the endless list of tasks she claimed she could not perform, despite the decent poultice she'd made for his leg. "I thought you didn't know anything about nursing wounds and such."

"I don't," she said, climbing off the bed. "Tending to something as insignificant as this must be instinctive. Hold still a minute. I'm going to get a rag or something to help stop the bleeding."

Josie made short work of cleaning and patching him up after that, and even donated a strip of her petticoat, figuring it was the cleanest thing in the cabin with which to bind the wound. It was. Thanks, Daniel assumed, to the accidental shooting, her defiant attitude had also undergone a welcome transformation. In fact, Josie seemed most agreeable, a situation he figured he'd best take advantage of while she still felt that way.

"I'm about starving to death," he said, urged on by his growling belly. "I also feel kinda weak after being shot in the head and all. Think you could rustle me up some flapjacks?"

Daniel could see that a refusal was perched on the tip of her tongue, the automatic response he'd come to expect no matter what was asked of her. After that moment's hesitation, however, she surprised him.

"I suppose I could try. How do I make them?"

Directing her to the shelf above the stove and the bin of flour beside it, Daniel gave her step-by-step instructions that culminated in a reasonably edible meal. The flapjacks weren't particularly light, but not too bad for someone untrained in the culinary arts. He'd warned her to keep a close watch on the cakes as they cooked, but somehow Josie managed to burn them anyway, frying them to a deep charcoal color that matched the layer of soot covering her face and clothes. He'd been meaning to fix that stove pipe for a while now, but with the busted-up leg and all, hadn't quite gotten to it.

"Who put this stove together?" she asked irritably, eyes glowing through soot like a cat's in the dark. "Whoever did it ought to be shot."

"You've already taken care of that," Daniel said, drawing the first burst of laughter from her. It was a pleasant sound and made him feel comfortable enough to add, "Why don't you drag up one of the chairs and eat with me?"

She hesitated, looking at him cockeyed for a moment before grabbing a chair and settling in next to the edge of the bed with her plate. "I do have a couple of questions about you and Long Belly, if you don't mind."

Daniel couldn't think of anything to do with their relationship that would make him uncomfortable, so he gave her free rein. "I don't mind a bit. What do you want to know?"

"For one thing, you two call each other brother. You don't look that much like brothers—are you?"

"We're not related by blood at all. My wife was his sister, so he's my brother-in-law. We've been calling each other brother since the wedding."

"You have a wife?" She said it as if finding a woman to marry him had been a miracle.

"Had," he snapped. "She died a couple of years ago."

"Oh." Head bowed, Josie generously added, "I'm sorry."

"No need to be."

Obviously eager to move onto a new topic, she asked, "Is that why he doesn't listen to you, even though you are the agent in charge of his tribe—because you're not Cheyenne?"

"Oh, but I am." Daniel supposed he ought to be insulted by her insinuations, and in some ways he was, but most of what she assumed was true. Crunching his way through the remains of a flapjack, he said, "He probably only half listens to what I tell him because I'm only half Cheyenne."

"Then you two were raised together?"

Daniel shook his head. "I never even met Long Belly or the other members of the tribe until they were rounded up and sent to this reservation a few years ago—you know, after that Custer mess at the Little Big Horn. That's when I decided the Cheyenne needed my help more than the soldiers did."

He paused there, waiting to either see or feel her revulsion over the fact that he was aiding the very band of cutthroats who'd helped annihilate the white man's fair-haired general. It took less than a minute for her to come through with a properly offended expression.

"I'm not sure I understand what you're saying." Josie's mouth was pinched and her cute little nose tilted upward. "You mean that you and Long Belly actually took part in Custer's defeat?"

Daniel was sorely tempted to answer in the affirmative, to claim that yes, he and Long Belly had fired the fatal bullets that ended the general's life, but instead, he hit her with the truth.

"Long Belly's family was there, camped on the Little Big Horn, but he wasn't much more than a boy back then and didn't participate in the battle. I was still scouting for the army at the time, though not for the Seventh, and helped Mackenzie's troops locate and nearly annihilate the Cheyenne camp a few months after Custer's defeat."

Josie's expression softened dramatically and her eyes lit up. "Then you must be some kind of war hero."

Daniel smiled, but an ache filled his throat that started from his heart. "That depends on how you look at it—through white or Cheyenne eyes."

His appetite gone, Daniel dropped his plate on the bed and thought back to the revelations that made him the man he was today. That was back when he first realized that the military had figured out that one of the quickest ways to bring Indians under control, and thereby dependent and subject to the white man's regulations, was to destroy their main source of survival and independence—the buffalo. To his everlasting shame and horror, Daniel, along with his father, took part in the destruction of the great bison herds, at least until he realized what was happening to his own mother's people. By then, it was nearly too late.

Leaving those details out, he explained, "It wasn't until after a large group of Cheyenne were sent back here to starve to death that I decided they needed and deserved my help more than the army did."

"Starve to death?" Josie dropped a bite of flapjack back onto her plate. It landed with a hollow *clunk*. "But how can they be starving to death here in these mountains, of all places? Surely these people know how to hunt."

Trying to hang on to his private feelings on the subject, Daniel said, "It's impossible to hunt game that's been slaughtered to extinction by your enemies, the way the buffalo and antelope have been here in these mountains."

"There's no game left?"

Daniel shrugged. "A couple of elk and deer, I suppose, but they're few and far between. Sometimes the Cheyenne resort to picking off a few head of stray cattle from the ranches along the Tongue River—and that, as you might imagine, doesn't set too well with the ranchers. That's one reason Long Belly and I are trying to start up our own cattle ranch. If we do well enough, we plan to turn it over to the tribe."

Josie considered all this a minute, then frowned. "I still don't understand how they can be starving with all the supplies you bring them on behalf of the government. I know several white families that could have used a little free flour last winter."

"They're welcome to it," he said, barely hanging on to his temper. "Of course, to qualify they have to have been driven at gunpoint off the land where they were born and raised, then agree to live under conditions that make them sick and to adapt to ways of life they detest, such as farming. Oh, and they also can't complain when the government breaks promises and treaties, or when it expects them to suffer quietly at the hands of crooked traders and white horse thieves. And forget about religion as you know it—they have to change all those beliefs, too. Still think you know some white folks who deserve free flour?"

Daniel suspected he'd gone a little too far even before Josie grabbed his plate off the bed, then flounced over to the counter and dumped the remains of both their meals there. When she marched over to the table and glanced out the window, he thought she might even try to make a break for it.

She didn't, but surprised him by completely ignoring the previous subject to ask, "If this is a cattle ranch, where are your cattle and hired hands?"

As happy as she for the change of topic, Daniel laughed as he said, "We're just getting a start in the business. Long Belly *is* my hired hands."

Turning back to him, Josie asked, "Then why is he off chasing buffalo that aren't there instead of tending the herd?"

In no mood to get back on such a personal level, Daniel made quick work of his explanation. "Buffalo have always provided food, lodging, tools, and other goods to the Cheyenne, and are the most worshiped animal in that tribe, second only to their God, *Heammawihio*. Since Long Belly can't fill his people's bellies just yet, he dreams of finding at least one living buffalo to fill them all with hope."

Her expression thoughtful, Josie nodded, then went back to staring out the window. After that, the morning and afternoon flew by as Daniel dragged himself outside to tend the livestock with his surprisingly cooperative assistant, Josie, by his side.

Not only did she muck out the stalls without complaint, she didn't even balk when he filled a wheelbarrow with fresh pine logs and asked her to push it back to the cabin. Whether she realized he was laying in supplies against what could be one hell of a storm, he couldn't say. All Daniel knew for sure was that scattered snowflakes had begun falling at noon, and if the darkening clouds were any indication, his ranch would be covered in at least a foot of snow by morning.

That night they ate a supper of ham and leftover flopjacks, as Daniel thought of them. Although Josie continued to do pretty much what he asked of her, as the evening wore on, he could sense a little of the former defiance creeping back into her manner. He went so far as to complain about his aching head, holding it and moaning like the baby she'd accused him of being, but even that performance wasn't enough to bring her back to a contrite, fairly obedient female. What little remained of Josie's agreeable nature abruptly vanished about the time she crawled under Daniel's blanket. Then, once again, he found a lodgepole pine lying next to him.

"So, Josie," he said casually. "I realize it wasn't your idea to come here and all, and that whatever Long Belly paid, it probably wasn't quite enough for all you've been through. How much more do you want to take the starch out of my hide?"

Beside him, incredulously enough, she grew even stiffer. "What the *hell* is that supposed to mean?"

Daniel cleared his throat and reached for her. "I was hoping to buy a little of your time. It's been a while since I've known the feel of a woman."

She slapped his hand away the minute it touched down on her breast. "It's gonna be a hell of a lot longer if you're counting on me to ease your suffering. Now shut up. I'm tired and need some sleep."

By the next morning, Josie wondered how much longer her own belly would let her hide her considerable cooking skills. Though she'd intentionally burned the pancakes just to make sure that she wouldn't called on to cook again, she found to her chagrin that even she couldn't stand them. Her sensibilities were also offended enough by the mess in the cabin that she considered tidying the place up a little. Then again, it could be a waste of time. Cleanliness may have been next to godliness, but Josie thought that maybe this cabin was too ungodly to ever be clean again. Maybe if she stayed outside more, she wouldn't notice so much.

Taking Daniel's heavy coat from the rack, Josie slipped into it, and while she was at it, helped herself to his deerskin boots. They were thigh-high moccasins with fringed flaps that were more than big enough to pull on over her shoes.

"I'm going out back to use the privy," Josie announced over her shoulder. "Is there anything I should do for the animals while I'm outside?"

"Well, you could milk the cow, if you don't mind, and maybe toss a little hay to the horses. Everything else should be all right until tonight, unless you want to trouble yourself to look for eggs."

Josie kept both her smile and her delight to herself. "Oh, all right," she said with a forced sigh. "I'll do what I can."

Then she opened the door and stepped out into a thick, invigorating blanket of glistening snow. Daniel's boots proved to be surprisingly warm, even though Josie did have to stop now and then to pull them up, but they kept her dry as she trudged to the outhouse and then to the barn, all without spotting a bear, thank the Lord. She'd left the gun on the table where she'd dropped it, too skittish after shooting Daniel to even think of touching it again so soon.

When Josie finished tending the livestock, she took a few minutes to just stand out in the cold and breathe the frosty mountain air. Unlike her mother, who had bundled herself from head to foot at the first sign of fall, Josie thrived in cooler temperatures. She came alive at the first flurries of snow, her pulse racing through her body with renewed vigor, and felt a certain bond with the out of doors each time her breath left its imprint in the frosty air.

Loathe to return to the cabin, Josie finally forced herself to collect the eggs and a half a pail of milk, then headed for the house. As she stepped across the threshold and kicked the door shut, Daniel greeted her with pretty much the same words he'd used the morning before.

"I'm starving," he said, patting his belly through a clean buckskin shirt—well, cleaner than the last, anyway. "Why don't you fry up those eggs and maybe try to make us some biscuits today. Sure would go good with what's left of that ham."

Josie set the supplies on the counter. "If you want breakfast, you're going to have to cook it up yourself. I've got stalls to muck out."

"But what about you? Aren't you hungry?"

Since Josie had come across a barrel of apples in the barn while looking for eggs and had nearly eaten herself sick on them, she found it easy to smile and say, "I couldn't eat a bite. Besides, I'd just as soon get the chores done."

By late afternoon, the wind had picked up dramatically, howling like a thousand wolves in the depths of despair. Where there had been pristine snow and a quiet preparation for the winter ahead, came a blizzard of freezing proportions, a display to show them all, man and beast alike, that Nature danced to her own tune and in her own time. No one was more surprised than Daniel at the sudden, extensive display of raw power.

"My Lord," Josie blurted out as she peered through the window. "If this keeps up, I'll never get back to town. Never."

"Oh, it can't be that bad."

But just to make sure, Daniel pulled himself up on his crutches and hobbled over to join Josie at the window. When he looked out, all he could see was sheets of ice. There were no trees, no barn, no nothing. It was as if white had erased the entire world beyond the cabin.

"Damn," he said, amending his previous statement. "That

is an unusually big storm for so early in November. I sure hope Long Belly and your friend were able to find shelter before all this started.''

Damn fool Cheyenne, was what he thought, but Daniel kept that sentiment to himself. No good worrying Josie, even though she would have every reason to be concerned if she realized the kind of jeopardy Sissy might be in by now. She was already worried enough on her own behalf. He wasn't any too comfortable with the looks of the weather himself.

Making a show of nonchalance, Daniel went to check on the big pot of elk stew he'd started earlier, a meal he hoped would taste as good as it smelled. About then he picked up the sound of something other than the wind. He thought he heard a high-pitched whinny, and was beginning to think that maybe he heard the sound only because he wanted to so badly, when something heavy *thumped* down on the porch. A moment later the cabin door crashed open, and in blew Long Belly with Sissy and the storm close behind.

"We have returned," he announced unnecessarily. "My woman has found the place where the great buffalo sleeps."

Daniel almost fell off his crutches. "You came across a buffalo wallow?"

Grinning like a fool, Long Belly became quite animated, even for him. He spread his arms wide and said, "It was the bed of a huge bull, bigger and deeper than any I have ever seen."

Daniel scoffed at the idea. "You probably stumbled across the sleeping spot for a bull elk, or maybe a steer."

Long Belly shook his head resolutely. "It belonged to the buffalo, my friend, and he had recently rolled his great body there. I found his tracks leading away from this place, but lost them when the storm came."

As Daniel stood there in shock, his mouth agape, Long Belly took Sissy by the shoulders and began to rub her arms vigorously. "Buffalo Hair has the spirit in her as I thought," he went on. "When the storm leaves us, she will return with me to the sleeping place and lead me to the great one."

Daniel still couldn't quite buy the story, but he withheld comment. He didn't dare believe it, not yet, not on so little grounds. Even if it were true, Long Belly would have one hell of a time catching such a beast if he ever spotted it, especially since this lone bison had apparently eluded hunters and ranchers for so long. Because Long Belly, a tracker without equal, had identified hoofprints that couldn't easily be mistaken for another animal's, Daniel had to at least make a show of rejoicing with him.

"Congratulations, brother. May your next hunt be a complete success."

The Cheyenne patted Sissy's hair with near reverence, as close to affection as he ever got. Then he said, "Buffalo Hair should be congratulated, not me. She is like a goddess and will be treated as one."

He then led her to a chair and carefully eased her onto the seat. Daniel couldn't help but notice that through it all, the dusky-skinned whore had kept her thoughts to herself. Even her expression was a careful blank, revealing nothing of the woman within.

Josie, who'd been as silent and stunned as Daniel throughout Long Belly's passionate explanation, moved over by the table and stared down at her friend.

"Are you all right, Sissy?" she asked.

Long Belly immediately stepped between the two women. "Buffalo Hair is weary and must rest. You may tend to her needs, but do not bother her with your woman's chatter."

With that he turned away from an even more stunned Josie and said to Daniel. "One of these cattle who roams the hills, a small one that won't be missed by his owner, insisted on following this great warrior on the return home. We will eat well during this bad storm."

"Oh, hell, Long Belly." Daniel rapped the floor with one of his crutches. "How many times do I have to tell you that stealing cattle from the ranches around here is not the same thing as stealing horses? It is not a test of your bravery and skill. All it does it irritate the white folks and make them more determined than ever to run us off this land. Is that what you want?''

His head held high, long broad nose pointed regally upward, Long Belly ignored the entire complaint. He turned to Josie instead, sounding as imperious as he looked, and said, ''This calf who sacrificed himself for our table is waiting for you in the barn. You will clean him, taking care not to damage the hide.''

Josie, who'd worn a frightened, cornered look since Long Belly strode into the room, was suddenly a mass of conflicting expressions—chief of which was that damned defiance that reminded Daniel so much of his departed wife. Unlike Tangle Hair, this woman didn't seem to recognize her place.

Cheyenne women never forgot their status and unfailingly performed the tasks expected of them—fixing meals, tanning hides, sewing clothing, and even setting up the tipis in which they lived. Long Belly was raised in such a manner, his every need tended to by the women of his tribe, and unfortunately he expected the same of all females, white, brown, or red.

Daniel knew better than that, of course, not that the knowledge made Josie's presence any easier to bear. Tangle Hair would never, ever have refused to cook his meals or sew and clean his clothing. Like Josie, however, she was given to fits of insolence. If the woman smelled so much as a drop of whisky on Daniel's breath or took exception to something he said, she would chase him out of his own tipi until she was good and ready to let him back in again. So strong of will was she, in fact, that Tangle Hair had once actually fed Blackrobe, the Catholic priest at the mission, then thrown him out of her tipi in a rage because he failed to compliment her cooking.

His Cheyenne wife's attitude was one of defiance. The same was true of Josie. Daniel watched her carefully, wondering if fear or insolence would run her tongue when she finally addressed Long Belly's demands. And what his stubborn brother-in-law would do in return should defiance win out.

Growing impatient, Long Belly clenched his fists and took a step toward Josie. "You will do this now," he demanded of her. "Or you will be punished."

Chapter Six

When Josie first saw the Cheyenne come through the door, his great robe, hair, and face dusted with snow, the usual cold fear crawled through her veins, freezing her to the spot. At the arrogant demands he made, her blood suddenly thawed then heated until it bubbled like the stew on the stove.

"Make me." Josie dropped into a crouch and raised her fists. "I grew up with fourteen brothers—fifteen if you count the one a no-account murdering Indian killed. Just because you're bigger than me doesn't mean I can't get a few good licks in before you beat me to a pulp. And that's what you're going to have to do to make me go out to that barn and butcher your supper."

The savage looked to his brother in surprise.

Daniel glanced at Josie, hesitated, then laughed. "You'd best believe her, Long Belly. She damn near blew my head off this morning just because I fell asleep while she was talking."

This, unfortunately, drew the Indian's attention to the strip of petticoat strapped to Daniel's scalp. "What did happen to your head?" he asked.

"It's like I said—she shot me. I wouldn't get her all riled up if I was you."

Long Belly's skeptical eyes went to Josie. "This is true? You took a gun and shot my brother?"

She threw back her shoulders, a mouse standing up to a puma, then dared to say, "Darn tooting I did."

To her relief, the big Cheyenne turned away from her, slowly shook his head, and apologized to his brother-in-law. "This gift I have brought to you is truly worthless. She cannot cook, is no good at washing dishes, and now she has tried to kill you. Perhaps I should leave her in the forest for the wolves."

"Hold on a minute." At last, Daniel came to her defense. "I didn't say she meant to shoot me, just that she did. It was an accident, and she did turn out to be a pretty good doctor when it came time to patch me up."

Long Belly turned to stare at her again, not exactly glaring, but making Josie feel as if he were measuring her for a pine box.

"She is a bad gift, this white woman who can do nothing. Until I can return her to her people, she must be taught to obey. Perhaps it would help if I were to beat her."

Josie dropped back into a crouch, fists raised as before. "Go ahead," she challenged. "Try it."

"All right, you two," said Daniel. "Why don't you both go to your own corners a while and cool off. Maybe in the meantime, Sissy can go to the barn and take care of that calf. The stew ought to be about done by the time she gets back."

Long Belly shook his head, rattling the arrowheads and strips of wolf hide woven into his braids. "Buffalo Hair must rest. She is not to be disturbed by such tasks. I will see to this lost animal myself."

Grumbling something about women's work, Long Belly started for the door, pausing long enough to say to Josie, "When I return, you will be punished for what you have done to my brother's head—and for what you have not done for him." Then he disappeared into the storm.

Although she'd halfway expected a little show of support

from Sissy, it didn't take long for Josie to discover that it wouldn't be forthcoming. While Daniel continued to work on a large piece of deerskin, Sissy snuggled quietly in her chair, eyes downcast as she warmed herself by the stove. Her casual, unconcerned attitude irritated Josie at first, but then it occurred to her that she hadn't so much as given a thought to poor Sissy when she'd been out in the storm. Hadn't even considered her safety or the terror she must have felt to be lost in a raging blizzard.

Realizing this about herself made Josie feel awful enough on its own. When she remembered some of the things Sissy had said the morning she'd gone with Long Belly on his insane journey, she felt even worse. Maybe Sissy was right, Josie thought with a jolt. Maybe she was a terrible excuse for a friend. She'd certainly taken for granted the overtures Sissy had made on her behalf at the pleasure palace. Never once had she done anything for the woman in return.

Hoping to make up for the unintended slights, Josie turned to her and asked, "Are you warmed up yet?"

She shivered a little. "Almost."

"Would you like me to heat some water to warm your hands and feet?"

"Huh?" Sissy looked up at Josie, the whites of her eyes exposed. "Well, sure. That'd be real nice."

"I'll get right to it."

As she searched through the rubble of dirty dishes on the counter by the stove, Josie realized that something fundamental had changed in Sissy, a subtle yet obvious difference. The woman had always been distant, very much within herself, almost to the point of being secretive. Now she seemed more aloof than cold, as if her stoical nature was by design rather than by rote. Gone was the slight droop of her chin, the subservient manner. She even displayed a touch of ego, as if her new role as Long Belly's great buffalo goddess had gone to her head.

Of course, part of that ridiculously imperious manner surely stemmed from the way the damned savage had worshiped her since their return. The way he'd fussed over Sissy, insisting that she couldn't be distracted from the buffalo spirit long enough to help do anything would be enough to turn any woman's head. Even Josie's. Why couldn't *she* have been the one to have found a damned buffalo wallow?

Aware that jealousy was creeping into her heart again, Josie shook off those covetous thoughts and filled a fairly clean kettle with water. Not long after Sissy cleaned her face and hands, and soaked her frozen feet in the warm water, Long Belly returned from the barn. Dusted again with the snow that was still falling, he shook himself like the dog that he was, turning the dirt near the threshold into a puddle of mud. Then he stripped off his coat and boots and plodded barefoot over to Daniel's bed, where he still sat working the piece of deerskin.

"So, my friend," Long Belly said. "Before I punish your foolish woman, I must ask—how well does this perfect gift warm your bed these cold nights?"

Daniel glanced at Josie, who was holding her breath, then hesitated just long enough to rob himself of an answer.

"It is as I thought," surmised Long Belly. "She is no good for pleasure either. For this, I am sorry, brother. Perhaps you will accept my gift of Buffalo Hair in your bed tonight."

"Ah, thanks . . . but no thanks."

"But you must," Long Belly insisted. "My woman knows much about the pleasure of men. I will take this worthless female to my own bed and show her what it means to please a man."

Josie gasped, terrified to think that Daniel might encourage such an arrangement. And why wouldn't he? Sissy was a much better bargain in a man's bed than Josie was or could ever be.

"I should have beaten this worthless female before I left on my journey," Long Belly continued, his features set like stone. "I will beat her now and send her to my loft."

"You do," she said, not crouching, but backing up, "and I'll kill you. I swear I will."

"Hold it right there." Daniel came to her rescue again, as before, on the late side. "Don't I have anything to say about who sleeps in my bed?"

The savage turned away from Josie. "Of course, but I know you will prefer my woman to yours. She will make you very happy. I owe you this and more."

"Dammit, Long Belly, you owe me nothing, you hear? Nothing." Daniel glanced at Josie, making up his mind about something, then turned back to the Cheyenne. "As to your offer of Buffalo Hair, I really can't accept. If there's one thing my perfect little gift knows how to do, it's take the chill out of a man's blanket. Besides that, she cooks up a mean batch of flapjacks. Leave her with me."

Before then, Josie had felt a distinct separation from the other three, a sense of isolation that she hadn't even felt when her stepfather dumped her at the pleasure palace. Until that moment of awareness, she hadn't realized how truly alone she was in the world. Now she figured that Daniel must care a little about her, no matter how deeply those sentiments were rooted in his own behalf, his own comfort. There was something more to his feelings, she just knew there was, some little piece of sympathy for her or her situation. Maybe both.

If she were to survive this nightmare—and suddenly, Josie wanted nothing more than that—she would have to figure a way to nurture those sympathetic feelings in Daniel. To gain or keep this man as an ally, she had to do something to ensure his loyalty, to build on that tiny base until he was willing to see things her way. At least until he could find it in himself to make Long Belly take her back to civilization. Besides, she still didn't know very much about this business between men and women. Maybe Daniel wasn't such a bad way to learn. He wasn't handsome in the usual sense, but sensual in a kind of uncivilized way, a man who made promises with his eyes she thought he might keep. Cheyenne blood aside, he promised to be an improvement over the fumbling, inept Henry.

For the first time since her abduction, Josie not only felt as if she could live through the experience, but take it into her own hands and control it. Besides which, she finally had a plan, one she intended to put into motion tonight—the very minute she and Daniel were alone.

* * *

After a meal that turned out a whole lot better than Josie had expected it to be, an exhausted Long Belly stoked the fire for the night; then he and Sissy went directly to the loft. Daniel eyed the pile of dirty plates and pans on the counter and smiled at Josie as if to suggest that she ought to wash them. While she intended to become more genial around him, she had no plans to turn into anyone's housemaid, ever again. If the dishes got washed, someone besides her in this bizarre little quartet would be getting the chapped hands.

Ignoring his hints, Josie looked down at the dress she'd worn and slept in since the savage kidnapped her, a gown that wasn't merely wrinkled, but covered in soot thanks to Daniel's dreadful stove. As long as she was going to be relaxing her standards in other ways, she figured it couldn't hurt to ease them in regards to modesty as well. After setting a clean bucket of water on the table and dropping the robe Sissy had brought along from Lola's onto the chair beside it, she blew out the lantern and proceeded to wash up in the dark.

"Hey," Daniel called from his bed. "Why'd you douse the light? I'm still working on this deerskin."

Her face as clean as it was going to get under these circumstances, Josie patted her skin dry with a rag she'd washed just for that purpose, then said, "I prefer to tend to my toilet in private. If you must have the light, I'll bring the lantern over when I come to bed."

She heard Daniel's sigh echoing in the darkness. "Never mind," he muttered. "I guess I'm about ready to turn in myself."

In the silence that followed, save for the howling wind, Josie washed out her dress, then draped it over the antlers next to Daniel's coat. Still wearing her chemise, drawers, and stockings, she slipped into the red satin robe and hurried across the frigid room to the warmth of the bed.

Josie had barely settled into her spot at the far edge of the mattress when Daniel's voice came to her on a whisper.

"I've been cutting a pattern in that piece of deerskin to make some high boots for you. With the weather the way it is, it looks like you'll probably be here at least another week. I figured you could use your own pair."

Josie was so surprised and touched, at first she didn't know how to respond. She didn't want to appear to be too grateful, thereby losing the upper hand, and yet she could hardly brush off such a thoughtful gesture.

"Why, thank you," she finally said, settling for something in between. "I appreciate your going to the trouble. When will they be done?"

Josie felt him shrug against the mattress. "Depends on how long it takes you to sew them up. You do sew, don't you?"

"Well . . . no."

"God almighty, woman, what *can* you do?"

It wasn't easy, but somehow Josie managed to keep from laughing as she said, "Muck out the stalls?"

He sighed. "All right. I'll sew them up good and tight, but if you want beads or other decorations, you'll just have to learn how to sew well enough to put them on yourself."

"It's a deal." Josie inched a little closer to Daniel, hungry for his warmth and something she couldn't define so easily. "I expect I ought to thank you for keeping your crazy brother-in-law away from me earlier. I think he might have killed me if we'd come to blows."

Before answering, Daniel rolled to his side, facing her. He was so close, their noses were practically touching as he said, "Long Belly wouldn't really have beaten you. He just wanted to put a scare in you. He's got it in his head that all women should behave the way his own mother and the other female members of his tribe do. He figures threats will frighten you into doing what he thinks you should do."

Knowing the relationship between the two men, Josie's best move would have been to swallow her hatred and keep her thoughts to herself. Somehow it didn't work out that way.

"Long Belly makes threats because he's nothing but a no-account, bloodthirsty savage."

She said it with a sneer that must have been audible. Until then, the air around Josie had felt cold. Now it seemed as frozen as Daniel's voice when he finally replied.

"You don't much like Indians, do you?"

"I *loathe* them," she said, unable to stop the torrent of hatred. "You would too if your father and brother were murdered by savages like Long Belly during an attack on your wagon train."

Again he was quiet a long moment before answering.

"I'm sorry. I didn't know," Daniel said softly. "I'm not saying this is the same thing as what happened to you, but as an army scout, I saw soldiers murdering Indian women and babies. I could feel much the way you do after witnessing such brutality, but I don't hate all whites just because of the acts of a few."

Pausing to think over Daniel's rationale, Josie couldn't argue the point. She did manage come up with another case against Long Belly.

"All right," she said easily. "I agree that hating all Indians doesn't make much sense, but I think I have a damn good reason to loathe your no-account brother-in-law. He kidnapped me, remember?"

"That's right," he admitted. "You also know damn good and well that's not what he set out to do. He still believes that he bought you as a gift—and so far, you haven't been much of a bargain."

Daniel slipped his arm around Josie's waist then, catching her off guard. Surprising her even more, he pulled her fully into his arms and kissed her. It wasn't a sudden smashing of lips, the way he'd done their first morning together, but a more gentle embrace, almost a caress. She allowed the kiss, and even met it with a decided burst of enthusiasm, figuring this might be a good time to add a little show of appreciation to her plan.

Daniel pulled away from her lips briefly, gasping as he said, "God in heaven, Josie. I think we've finally found something you can do."

Her cheeks were burning, and strangely enough she wanted

another of Daniel's kisses, but she made herself say, "Thanks, and good night."

"Good night?" Instead of letting go of her, Daniel tightened his grip on her waist. "But I thought . . . hell, woman, the way you just kissed me and all, I thought you were finally ready to be a little more friendly in bed."

"I don't know why you would think that. I told you once that I don't consider this cabin a brothel, and therefore—"

"I know, I know," he grumbled. "You're not on duty."

"That's right. I'm trying to think of this unfortunate incident as a vacation of sorts."

"Well, so am I, lady, so am I." He pulled her closer, snuggling her breasts up tight against his chest. "What's so wrong with the two of us having a little fun together? Your friend in the loft doesn't seem to mind the arrangement."

Daniel kissed her again, growing bolder in both touch and manner, enough anyway to take Josie's breath away and fog up her mind a little. It occurred to her, and none too soon, that maybe she didn't have quite as much control of him, the situation, or even herself as she assumed she would have. When she realized that she'd actually wrapped one of her legs across his hip and was pressing her intimate self against his knee, panic set in. Afraid of what she might do next, Josie called on one of the complaints she'd overheard from the working girls at Lola's, hoping that would convince Daniel to leave her alone.

"I guess I should have told you before now," she blurted out the next time his lips left hers. "I'm afraid I've gone and caught a pox from one of my customers."

This worked so well, Daniel all but left his fingers behind in his haste to get as far away from Josie as he could. In fact, he clung so closely to the edge of the mattress throughout the night, she worried that he would fall out of bed and re-injure his leg.

The following morning, Josie crept out from under the covers while Daniel was still sleeping and tiptoed over to check on her dress. Not only was it still damp, but even in the vague light she could see that all she'd done while trying to wash it was grind the soot into a great dark cloud that covered up most of the bodice. She was too cold to parade around the cabin in nothing but her underwear and the satin robe, attire that was too revealing to wear around the men anyway.

Left with no alternative, she slipped into Daniel's heavy coat, then reached for his high boots. Josie was just pulling on the second moccasin when she heard the ladder squeaking behind her. In the next second, Long Belly stood over her.

"I will put wood in the stove," he said quietly. "You will make coffee."

The boots firmly in place for the time being, Josie clung to the hope that Daniel's claims about the savage were true. Then she rose to her full height, still several inches shorter than Long Belly, and said, "Maybe later. Right now I'm on my way out to the barn."

"What concerns do you have in the barn?"

"I thought I'd feed the animals, milk the cow, and collect some eggs. All right?" Dismissing him, she turned toward the door and reached for the latch.

Long Belly's hand suddenly trapped Josie's between him and the rough pine planks. "I will tend to the animals as I always do," he said doggedly. "You will make coffee and clean our dishes."

"Damned if I will."

The Indian looked as if he'd been gut-punched. Josie used his paralysis to her advantage by pushing on the latch and freeing the door. As she stepped over the threshold, Long Belly was suddenly himself again. He leapt up beside her and used his arm as a barricade to lock their two bodies into the confines of the door frame.

"You will do as you are told," he said, loud and demanding.

Josie struggled, trying to pop free of the brute. "I'm going to the barn. Now get out of my way."

"What the hell is going on?" said Daniel from behind them.

"Shut the damn door. It's already cold enough in here to freeze a witch's ass without inviting the storm inside, too."

Giving into the Cheyenne's superior strength as well as Daniel's request, Josie backed into the room, complaining loudly. "I'm trying to go out to the barn and take care of the livestock, but Long Belly won't let me pass."

The Cheyenne pulled the door shut, then shocked Josie by grabbing her arm and dragging her over to the stove. "You belong here, cooking and cleaning. Here you will stay."

"Let go of me," she warned, kicking the savage in the shins.

Long Belly hollered, but tightened his grip.

"Dammit, you two." Sounding exasperated, Daniel reached for his crutches and climbed out of bed. "What do I have to do? Dump a pail of ice water on your heads to get you to calm down?"

Ignoring Daniel, Josie brought her heel down hard on the Indian's toes. Long Belly immediately released her, then lit into her with a string of Cheyenne curses.

By now Daniel, who was clad only in his drawers, had hobbled over to where they stood. "Now what?"

Long Belly, paying about as much attention to him as Josie had, reached into the pile of dirty pots and pans, grabbed a plate crusted with grease and God knew what, and thrust it into Josie's hand.

"When I return from the barn," he said. "You will have coffee made and these dishes clean."

Intent on only one thing, refusing to be a slave for either of these men, she let the plate slip through her fingers and shatter against the plank floor.

"Christ, Josie," said Daniel. "Anyone can wash dishes. At least give it a try."

He then made the mistake of reaching into the pile and handing her a second plate. Like the first, she let it fall through her fingers and smash against the floor.

"Josie—what the hell is wrong with you?"

"I will not be your slave," she said defiantly. "Damned if I'll ever be anyone's slave again."

With that, she ran past the two men and headlong into the storm.

After closing the door behind her, Long Belly cast a long glance Daniel's way and said, "Broken Dishes. I think we should name your woman Broken Dishes."

Daniel regarded the shattered crockery at his feet. "That sounds about right. Broken Dishes, it is."

"Forgive my bad judgment, brother." Long Belly limped to the counter, his leg dragging. "This gift has been worse than no gift at all. If it takes the rest of my life, I must—"

"Don't say it, you red-skinned son of a bitch. If you say that you owe me one more time, I swear to God, I'll throttle you till your eyeballs pop out."

Long Belly just smiled, promising nothing beyond the moment.

Hearing a familiar squeak, Daniel glanced up to see Sissy climbing down the stairs.

"What's all the commotion?" she asked, joining them near the stove.

Grumbling to himself, Daniel said, "Long Belly here was trying to teach Josie how to wash the dishes. She didn't take too kindly to the job."

"I don't mind washing no dishes." Glancing at the mess on the floor, Sissy dropped to her hands and knees and began picking up the fragments.

"You will not do this," said Long Belly. "And you will not wash dishes. You will think only of finding the buffalo's sleeping place again."

"I didn't find no sleeping place." Sissy sat back on her heels. "All's I did was fall in a hole."

Long Belly refused to believe this. "The buffalo spirit led you there."

She shook her great tumbleweed of hair. "If anything led me there, it was them big boots you gave me. That's why I tripped and fell in the first place."

"You are the keeper of the buffalo spirit," he stubbornly insisted.

In exasperation, Sissy looked to Daniel.

He leaned forward, resting more heavily on his crutches, and said to his brother-in-law, "If Buffalo Hair wants to wash the dishes, let her. I don't see how that can defile the precious spirit inside her anymore than you do when you take her to your bed."

Long Belly bristled. "That is different."

"Oh?" It wasn't often that Daniel actually backed the man into a corner. He rather relished the opportunity. "How do you figure that? If I remember correctly, the Cheyenne set a high store on keeping their women chaste outside of marriage."

"Buffalo Hair was not chaste when she first came to me, and she was not chaste with me before I realized she had the spirit in her." Proud of his logic, Long Belly went on to say, "If I do not touch this woman again, she will not become chaste again, so why should I deny myself her pleasure?"

Daniel laughed, impressed with his rapid rationalization of the situation.

Encouraged, Long Belly added yet another bit of logic. "Besides, Buffalo Hair is not a Cheyenne woman. She does not have to follow our customs."

"It seems like none of the women around here have to follow our customs," Daniel said in complete agreement. "Why do you suppose that is?"

Long Belly pondered this. "Ah, my friend, Broken Dishes is a very difficult woman, one who needs to be taught many lessons. Shall I go to the barn and beat her for you?"

The idea had merit. Hell, thanks to Josie's conniption fit, Daniel was down to his last three plates. He hobbled over to the window, looked out on the raging storm, and said, "Thanks for the offer, brother, but I'm afraid beating a woman like that would only make her madder. She'd probably shoot us both in the head—on purpose."

Snow was blowing so thick outside, Daniel guessed it would be hard for a man to see his hand in front of his own face. The odds of Josie losing her way under such conditions and freezing to death seemed too likely to ignore.

Turning back to Long Belly, he said, "Maybe you ought to go out to the barn and check on Broken Dishes. She might have gotten lost the way that storm is blowing."

"I will be happy to do this for you. I owe—" He stopped himself short of uttering the entire foul sentence. "I will be happy to do this for you."

"Thanks." Watching as Long Belly pulled on his coat, Daniel waited until he had started for the door before adding, "And brother? Be nice to the lady."

Chapter Seven

She was lost.

She was hopelessly and frantically lost in a swirling flurry of snow so white, its glare was as blinding as the sun.

Josie wasn't new to this sort of weather. She knew full well the dangers of being lost in a blizzard. The Baum Ranch outside Miles City couldn't have been more than sixty miles to the north. Conditions there wouldn't be a whole lot different than what she was facing now. What did vary was the fact that had she been home, she'd have been able to make her way from the house to the barn easily. Here she was a newcomer, more easily disoriented than she ever would have imagined.

Pulling the hood of Daniel's jacket well around the sides of her face, Josie paused to get her bearings. How far had she run? Ten or fifteen feet? Since she couldn't see anything but white anyway, there was no sense exposing her eyes to the needle-like shards of snow. Josie kept her head down, changed her direction slightly, and used her right hand as a divining rod of sorts.

Her efforts were rewarded a moment later when her fingertips smashed into something solid. Feeling her way along the rough wooden planks until she came to a corner, Josie quickly discovered that she'd come across the wellhouse, a small building erected over an underground spring. Using its location as her guide, she followed the slight incline down from the back of the wellhouse, veering slightly to the right, and ran straight into the side of the barn, as she'd hoped.

Once she was inside the cavernous building and safe again, she leaned against a stall and let out a relieved sigh. The next time she lost her temper, Josie muttered to herself, she would go stand in a corner like any other recalcitrant child. Trying to relax, she inhaled, pulling in the warm scent of grain and alfalfa along with the clean, yeasty aroma of the animals themselves. In the chill of the frigid morning, she could see steam rising off the backs of the livestock and the trail of her own breath mingling with the animal heat in the frosty air. Her heartbeat back to normal, Josie went happily about feeding the horses, pausing to rub their noses and murmur silly greetings to each in turn, and then settled herself over the stool to milk the cow. She'd collected about a half a pail of milk with the promise of more to come when the barn door suddenly clattered open.

Glancing around the end of the stall, she saw Long Belly standing in the doorway, his hair and face framed in snow. In his hand, he carried a big axe with feathers hanging off the handle.

Gripped with a very clear picture of who his intended victim must be, Josie leapt off the stool and ducked down in the stall. The cow, apparently unhappy about the fact that she hadn't finished the job, turned its big eyes on her and bellowed.

"Hush, please?" Josie whispered, grabbing the milk pail.

The cow, of course, didn't answer, but Long Belly did.

"Broken Dishes?" he shouted. "Is that you?"

That didn't make much sense—was the bastard still going on about the plates she'd smashed?

"I come for you," the Indian said, his voice drawing closer.

Trembling in her hiding spot, it occurred to Josie that if she didn't take some kind of action, if she just sat there until the savage finally came across her, she would die like her father and brother had, a helpless victim waiting to be ravaged and scalped. Looking frantically around inside the stall, she couldn't find anything to use as a weapon except the pail she held in her hand.

As Long Belly's shadow came into view, Josie leapt out of her hiding spot, swung the pail high over her head, then brought it down as hard as she could on top of the Cheyenne's skull.

Long Belly groaned, milk running down his face and braids, then staggered backward and collapsed in the straw.

Josie didn't stick around long enough to find out if he was simply stunned, out cold, or even dead. She darted out of the barn and ran straight for the cabin.

When the door crashed open and an ashen-faced Josie dashed into the room, Daniel's first thought was that she'd crossed paths with one of the bears he'd warned her about. She wasted no time informing him that she'd come across an animal of a whole other kind.

"Daniel!" she said, breathless. "Your brother-in-law followed me into the barn and tried to kill me!"

"Kill you?" Daniel tried not to laugh, even though he was sure there must be some kind of joke coming next. "What did he do—sing?"

Josie's eyebrows drew together and held. "I'm serious. He came into the barn while I was milking the cow and went after me with his axe."

"*After* you?" Daniel exchanged a glance with Sissy, who looked troubled. "I sent Long Belly to the barn for you because I was afraid you might have gotten lost in the storm."

"Hah!" She laughed, but there was no mirth in her expression. "How did you figure he was gonna save me with an axe?"

Daniel chuckled, understanding how she might have gotten the wrong idea. "Long Belly took the axe to split a few more logs because we're running low on firewood."

She thought about this a moment, then glanced at Sissy. "He really wasn't planning to kill me with that axe?"

Sissy shook her head. "It's like Dan'l says. We thought you was lost."

Feeling like an idiot, Josie sighed heavily. "I sure thought different, especially since he was still going on about those damned dishes I broke."

"I don't know why Long Belly would care about the dishes," Daniel said. "They're mine."

She looked up, only mildly repentant. "Oh. Sorry."

He came a little closer, bearing some weight on his bad leg. Thanks to the job she'd done cleaning the infection from his wound, Josie figured Daniel wasn't but two, maybe three weeks away from being healed. That seemed payment enough for a couple of broken plates. Unless, of course, she'd managed to kill his brother-in-law—a definite possibility considering the fact that she'd pasted Long Belly so hard with that pail.

Assuming she hadn't out and out killed the savage, Josie knew that sooner or later he would return to the cabin. What then? Long Belly may not have had murder on his mind when he went to the barn, but he most surely would be thinking along those lines when set eyes on her again. And there would be no one to come to her rescue. There was no way that Daniel would be so quick to come to her defense once he realized that she'd been the one with murder on her mind.

"Where's the milk and eggs?" he asked, back to the subject of the barn.

"The . . . ?" Josie slapped her forehead. "I was so frightened, I forgot all about my chores. Maybe Sissy can go after them."

Daniel glanced out the window and shook his head. "The way this storm is blowing, I think we'd better leave the outside chores to Long Belly for the time being. It's easy to get disoriented in a blizzard like this. I'm surprised you made it to the barn and back without getting lost."

Of course she had no intention of telling him now or ever that she'd done just that, but Josie used the opening to bring up a worrisome problem.

"Since things are so bad out there," she said hesitantly. "Maybe someone ought to go check on Long Belly—you know, to make sure he's all right."

"Check on Long Belly?" Daniel hooted a laugh.

"But what if he's fallen . . . or had an accident?"

"If he's fallen, he'll get up. As for an accident—" Daniel eyed her with suddenly suspicious eyes. "Is there something else I ought to know about?"

Wide-eyed, Josie felt her entire face tighten with feigned innocence. "No, no, it's just that anyone can have an accident in a barn full of tools and such."

Daniel kept coming at her until he'd trapped her between his body and the table. "Sissy," he said, never taking his eyes from Josie's face. "If you walk in a straight line from the porch, you can't help but run into the barn. Think you can manage to go out and check on Long Belly?"

"Sure."

Without so much as asking Josie's permission, Daniel spun her around and stripped his jacket off her shoulders. Then he handed it to Sissy, saying, "Wear this, and remember—a straight line."

After she'd gone, Daniel spun Josie back around and turned his attention on her with particular interest in her apparel—the red satin robe. "What really happened out there in the barn?" he asked.

"Nothing." Time for a change of subject. No question about it. "You sure look nice this morning. Did you shave or something?"

Although Daniel didn't entirely lose his skeptical expression, he rubbed his jaw and nodded self-consciously. She'd meant to distract him, not herself, but suddenly all Josie could think about was his damp, clean hair and the expanse of smooth, swarthy skin from his forehead to his waistband. Now that she could see his entire face, she also noticed that he was far more handsome than she'd realized. She could almost forget about the Cheyenne blood thundering in his veins.

Even Daniel's eyes seemed a brighter shade of blue this

morning, and clean-shaven, there was nothing to disguise his wicked smile or the way his full lips parted at her undisguised appraisal of them. Josie could hardly believe that she'd kissed those sensuous lips last night. Would he offer more of the same tonight?

The storm couldn't last much longer, she figured, a day or two at the most. In the meantime, why not enjoy a few more stolen moments in Daniel's arms? She suppressed a little shiver of pleasure at the thought, recalling the way he'd kissed her, his lips gentle and teasing against her mouth one minute, passionate and demanding the next. He wouldn't be pressing her for more than kisses, believing her diseased. It would be safe to indulge her curiosity. Suddenly Josie could hardly wait for the night to come.

Daniel leaned into her then, his mouth moving toward hers in a way that promised the delights of the night were hers for the taking now if she'd wanted them that badly, and then suddenly the cabin door banged opened, robbing her of the opportunity.

Daniel wheeled around with the aid of his crutch to see that Long Belly and Sissy had returned. The Cheyenne's arms were full of wood, and a lump the size of Texas stood out on the left side of his forehead. Buttery milk stained the front of his glorious buffalo robe, and clumps of it were curdled in his braids. He also, Josie couldn't help but notice, had a firm grip on his axe. She began to back toward the stove.

"Holy Christ," said Daniel, horrified by Long Belly's appearance. "What happened? Did the cow decide she didn't want you to milk her after all?"

Long Belly dropped the load of wood near the door. "The cow was calm. I was clumsy, an accident."

"An accident, huh?" Daniel shot Josie a suspicious glance.

Sissy, who carried the milk pail and a few eggs in the pocket of Daniel's jacket, headed for the counter to dump her load. Josie slinked along behind her, using her buffalo hair as a shield.

"An accident, yes," said Long Belly, protecting Josie for reasons she couldn't imagine.

After that statement, the savage finally cast a furtive, wary glance her way, but didn't meet her eyes or make a move in her direction. Instead, he crossed the room and disappeared up the ladder. What was his game? Josie wondered. Was he waiting to get her alone before lighting into her, too embarrassed to let Daniel know that a female had ambushed him? Or figuring on sneaking up as she slept to get his revenge? She had no doubt he'd be seeking his pound of flesh, one way or another.

As Sissy lined the eggs up on the counter, Josie impulsively said, "Need some help?"

"Cooking? I thought you'd rather die than get stuck fixing us a meal."

Keeping her voice low, she said, "I meant that I'd rather die than take orders from that savage, not that I expected you to do everything. Besides, I was under the impression you weren't supposed to lift a finger around here. Aren't you afraid the buffalo spirit will sneak out of you if you get to working with the pots and pans?"

Sissy, not one prone to frivolity, chuckled under her breath. "I figure if I don't want to get poisoned by the food or the filth on them dishes around here, I'd best tend to such chores myself."

"I have to admit that I've been kinda washing the dishes up before I eat off them, too. Have you taken a good look at the stove?"

Sissy didn't bother to look at it. She simply nodded. "There's enough grease stuck to its topside to sweeten every skillet in all the Territories."

Josie snickered, still hiding behind Sissy's hair. "They're a couple of pigs, aren't they?"

For the first time that Josie could remember, Sissy actually laughed. Not a gut-rolling chortle, but open-mouthed giggles, the way Josie figured girlfriends behaved. Feeling close to Sissy in ways she never imagined she would, she took up the plate she'd washed and began to dry it with the sheepskin lining of Daniel's coat.

"When's your birthday?" she asked, caught by a sudden idea.

Sissy stopped in the middle of the pan she was scrubbing, and frowned. "Don't have one."

"Of course you do. You must know how old you are."

This time Sissy kept on scrubbing. "Don't know for sure. About twenty, I expect."

This was a shock to Josie, and not just because Sissy obviously didn't know her true birthday. She had assumed that Sissy was older, certainly beyond her own twenty-three years. Her skin was surprisingly smooth and bronzed, but her eyes and general manner were aged, too hollow for a woman of twenty.

Wanting to make up for the void somehow, Josie said, "Everyone should have a birthday. Since we don't know the exact date of yours, why don't we proclaim Thanksgiving as your official birthday? That way you'll always remember when to celebrate."

Instead of the response Josie had hoped for, Sissy merely shrugged. "Don't make no never mind to me. I ain't never had no reason to celebrate the day I was born, and I don't expect that I'll have reason to in the future."

Instead of discouraging Josie, Sissy's lackadaisical attitude only served to fire her imagination. She vowed then and there to make sure that Sissy was remembered on her birthday— even if, heaven forbid, they were still stuck in this godforsaken cabin on Thanksgiving Day.

Across the room, Daniel made a show of putting the finishing touches on Josie's boots, but mostly he was just trying to listen in on the women's conversation. All he'd heard so far were murmured exchanges and a few giggles, nothing that made any sense. Then, adding to the confusion, Long Belly returned to the group carrying one of his long-sleeved shirts and a pair of fringed leggings—which he then gave to Josie.

"What the hell are you doing?" Daniel blurted out, surprised he'd voiced the thought.

"Broken Dishes needs something to wear other than her skinny dress or your heavy coat."

"Broken Dishes?" said Josie.

"Your new name," Daniel explained, irritated all at once. "How do you like it?"

Instead of answering him, she turned to Long Belly and thanked him for the clothes, then huddled with Sissy again.

Daniel had, of course, recognized that Josie needed something other than the flimsy dress—why the hell did she think he was sitting here stitching up a pair of damned boots? The fact that Long Belly, whom Josie feared and loathed, had thought of a solution to her lack of clothing, much less provided that solution out of his own meager wardrobe, stuck in his craw like the thigh bone of a chicken.

"Shall we go outside, my brother?" Long Belly suggested, heading for the door. "And leave Broken Dishes her privacy for dressing in her new clothes?"

Irritated all over again, this time by the fact that he hadn't thought of the simple courtesy himself, Daniel nearly broke his other leg in his haste to join his perplexing brother-in-law outside.

"All right, you sneaky bastard," said Daniel the minute the cabin door was closed behind them. "Why the sudden change of heart about Josie? It wasn't an hour ago that I had to all but chain you to the wall to keep you from beating her."

Laughing to himself, Long Belly stepped off the porch and took the opportunity to relieve himself as he explained. "You said to be nice, did you not?"

"Well, yes." Daniel joined him, even though working his way down the icy steps was slow work. "I figured nice couldn't hurt, but the way you're spoiling her, she won't be worth a damn. Hell, she already wasn't worth a damn when you brought her here—now she'll be even more worthless."

Turning his back to the furious snowstorm, Long Belly said, "Broken Dishes was a very bad gift. I have already told this to you, and I believe it still, but I also think she may be a good woman yet. A very strong woman, in the Cheyenne way.''

Daniel stood there staring in shock for so long, his dick damn near froze in his hand. As he adjusted his clothing, he recognized that something ugly and foreign was warming inside him, an insidious thing he ought to stamp out before it caught fire. Still, he couldn't help wondering—was Long Belly trying to claim Josie as his own? He had, after all, and on more than one occasion, offered to take her to his bed and teach her a thing or two. The very thought made Daniel want to tear out the man's throat.

''Just what happened out there in the barn, brother?'' he demanded. ''The truth—all of it.''

Long Belly's head snapped up as if he'd been slapped— something Daniel sorely wanted to do. ''I do not know what you speak of.''

''Yes, you do.'' Daniel hobbled a step closer to him. ''You think I don't know that Josie somehow put that lump on your head? What did you do to make her so mad?''

The big Cheyenne simply stood there, his outline a fading photograph in the swirling snow. ''I did not beat Broken Dishes, nor shall I.''

Of that, Daniel had no doubt. Feeling both hot and cold, a madman in a suit of ice, he shouted, ''How about this, you red-skinned son of a bitch? Did you try to sample her, maybe show her the proper way for a woman to bed a Cheyenne warrior?''

Long Belly's mouth dropped open. ''Why do you think this of me, brother?''

''Because you know that Josie's the Deadwood Stage—any man can ride her.'' Out of control, Daniel raged on. ''Maybe you ought to know something else about her before you go dipping where you're not wanted again—that gal has the clap. How'd you like to take that back to your friends on the reservation?''

"The clap?" Long Belly puzzled over this a moment.

"Disease," Daniel said, all too happy to clarify the situation for him. "You go poking around in that one and you'll get a disease guaranteed to rot your pecker right off your body. Now how much do you want her?"

Long Belly shuddered. "My Brother, I do not want your woman now, and I did not—"

"What you did," Daniel said, interrupting, "was bring those two here in the first place. It was the worst, the stupidest thing you've ever done, you hear? You owe me for this—and one hell of a lot more than your miserable hide is worth."

After that damning statement, the rest of the morning went by in an angry blur. Long Belly didn't say another word. Not to the charges Daniel had leveled at him. And not to the women, who fed and fussed over the big Cheyenne as if he were the one with the broken leg. Sick to death with the entire group— himself in particular—Daniel dragged his aching body back to bed after breakfast. To his surprise, he fell asleep almost immediately.

When he awoke some time later, it was to a much brighter room. And a disturbing quiet. Sitting up in bed and gathering his wits, Daniel glanced out the window to see that the sun was peeking through the clouds, if not quite shining. A brief respite, he wondered, or the end of the early storm? A quick look around confirmed that the cabin was deserted except for him and his useless body. Assuming at first that his housemates had gone out for some air, Daniel climbed out of bed and made his way to the door.

He paused there, noticing the fresh supply of firewood, then turned to see a new clod of ham on the counter along with a bowl of eggs and a full pail of milk. Provisions that Long Belly usually left behind each time he went on one of his insane buffalo hunts. Daniel checked the corner and saw that the Cheyenne's parfleche was gone, along with Josie's dress, shoes, and satin robe.

He opened the door and stepped out onto the porch, knowing

somehow what he would find. He didn't even need to make
the trip to the barn to understand that a couple of the horses
and the mule were gone. Their tracks stood out in the snow
like signposts.

And each of them pointed the way to Miles City.

Chapter Eight

The ride up into these hills a few days before had taken place at night with Josie aboard the miserably uncomfortable back of a sure-footed mule. She'd been terrified then, most of her fears centered on the savage and his unknown plans for her, but also because she couldn't see the path ahead or judge its dangers.

Josie was terrified all over again, and not because of Long Belly, who'd been downright agreeable ever since she'd clobbered him with the milk pail. In fact, everything seemed to have reversed itself. Now that she could actually see where she was going, gazing down on snow-covered valleys and ahead to impossibly high mountaintops, Josie longed for the ignorance of darkness, the cloak that had shielded her from the dangers ahead. These slopes were not only thick with snow, but icy beneath that fluffy white layer, treacherous in spots for even the sure-footed mule.

Unfortunately, Josie had refused to mount the bony-backed creature that morning. She'd insisted instead on riding the big, beautiful horse that Daniel simply called The Black, sure that her hours spent on the back of the family's plow horse made her an experienced rider. Long Belly had explained that The Black was the young breeding stallion Daniel planned to use in improving the small herd of horses he planned to raise. He also tried to convince her that he was an unsuitable mount for her, but Josie couldn't be dissuaded.

Now as she clung to the reins and neck of the nervous, high-strung animal, she realized much too late that she was no match for a horse such as this. Duke, with all his high-stepping ways, was simply a candidate for the glue factory compared to the spirited half-ton of horseflesh between her thighs now. Why had she been so damned stubborn?

At first Josie had no idea what Long Belly was up to this morning when he sent her and Sissy to the barn to tend the horses and brush them down. She enjoyed such activities immensely and didn't think too much about it until the big Cheyenne joined them with all his traveling gear, including hers and Sissy's clothing. She'd wanted to go back to Miles City all right, but this didn't seem right, riding off without so much as a word to Daniel. It hadn't been his idea to kidnap her, and he had tried to make her as comfortable as possible while she was a captive in his home. How could she take off without saying good-bye?

Josie mentioned her desire to return to the cabin in order to bid Daniel a brief farewell, but Long Belly wouldn't allow it. They would leave with him now while there was a break in the weather, he'd said, or they wouldn't be leaving the reservation at all. With freedom so close at hand, Josie reluctantly agreed to his terms. Sissy, on the other hand, while uncomplaining and acquiescent, was a sullen and unenthusiastic traveling companion. Josie had an idea that she'd rather have wintered in the cabin than back at Lola's.

On the trail, the winds were still calm, but a light snow had begun to fall. The sun ducked behind a cloud to become only a teasing glimpse of daylight, a distant memory of warmth. Yet Long Belly plodded onward astride his own paint, and began to lead them down the sheer side of another mountain. Sissy rode close behind the savage on a little brown mare.

Since Josie had foolishly done such a good job of convincing
him that she was at home in the saddle, not bothering to mention
that she was used to a sidesaddle, she'd been left to bring up
the rear.

That mighty restless stern suddenly decided that he'd gone
far enough. At the edge of the steep trail, The Black dug his
hooves into the snow and refused to budge. Josie kicked the
stallion's sides as hard as she dared, urging him on, but her
efforts were wasted.

"Long Belly!" she called, terrified of being left behind.
"The Black won't go down the hill."

Without stopping or even slowing the paint, the Cheyenne
turned on his saddle blanket and shouted, "Whip his rump as
hard as you can with the reins. He will move."

Afraid of the big stallion, Josie feebly slapped the reins
against his backside. He jumped in place, dancing side to side,
but didn't move forward.

"Come on, Black," she said, trying to wheedle him into
complying. "How can you be such a loving, cuddly thing in
your stall and so damned bullheaded on the trail?"

The stallion snorted, then continued to toss his head and
dance in place.

When Josie glanced up to call out for help again, she saw
to her horror that Long Belly had already disappeared into the
forest and that Sissy's mount was a mere smudge against the
deep green of the trees.

"Stop!" she shouted. "Don't leave me."

Hearing her cries, Sissy pulled up the little brown mare just
before they both disappeared into the forest and snow, then
wheeled the animal around and started back up the hill. She'd
almost reached the spot where Josie sat stranded on the back
of the unruly stallion when the mare's footing suddenly gave
way to a treacherous patch of ice. Then everything seemed to
happen at once.

Sissy's mount reared in panic, but her small back hooves
were useless against the patch of ice. Her legs wrenched out

from beneath her, the mare tumbled over backward with her rider still clinging to the saddle.

Both Sissy and the mare screamed as they fell, their voices and bodies eerily entwined, and then they began a deadly slide down the side of the hill.

This was way too much excitement for The Black.

He got moving at last, but now he was in a panic of his own. The stallion uttered an ear-splitting scream, vibrating Josie in the saddle, then leapt to the right, pawing the frosty air with his front hooves. In almost the same instant, he abruptly spun around on his back legs and took off at a dead run. Through it all, Josie somehow managed to hang onto the saddle horn and the horse's thick mane, although twice she felt her entire body slip sideways, mere inches from The Black's deadly hooves.

Now it was Josie who screamed, begging the animal to stop, to whoa, to free her from his panicked flight. When that didn't have any effect on the stallion, she heard herself hurling oaths at him, screaming the vilest curses she could think of and then some. The Black ignored her and continued to race on, galloping through a blur of trees that slapped Josie's face and arms, and through drifts of snow that kicked up shards of stinging ice.

Incredulously enough, the horse continued to gain speed, making it all the more impossible to convince him to stop. He wouldn't stop . . . no matter what she did, he would not stop. Couldn't stop.

Sissy's first sense of awareness came when she tried to roll over and found that she couldn't move. She'd thought herself asleep, dreaming of an endless sea of brilliant white clouds, thinking perhaps that she'd joined her mother and baby daughter there, lounging in all that puffy softness and grooming their angel wings. She wondered if babies butchered from their mother's wombs before they were even half-formed got to go to heaven. Lola, who'd done the abortion and made sure that Sissy would never conceive again, had scoffed at the idea, insisting that all she'd done was scrape out a mass of formless, insignificant tissue.

Sissy wasn't so sure.

Her mother had told her about heaven and angels, convincing her they were real in the weeks before syphilis had claimed her in both body and mind. Sissy wanted to go there now, to the place where broken spirits were miraculously healed and everyone was equal. A place where she might reunite with her mother and find her daughter at last.

Determined to take her place in the untroubled world her mother had promised, Sissy tried to slip back into the dream, to drift forever among the clouds.

The voice of God suddenly came to her, shouting words she'd have expected to hear from His lips as a golden whisper.

"Wake up, woman," He demanded of her. "You must wake up now or you will die."

Wasn't that the point? she thought, and laughed. That tiny movement brought an explosion of pain that ran the length of Sissy's body, centering its cruel claws somewhere in the area of her chest. She moaned, disheartened to think that she might still be alive, and again tried to roll to her side. As before, her body refused to move. No longer in the clouds, she was caught in a bog filled with pins and needles, a mountain of barbed clay that made it next to impossible to breathe. Had she tripped and somehow fallen into hell?

"You must fight hard, Buffalo Hair," said God, leaning over to kiss her forehead, and Sissy's first thought was to correct Him.

"I'm ... Sissy," she said, surprised to find speaking so difficult. "I'm—"

"Yes, Sissy, I know. You must rest. Do not talk. Can you open your eyes for me?"

A simple thing to open one's eyes, but when Sissy tried, her lids seemed stuck, as if held shut by a whole pot of glue. She tried harder, frantically rolling her eyes behind lids that wouldn't obey, until finally they cracked, then hung there at half-mast. God, she noticed right off, was a blur of buffalo fur and cinnamon skin.

"Focus," He said. "Look at me and focus."

Sissy blinked her eyes and glanced up at Him again. Although she'd never seen an image of God, she hadn't expected Him to look so much like Long Belly. Or to find a single tear running down his cheek.

Memories flooded her then, thoughts of the cabin, of Josie and Daniel, of the big Cheyenne who took her to his bed and used her body each night. She was alive. Hurt, but alive. In pain, but comforted by the man who'd dragged her to these hills in the first place. A man, she thought with wonder, who had tears in his eyes.

Never, as long as Sissy could remember, had anyone, not even her mother, shed a tear on her behalf. As much as the sight touched her, it disturbed her even more, enough to make her want to jump up and run away. If only she could.

"What happened?" Sissy asked, trying to get her bearings.

"You fell down the side of the mountain. Your horse fell with you and landed upon your body."

There was no horse lying across her now. "I can't move. Why can't I move?"

Long Belly looked away, staring intently at the blanket of snow beside her. "You have been injured," he said at last. "Badly bruised. Do not try to move again. I will make a travois to take you home."

As he got to his feet, Sissy said, "Did you kiss me a while back?"

Long Belly lowered his head as if embarrassed, then slowly nodded.

She remembered then the reason for his grief, the thing that must have prompted both the tears and the first kiss he'd ever given to her—Long Belly actually believed that she'd been touched by the spirit of a buffalo, and that if she died, the spirit would die with her. Sissy had no way of knowing if that were true. The one thing she did know was that she couldn't allow this man to touch her heart.

Filling her lungs with all the scant air they could hold, she said, "Well, don't do it again, you hear?"

At the cabin, Daniel and his crutches had been pacing near the door for what seemed like hours. He was half-tempted to go on out to the barn, splinted leg and all, saddle up The Black, and ride after Long Belly and the women he'd kidnapped all over again.

Not that he wanted to keep Josie here against her will any longer than necessary. And not that he enjoyed having her around. At least, that was what he told himself. And that was what Daniel thought about when he wasn't worrying about the weather and his cattle.

Daniel's herd was small, around twenty head. Summer had come hot and dry in the spring and never looked back, which meant that feed grass was inferior. Between the poor feed, brush fires that took much of it, and the lack of rain, Daniel's cattle and those of other area ranchers were not in good enough condition to go to market. Opting, as most of his peers did, to hold the entire herd over with hopes of fattening it up next spring, he had laid in a good supply of hay to help the cattle through winter by the time the first snow hit in October. If what he'd seen of November so far was any indication, he hadn't bought near enough hay.

Daniel stepped outside to get a better idea of the sky and stopped just beyond the porch. Instead of checking the weather right then, he found himself again fighting the urge to continue on to the barn and saddle up The Black. About then, and much to Daniel's astonishment, the stallion trotted into the yard. The horse was saddled and bridled, but riderless.

Whistling for his prized stud, Daniel snapped his fingers, the signal to come. The Black, winded and weary, hung his head and plodded over to where his master stood. His flanks were heaving, his nostrils blowing, and his body was damp and foamy with exertion. Daniel couldn't make sense of it. Who would have ridden this particular horse to such extremes, and why? Surely not one of the women. Long Belly would never have allowed a female to ride what amounted to a green-broke stallion, and his paint would have had to come up lame before he'd have ridden The Black himself.

Concerns about the animal nudging his curiosity aside, Daniel left one of his crutches behind and led the stallion to the barn. After drying him off and giving him a good rubdown, he fed and watered the horse, then went to check on the other animals. Only the mule was left behind, but oddly enough, it appeared to be sound. Why, he wondered again, had Long Belly taken The Black on his journey instead?

Daniel got most of his answers within the hour. By then the wind had picked up, not enough to blow the snow from the trees, but enough warning that another blizzard was headed their way. Almost a foot of snow had fallen since morning, and it showed no signs of letting up. Daniel was staring out the window, judging the clouds, when Long Belly rode into his view.

He was leading the brown mare, and his own paint was dragging a crude travois behind its heels. He seemed to be alone.

Dreading the news, Daniel made his way outside and down the porch. "What the hell happened?"

"Buffalo Hair has been injured in a great fall." Long Belly climbed off the paint and went to work on the bundle lying on the travois. "I must get her inside. Can you tend to the horses?"

Daniel hobbled across the yard, reaching Long Belly as he gripped the poles of the litter between his hands and began dragging it toward the cabin. He glanced at Sissy to see that her eyes were closed. She was either unconscious or asleep.

"Where's Josie?" Daniel wanted to know. "Didn't you take her with you?"

Long Belly avoided his gaze and continued on his way to the house. "She rode The Black. He spooked and ran off with her."

Daniel reached out and snagged the Cheyenne's arm. "You put a woman on that crazy stallion?"

"She insisted that it be so."

"Insisted? You would never have allowed her or anyone else to ride your own damned horse. How could you let her take mine?"

He hung his head. "It seemed the quickest way to get her out of the barn. Do not worry," he said, although he sounded deeply concerned. "I am sure that your great horse will find his way back with her soon."

Daniel gritted his teeth and squeezed Long Belly's arm so tightly that he yelped. "The Black came back to the ranch over an hour ago. Josie wasn't on him."

Long Belly's skin paled in horror. "How can this be? I saw no signs of her on the trail."

"She's got to be out there somewhere."

Long Belly glanced over his shoulder in the direction from which he'd just ridden in. "How will I ever find her now? The storm has already covered my own tracks."

PART TWO

If the adder could hear
and the blindworm could see,
Neither man nor beast
would ever go free.

—Nineteenth-century proverb

Chapter Nine

Semiconscious and dazed, Josie snuggled deeper into her bed of snow. She was surprisingly warm—so content, in fact, that she felt as if she could lie there forever. Something at the back of her mind pricked at her more conscious self, urging her to get up and save herself before it was too late. Josie was so darned comfortable, she couldn't bring herself to pay heed to the warnings. All she wanted to do was lie there in the soft, warm snow dreaming of springtime and wild roses and sweet, sweet perfume.

Scattered memories came to her as she dozed, images of racing through the forest on the back of a runaway stallion, of glimpsing hoofprints in the snowy path ahead. She remembered thinking that The Black must be following the trail they'd left earlier, and that now he was headed straight for home. Soon she would be safe inside Daniel's cabin, his strong arms around her, soothing her fears, his lips pressed to hers. Soon, very soon . . . and yet. Something was wrong.

When it came to her—a terrifying memory of The Black rounding a bend in the icy road at top speed—Josie gasped and choked on a mouthful of snow. Something had spooked the stallion, she recalled. She thought it might have been a bear, but she didn't know for sure because when the horse shied, she was catapulted right out of the saddle. She'd been airborne, a lovely memory of floating like an eagle for a few seconds, and then found herself rolling down the side of a hill, tumbling end over end in the snow until she connected with something hard.

Josie breathed deeply, catching the pine-scented mulch of the earth beneath her, and surmised that her fall had been stopped by a tree. Was she hurt? She didn't think so. All Josie could feel at the moment was safe and warm. And that something wet was nuzzling the back of her ear.

The Black. Of course.

That no-account excuse for a horse was standing guard over her, no doubt filled with remorse over his brutal treatment of his rider. It was the least he could do after nearly killing her. Josie shook her head, hoping her fragmented mind would come together again the way pieces of a puzzle fell into place. She blinked several times, raised her chin a bare inch above her warm bed, and tried to focus on the landscape before her.

A sea of white stretched out as far as the eye could see, the blinding waters disturbed by several tall ships. That didn't make any sense. She'd never even been to the seashore. Josie blinked a couple of more times, forcing her eyes to focus, and when she looked again, she realized the vessels were nothing more exotic than trees. Beneath some of those majestic pines stood a few head of cattle, each pawing through the crusty snow for the fodder beneath. Assuming this was Daniel's herd, that meant the cabin could be very close.

The horse's muzzle left Josie's ear, and in its place, came a raspy tongue that licked the entire side of her face.

"All right, all right," she said, struggling to her hands and knees. "Just give me a minute."

Actually, Josie soon discovered, she needed more like five or ten minutes. Now that she was fully conscious and aware of her predicament, she no longer felt warm or safe. She shivered inside Daniel's jacket and shook off the layer of snow that had collected on her back. Movement brought the first of several aches and pains, none of which, she deduced, were caused by broken bones or life-threatening injuries. She was lucky, and she knew it. Still, Josie had her doubts about throwing her battered body up on the back of that wild stallion again. Even if she were fool enough to try and mount him, what guarantee was there that she could stay on him any better than she had the last time?

The Black nudged her then, good and hard, with enough force to knock her off balance and onto her side.

"Hey!" she cried, determined to gain at least a little dominance over the ornery horse. "Don't you think it's about time you learned who's in charge? From now on—"

The words, her heartbeat, everything seemed to die in her throat as Josie got a good look at the belligerent stallion—and saw that it was no horse at all.

Utterly dumbstruck, the only words she could think of fell out of her mouth in a husky whisper. "My God."

In the barn, Daniel finished grooming the mare and the pinto, then gave them an extra ration of feed. As much as he hated to admit it, all three horses were exhausted, unable to take Long Belly on a search for Josie until they'd had a chance to rest up. The only option was for the big Cheyenne to take the mule and make do as best he could.

The sooner the better, thought Daniel as he stepped out of the barn and into a blast of frigid air. If Josie wasn't found in the next hour or so, she couldn't possibly survive in the freezing winds that were kicking up, never mind the blizzard that was sure to follow.

Moving as quickly as he could with only one crutch to aid him, Daniel returned to the cabin to find Long Belly fussing over Sissy, who remained in the travois on the floor.

"You'd better get going," said Daniel. "Another storm's coming in, fast and hard. The horses are spent, so you'll have to take the mule."

"I will go," Long Belly assured him. "But first I must see if Buffalo Hair is well. She worries me greatly."

"You get your butt on that mule. I'll take care of Sissy if she needs doctoring."

"But you cannot do what must be done." Long Belly rose, facing Daniel with more defiance than he'd ever seen in him. "Even I cannot tend to Buffalo Hair alone. We must move her to your bed, gently, so we do not cause her pain or further injury."

Biting back words he knew he might regret, Daniel kept a grip on his temper long enough to take another look at Sissy. Long Belly had removed the rope he'd used to lash her to the travois and unwrapped the horse blanket that had shielded her from the elements. She was moaning softly, her eyes rolling and twitching beneath fluttering lids, and her lips were taut, rigid with pain. Since she'd been crushed by a horse, Sissy could be suffering from all manner of injuries, some of them potentially fatal.

"All right," he said, resigned to this much. "How do you propose we get her on the bed?"

"I will drag the litter to the edge of the mattress. Then each of us will lift the ends of the poles at the same time. Can you do this with your broken leg?"

Daniel had an idea it wouldn't be any too comfortable, but figured he could manage. "Drag it on over here. Time's a-wasting."

By pushing his splinted leg out behind him, Daniel was able to bear most of his weight and his half of the travois by using the strength in his right leg alone. Once they got Sissy on the bed, it was a simple of matter of dismantling the pine branches Long Belly had used for poles, then sliding the horse blanket out from beneath her.

"There," said Daniel, wiping the perspiration from his brow. "I'll take over from here."

To his consternation, Long Belly shook his head and sat down on the bed next to Sissy. "I must feel her bones to see where she is broken," he said, unbuttoning her buckskin shirt.

That's when Daniel's patience ran out. "I said I can do that, dammit. You should be out looking for Josie, who wouldn't even be lost if you hadn't done something so stupid as drag her out in this weather, on my half-broke stallion, no less."

Long Belly's eyes twitched, but he didn't look up at Daniel. He remained silent and continued running his hands over ever inch of Sissy's nude torso; then be examined each arm.

Exploding with frustration, Daniel lit into him. "What the hell were you thinking when you took those two women out of here? Were you thinking at all? You could have gotten the both of them killed—hell, maybe you have."

His examination of her upper body complete, Long Belly buttoned Sissy's shirt, then turned to Daniel and glared. "It is you who drove me to take them away, you who forced me to make such a journey before the storm had finished with us."

"Me? *Me?*" Daniel kicked at the bed with his good leg, forgetting in his anger that he'd be putting his entire weight on the bad one. He groaned, then fell heavily on the mattress beside Sissy.

"Careful you do not disturb her," warned Long Belly. "She has two bad ribs, one broken, the other torn loose from the others."

"Sorry," he said, meaning that much, but then he was right back at Long Belly's throat. "I just wish you'd show as much concern for poor Josie, who's probably frozen half to death by now."

The Cheyenne removed Sissy's leggings, then slipped his hands under the long shirt and began to probe her pelvis and hips.

As his fingers glided over the smooth contours of her body, Long Belly turned to Daniel and said, "I am very concerned for Broken Dishes, as I am for Buffalo Hair. I agree it was a stupid plan to take them to Miles City at this time, but you are as responsible for what has happened as this sad Indian."

"Why do you keep trying to blame me? Hell, I didn't even know you were leaving."

"It was you, was it not, who said to this foolish Cheyenne

warrior that the worst thing I ever did was give a diseased woman to you?"

Daniel hated that Long Belly chose to bring up this point, especially since he'd used his own words against him. "Yes," he admitted, "I suppose that I did. But I never said that you ought to just up and take them back without consulting me."

Long Belly had worked his way down Sissy's thighs, and was feelings the bones of her knee as he said, "You told me that I owed you more than my miserable life for bringing Broken Dishes here. I did not think that I should bother you with the task of removing her and her disease from your bed."

Daniel suddenly felt like the back end of the mule. "Sorry, brother. You're right. Most of this is my fault, not yours."

Long Belly got up off the bed and put a hand on each of Daniel's shoulders. "I am as you say, the stupid red-skinned son of the bitch who made all this trouble. Do not blame yourself."

"But I never meant for—"

"Stop," said Sissy, drawing a rasping breath. "You fellahs are making me sick."

Daniel exchanged a quick glance with his brother, then he tiptoed away from the bed, leaving the pair in peace.

"I must go now," said Long Belly to his patient. "You have many bruises and ribs that must heal, but I think you will be all right. My brother will tend to your needs while I search for Broken Dishes."

Sissy nodded, then drifted off again.

Long Belly headed for the door. "I go now."

"And hurry, would you?" said Daniel, hobbling along behind him. "If you don't find Josie soon, I'm afraid that . . . well, she might be . . ." He left that final, unthinkable thought unsaid.

"Do not worry, my brother. If you wish this worthless woman returned to your lodge, I shall find her."

Daniel smiled. "It is my wish. Now go, make haste."

He stood there in the doorway even after Long Belly had disappeared into the barn. Snow was falling harder now, not quite in blizzard proportions, but piling up in drifts as high as his waist. Daniel could barely stand to think of Josie out in this storm, cold, alone, probably frightened out of her mind. He closed his eyes, praying to God in a rare act of faith that she would be found alive and well. When he opened them again, he nearly collapsed in disbelief.

It took a minute or two to convince himself that his eyes weren't playing tricks on him, but there by the wellhouse he swore that he'd caught a fleeting glimpse of a woman with long auburn hair. Daniel moved to the edge of the porch, straining to see through the flurry of snowflakes, and there she was again, hurrying toward the open door of the barn.

"Josie!" he called, his heart in his throat.

But she continued on, apparently unable to hear him over the storm. Then she scurried, or rather limped, into the barn.

The last thing Josie expected to find when she ducked into the barn was Long Belly. But there he was, one hand fisted in the mule's mane as he prepared to mount the animal.

"Long Belly," she said. "You've got to listen to me."

He turned to her in surprise. "You are here."

"Yes, it seems that I am. Please take the mule back into his stall and stay there with him, out of sight, until I tell you it's all right to come out again."

"Where did you come from?" he asked, completely disregarding her request. "How are you here?"

"I don't have time to explain anything right now. Just take the mule and go hide in the stall."

Still ignoring her, he said, "Does my brother know you have returned? He will be very—"

"Long Belly!" Remembering his docile behavior after she'd clubbed him with the milk pail, Josie dared to use that reaction to her advantage. "Do as I say, and do it now, you no-account bastard, or I swear to God, this time I'll take your head off with that pail."

The threat, as she'd hoped, had the desired affect. As the

stunned Cheyenne retreated with the animal into the stall, she helped herself to an armful of hay, then rushed back out into the storm. Daniel, who'd been standing on the porch, was nowhere in sight.

Hoping he'd stay that way, in the cabin where he belonged, Josie hurried back to the small clearing just beyond the well-house, to the place where she'd left her new friend.

Chapter Ten

Daniel returned to the porch, both crutches in hand, only to see Josie disappear into the forest again. As far as he could tell, Long Belly hadn't ridden out after her. Frustrated and confused, he hobbled down the steps and made his way to the barn to get some answers. A single lantern hung near the entrance, illuminating the enclosure in murky light. Even in those poor conditions, Daniel could see that with the exception of the livestock, the barn was deserted. What the hell was going on?

He made his way down the center aisle, heading for the last stall to check on the mule's whereabouts, when Long Belly's voice came to him from out of nowhere.

"May I come out now?" he asked, oddly enough.

"Long Belly? Where are you?"

He poked his head around the corner of the mule's stall. "Broken Dishes has returned."

"Yes, I know. I saw her run in here, but where is she now?" Daniel closed the gap between them and stood just outside the stall. "Why are you hiding in here? Have you done something to her?"

The embarrassment of explaining the situation lay in sullen wrinkles across the Cheyenne's brow. "She said if I did not obey her wishes, she would remove my head. I believe this women means to do me harm."

"And what wish was that?"

"She said I must hide in the stall and not come out until she said I could."

Daniel didn't know whether to laugh or beat the facts out of the man. At the moment, the latter seemed the more attractive option. "You're not making a hell of a lot of sense. What'd you do, scare her again?"

"I have done nothing," Long Belly insisted. "It is Broken Dishes who wishes to—"

The barn door squeaked opened, effectively closing the formerly fearless warrior's mouth. Without another sound, he ducked back into his hiding place. Utterly confused by now, Daniel turned to see that Josie was backing into the barn. She was slightly hunched, bending toward something. Her hands were full of hay and stretched out in front of her as she inched her way along the straw corridor.

Then, to Daniel's surprise, the nose of an animal appeared at the edge of the door, its nostrils flared, as black as pitch against the flurries of snow behind it.

"Come on," Josie cooed, still backing into the barn. "You're almost here, safe and warm."

A moment later the great matted head of a buffalo rounded the corner.

"Holy Christ!" Daniel staggered backward and nearly fell off his crutches.

At the sound of his voice, the beast raised its head from the temptation of the offered hay, planted its hooves, and grunted.

Josie glanced over her shoulder, shouting to Daniel in a whisper, "Be quiet, and please go hide—now!"

Astounded, unable to believe his own eyes, Daniel woodenly went along with her request and hobbled into the stall with Long Belly.

"Perhaps you understand now, my friend," the Indian said.
"Broken Dishes has gone crazy, no?"

Daniel shook his head, but decided against explaining what
he'd seen. If Long Belly knew that a buffalo—*a buffalo!*—
was following Josie into the barn, he wouldn't believe it until
he'd seen, and undoubtedly startled, the great beast for himself.
Daniel had seen, and he still wasn't convinced. Surely it had
been an illusion.

After a few more moments of silence save for the soft sounds
of Josie's encouragement, the barn suddenly came alive. The
door squeaked to a close, the buffalo grunted like a hog in
slop, and the horses began nickering in deep, nervous tones.
Behind Daniel and Long Belly, the mule pawed the ground,
its eyes big and white, rolling with anxiety.

Concerned about the ensuing chaos should the mule break
loose and confront the strange beast in the barn, Daniel whispered, "Tie that lop-earned animal up before he tramples us."

Long Belly wasn't in a mood to listen. "What are these
noises I hear? Is Broken Dishes—"

"You'll find out soon enough. Take care of that mule. Do
it now."

Daniel didn't waste time checking to make sure that the
order was followed. He had to be sure of what he'd seen. His
movements slow and careful, he inched his head around the
corner of the stall. The buffalo, no illusion or apparition after
all, stood in the center aisle, its great head swinging back and
forth. It *was* true. Despite the horrendous mistake he and hunters
like him had made, at least this one great beast still lived to
roam the plains. Daniel's relief was palpable. Redemption, it
seemed, was finally within his reach—assuming the thing didn't
trample them all to death first.

Concerned about Josie and her proximity to the wild beast,
Daniel sought to gain her attention—and only hers.

"Psst."

The buffalo raised its head right along with Josie.

"What?" she whispered back.

Daniel motioned for her to join him in the stall, then stepped back out of sight. Turning to Long Belly, he pondered ways of explaining the situation while keeping the Cheyenne relatively calm at the same time. It seemed an impossible task.

Josie crept up behind him then and said, "So what do you think of my new friend?"

"I see, but I don't believe."

She laughed. "I thought he'd be happy inside out of the cold, but now he seems awfully nervous. What can I do to calm him down?"

"Her," corrected Daniel. "It's a female."

"It is? How can you tell from so far away?"

"Has to do with the horns. I'll explain later."

"Who do you speak of?" asked Long Belly, heading out of the stall. Daniel raised a crutch, barring his way.

"Quiet," he said. "And I'd advise you not to rush out there for a look at our . . . guest. You know how skittish buffalo can be."

Daniel had assumed that Long Belly would go wild when he learned that the buffalo of his dreams had been found, not that he would lapse into a stupor. The big Cheyenne was beyond excited, unable to say or do more than clutch his chest and sag against the wall, as mute as the planks of wood that held him up. Guessing that he wouldn't remain silent or immobile for long, Daniel took those precious few seconds to come up with a plan.

Whispering to Josie, he said, "If any of our horses get loose with your new friend, they'll be ripped to shreds in minutes. Can you sneak back out there and check to make sure the stall doors are secure so the horses can't get loose? The cow will just have to fend for herself."

Josie shrugged. "I doubt you have to worry about her. I think the buffalo has been living with some cattle—yours, I guess."

"Buffalo?" said Long Belly, looking and sounding hollow. "Where is this buffalo you speak of?"

"Go now," Daniel urged Josie. "Toss a little more hay on the ground to keep it busy while you're securing the stalls.

And hurry," he added with great meaning, "before our other friend here decides to help you."

As Josie quietly went about her tasks, Long Belly regained most of his senses.

"I must see this buffalo you speak of," he said to Daniel. "I must see it now."

"You will," Daniel assured him. "But not until the three of us are sneaking out the rear door on our way back to the cabin. You can take a quick look at it as we leave, but be sure to keep quiet and don't make any sudden movements. It's a little nervous and might charge us."

Long Belly nodded in agreement, but his eyes were so huge and glazed over, Daniel would have bet that he'd forget his vow once he saw the great beast. When Josie returned to the stall, he urged her through the back door first, then tucked both of his crutches under one arm in order to keep a firm grip on the Cheyenne's jacket as he stepped out into the aisle. It seemed like a good idea, keeping control of Long Belly in that manner, but Daniel might as well have tried to control the buffalo.

When Long Belly actually caught sight of the great beast, he fell to his knees in prayer, dragging Daniel down with him. He landed face down in the straw, kicking his splinted leg out behind him. That foot then hit the edge of the open door, prompting an involuntary howl Daniel couldn't have contained under the threat of death.

His agonized cry got the buffalo moving. Trotting down the corridor toward the men, the beast grunted several more times, a strange sound that sent The Black rearing in his stall and turned the other horses into high-pitched, whinnying maniacs. About the time Daniel thought he would be trampled to death by the last living buffalo on earth, Josie stepped between him and the beast.

"Get out of the way," Daniel shouted.

She, of course, didn't listen.

Instead, Josie held her ground and began making cooing noises which, surprisingly enough, slowed the animal's approach. Although still highly agitated, the beast stopped in its tracks mere inches from where she stood, its tail raised in challenge to the two men behind her. That was enough to get Daniel going, but Long Belly was still caught in the animal's spell.

"Broken Dishes has mastered this great beast," he said, awestruck. "She must be a goddess or a—"

"Shut up, you fool," Daniel said, cutting off the Cheyenne's benediction. "Get me out of here before your great beast runs through her to get to us."

This got Long Belly moving at last. He helped Daniel to his feet, then dragged him through the narrow opening Josie had left in the door. A moment later, she followed them outside and secured the barn door. Then the group trudged through the field of snow carpeting the corral and made their way back to the cabin.

Once they were all inside again, Daniel insisted that Josie warm herself by the stove before he would allow any further discussion about the buffalo. Now that he could concentrate on her, he saw that her face was scratched, a couple of gouges almost matching those she'd left on him their first morning together. Her cheeks were blotched with angry patches of red—frostbitten, no doubt—and her hair had come loose of its braid, leaving it to fall every which way across her back and bosom in a mass of auburn tangles. She looked as if she'd picked a fight with a wolverine.

"Are you all right?" he asked, removing his jacket from her shoulders.

Josie paused, warming her hands over cook top, and considered the question carefully. She'd been so cold, she hadn't really been able to feel her extremities until now. As she warmed up, her fingers and toes began to tingle and sting, yet she didn't think they suffered from frostbite. She also ached from one end to the other—and knew exactly what had caused her injuries.

"Thanks to that no-account crazy horse of yours," she said, shooting Daniel an accusing glance, "I'm tired, cold, and bruised from my toes to my head. Other than that, I guess I'm all right."

Long Belly pushed his way into the conversation. "Where did you find the great buffalo? Why did he come here with you?"

"*She* followed me," Josie corrected. "At least Daniel says he's a she."

"She is," he confirmed, before going back to her previous comment. "As for my crazy horse, I would never have allowed you to ride him—that fool did." He pointed at Long Belly. "So what happened? Did The Black throw you?"

Josie nodded and rubbed her backside. "We were almost back to the cabin when something in the trees spooked him. I went flying out of the saddle, then rolled down a hill and crashed into a tree."

"And then you found the buffalo?" asked Long Belly, focused on only one topic.

"No," she said. "The buffalo found me. Actually, I guess you might say that she also saved my life."

The men glanced at each other. The look they exchanged said they thought her quite mad.

"I passed out after I hit the tree," she explained. "When I came around again, the buffalo was trying to nudge me up out of the snow. I think I might have laid there forever if she hadn't been so persistent."

Again they exchanged a glance, this one of both doubt and wonder. Then Daniel said, "All right. Assuming the buffalo saved your life—and I'm not saying that she didn't—how did you get her to follow you back here?"

Until then, the enormity of the experience and the apparent rarity of a wild buffalo taking to a human being hadn't really crossed Josie's mind. She'd seen buffalo herds at a distance during the family's trek out West, but knew very little about the nature of the animals. She'd certainly never been close enough to one of the beasts to actually see its dark purple tongue or feel it rasp up the side of her face like the dull blade of a razor. Did that make her special somehow?

Turning to warm up her backside against the stove, Josie drank in the marvel of the men's expressions, unaware until then how thirsty she'd been for respect—theirs or anyone's. Never had she been an object of such admiration, much less the near reverence with which Long Belly was regarding her. While she could hardly call Daniel's expression worshipful, he also seemed to be holding her in much higher esteem than he had that morning. Knowing these things made Josie feel aglow inside, as if an ember of coal burned close to her heart.

Smug as she relayed the tale of her arduous trek, she said, "After I got over the shock of seeing a buffalo standing over me, I started back up the hill, figuring I could follow the tracks of that idiot horse of yours—assuming he was smart enough to head home. I heard something behind me, and when I looked back, I saw that my new friend was following me."

Long Belly sighed, or something close to it, and then his eyes rolled to a close.

Daniel was less convinced. "You expect me to believe that buffalo followed you like a pet dog all the way back to the cabin?"

"Well, she did stop here and there, but I just dug around in the snow until I found a handful of grass, and along she came, nibbling out of my hand until we got near the barn. She wouldn't move after she saw the building no matter how much grass I tempted her with, so I ran inside and got some hay. She couldn't resist it."

"Well, I'll be damned." Daniel shook his head with wonder.

Josie turned to Long Belly, assuming he had a few questions for her, too, but he stood there staring somewhere over her head, in a world of his own.

From a distant part of the room came a sudden groan.

Glancing between the two men, Josie saw that Sissy was lying in Daniel's bed. In all the excitement, she'd somehow forgotten about her.

"What happened to Sissy?" she asked, alarmed.

"She and her horse took a pretty bad fall."

Josie didn't care for Daniel's tone or his expression. He reminded her way too much of an undertaker.

"She's got some broken ribs," he went on to say. "And she probably has a concussion, too."

It all came back to Josie then—the fall, the screams of both Sissy and the mare, The Black nearly unseating her in his own panic. How could she have forgotten any of it—especially the accident that could have cost her the only friend she'd ever known?

Almost afraid to hear the answer, Josie asked, "Is . . . will Sissy be all right?"

He shrugged. "Might take a little while, but I think she'll be just fine."

Josie tried to squeeze past the men in order to go to Sissy and assess the damage herself, but Daniel blocked the way. "She needs her rest now. Leave her be until she comes around on her own."

It wasn't easy, but she bowed to his judgment. If those were Sissy's only injuries, there wasn't much else to be done for her anyway. Besides, Josie was too tired and achy to argue the point. Suddenly, she could hardly stand, much less make it across the room. She swayed on her feet and willingly allowed Daniel to help her to a chair, which he did by using only one crutch to aid his own ailing body. Long Belly, who remained trancelike, went to the bed, looked down at Sissy, then slowly made his way up the ladder to his loft, all without speaking a word.

Outside, the storm raged on, building rapidly toward blizzard proportions. Soon, Josie thought, feeling neither happy nor sad, but resigned, they would all be trapped in a cage of snow. Caught as surely as the great beast in the barn.

An hour or so later, after Daniel had warmed a kettle of water for Josie to use in washing up, he set his mind to fixing a hot meal—soup, he thought, given the fact that invalids suddenly outnumbered the healthy. Although he'd laid in extra rations for the livestock, he hadn't had much chance to consider his own needs, especially after he broke his leg. At the time, winter had seemed a long way off.

Now, with two extra mouths to feed, Daniel realized how truly meager the cabin's store was. The shelves above the stove contained a tin of coffee, a sack of sugar, a jar of salt, a bowl of acorns, and two bottles of whiskey. A bin of flour sat to one side of the stove, enough to see them all through for months. To the other side of the stove, away from the heat, sat a barrel loaded down with potatoes and onions. Larder enough for a while, he supposed, but soon he would have to make a trip to the St. Labre Mission for more supplies.

Settling on the few ingredients at hand, Daniel filled a kettle with water and added potatoes, onions, and a nice fat clod of beef from the calf Long Belly had "accidentally" rounded up.

As he tossed in a measure of salt, Josie, who'd been dozing in her chair, suddenly said, "I think I'll call her Sweetpea. How does that sound?"

Daniel glanced over his shoulder. "What?"

"The buffalo. Don't you think the name Sweetpea suits her?"

With a roll of his eyes and a shrug, Daniel turned back to the kettle and began to stir the watery soup. Why, he wondered, did women always think they had to come up with names for their animals, especially the ones that sooner or later wound up as someone's meal? Men didn't indulge in such foolishness as a rule, unless the subject was a horse. Even then, Daniel didn't see the need for fancy names.

The mule was the closest he ever got to naming an animal, referring to the cantankerous beast, depending on its mood, as Lop-ears, Knothead, or Buzzard Bait. The Black was The Black because he was black. The mare was known as the mare, the cow a cow, and the chickens were, of course, chickens. Long Belly called his paint Spots That Fly with the Wind, chiefly because his owner was a fool. Daniel occasionally referred to the horse as Spots That Break Wind, simply because he enjoyed irritating his brother. Otherwise he called him The Paint, what else? Now it seemed the ranch was blessed with a grumpy buffalo named Sweetpea, a ridiculous moniker if ever there was one. What was next, he wondered, a grizzly called Baby?

"Well?" said Josie, drawing Daniel's attention again. "Can you think of a better name for her than Sweetpea?"

With a final stir of the soup, he propped the big wooden spoon against the edge of the kettle and turned to her. Josie was dragging her fingers through her hair in an effort to undo all the tangles and knots, grimacing as if it were an ordeal. It suddenly occurred to Daniel that the poor woman didn't have her usual grooming aids with her.

Heading to his possibles bag, Daniel suggested, "If you just have to name it something, why not call her Bison? That's what she is, you know."

"What kind of name is Bison? That would be like naming a child Kid or Ragamuffin, don't you think?"

"What I think," he said as he dug out his bristle brush, "is that naming animals is a foolish waste of time."

"In that case, I'm sticking with Sweetpea whether you like it or not."

There was something new in Josie's attitude, Daniel thought as he approached her chair, a heightened sense of superiority above anything he'd noticed in her before. It made him want to take the backside of the brush to her bottom, to destroy that obstinate streak once and for all. But then she turned to him and grinned, an adorable smile that wasn't so much crooked as slanted, angling to the right with a little catch that prompted an involuntary wink. The expression made Daniel forget all about her defiant nature. The next thing he knew, he was playing the handmaid.

"Let me help you with those tangles," he suggested, positioning himself at the back of her chair. "You'll never get them out yourself."

"What a nice surprise," she said, eyeing the brush. "Thank you. I'd appreciate that very much."

As he began to draw the bristles through her hair, Josie settled into the chair with a request. "Tell me about the horns. How did you know that Sweetpea was a female?"

"Easy," he muttered, distracted by her hair as it slid through his fingertips. "Cow horns are skinny and the tips point forward. A bull has much thicker horns with tips curving upward—all the better to rip a hunk out of another bull. Or a man."

She made an odd noise, a cross between a groan and a gag, then went silent, giving herself up to his ministrations.

Since he'd never groomed a woman's hair before, not even his wife's, Daniel was unprepared for the response it pulled from him or the deep sense of intimacy the act suggested. As he drew both the brush and his free hand through her hair, he marveled over the texture, the coarse, full-bodied, but surprisingly soft feel of those locks slipping through his fingers. After he'd brushed out most of the tangles, Daniel continued to stoke Josie's mane of auburn tresses, making them shine until she relaxed enough to let her head fall back. Then she began to moan with undisguised pleasure.

"No one," she murmured softly, "has ever done this for me—at least, not since I was a very small child at my mother's knee. It feels so wonderful, I could almost fall asleep."

Sleep by then was the last thing on Daniel's mind. He wanted to raise Josie up out of that chair, wrap himself in those shiny locks, and kiss her until they were both crazy from wanting each other. He'd almost convinced himself to do just that when Long Belly spoiled the whole mood by climbing down the ladder and making his way to the table.

Glancing at Daniel, the big Cheyenne eyed the brush in his hand with amusement, then said to Josie, "If this maiden has finished grooming you, I have gifts to offer in your honor."

Josie sat bolt upright, cutting off Daniel's indignant response. "Gifts?" she said. "What kind of gifts?"

"Things to keep you safe." The warrior then hunkered down before her, playing the humble apostle. "These are charms meant only for a woman of your great powers."

He reached out and took into his hands a small length of hair that ran from Josie's temple down to the tip of her breast. She flinched at first, frightened perhaps, then relaxed and allowed the fawning Indian to continue with his revolting dis-

play of devotion. Daniel thought he might be sick as he watched
the overly dramatic ceremony Long Belly made of plaiting the
hair at each side of Josie's head. When he fastened the ends
of the braids with an arrowhead attached to a leather thong,
then set out to explain what he'd done, Daniel thought for a
moment that he really might throw up.

"These are stone arrowheads," Long Belly said, carrying
on as if he were truly besotted. "They will ensure you a long
life. Wear them always."

While Josie studied the crude charms, the Indian reached
inside his buckskin apron and withdrew a tiny leather bag
attached to a long strip of rawhide.

"This," he explained, "is the greatest gift of all, an amulet
to protect you against accidents or illness. Never let it leave
your slender neck."

As Long Belly rose to tie the medicine bag around Josie's
throat, Daniel's gut rolled and he clenched his fists against a
sudden burst of rage. This had to be a false gesture, one calculated to ensure that her power over the buffalo could be trans-
ferred to him. To offer a white woman such a gift was unheard
of in the Cheyenne tribe, a gesture that usually carried far more
significance than Josie could ever understand. Daniel had never
been given a medicine bag. Not only was he half-Cheyenne,
he was also Long Belly's brother-in-law and the father of his
nephews.

With the amulet properly tied at Josie's throat, she looked
up at Long Belly and said, "What's in the bag?"

"Never ask such a rude question of any Cheyenne." At this
breach of etiquette, Long Belly was properly indignant. "The
medicine contained in this bag is known only to the warrior
who makes it. It is not for your eyes or ears."

Josie shrugged indifferently. "Oh, well, in that case, thank
you."

"You must not thank me for these gifts, Broken Dishes. I
owe you much for bringing the great buffalo to me—even my
life."

Daniel couldn't keep silent any longer. "For Christ's sake,

you fool, will you stop all that beholding nonsense, once and for all? I'm getting damned sick of it.''

Long Belly ignored his complaints. ''Broken Dishes and her powers deserve these gifts and even more for what she has done. I will go to the barn now and thank this great beast also for allowing her to lead it to me.''

Josie jumped out of her chair so fast, Daniel almost fell off his crutches.

''Oh, no, you won't,'' she said. ''I don't want you anywhere near Sweetpea.''

Long Belly looked to Daniel. ''Sweetpea?''

He smiled, sensing a sudden turbulence in the Cheyenne's great plans for the bison. ''That's what she named the buffalo. Kinda cute, isn't it?''

His features suddenly set in stone, Long Belly turned back to Josie. ''I must go to the beast and make myself known to her.''

Josie held her ground. ''Sorry, but I can't allow that. Sweetpea is afraid of everyone but me. That buffalo is mine. I found her, she followed me, not you, and nobody is going to disturb her without my permission.''

Daniel could see the muscles of Long Belly's neck tense up as she spoke, and when he added a most murderous glance to his demeanor, it seemed time to referee.

''Josie,'' said Daniel. ''You can't keep that buffalo to yourself.''

''Oh, yes, I can.'' She stamped her foot as she added, ''When I'm finally able to go back to Miles City, Sweetpea is going with me. And that's that.''

The rest of the afternoon passed with suspicious glances and a few hot glares divided among them, but the trio somehow managed to take their supper around the same table. Josie and Daniel claimed the chairs, leaving Long Belly to balance himself on the potato barrel.

They ate Daniel's tasty beef soup in silence, which was just

fine by Josie, who'd heard all she wanted to out of the sullen
Cheyenne. After they'd finished their meal, she woke Sissy
long enough to get a few spoonfuls of warm broth down her,
and then let her drift off to sleep again. Long Belly made a
grand show of washing the dishes, making sure everyone knew
that such tasks were beneath him. Daniel sat at the table working
beads into the pair of leather boots he'd promised to make for
Josie—the same beads he'd sworn that she would have to sew
in place herself. In the face of all Long Belly's gifts, she figured
he no longer felt justified in demanding that she should do
something so lowly as sew on her own beads.

It was as Josie was spreading an extra blanket over Sissy
that Long Belly made the mistake of trying to sneak out of the
cabin behind her back. Right behind him, she threw on Daniel's
coat and boots, and braved the storm. The wind was blowing
so hard, it was driving snow as if it were stakes, making it
difficult to see. That was why Josie ran straight into Long Belly,
who was relieving himself to the side of the porch.

"Oh," she said, eyes averted. "Excuse me. I'm just on my
way to the barn to tend the animals."

Lowering her head to hide her embarrassment, she went on
her way, struggling to keep herself upright through the stronger
gusts as she made a beeline for the barn. Sweetpea, Josie
discovered, had made herself at home against the big sliding
door, which made it nearly impossible to open. She tugged
until there was a crack in the door just big enough to squeeze
through, and saw that the buffalo was still munching on the
hay she'd tossed to her earlier. The animal seemed perfectly
content in her new home.

Moving quietly to make sure the beast stayed that way, Josie
lit the lantern and went about the business of feeding the horses
and milking the cow. Through it all, Sweetpea kept a close
watch on her, but didn't appear to be ruffled by her presence.
She prayed the animal would always feel so calm around her,
at least until she'd put all of her grand plans into motion.

Josie knew that Daniel and his savage friend must think her
selfish, or maybe even insane, but they had no way of knowing

that Sweetpea might well represent the kind of freedom Josie had long dreamed of—a ranch of her very own. What banker in his right mind would refuse to stake the woman who owned the last surviving buffalo, especially if she somehow managed to find Sweetpea a mate? The very thought filled her with a sense of power she'd never felt before, but also weighed Josie down with the burden of taking on such a responsibility.

At what magic age, she wondered, did a person know, inexorably, when she was right and the world was wrong? Was there ever a time to be completely sure of one's convictions, or was this the norm, this living in a constant state of anxiety over decisions made in the heat of the moment? All Josie knew for sure was that this apparently unusual buffalo had bestowed on her the means to become independent as well as a certain power over the men inside the cabin—the savage in particular. Right or wrong, it wasn't a gift she intended to relinquish easily.

When Josie returned from the barn, pail of milk in hand, Daniel had put away his sewing supplies for the night, and Long Belly was sitting on the edge of Sissy's bed.

"The animals are taken care of for the night," she announced. "And Sweetpea is resting comfortably."

"Good," said Daniel, rising from his chair. "I think it's about time we all had a good rest, too."

"I am ready to have a long sleep," replied Long Belly as he got off the bed and headed for the ladder.

Milk pail still in hand, Josie's gaze went suddenly to the bed where Sissy slept. Long Belly stopped in his tracks and turned his eyes on the same spot, as did Daniel, who'd been hobbling across the room.

As one, their attention shifted from the bed and settled on each other.

Then Daniel draped his arms over his crutches and said, "Well, hell. Where're we all gonna sleep?"

Chapter Eleven

Long Belly was the first to offer what he considered the simplest solution. "My brother and his bad leg must sleep with Buffalo Hair. I will share my loft with Broken Dishes."

Daniel jabbed Long Belly's ribs with the end of his crutch. "The hell you will, you horny bastard."

"I meant only to share my blanket," the Cheyenne insisted.

Josie, who wasn't going to accept any solution but her own, said, "I'll just stay down here with Sissy. You two fellahs can bunk together in the loft."

"Over my dead body," Daniel declared.

A sudden ally, Long Belly agreed. "This great warrior does not share his bed with other men. I will sleep with Broken Dishes or I will sleep alone."

She gave them both a quick smile. "You two figure it out. I'm turning in."

With that, she marched over to the bed, drew back the spread, and climbed in next to Sissy, buckskins and all.

A pregnant silence settled over the room after that. Moments later, Daniel thumped up to the end of the bed.

"Even if I wanted to sleep with Long Belly, which I don't,"

he complained. "I can't climb up to the loft with this leg. Where do you suggest I bed down?"

Although she regarded him with a certain amount of empathy, Josie wouldn't budge. "It wasn't my idea to come here, remember? If you can think of a better solution than this—one that doesn't have me lying on the floor or with that savage—I'm willing to listen. Until then, if you don't mind, I'd like to get some sleep."

More silence, this time accompanied by the muted sound of Long Belly's pacing. Josie closed her eyes to the men and the light still glowing from the lantern. Instantly drowsy, she let her mind wander into the future, where she entertained herself with visions of her buffalo and cattle ranch. Pondering a name for the enterprise, she first thought of calling it The Flying Josie. No, that was far too simple for such a big change in her life. Freedom Rings came to mind. The brand would be unique, but the name was definitely too patriotic. How about The Buffalo Queen Ranch? Not only in the running, but the leader. It was as she tried to imagine the sort of brand that might go with such a name that a male voice suddenly rattled Josie's eardrums—and her nerves.

"You will sleep in the loft."

Her eyes flew opened to see the big Cheyenne hunched over the bed. Josie clutched the buffalo spread at her throat and held tight. "What did you say?"

"We have discussed it." Long Belly inclined his head toward Daniel, who was sitting at the table. "You will sleep in the loft, alone. My friend will go to his own bed with Sissy. I will rest these weary bones on the floor before the fire. Go now."

Since she couldn't think of a rational argument against the plan—a sudden and miserly resentment over the idea of sharing Daniel with Sissy, never mind that she was unconscious, didn't seem at all rational—Josie got out of the warm bed and scrambled up the ladder to the loft.

Once inside the Indian's lair, she immediately noticed that the ceiling was too low for her to stand upright and that she could barely see, even though the lantern still burned brightly on the table downstairs. Following shadows, she crawled on her hands and knees across a large buffalo rug and discovered an apple crate against the back wall that was masquerading as a night table. A fat candle in a chipped saucer sat on the top of the crate along with a box of matches.

Josie put a flame to the wick and saw that the wall to her right was home to stacks and stacks of rolled-up hides, most of them buffalo, along with elk, deer, and an assortment of smaller bundles she couldn't identify. The rug she'd crawled across turned out to be a bedspread covering yet another buffalo hide stretched out on the floor beneath it. A pair of thick woolen blankets were sandwiched between these two hides—sheets, she surmised. No wonder Long Belly dreamed that buffalo talked to him in the night.

Josie brought the light around to shine on the wall to her left and saw that it was the resting place for a pile of clothing. Among those articles, she spotted a couple of small bows, miniatures of authentic weapons, and what looked like it might have been a crude stick horse. Long Belly's childhood toys? Next to them in the corner stood the Indian's weapons of war— a full-sized bow and quiver of arrows, some kind of club with a vicious looking spike at the end, and a huge rifle.

Not at all ready to trust the owner of those weapons, Josie crawled over to the corner and helped herself to the club. Once she'd stripped down to her chemise and blown out the candle, she climbed, weapon in hand, beneath the blankets. By then the lantern downstairs had been doused for the night, leaving only the glow from the stove to light the cabin, a faint reddish tinge that clung to the ceiling like a bloody sunset. It looked as if the fires of hell were banging at the gates of heaven.

As Josie slept, she dreamt of buffalo, of a great herd of the beasts thundering across the grasslands that encompassed The Buffalo Queen Ranch. She rode among the bison atop a sleek ebony stallion—The Black, who continuously glanced back at her through a pair of bright blue eyes. A sparkling crown of diamonds and pearls adorned her hair, proclaiming her the

Queen, and ranchers came from miles around in hopes of observing the secrets of her success.

The Black, adoration clearly showing in his dazzling blue eyes, nuzzled her ear, odd considering the distance between his muzzle and her head. And then the dream became even more confusing. More real. It wasn't the muzzle of a horse that caressed her, she realized, but lips. Male lips. As the night and consciousness came back to her, and she realized that this was no dream, but real, Josie knew the man lying beside her could be no one but Long Belly.

Her hand firmly clasped around the club, she pulled it out from beneath the covers and swung it hard against the bastard's body.

"Oh, shit!" he cried.

Josie arced the club above her head, preparing to deliver another blow. "Get away from me, you no-account bastard. If you don't leave right this second, the next one'll be right between your eyes."

"Christ, Josie. What's got into you?"

She paused in midswing. "Daniel? Is that you?"

"Yes, it's me," he muttered. "What's left of me anyway. I think you crushed my chest."

"Oh, Lord—I thought you were Long Belly."

"I kinda wish that I was." He uttered a short laugh. "At least then I'd be safe in bed with Sissy."

"And why aren't you—in bed with Sissy, I mean?"

"Because," he said, taking the club from her hand and flinging it across the room. "Things weren't working out downstairs. Sissy moaned every time I so much as moved my foot, and who could sleep with Long Belly rolling around, carrying on like a lost calf because he got stuck with the floor for a bed?"

Josie didn't see how there could be much different between that and the plank flooring in the loft. She was also curious about Daniel's sudden recovery. "How did you manage to get up here with a broken leg?"

"I took the splint off. Since the infection cleared up, that contraption has been more hinderance than help. I figure I ought to be able to do without the crutches in a week or so—if I don't freeze to death first. Is it all right if I get under the blanket with you?''

Since it hardly made sense to turn him away now, Josie lifted the buffalo spread and guided him between the sheets. Warming himself, Daniel snuggled close to her, making her all too aware that he wore nothing but a pair of woolen drawers. Josie had prepared herself against an attack by the Indian, not an attack on her senses by this man. But Lord, it felt good to have him lying next to her again, to be safe and snug in his arms. She almost wished she hadn't told the fib about her nonexistent sickness.

''That's a hell of a lot better,'' Daniel said, slipping his arms around her back and waist. ''There's nothing like body heat to take the chill out of a fellah.''

He draped his good leg across her then, pressing his body against hers, hot and hard, and then his hands went to her hair. Stroking her locks, slipping his fingers through them as he'd done earlier, he sighed.

''Your hair is so soft,'' Daniel murmured, kissing the braid at her temple. ''I can't get enough of it, the way it feels or the way it looks. The red in it reminds me of the sun breaking through a storm cloud. It's such a beautiful, coppery chestnut, it doesn't seem real.''

His words were like liquid tremors pouring down Josie's spine, saturating her entire body with a nameless, heated desire. She moaned, hardly aware she'd vocalized the sensation, then breathed deeply of Daniel's scent—pure, natural male with only a hint of the out-of-doors to season his unique flavor.

''Josie,'' he whispered, his voice a flame in the dark. ''Sweet, sweet Josie. It wasn't just Long Belly's complaints that drove me up here. I missed you next to me. Did you miss me, even a little?''

She'd missed him all right. His warmth, his scent, the things he said to her in the darkness, the things he *didn't* say, even though he thought her a diseased whore.

Daniel seized Josie's moment of hesitation with a kiss, rimming her lips for an eternity with his own before sliding his tongue into her mouth. She'd once tried this kind of kiss with Henry, an experience he'd promised would send her soaring to the stars. It nearly sent her heaving into a bucket instead. There were stars to be had, she now realized, when kissed by a man, not a boy. Especially if that man had a very good idea about what he was doing. Doubts aside, she threw herself into the experience, mimicking the thrusts of Daniel's tongue, then grew brazen enough to add a few twists of her own.

This prompted a new boldness in him, and the next thing Josie knew, Daniel's hands were fumbling with the buttons of her chemise, his lips nibbling her earlobe as he whispered, "I know you're sick and all, but I want you, lady. I want you so much, I'm about to bust. I'm begging you—put me out of my misery some other way."

She had no idea what he meant. "What are you talking about?"

He laughed from deep in his throat, a dark, rich sound. "I'm talking about pleasuring each other a little. You first, then me."

Josie wasn't exactly sure what he meant by pleasure. There were all kinds, weren't there? Like the cries of a baby ranged from fussy to angry to rage, she assumed that pleasure ran the gamut from comfort to quiet happiness to delight. Whatever kind he had in mind, the idea intrigued her, but it also worried her a little. Unwilling to step into territory she knew next to nothing about, Josie settled on borrowing one of Sissy's comments as an excuse.

"I don't think so—I've never known pleasure from any man."

"*Never?*"

"No, never."

Josie thought that would be the end of it, but Daniel wasn't so easily dissuaded. "Then it's damn well time that you did."

Before she could figure his next move, Daniel slipped the chemise from her shoulders and began caressing her bare breasts. She gasped, wondering if she was as safe as she'd assumed she was and how long she should allow this to go on, and then his mouth moved to her nipples, kissing and suckling each of them in turn. Josie drew a tortured breath, trying to form the word "enough," but could only manage a breathy, "Ohhh, Daniel."

"That's me, beautiful," he whispered against her naked skin. "Say it again. I love to hear you call my name."

Too dizzy from wanting him to form a lucid thought, she did as she was told. "Daniel."

His mouth still at her breast, he moaned against her rigid nipple, then slid a hand across her belly, pausing to caress her there. Daniel's thumb circled her naval several times, teasing, and then dipped into its center. The next thing she knew, his probing fingers had worked their way into the thatch of hair protecting her sex.

"Oh, Daniel—no, stop."

He hesitated, but did not remove his hand. "Am I hurting you?"

"No, but I—I told you, I caught a pox."

"I know," he whispered, his fingers working a kind of magic she'd never even dreamed about. "This won't be dangerous to either of us. Open your legs. I'll show you what I mean."

The next morning, Josie reluctantly emerged from the depths of slumber. She was warmer than she'd ever been since coming to this cabin, even warmer than standing in front of the stove with the flames of a roaring fire licking away at its doors and cooktops. She could hardly move, so tightly swaddled was she in erotic memories and the buffalo spread, and she thought for a fleeting moment that this must be how an infant feels curled up in its mother's womb. She stirred, feeling a distant rush of pleasure, a reminder of the night and Daniel . . . and magic.

She felt herself blush as she thought back to the shameless way she'd behaved beneath his touch, and grew warmer still as she recalled her own boldness when it came time to return the favor. Giggling to herself, Josie yawned, then tried to raise her arms to stretch. They wouldn't budge. It was then she realized that she wasn't simply wrapped up in the blanket, but wedged between two immovable objects.

She glanced to the object on her left—Daniel, who slept on. Then she turned to her right—and came eye-to-eye with Long Belly, who was beneath the blanket with her. *"You!"*

Brazenly draping one arm across her waist, he said, "Did you sleep well?"

"Get out," she said, giving him a shove.

Daniel stirred, muttering, "What's all the racket about?"

"Your brother the savage climbed into bed with me while I was asleep, that's what."

Daniel sat up. "Long Belly? What the hell are you doing in here, you son of a bitch?"

"Do not worry that I am trying to steal your woman," he said. "I am only here to protect Broken Dishes as she sleeps."

Josie slugged his shoulder. "The only thing I need protection from is you."

Then she pulled the pillow out from under her head and whopped him with it. That got him moving. Long Belly popped out of bed and headed on hands and knees to the ladder. About that time Daniel threw his own pillow at the sneaky bastard, nailing him alongside the head.

"And stay out," he shouted as Long Belly slinked off downstairs. Turning to Josie, he touched her cheek and said, "How long has he been up here?"

She shrugged. "I don't know, but now that he's up, I'd better get downstairs and keep an eye on him."

"But first . . ." Daniel pulled her across his chest with a kiss that stirred up lusty memories and promises of more to come. When he released her, he tapped the tip of her nose, then dragged his finger across her cheeks. "Even your freckles have turned red. How long's it been since you blushed in front of a man?"

Josie laughed as she crept out of bed. "Since before either of us was born."

Chuckling along with him, she slipped into her buckskins,

blew Daniel a kiss, then quietly made her way down the ladder and into the chill of the room below. Long Belly was stoking the fire, but the minute he saw her, he hurried out of the cabin. Sissy was still in bed, awake at last.

"How are you feeling?" Josie asked, approaching her.

Sissy turned listless eyes her way. "Like a horse sat on my chest."

"One did, remember?" Josie eased onto the bed and slid her hand across Sissy's brow. "How's your head?"

"Aches a mite, but nothing I can't stand." She fixed her gaze on Josie's cheek and frowned. "What happened to you?"

She'd almost forgotten that she was scratched up. "That crazy horse I was riding dragged me through a couple of trees, then pitched me off the side of a mountain. Didn't break anything or get hurt too bad, but I don't think I'll be riding out of here on that animal again."

Sissy started to laugh, then thought better of it and clutched her ribs. "I guess I wasn't so lucky. Feels kinda busted up in there."

"You apparently have one broken rib and another that's separated."

"Figured it'd be worse." She then gave Josie a narrow look. "You taking care of both fellahs now, are you?"

"You mean cooking for them? Not me."

"No, I mean I know that Long Belly was up in bed with you most of the night."

"Not at my invitation, he wasn't. He came up to 'protect' me because he thinks I'm some kind of buffalo goddess like you."

"Why would he think that?"

Josie glanced around the cabin, realizing that Long Belly had been gone for some time now—far too long for a man who'd gone outside simply to relieve himself.

Josie leapt off the bed. "I'll have to explain the rest later, but I will tell you that I found a buffalo yesterday, and that right now Long Belly is probably trying to steal it from me."

''A buffalo?'' Sissy's voice sounded dazed and as if it were fading.

Leaving her to draw her own conclusions, Josie tugged on Daniel's boots and jacket, then headed out the door. Once in the fresh air, she was amazed to see how much snow had fallen during the night. Drifts were piled up to the railing on the porch, and still the snow fell, albeit in gentle flurries rather than the blizzard proportions of yesterday. Although visibility was poor, she could see that Long Belly had carved out a narrow trail that led to the barn. A path right to Josie's precious buffalo.

Head down against elements, she followed that trail. Even before she reached the barn, she could see that the door stood open wide enough to emit a man—or a full-grown buffalo. Her heart in her throat, she stepped inside the building. The lantern was lit, the horses and cows were quietly munching away on their morning feed, and the chickens argued over the fattest hunks of grain. Nothing was out of place, and yet everything was.

Sweetpea was gone and, with her, Josie's hopes for the future.

Chapter Twelve

Inside the cabin, Sissy kept a furtive eye on the spectacle Daniel was making of himself as he half fell, half climbed down the stairs. Beside the fact that he could barely manage the descent on only one leg, he was practically naked, dressed only in a pair of gray drawers. By the time he was on solid ground again, crutches tucked neatly under his armpits, he was turning the air blue with an endless stream of curses. Giving him a chance to calm down, it wasn't until Daniel had reached the stove and put on a pot of coffee that Sissy let him know she was awake.

"Josie says she found a buffalo. That true?"

He turned to her in surprise. "Beg your pardon for my foul mouth, Sissy. I didn't think you'd come around yet."

"I've heard them words before and plenty more like 'em. Is it true?"

He nodded wearily. "It sure is. Even more amazing, she somehow managed to get the thing to follow her back here. Put it up in the barn like it was an orphaned calf."

Something new ached inside Sissy at this news, a pain that

had nothing to do with her injuries. "Didn't know you could get a wild critter like that inside a barn."

"Neither did I." Daniel gave off a feeble chuckle as he hobbled over to where he'd left his clothes. "According to Long Belly, Josie has some kind of magic touch with the damn thing."

The ache in Sissy's breast intensified. She tried to swallow the pain as she said, "Well, I guess that makes her the new Queen of Buffalo around here. 'Bout time. I was getting kinda tired of wearing the crown."

"I wouldn't hand over your throne just yet, at least not until we talk some sense into her."

"What's she gone and done?"

"Josie has taken it into her head that the buffalo belongs to her, and only her." Daniel slipped on his shirt and buckskin trousers. "She won't let me or Long Belly get near it."

"But she cain't do that." Sissy tried to sit up, forgetting about her ribs, and set off a fresh explosion of pain. Again clutching her midsection, she eased back down on the pillow.

"Hey—better take it easy." Daniel leaned over the bed. "You've got a couple of broken ribs."

"I know," she whispered, waiting for the pain to ebb. "Lord knows I know."

She organized her breathing, then said, "Josie's gone off after Long Belly—I don't know what he'll do if she don't let him get at that buffalo."

Daniel turned quickly toward the window, but not fast enough to hide the concern in his expression. She thought she'd seen a little more than simple worry lining his face, too. Sissy didn't mind so much that Daniel had feelings for the gal, but it irritated her some to realize that suddenly everyone loved Josie with little or nothing left over for her. Not that Sissy was used to or expected anything more. She supposed this sudden burst of jealousy, or whatever it was, had something to do with those few days of respect she'd enjoyed as a woman graced with the buffalo spirit. As silly as Long Belly's claims were, they had given her a fleeting glimpse of what it must be like to be cherished rather than scorned, a woman of pride.

At the window, Daniel said, "I can't be sure with all the snow out there, but it looks like the barn door might be open. Maybe I ought to go out and check on them."

Sissy considered this along with the stubborn, selfish side she'd witnessed in Josie, and figured if the new buffalo goddess really cared about keeping that damned animal to herself, she'd probably find a way to stand up to the warrior. After all, Long Belly had proved more than once that he responded much better to female threats than he did to tears or passive displays.

With a little sigh, Sissy said, "Now that I think on it, I'd be more worried about that injun than Josie. When that gal found out he'd gone to the barn, she lit on out of here like a swarm of bees was on her ass. I hope she ain't packing that gun of yours."

Inside the barn, Josie stood in the center aisle in stunned disbelief. Where could Sweetpea have gone? Snow had been piled high against the barn, the drifts covered with frozen shards of ice. If a buffalo had recently broken through that frozen crust of snow, Josie most surely would have noticed the trail. That aside, how could a buffalo have opened the door in the first place? And where the devil had Long Belly gone—on foot, no less? None of it made any sense.

She took another look around the inside of the barn and realized something else was amiss. The ground near the entrance was dug up, and the backside of the barn door was splintered, looking as if someone had taken an axe to it.

As she focused on the door, trying to understand what might have happened there, Long Belly stepped though the opening. His expression had been bright compared to the weather, satisfied, until the moment he saw her. Then suddenly he was all worry lines and wary eyes, looking as guilty as Judas Iscariot.

Thinking only of her future plans and how this man might

have ruined them, Josie snatched up the shovel leaning against the cow's stall and advanced on him.

"What have you done to her?" she demanded. "Where is Sweetpea, you, you . . . *bastard!*"

Long Belly held up his arms and retreated to the open doorway. With the background of snow flurries framing him, he looked like the angel of death.

"I have done nothing to harm this buffalo," he insisted. "She is safe in the corral outside."

Josie lowered the shovel to half-mast. "Why did you put her out there?"

"I did nothing. The buffalo put herself in the corral." He dared to take one step back into the relative warmth of the barn. "When I came outside, I heard the beast banging against the door. I was afraid she would tear the barn down in her efforts to escape. I went around to the back and opened that door. When she saw the snow and the trees, she ran outside."

"Then Sweetpea is all right? She isn't hurt or lost?"

"The buffalo is content." Long Belly did something after that comment that Josie had never witnessed before. He smiled. "You must remember that I have great concern for this buffalo and would never bring harm to her. My people and I are most grateful for the gift you have brought to us."

Josie thought about setting him straight right then and there, and she was sorely tempted to inform him that his people would just have to worship both Sweetpea and herself from afar. Something in his expression made her hold her tongue. It was as if Long Belly were in another world as he spoke of his people and the buffalo, a magical place that made his dark eyes shine and his cinnamon skin glow from within. She knew then that she need never fear that the savage would harm Sweetpea. Stealing her was another matter.

Josie propped the shovel against the feed room wall. "I'm going out to see Sweetpea now," she said, turning toward the back of the barn. "I have to at least say good morning to her."

In a hurry to do just that, Josie slipped quietly through the back door and saw the buffalo huddled under a lean-to attached to the back of the barn. She was happily munching away on the pile of hay Long Belly had apparently set out there for her until she heard Josie's approach. Then she began to grunt, a sound that Josie took as "I missed you."

Speaking in low, cooing tones as she drew closer to the animal, she said, "So, you didn't like the cozy accommodations in the barn, huh?"

Sweetpea turned to look at her, swinging her great head and still grunting.

"I don't want to disturb your breakfast. I'm just checking to make sure you have everything you need." As far as Josie could tell she did, with the exception of water. "I'll be right back."

Returning to the barn, she grabbed an empty pail and filled it from the water barrel just outside the feed room. About then, Daniel limped in through the front door.

"Everything all right in here?" he asked, looking from her to Long Belly, who was busy milking the cow.

"Yes," she said, "even though your brother-in-law was forced to put Sweetpea outside in the cold."

"The beast is wild," Long Belly muttered. "She would tear down the barn if kept inside. See the door for yourself."

Daniel glanced behind him. "Jesus, what'd she do, go crazy?"

"You make it sound as if she's insane," Josie said. "She's fine around me. She only gets wild when you or Long Belly tries to interfere with her."

"That's because she *is* wild," warned Daniel. "No matter how much she may seem not to mind your presence, you've got to remember that this buffalo is a wild beast, not a cow in a field. She could be very dangerous."

"To you and Long Belly, perhaps," she said over her shoulder as she turned and headed back out to the corral. "But Sweetpea would never hurt me—she adores me."

This time when Josie approached the buffalo, metal pail in hand, Sweetpea's grunts grew louder, more serious, and she turned the whites of her eyes on her. The behavior gave Josie pause, but she continued to speak to the animal in soothing tones.

"Easy, girl. I've just brought you some water." Then she held up the pail.

Ungrateful as only a wild beast could be, the buffalo lowered her head and charged.

Josie flung the pail in the air, not bothering to stick around long enough to see where it landed, and ran as fast as she could for the safety of the barn. As she closed the door behind her, she could hear the sounds of horn against metal, shuddering to think Sweetpea could just as easily be tossing her around.

"If that buffalo adores you so damn much," came Daniel's voice from behind her. "Why isn't she a little more grateful that you brought her a pail of water?"

Josie spun around, still trembling, but indignant. "She likes me fine. She simply wasn't thirsty."

He smiled. "Then where's your bucket?"

Head held high, Josie started up the aisle toward the front of the barn, sashaying by Daniel and Long Belly as she said, "I left it with Sweetpea. I figured she could use a toy."

Then she headed for the cabin, humbled by the knowledge that if she hoped to make The Buffalo Queen Ranch a reality one day, she was going to have to learn a whole lot more about the species.

The blizzard raged for another week. To Daniel, who spent those nights sharing the loft with Josie while Long Belly stayed in the bed with Sissy, it was a time of both pleasure and pain. Although he and Josie continued to satisfy one another, each of them ferreting out the most responsive places on their bodies, his frustration grew.

Even while he'd been married, Daniel had never been much of a kisser. Tangle Hair had it in her mind that mouths and tongues mingling was something unclean. With Josie, who couldn't seem to get enough of his kisses, Daniel felt as if he were getting a whole new education in matters between the sexes and had discovered the kind of desire that started from somewhere other than his groin—a desire so strong, he wasn't sure how much longer he could go on wanting her, but not having her.

Adding to his frustration was his general physical condition. Although his leg was much stronger, it still couldn't support his weight. That meant Daniel was basically stuck in the cabin until the weather cleared. Josie had pretty much appointed herself as tender of the livestock, a situation that kept her out-of-doors for long periods and prompted occasional battles between her and Long Belly over who would see to the buffalo's needs. Sissy was on the mend, but not much use with the household chores. Daniel, much to his aggravation, was the only one left who could prepare the meals, such as they were.

It was as he was trying to decide between cooking up some hamhocks and beans or frying a couple of elk steaks for supper, that Josie came back to the cabin, bringing with her a cloud of snow. She shook herself out of his jacket, then brushed the excess flakes from her hair. The arrowheads Long Belly had attached to her braids bobbed against her breasts, constant reminders of her newly exalted status.

"When is this storm ever going to stop?" she asked breathlessly. "I swear, I've never seen anything like it so early in the season."

Long Belly, who was working on his handwriting skills at the table, looked up to say, "The buffalo—she is well?"

Josie nodded. "So far, but if this keeps up, I'm afraid she'll freeze to death out there in that corral. She's got icicles hanging off her fur."

"Don't worry about her," said Daniel. "Buffalo are made for weather like this. If you want to worry, concern yourself about my cattle. They didn't get a chance this year to put on much by way of winter fat. I'm told they could have a pretty rough time of it out there."

"You heard right," she said. "Between prairie fires and lack of rain this summer, everyone's cattle suffered. My father—

stepfather's—herd is in the same shape. If these storms don't let up soon, I'm afraid he's going to lose a few head.''

"Your family raises cattle around here?" asked Daniel.

She nodded. "It's the Baum Ranch, just east of Miles City. We had around five hundred head, last I heard.''

This so surprised him, Daniel almost blurted out the obvious—what were you doing working in a whorehouse if you have family so close by? He didn't, but the question remained in his mind as he said, "You know a lot about cattle ranching, do you?''

Josie shrugged as she headed to the stove to warm herself. "Some. Enough to know that you don't have anything to worry about yet. Your cattle have the forest to help shelter them from the cold. All those trees also keep the snow from piling up so high they can't forage. Surely you know that.''

At the table, Long Belly chuckled. "My friend knows nothing of cattle. He is, as he has told me, a blind man who wishes to teach those without eyes. I do not understand this.''

"It's the blind leading the blind, you fool," said Daniel, frustrated with far more than Long Belly's attempts at levity. "And it simply means that I, someone whose knowledge of cattle is pretty much restricted to how thick my steak is, am trying to teach you and your starving tribe how to raise beef so you can support yourselves.''

Josie looked from the Cheyenne to Daniel. "So this is your first herd, that scraggly little group I saw when Sweetpea found me?''

Daniel felt somehow less a man to admit, "Yes, all twenty head of them, give or take. I'd have a better idea of how they're doing if I hadn't broke my leg and this damned fool here didn't go off looking for buffalo every time I ask him to go check on the herd. Maybe all of that will change now that we've got good old Sweetpea out in the corral.''

Long Belly sat back in his chair, pencil to his lips in thought. "Broken Dishes says the herd will be fine. This means that I can continue my search for a great bull. Sweetpea must have a mate.''

His frustrations mounting, Daniel felt something inside him snap. "You're done looking for buffalo, you hear me? It's about time you faced your responsibilities."

As he hobbled over to the table, still scolding Long Belly over what he saw as his shortcomings, Josie shut her ears to the noisy argument. She was more concerned with her own problems. In order to ensure her future success, she probably *would* have to breed Sweetpea. How was she to do that without a bull? Even though Josie planned to raise cattle as her main business, the fact that she also had buffalo was the one thing she counted on to set her ranch apart. It was the very reason, and probably the only one, that could convince a banker to take a chance and back her.

Turning to the men and their ongoing argument, Josie joined the fray. "I think Long Belly should be allowed to search for a bull. After all, if we found one buffalo, why not two?"

Daniel blew out an exasperated sigh. "I think you should just stay the hell out of this. It doesn't concern you."

"It concerns me as much as anyone in this house."

"Broken Dishes is right." That said, Long Belly climbed out of his chair and directed his next comment to Daniel. "I will not allow you to speak to this woman in such a manner. She is to be respected above us all."

"*You* won't allow *me?*" The veins in Daniel's throat stood out like the ribs of a tipi. "Why, if I had both my legs under me, I'd march you outside right this minute and give you the beating of your life."

"And I," said Long Belly, "would accept this beating. I owe you this much."

Hands gripping the edge of the table, Daniel kicked his crutches aside. "Then maybe I ought to just beat you where you stand."

Sissy, who'd been resting, groaned and climbed off the bed. "I kinda wish that horse had squashed my head," she muttered, moving stiffly to the stove. "At least then, I wouldn't have to listen to all this shit."

Josie burst out laughing. "You hear that, fellahs? I think you've disturbed the patient."

"So have you, princess," said Sissy as she joined Josie. "If you'd just give 'em their damned buffalo and be done with it, none of us would be disturbed around here."

"But it's my buffalo." Why didn't anyone see that but Josie? "I can't think of one good reason to give her up."

"I can. They're men and know what to do with her. What's a slip of a girl like you gonna do with a big ole stinky buffalo, anyway?"

Josie thought of telling her exactly what she planned to do, but held her tongue. Sissy would only laugh at her plans for a ranch, and at the moment, the last thing she needed was hers or anyone's ridicule.

"How are your ribs feeling?" she asked, changing the subject.

"Fine, now that you got 'em bound good and tight. It's my ears that's suffering." After a meaningful look, Sissy glanced toward the window. "Cain't even go outside for a little relief from all this fighting over a stupid buffalo. It's blowing hard enough for December out there. We been here that long already?"

It struck Josie that she didn't know. She glanced at Daniel and Long Belly, noting that their argument had simmered to vicious glares and muttered insults, and asked, "Do you fellahs have a calendar or know what day it is?"

Daniel turned to her with a shake of his dark head. "Don't have much use for a calendar, but I'd say we're about done with November, give or take a few days. Why?"

"You ask why?" she said, remembering a promise she'd made to herself. "It's Thanksgiving, that's why! We have to have a celebration."

After that startling announcement, Josie didn't allow anybody to get in her way. She sent Long Belly to the smokehouse for a ham and some beefsteaks, then set a pot of potatoes to boil on the stove. After the Cheyenne returned with the meat, Sissy joined him at the table, an interested observer as Daniel continued teaching his brother-in-law how to read. This left Josie in relative privacy to cook up her surprise. One, she hoped, that would somehow make up for Sissy's loss of status as the buffalo spirit. Not a word had been spoken about the transfer of power between the two women, but Josie had felt Sissy's envy and accepted the guilt, deserved or not. This was her chance to help the woman shine again. A chance to show them all that she knew how to be a true friend.

Using the meager supplies at hand, Josie mixed up a batch of biscuits, then set to making a cake, leavening both baked goods with sour milk and molasses. Although no one disturbed her as she worked, she couldn't help but notice that Daniel was watching her with interest as she fluttered about the stove. He wondered about her sudden prowess as a cook, no doubt, but she would have to worry about an explanation later. For now, she had a birthday supper to prepare.

When the meal was ready and the group gathered around the table, the women sitting on chairs, the men on barrels, at first the others were too stunned to fill their plates. They just sat there staring at the sliced ham, steaks, mashed potatoes and gravy, and the skilletful of fluffy biscuits. Finally, Josie got things going herself.

"Isn't anyone hungry but me?" she asked, dropping a blob of potatoes into a bowl. Thanks to her conniption fit over washing dishes, she no longer had a plate. "Dig in while it's still hot."

This got the others moving. Daniel was the first to load his plate, but it wasn't until after he split one of her biscuits and slathered it with butter that he commented on the meal.

"Jesus, this is good!" Butter dripped off his chin as he savored the first bite. "I haven't had real biscuits like these in so long, I forgot what they tasted like."

"Mmmmm," Long Belly agreed after stuffing an entire biscuit into his mouth.

Sissy, who was slow filling her plate, simply said, "Looks good, Josie. Best I've seen since we left Lola's."

"Hell," said Daniel, talking through a mouthful of mashed

potatoes and gravy. "This is the best grub I've had since— well, since I can't remember. I thought you couldn't cook."

"I can't," Josie claimed, expecting the question. "So don't get used to this. These are just a couple of recipes I picked up here and there."

Daniel was working on a chunk of ham he'd sandwiched between the halves of a biscuit, but that didn't stop him from saying, "Here and there, or on your father's cattle ranch?"

"Here and there." She looked at him sharply, hesitating a moment before she added, "Now shut up and eat."

The old Josie Baum would never have delivered such a rude comment, but then the person she'd once been had spent a lifetime hearing her stepbrothers and Peter Baum let her know in those same words that her thoughts and opinions were unwanted. To deliver rather than receive the foul reprimand felt much better, if not proper.

Daniel apparently had no problem with Josie's insolent tongue. He simply dove into his food, finishing the rest of the meal in silence, save for the slurping and gobbling of men unused to sharing their table with women. When the last fork was laid in surrender across an empty plate, Josie cautioned the group to remain in place.

"Don't move," she said, heading to the stove. "I have one more surprise, so I hope you saved room for it."

She'd left the cake at the back of the cooktop hidden beneath a scrap of clean toweling. It hadn't risen as high as she'd have liked, but after drizzling the top with a mixture of sugar and water, then sticking a wooden match in the center to serve as a candle, she thought it didn't look too bad under the circumstances.

After lighting the match, Josie turned to the group at the table and said, "Happy birthday, Sissy!"

Daniel joined in offering muttered birthday wishes as Josie brought the cake to the table. Long Belly just sat there looking puzzled.

"Make a wish," Josie urged, pushing the cake beneath Sissy's nose. "Then blow it out quick before the match burns down."

Sissy made a funny little sound in her throat, something close to a sob, then pushed out of her chair. She hardly looked up at Josie, but what she could see of her eyes looked wet.

"I ain't never had no birthday before, and I don't see the need for one now. I'm tired. I'm going to bed."

With that, she went to the ladder and made her way up to the loft, damaged ribs and all.

Later that night, after Josie had finished scrubbing the kettles and dishes she'd insisted on cleaning herself, she finally joined Daniel, who'd been lying in bed for what seemed like hours. Until Sissy's disturbing reaction to the birthday cake, he'd figured he'd seen the last of his own bed until the women were finally able to go back to Miles City—a thought Daniel would just as soon not contemplate.

The fact that Josie had a whore's disease should have been enough to make him glad she'd be leaving soon, but dammit all, he still wanted her. How could she have wound up in such an occupation in the first place? he wondered, again thinking about her family in Miles City. He didn't know much about the whoring profession, but he had heard that most loose women were either orphaned, abandoned, or just plain booted out of their families. He couldn't imagine Josie in any of those circumstances, but then again, he had trouble picturing her as a whore, too. She was, at the least, a very complicated female. One that he wanted so badly, he'd finally figured out a way to have her. Earlier Daniel had dug through his possibles bag and found a little item that would smooth the way toward easing both their frustrations.

When she finally blew out the lantern for the night and joined him in bed, Josie surprised Daniel by going back to her old posture—as rigid as a lodgepole pine. And just as quiet. Now what the hell was wrong?

He took a stab at the cause. "That cake you baked was good. Real good. Best I ever had."

In the darkness came one word. "Thanks."

Digging deeper, he said, "It's too bad Sissy didn't appreciate it more."

"Yep."

He tried another tack. "Think maybe she's got a burr in her saddle because you found that buffalo, and not her?"

"Maybe. I don't know. I just know that I was only trying to be her friend tonight."

Success at last, or so he thought. "Well, I just want you to know that I think it was a right friendly thing you did baking up a birthday cake like that, especially since you don't—er, cook."

Josie sighed heavily, the first real sign that he was getting to her. Then, unfortunately, she let him know exactly what she was feeling.

"Shut up, Daniel. I want to go to sleep."

Undeterred, he rolled onto his side and wrapped his arm around Josie's waist. She wore only her chemise, her body soft despite the rigid core, and she smelled sugar-sweet, just like a birthday cake. Best of all, no longer would he have to lie next this woman, touching, holding, but not really knowing her— at least not in the way he needed to so badly. It was time to let her know that.

"You've been seeing to everyone else's needs tonight," Daniel whispered. "Would it interest you to know that I've been thinking of yours?"

"What's that mean?"

"I want to make love to you, Josie—real love and real pleasure, not what we've been doing."

She stiffened in his arms. "B-but we can't. I told you why."

"I know," he said, barely able to contain his glee. "You're sick and all, but what if I told you I figured a way around that?"

He wouldn't have thought it possible, but Josie grew even more rigid. "You have . . . but how?"

Daniel reached under his pillow and withdrew the item he'd hidden there. Dangling it between them, even though she couldn't possibly make it out in the darkness, he said, ''Guess what I found?''

Chapter Thirteen

"Christ, Josie, it's a rubber, not a snake. Since I got it from a gal in your line of work, I assume you've seen a couple before. Quit playing around and get back over here."

She didn't know exactly what a rubber was or how it could be used to save a man from a diseased woman, but Josie knew precisely what Daniel had in mind. That was why she'd jumped out of bed and run over by the stove.

"Come on, sweetheart," he urged. "Don't tell me you'd rather stand there freezing in the dark than climb back in this bed with me for a night of unbridled pleasure."

She stifled a moan, understanding at least what he meant by pleasure. She wanted nothing more than to lie in bed with Daniel while his lips and hands did what they would to her. But tonight he wanted more, and apparently he had the means to take it. How to turn him away this time? After all the lies she'd told, Josie doubted that Daniel would appreciate the truth at this late date. Trouble was, she couldn't think of another lie.

"Go to sleep, Daniel," she finally said, hoping that would do the trick. "I want to sit here by myself and think a while."

He took a long time replying, and when he did, Josie wasn't

honestly surprised by his reaction. "Well, to hell with you, Miss Baum, and to hell with your thinking. In fact, to hell with playing the gentleman. You like that chair so much, you can just stay in it for the rest of the night."

"What?"

"You heard me. If you can't bring yourself to make love to me, then I sure as hell can't imagine why you'd want to sleep with me."

"B-but—"

"That's it, Miss Baum. I'm going to sleep."

While things hadn't turned out exactly the way she'd hoped they would, Josie counted herself lucky—for tonight, anyway. Wrapping herself in Daniel's coat, she curled into the chair nearest the stove, and tried to make herself comfortable.

Fuming, Daniel lay on his back trying to figure out what it was that made Josie Baum the woman she was—and why he couldn't stop himself from wanting her.

She was still an enigma in certain areas for sure, that frustrating virginal whore act, in particular. With the exception of her friendship with Sissy, she seemed to care about only one thing—that stupid buffalo. On the other hand, Josie had more than enough hate to go around. Near as Daniel could figure, she hated all Indians with cause enough to hate only a few; hated being told what to do, especially in regard to what most sane people would consider female work; hated her life as a whore; and most of all, hated him. Daniel figured he knew why, too—his Cheyenne blood. Why else would she continue to refuse him what she'd probably done for a thousand others?

Fuming all over again, he tried to look for another reason that she might have refused him. Could be, he supposed, that Josie had decided to find another way to support herself once she got back to Miles City, an admirable plan if it were true, but also damned inconsiderate. Fact was, he wanted her now, dammit, and no matter how hard he tried to convince himself that she wasn't worth the humiliation, he knew he wouldn't be happy until he'd had her. So what had he done toward that effort? Tossed her right out of his bed.

"You stupid ass," Daniel muttered to himself as he felt along the night table for the box of matches. He'd half hoped that Josie would come creeping back to bed on her own, begging and pleading for sanctuary, apologizing for putting him through this endless agony. Now it seemed plain that if she were going to join him beneath the blankets again, he would have to go get her and drag her back to bed.

After he got the candle lit, Daniel squinted into the darkness across the room. He could barely make out her shape in the scanty light, but he could see that she had curled up on a chair and fallen asleep. Guilt pricked at him as he limped over to where she sat. She would be as stiff as a poker and kinked up like a ball of barbed wire if she stayed in that position much longer. And it was his fault. All his fault.

"Josie?" he whispered. "Wake up and come to bed. This is no place for you to sleep."

Her head bobbed against her chest; then she abruptly looked up at him. "What?"

"I want you to come back to bed."

"Oh, no, you no-account bastard. I'm staying right here."

Daniel wrestled her out of the chair, bad leg and all. "Come on to bed now."

"No."

Josie struggled against him as Daniel peeled her out of his coat. Then, sparing his tender leg as much as possible, he began to drag them both across the room. "You're getting in that bed with me now, or I'm—"

The door to the cabin crashed open then, a chill wind blowing the rest of Daniel's words right out of his mouth. The lean shadow of a stranger filled the doorway for a split second, and then it pounced into the room.

"Turn her loose!" the intruder demanded, sounding young and unsure of himself. This curious announcement was immediately followed by the blast of a shotgun.

"Oh, shit! Oh, shit!" The shadowy figure howled and began hopping up and down.

Using that moment of agony and confusion to his own advantage, Daniel shoved Josie aside and reached for the intruder's gun. As his fingers curled around the barrel, the stranger raised the weapon and fired a second round. For a horrifying minute, Daniel thought his hand might have been blown off by the blast. Then he realized that the stinging vibrations came from the repercussions of the shot, and not because his fingers were hopping around on the floor like five little headless chickens.

In the time it took for Daniel to contemplate the condition of his hand, the intruder regrouped and launched another attack. The empty shotgun fell to the floor with a clatter, and then the willowy shadow was on him like a cat on a hare. Since Daniel's mending leg could barely accept his own weight, it was a simple matter to bring him down. Fists flying, the man sprang onto his prone body the minute he hit the floor.

"I'll kill you, you dirty no-account bastard!"

Slender fists pummeled Daniel's face, but even in the midst of warding off the beating, he recognized the phrase as one that Josie had used on him—often.

"What have you done to her, huh?" cried the stranger.

Something hot and wet splashed down on Daniel's face.

"Is she raped?" he went on, his voice wavering.

The utterly bizarre reality that he'd been shot at and then attacked by an assailant who was crying—*crying*—struck Daniel in the funny bone, even as he took a blow to the nose. He might have laughed if something heavier than the sobbing man hadn't piled on top of him then, crushing him so that Daniel could hardly breathe.

Long Belly, who'd thrown himself onto the stranger's back, all but growled as he said, "I have never counted coup on such pretty yellow hair before. Prepare to die."

Daniel looked up to see that one of Long Belly's hands was filled with a clump of blond hair, the other with the handle of his scalping knife. When the blade touched down on the man's pale white skin, he shrieked in horror. That drew a high-pitched scream from Josie. Racing across the room, she threw herself on Long Belly's back.

"Leave him be!" she cried. "Don't kill him! Please don't kill him."

Bodies piled three-deep on his chest by now, Daniel mouthed the words "get off," but all that came out was a guttural wheeze. From the corner of his eye, he saw Sissy's purple satin slippers approaching. Why not climb aboard? he thought irrationally, little stars popping behind his eyes as he slowly began to lose consciousness. The slippers disappeared, no doubt to join the fray, and then a moment later, Daniel heard a muted *clang*. Two of the bodies immediately rolled off his chest— Long Belly and Josie. The third, his attacker, just lay there like a sack of mud, out cold. Daniel heaved the man to one side, then climbed to a pair of very unsteady feet.

"Christ," he said. "What in hell was all that about?"

At the table, Sissy lit the lantern. Now that he could actually make out the intruder's features, Daniel saw that he was just a kid, fifteen, maybe sixteen—and that Josie had thrown herself across his prostrate body.

"Caleb!" she cried, slapping the boy's cheeks. "Caleb, honey, are you all right?"

"You *know* this son of a bitch?"

Through her tears, she admitted, "H-he's my brother."

Daniel barely had time to digest that surprising fact before he noticed that Long Belly was still face down on the floor with Sissy kneeling beside him.

"What happened to him?" he asked.

"I thumped him with a frying pan before he could do something stupid to that boy." Sissy glanced up at Daniel with worried eyes. "Mighta whopped him a little too hard."

Pausing just long enough to determine that Long Belly was still alive, Daniel said, "He'll be all right. See if you can't bring him around." Then he limped over to where Josie struggled to do the same for the kid.

"Is that really your brother?" he asked, even though he could clearly see a resemblance. The kid's hair was blond where

Josie's was auburn, but they both had the same high forehead and stubborn square jaw. His features were delicately carved like hers, and would have been too feminine for a male if not for the boils of impending manhood rising up along his throat and cheeks. The pale white skin there looked like a sockful of marbles.

"He's not just my brother," she said, patting the young man's head. "He's my favorite."

"Is he hurt?"

Josie shook her head. "I think he just fainted."

About then the kid's eyes opened, revealing the same mink-brown color as Josie's. He cast a wild glance around the room, sat straight up, then howled in pain.

"Oh, shit, shit," he said, grabbing at his leg. "I think I blowed my foot off!"

Daniel glanced at the damage. "You sure as hell blew off the side of your boot and maybe one of your toes, but that shouldn't keep you from getting your butt off the floor and telling me why you waltzed in here and took a shot at me."

"He's hurt," Josie complained, taking a look at the injury for herself. "Can't you just let him be for a minute?"

Daniel grumbled, but grudgingly allowed her the time to examine the wound. When she was apparently satisfied that her brother would live with most of his extremities intact, she helped him to his feet and then onto the chair by the door. That was when Daniel noticed that the kid had splintered his floor boards with the first blast, and with the second had blown off a corner of the loft, leaving part of it to dangle in midair.

Daniel stepped around his brother-in-law, who was conscious by now, but too groggy and disoriented to realize what had happened, and joined the Baum siblings at the table.

Pointing directly at the kid, he said, "You've got some explaining to do. Get to it."

Caleb glanced at Josie, who was shivering in her chemise, then at Daniel, who wore nothing but his woolen drawers. "Looks to me like you're the no-account bastard who'd better get to explaining. You been raping my sister?"

Son of a bitch. Why would the kid think a thing like that when his pristine sister could be had for a price in a whorehouse? Unless, of course, he didn't know that about her.

Changing his strategy a little, Daniel set the young man straight. "I haven't been raping your sister, dammit. Do me a favor and stay put a minute while I get a few things figured out." He crooked a finger at Josie. "Put your coat on and come with me."

For once, she did as he asked with no argument. When they were over by the loft, out of earshot, he whispered, "Doesn't your brother know you've been working in a whorehouse?"

She stammered a little, then said, "Mmmm, not exactly."

"I see." Not that he did. "I'll keep that information to myself for the time being, but in exchange, you'd better make damn sure that he understands the way things have been between us. The truth."

She sighed heavily. "Can I go back to him now?"

Daniel thought she was being awfully uppity considering the circumstances, but he gave her a short nod and escorted her back to the table. Then he continued interrogating her brother.

"Why did you shoot at me?"

"I already told you. To rescue Josie from you dirty bastard kidnappers."

That would have made sense given the fact that she had actually been kidnapped, but how had the kid found out? "Who told you what happened to her, and that you'd find her here?"

Caleb's hateful glare remained steady on Daniel's face as he easily said, "I went asking about her at Lola's. They told me she got kidnapped by a pack of wild Indians that were headed upriver. When I got to the mission, the folks there said she mighta come up here with a Cheyenne fellah that borrowed a boat. They also give me directions to this cabin."

Daniel shot Josie a puzzled glance, but she refused to meet it head on. Turning back to Caleb, he asked, "Then you do know that your sister has been working at a whorehouse?"

"Working?" The kid's pale skin went even whiter, almost

transparent, as he stared at Josie and said, "God in heaven, was you actually working there . . . as a whore?"

There wasn't a drop of uppity in Josie now. Her lips were pursed and her gaze darted around the room like a starving mosquito, landing here and there but never quite finding the sustenance she sought. In this case, he thought, escape.

Josie finally said, "In a way, I guess."

Daniel turned to look her straight in the eye, but she still refused to meet his gaze. "What the hell does that mean, in a way? Did you or did you not have paying customers while you worked at Lola's?"

She shrugged.

Daniel persisted. "How many men, Josie? More than ten?"

She shook her head.

"Less than five?"

A little nod.

It began to make sense now, puzzling as it still was, the little incongruities in Josie's behavior, the way she'd driven him mad with what he'd thought was artful innocence, the way she'd teased him, then turned him away. Not precisely the actions of a seasoned whore.

"I'll bet you've been lying to me about everything since the day I first set eyes on you," Daniel accused her. "In fact, you've probably never had a paying customer in your life, have you?"

"Leave her be," said Sissy, climbing to her feet. "While she was at Lola's, all's she did was some clothes washing and such. It weren't her idea to work there."

"That's right," said the kid, suddenly full up with self-righteousness. "Weren't her fault a'tall. Our pa dumped her at the pleasure palace to teach her a lesson. I come to bring her back home."

"Then you've come all this way for nothing," Josie said, her belligerent self again. "I'm never going back home— never."

While the two argued about Josie's future, Daniel stood there in shock. She wasn't a whore! Josie Baum was not a whore.

She was just a rancher's daughter, probably a relatively innocent
one at that, before he'd gotten his hands on her. Just thinking
about some of the things he'd asked Josie to do—hell, the
things he *had* done, like spend night after night seducing her
with his mouth and fingers, not to mention the perversions he'd
talked her into doing for him—made him want to dig a hole
to China and climb into it. Daniel couldn't think of a punishment
worthy of the way he'd dangled a rubber beneath her nose.

In the midst of all his self-admonishments, he recalled what
Josie's misguided brother had said, something about their own
father dumping her at Lola's. How in God's name could any
man purposely force his daughter to move into a whorehouse
and then live with himself? That made less sense to Daniel
than just about anything that had happened in recent weeks—
and he had plenty to choose from in his bafflement pantry.
Only one thing was clear to him by now, and that was painfully
obvious—he didn't have any business keeping a decent young
woman like Josie in his cabin, much less his bed, for another
minute or another day. Somehow, if he had to fight bad weather,
his blasted leg, or even Long Belly, he would make sure that
she and her deluded brother were on their way to the mission
at first light.

The next morning, as they saddled the horses and prepared
for the journey down the mountain, Josie was nearly overcome
by a sudden sense of sadness. She breathed deeply of the horses,
picking up the scent of hay and other fodder, and realized that
she would miss this barn and all its animal smells, miss them
in a way she'd never missed the livestock she'd cared for on
the Baum barn, including Old Duke. She would also miss
Sissy, who chose to stay behind with Long Belly, a man who'd
developed new respect for her since she'd bashed him with a
pan. Somewhere in those musings Josie finally conceded that
she'd miss Daniel most of all.

Recognizing that about herself felt odd in light of the fact
that he was a half-breed, one who only wanted her for one

thing—well, two if she counted Sweetpea. The buffalo aside, Daniel wanted the same thing from her that all men wanted from women—a few moments of pleasure in exchange for a lifetime of hell. It was good she was leaving now before she got any more wrapped up in the man, better than good. After what they'd been to each other over the last few days, there was a terrifying, but very real possibility that she could actually fall in love with the mercurial man.

Last night Daniel had been wonderful, more than accommodating once things had gotten straightened out. In light of the fact that Caleb had tried to kill him, and all her lies were out in the open, Josie wouldn't have been surprised if he'd turned them out in the cold. Instead, Daniel not only helped to doctor Caleb's poor foot, he'd even gone so far as to insist that she sleep in his bed. This left him curled up in a chair opposite her brother for the night. When she'd awakened this morning to the sight of those two together, she'd gone all blubbery inside, her heart filling with love to the point that it felt cracked. Even now, at the memory, a tear rolled down her cheek.

"What's wrong, Josie?" asked Caleb, who was helping her to saddle the horses for the trip.

She quickly wiped her cheek. "Nothing. Got some straw in my eye, I guess."

Josie had almost forgotten how close they were. Caleb shot her a look that said he knew better.

"All right," she said, not exactly truthful, but bringing up an issue that deeply concerned her. "I was thinking about the others back home. How are the little ones doing without me?"

"Pretty good. Pa got old Beulah to come stay with them during the day, and the rest of us pitch in at night."

She nodded, relieved. With the exception of Caleb, Josie's only regrets had been leaving behind two-year-old Billy and four-year-old Matthew. Beulah, ironically, was Henry's grandmother, a kind, sweet woman, who wasn't up to many chores but would at least play with the boys and make sure they were properly fed and cared for.

Wiping away yet another tear, Josie kissed her brother's

cheek and said, "Go on and get your horse. I can finish with the mare myself."

"The little ones are doing good," he reassured her. "Honest."

"Go," she insisted, lightly slugging his shoulder, and so he did, muttering to himself as he made his way down the aisle.

Watching him walk away, Josie smiled, still amazed by the daring rescue attempt he'd made on her behalf. Barely sixteen, Caleb was seven years younger than Josie, and the fourth of Peter Baum's sons. She thought of him as her favorite brother for a lot of reasons, chief of which was the fact that Caleb reminded Josie the most of her mother and the least of her stepfather. More than once she had shielded this most fragile of her brothers from Peter Baum's whip. More than once, she had failed. How on God's green earth had he managed to convince the man to let him come after her in the first place?

As Caleb led his buckskin gelding out of the stall, she asked, "Does Pa know you've come after me?"

Head hung low, he quietly said, "No, I run off in the night. I was kinda hoping that he'd forgive me when I came back with you, though."

"Caleb," she said, going to him. "I meant it when I said that I'm never going back. You've got to understand that. I know that Pa'll beat you bloody if you go home without me, but I just can't go back there."

He looked at her with their mother's eyes, and smiled. "I guess maybe I knew that all along. If you ain't going back, then neither am I."

This suddenly didn't sound like such a bad idea. "You want to throw in with me?"

Caleb lit up. "Sure do. What's your plan?"

"I figure on starting up my own cattle ranch when we get back to Miles City, and just wait until you see what I found to get us going."

"Cattle ranching, Josie?"

Caleb's face fell into a pout, not entirely a surprise. Each morning when Peter Baum rode off with his sons to ride the range, Josie had longed to go with them instead of seeing to her endless household chores. Though he'd never actually said so, Caleb's expression often mirrored those thoughts in reverse. If she ever got any help around the house, it was he who offered his services, and with more enthusiasm than he ever showed mounted on the back of a horse. Often Josie had wished that she could just up and exchange skins with Caleb, a sentiment she suspected he shared.

"I've got an idea," she said, seeing a way to make both their wishes come true. "I'll ride herd over the cattle, and you can stay home and manage the ranch. What do you think?"

"I think," he said, extending his hand, "that we got ourselves a deal."

Laughing with him, she said, "Get your horse saddled up. I'm going to go get my buffalo."

"Your what?"

"My buffalo, Sweetpea. She's the surprise I was telling you about, the one that's going to get us started in the ranching business."

Caleb scratched his head. "You can't start a cattle ranch with a buffalo."

"Oh, yeah? Who the hell says I can't?"

"I do, for one," said a third voice.

Josie turned to see Daniel leaning against the open door of the barn. All the tenderness she'd felt for him earlier vanished. "And I say you're dead wrong. That buffalo is going with me and that's that."

He strolled down the aisle toward them, his leg so well mended, his limp was even less noticeable than Caleb's.

"Even if you figure out a way to herd that animal," Daniel went on to say, "and I don't think you can, with that buffalo slowing you down, you'll never make it back to Miles City before the next storm hits."

"Take another look outside," Josie said with a laugh. She'd been pleased to encounter the sun when she stepped from the cabin that morning, even though a few clouds lingered over the mountaintops like clusters of fat sheep. "The weather has warmed up so much, the snow is beginning to melt."

"I noticed." Daniel paused a moment to rub the buckskin's nose. "Unless this is your first winter in Montana, I think you already know how fast the weather can change in these parts. You'll be taking enough of a chance just trying to get yourselves back to Miles City before the next storm hits."

He had a point, but Josie wasn't about to concede it or Sweetpea to him. "It can also stay nice and warm for a couple of weeks or more. I'll take my chances."

Daniel turned to give her a particularly pointed look. "Long Belly says he heard some white owls calling last night. It sure as hell wasn't the sun that chased them out of the Arctic this early. Leave that buffalo here. I'll see that she's well taken care of."

Josie hated to admit that Daniel was right, but in this case, he was. Even then she stubbornly went out to the corral and made a feeble attempt at fashioning a halter for Sweetpea in hopes of leading her away from the cabin. The minute the buffalo saw the rope, she panicked and nearly ran Josie down. There didn't seem to be any way to justify the risk of taking the beast back to Miles City at her own, unpredictable pace, not with the weather every bit as unstable.

In the end, since she and Caleb were not welcome at the cabin any longer, Josie had no choice but to head back to town, leaving Sweetpea behind. She did so vowing to her and to everyone in earshot that she would be back come spring to claim what was rightfully hers.

Josie was not, however, a fool.

She knew that if she waited until spring to return, her hope for the future would be long gone. In fact, she was quite certain that the minute she rode out of sight this morning, Long Belly would be making plans to transport Sweetpea to the Cheyenne camp. She didn't know as yet how she would prevent this from happening, but she got to work on a scheme the minute she mounted the little brown mare.

The ride between the cabin and the Saint Labre Indian Mission was only about ten miles, but thanks to the heavy snowfall and drifts in some places as high as their mounts' withers, it took them a good four hours to cover the distance. Daniel, who had business at the mission, lead the way aboard The Black. Caleb and his mount brought up the rear, with Josie sandwiched between the two, her mind working every bit as hard as the mare's slender legs.

Early on in the ride she came up with a reckless plan that would keep Sweetpea by her side and to some extent ensure that she would retain ownership of the animal. Josie dismissed this insane idea time and time again in hopes of finding a less volatile, more viable alternative. By the time they reached the banks of the Tongue River and the long, rustic cabin that served as the mission, there didn't seem to be another choice.

She would go ahead with the daring plan, even though it was risky in ways Josie didn't want to think about. She would not only go ahead with it, but she would see the crazy scheme through to the finish, come hell or high water.

In fact, an entire herd of wild buffalos couldn't have stopped her.

Chapter Fourteen

Christmas preparations were under way when Daniel and his little group arrived at the Saint Labre Mission. There were two buildings on the property—the mission itself, a long three-room log cabin with a huge wooden cross rising from the roof, and a two-story structure known as "the White House." It served as convent for the Ursuline Sisters, who ran the school, housed classrooms and the girl's dormitory, and also supplied a small chapel for daily worship. Sister Ignatius McFarland was passing between the two buildings, carrying a miniature manger complete with crib, as Daniel rode up.

"Hello," she called, her long black habit flapping in the wind. "With that broken leg of yours and all this bad weather, I was worried we wouldn't see you again until spring."

Daniel swung down off The Black, careful not to land on his bad leg, then tore off his hat and canted his head. "I couldn't wait until spring to see you again, Sister Iggy," he said, using his pet name for her. "I'd have crawled through a blizzard long before then if I had to, just to see your pretty face again."

She chuckled, her round little cheeks crimson against the

stark white coif of her habit, and then turned to his companions. "Why, it's Mr. Baum, isn't it?"

"Yes, ma'am," Caleb said, dismounting. "I found the agent's cabin just where you said it'd be."

As Josie climbed down off the mare, the nun greeted her. "And you must be Mr. Baum's sister."

"That's right," she said, shaking her hand. "Josie's the name."

"I'm Sister Ignatius. Please, come to the White House with me, everyone. We were just about to sit down to hot chocolate and sandwiches."

"The rest of you go ahead." Daniel fitted his hat to his head. "I have some business to go over with Father van der Velden. Is he at the mission?"

She nodded. "I believe he's in the kitchen with some sickly boys who just arrived."

Daniel headed toward the log cabin, wishing there were at least three of Father Aloysius van der Velden, a Dutch Jesuit who not only offered the Cheyenne religious and educational instructions, but medical knowledge and pure unbigoted friendship. If there was a fault in the man or the mission system, it was the fact that he tried so hard to convert the Indians to Catholicism when they already had their own belief in God and their own religion, which was a part of their daily lives. Another problem was that the Cheyenne saw themselves as extensions of nature and related to it spiritually, which sometimes looked like pagan ritual to Christians. Daniel found those ceremonies no more primitive than the rituals Father van der Velden performed at the mission—especially when he went around swinging a smoke pot or sprinkling holy water on everyone who got in his way.

As rustic on the inside as it was on the outside, the cabin had no doors or partitions separating its three distinct sections, but each had a clear purpose. The smallest room was the rectory or priests' quarters; the middle, formerly the classroom, was now the boys' dorm; and the largest formed a combination kitchen and dining room. It was in this largest section that

Daniel found the Jesuit, who was serving bowls of soup to two young, pale-faced Cheyenne boys.

Father van der Velden looked up as Daniel stepped into the room. "Ah, if it isn't our awkward Indian agent. How is your leg doing?"

"Fine," he grumbled, anxious to move to another topic. "Has the government sent more supplies yet? We could sure use a fresh load at Lame Deer."

"We got some flour and a few more staples, but I'm afraid they didn't send money for meat this time. We barely have enough for us to survive at the mission this winter."

Daniel nodded, even though the priest's back was to him. "Just like last winter, huh?"

Father van der Velden looked away from the soup pot and turned to Daniel with a rare frown. Blue-eyed and fair-haired, the priest usually had a smile and a kind word, no matter the subject. "I'm afraid so, but also like last winter, we expect the Lord will provide."

Not much Daniel could say to that except, "Well, I'm sure the tribe will appreciate the flour and staples. I wrote another letter to the agency. Who knows, maybe they will provide this time and the Lord can take this winter off."

"We can hope." The priest returned to the soup pot and began filling a couple of bowls. "I could use a little fresh air. Why don't you join me outside for a stroll as soon as I have these boys settled in with their meal?"

A walk didn't sound particularly good to Daniel, not with the dull ache pounding in his shin, but he sensed the clergyman wanted a little privacy for the rest of their discussion. When the soup had been served, he followed van der Velden back to the grounds, a hundred and sixty acres of good farmland that was not officially part of the Cheyenne reservation.

With the mission so far away, it meant that members of the tribe had to travel upwards of twenty miles in all kinds of weather to get their supplies, making it difficult for most of them to receive the rations they needed so desperately. That was but one of the problems Daniel hoped to address here today. The other had to do with the persistent rumor that the government intended to put the Cheyenne Indians on the Crow reservation, merging them with the very people they hated the most. If Daniel had his way, this would never happen, at least not without a lot of bloodshed and needless waste of human life.

When Father van der Velden felt secluded enough to speak up, he surprised Daniel by addressing another issue entirely. "A young man came here a couple of days ago looking for an Indian who'd kidnapped a young white woman from Miles City a few weeks back."

Daniel groaned, unable to stop the involuntary reaction.

"Your brother-in-law came here about six weeks ago and asked us to look after his horses while he borrowed a boat and went into town." Father van der Velden linked his hands behind his back, and deep furrows cut into his forehead. "When he returned the following night, he collected his horses without alerting anyone. Do you know if he is the Indian in question?"

Again Daniel groaned. "Well . . . yes. He's the one all right, but Long Belly didn't exactly kidnap the women."

"Women?" The clergyman clutched his chest through his black robe. "He took more than one?"

Daniel nodded as he considered ways of explaining the situation without slinging mud on the ladies or on Long Belly. "My brother-in-law thought that he paid for the women, not just a few minutes of their time, and brought them home to me as gifts."

The priest raised his sandy eyebrows. "He believes that females can be bought and sold as gifts, Daniel?"

"Well . . . yes. At least, he did."

Falling all over himself, he then tried to explain the whorehouse away without actually explaining. "You see, because of this broken leg of mine, Long Belly decided that I needed more help than he could give me. When he heard that white men have places that—er, sell women, he figured he could get the help I need there. Understand?"

Father van der Velden held his gaze steady. "I am a priest,

Daniel, not a saint. I am aware that such places exist and I know why they continue to thrive. Do go on. Tell me about this second woman. Is her family also looking for her?''

"Not that I know of." Too embarrassed to look the priest in the eye, Daniel made a show of cleaning his fingernails instead. "Sissy has been working at the—ah, pleasure palace for some time, but she decided she'd rather winter on the reservation with Long Belly than return to Miles City right away."

Father van der Velden stopped walking. "And you're quite sure this was her choice, not something your brother-in-law forced her into?"

"Positive," Daniel was able to say. "Those two have what you might call a hankering for each other."

The priest nodded, thinking things over. "And what's become of the other woman?"

"Josie is her name." Just saying it out loud gave Daniel pause, a moment to reflect on how much duller his life would be without her around to keep him fired up. He cleared his throat before he could go on. "She's here now with her brother, the young man who rode into the mission looking for her a while back. Josie isn't like Sissy, if you get my drift. She isn't a—er, you know—"

"Prostitute?"

"Right."

Lord, how Daniel hated this conversation, especially now that it centered on Josie and her moral standards. He couldn't think of them without thinking about the shameless way he'd treated her—no matter that she hadn't straightened him out on her status. He should have known better somehow—in fact, *did,* but chose to ignore his gut instincts in favor of more lustful pursuits.

The priest looked him in the eye. "If Miss Baum wasn't employed at this sinful place, then what on earth was she doing at such an establishment?"

Daniel explained it clean and simple, leaving out all mention of her family. "Josie was just a laundress there who happened to cross Long Belly's path."

Father van der Velden eyed him thoughtfully. "So your story is that your brother-in-law inadvertently kidnapped a prostitute and a rancher's innocent daughter." He shook his head in amazement. "You do realize, don't you, that we're just barely hanging on to this mission because Sister Ignatius had the good sense to homestead the land in her own name?"

"Yes, of course."

"Then you must also know that the white ranchers in this area would love any excuse to drive us out of here, especially something as morally corrupt as this."

"I'm aware of that."

"See that you don't forget it."

Mulling things over, the priest began walking again, head bent in thought, until they reached the White House. Then he trapped Daniel in his trademark and very persuasive smile.

"May I assume that there will be no further problems with this young woman or her brother?"

Pleased with the way he'd handled everything, Daniel gave a resolute nod. "None whatsoever. You have my word on it."

Inside the White House, Josie struggled to contain her mounting nerves. Although she found the Cheyenne girls charming and very talented as they showed off their sewing and fancy work, her mind was on one thing—the plan. Over and over she questioned whether she was making the right choice. She could go back to Miles City and take her old job, she supposed, but what good would that do? A job as a laundress at a house of ill repute would hardly improve her chances of securing a loan with a banker, especially if she didn't have a buffalo to use as bait. That in turn made her think of Sweetpea and what Long Belly and his tribe might be doing to her at this very moment. It also convinced Josie that she'd made the right decision, crazy and risky as it might seem. She really had no other choice.

"Come on in, Calf Road," said Sister Ignatius, coaxing one of her young students into the room. "Show our visitors what you are making."

The shy young Indian girl finally came into the room, eyes pinned to the thin carpet beneath her feet, and held up a calico dress of faded blue. "I have made this Christmas gift for my mother, Pushed by Everybody, who cannot come to school and be taught by the *wihonas.*"

"By whom?" asked Sister Ignatius.

"By the nuns," she said, a giggle in her voice.

Turning to Caleb and Josie, Sister Ignatius said, "We try to make sure that the children speak only English to us, and as a rule, we speak only Cheyenne to them. We've learned much from each other that way. Have we not, Calf Road?"

With another giggle, the girl nodded, then dashed out of the room. She almost crashed headlong into Daniel and a very pleasant-faced man dressed in a long black robe—the sort who looked as if he might easily become an ally.

"Father van der Velden," said the nun as she rose from the couch. "Come say hello to our guests, Caleb Baum and his sister, Josie."

Climbing to her feet alongside her brother, Josie exchanged greetings with the clergyman, then chose to remain standing when the priest insisted they return to their seats. Taking what he thought was Josie's cue, and in some ways it was, Caleb remained standing, too, ready to start the journey to Miles City.

"Thanks for the hot chocolate and all," he said. "But we'd better be heading out if we want to cover any ground before nightfall."

Father van der Velden wouldn't hear of it. "Oh, but why not stay the night as you did before, young man? We have plenty of room for the two of you, and besides, your mounts will make much better headway if they start out fresh in the morning."

"Thank you kindly, sir, that's right friendly of you, offering to put me up twice." He glanced at Josie, eyebrows raised expectantly. "I'm sure my sister would appreciate your hospitality, too. Wouldn't you, Josie?"

All eyes went to her, including Daniel's. Avoiding that bright blue pair in particular, she shrugged and boldly set her plan in motion. "I suppose it would be best for the horses if we stayed here tonight—that is, if you have a place for me away from the girls in your care."

The nun and the priest exchanged a puzzled glance. Then Sister Ignatius said, "You're very welcome to stay here with the girls, Miss Baum. It won't be a problem at all."

"Not for me, maybe," she said, hanging her head. "But I don't think you really want someone like me around your innocent young students. You see, I've been . . . compromised."

Sister Ignatius's hand flew to her mouth, trying no doubt to mute a horrified gasp that escaped anyway.

Father van der Velden sputtered a minute, then turned to Daniel and said, "You assured me there would be no problems."

"I—well, sir, I didn't expect—"

"Was this woman compromised while she was in your home?"

Josie felt rather than saw Daniel's stare, knowing that he was waiting for her to set the priest straight. She did. "I wouldn't have said it if I didn't mean it, Father. Not only was I kidnapped and taken against my will to Mr. McCord's cabin, he forced me to get undressed and sleep in his bed with him, night after night."

"*Daniel?*" The priest's neck was mottled with splotches of red and his face was no longer kind or somber. In fact he almost looked capable of murder. "Is this true?"

"Well, yes, but—"

"Did you violate this unfortunate woman?"

From the corner of her properly downcast eye, Josie saw Daniel loosen his collar.

"Well," he said, his voice cracking. "That depends on what you mean by violate, I suppose."

Fanning the flames, Josie leaned toward the priest and whispered just loudly enough for all to hear, "He made me remove my clothing—isn't that violation enough, sir?"

Father van der Velden's eyes bulged as he sputtered, "I . . . ah . . . *Daniel?*"

"Well, I suppose I may have done a couple of things I shouldn't have, but she—"

"You're not," said the priest, cutting Daniel off, "going to stand there and tell me that your less-than-honorable behavior was the fault of this virtuous young woman, are you?"

"Well, no, but—"

"I know'd it!" shouted Caleb, surprising everyone. "I know'd that no-account bastard had been raping Josie all along, and now I got to kill him."

Catching all but Josie off guard, Caleb lunged at Daniel, and might even have knocked him to the ground if she hadn't stepped between the two, blocking his progress. Hands braced against Caleb's shoulders, Josie flashed a grin meant only for his eyes.

"Have you forgotten where we are, Caleb?" She heaved a dramatic sigh and pointed into the next room, where an elaborately garnished alter dominated the nun's chapel. "This is no place for talk of killing. I'll be all right . . . eventually."

"But Josie," Caleb objected, "what kind of brother would I be if I just stood here and did nothing to avenge your honor?"

"Never fear," said Father van der Velden. "Our friend Daniel McCord will be making amends for maligning your sister's good name. I'm sure he's already settled on a way to restore her honor, haven't you, son?"

The look Daniel shot Josie just before all eyes turned on him hinted that he'd figured out the exact method of her murder, not of making amends. He did an admirable job of hiding those feelings, however, when he turned to face the others.

"I reckon I do owe Miss Baum and her brother an apology," he said quietly, addressing neither of them directly. "In my own defense I do have to say that I was under the impression that Josie was a woman of easy virtue when Long Belly brought her to me. I treated her accordingly."

"And how did you treat her when you realized she was not such a female?" asked Father van der Velden. "Did you accord her the respect due a proper young lady?"

Daniel muttered something unintelligible under his breath before he said, "Well, I didn't exactly know until—"

"Daniel." The priest's tone brooked no argument. "There isn't but one thing you can do to repair the damage you've done to this woman's good name. I think you should stop wasting our time and get to it."

Inside the deep pockets of her buckskin shirt, Josie crossed her fingers.

After a long, tense moment, Daniel glared at her and said, "How'd you like to come live with me in my fine castle, princess?"

"*Daniel,*" chided the priest. "Surely that isn't the best you can do."

Still glowering, he grudgingly admitted, "No, I've got the bark to do this right, if I have to, but for the life of me, I can't understand why any 'lady of proper breeding' would even want an offer to tie herself to someone like me."

The priest's smile was sanctimonious, even for a man of the cloth. "Perhaps if for no other reason than the fact that she has the courtesy of a proposal coming?"

Daniel emptied his lungs with a dramatic puff of his cheeks, then stood there hat in hand and said the words Josie had been waiting to hear. "Will you do me the honor of becoming my wife, Miss Baum?"

Drawing his moment of agony out a few minutes, Josie twisted from side to side as if in the throes of indecision. Then she finally closed the jaws of her trap.

"I don't have much choice, since no other man is going to want me after what you've done. Yes, I'll dishonor myself by becoming your wife."

"W-what?" Daniel nearly strangled on the word. "Was that a *yes?*"

Josie nodded, unable to look him in the eye.

"But we can't get married—I don't want to get married."

"I'm afraid, Daniel," said the priest, "that it's not your decision to make. Miss Baum has agreed to become your wife, and I will personally see to it that you two are wed posthaste."

"Oh!" Sister Ignatius clapped her hands. "We're going to have a wedding. How wonderful."

"Indeed we are," said Father van der Velden. "How does six o'clock this evening sound to you, Miss Baum?"

Still avoiding Daniel's gaze, Josie ignored what sounded like a low growl coming from his throat and said, "That sounds perfect."

Caleb, who'd been scratching his head since Daniel's first, rather impudent proposal, finally had his say on the matter. "You sure about this, Josie, marrying up with a half-breed and all?"

"He's got a point," said Daniel, all too eager to agree. "Think about the kids. You don't want to be mother to a couple of wild Indians, do you?"

Since Josie had no intention of bedding Daniel in that way, much less bearing his children, she didn't see a problem. "It's already settled. We're going to be married tonight, and that's that."

"At six o'clock, no less," said Sister Ignatius, a sudden ball of nerves. "We have so much to do! First of all, we've got to find you something to wear, child. You can't get married in buckskin trousers!"

Josie glanced down at herself, unconcerned about her apparel. She'd worn the trousers and shirt Long Belly had given her as well as the deerskin boots Daniel had made simply because they were so much warmer than her stained yellow dress. She didn't give a damn about what she wore at her wedding, especially since she didn't intend to look on the marriage as anything other than a means to an end.

"This is all I've got, Sister," she explained, hoping that would be the end of it.

"Well, don't you worry. We'll come up with something a little more suitable." Her hands flew to her cheeks. "Oh, and

I'd better run get Sister Angela busy in the kitchen. We have a wedding feast to prepare.''

"I kin help with that, if you like," offered Caleb.

"Come on, then. Follow me."

As the nun hurried off with Caleb, all gangly legs and teeth, Daniel said to the priest, "If you'll excuse us, Father, I'd like a few minutes alone with my fiancée. I thought we'd go outside for a walk, if that's all right with you."

The last thing Josie wanted was to be alone with Daniel, especially before the wedding. "I really shouldn't leave. The nuns will be needing me for fittings and such."

"Go ahead, my dear," said Father van der Velden. "The sisters will be a while giggling over this unexpected event before they can get down to sorting through their sewing supplies. I'm sure you two have a lot to talk about."

Stuck in a mud pie of her own making, Josie had no choice after that but to allow Daniel to lead her out of the charming house and into the bright sunshine. Once they were alone, it took him until they'd walked all the way down to the banks of the Tongue River before he got to the point. Even then, he stood there a while, kicking at clumps of snow and staring out at the sluggish waters before he finally spoke his mind.

"Why in blue hell did you say yes to my proposal?" He turned to look at her, that blue hell he spoke of gleaming in his eyes. "I've been married once before, and believe me, once was enough. I don't want to get married again, especially to someone as worthless as you."

Josie wasn't exactly looking for romance out of Daniel, but his comments hurt. "I don't know why you're in such an uproar. It seems to me that we're about perfect for each other."

"Perfect? How do you figure that? Hell, woman, half the time we don't even like each other much."

"It's simple. You don't want to get married and neither do I."

Daniel looked at her as if all her brains had leaked out somewhere between the river and the mission. "Then why, if I may ask again, did you say yes?"

She supposed it no longer mattered if he knew her true motives—Father van der Velden was going to make Daniel marry her no matter how many excuses or stories he came up with.

"Because," Josie admitted. "It seemed to be the only way I could keep my claim on Sweetpea and get a start on my cattle ranch at the same time."

Daniel's expression remained the same—agog and perplexed. "Have you gone completely loco? If you marry me, the only thing you'll accomplish is keeping me good and pissed for the rest of my life."

"Not if you look at this wedding as more of a favor than anything."

Daniel took a step away from Josie, then dramatically looked her up one side and down the other. "You really have gone loco, haven't you."

"If you'll shut up a minute, I'll explain."

"Please do."

"The first reason for getting married is that I'm not letting that buffalo out of my sight long enough for you and that heathen brother of yours to steal her away from me. That means I have to stay at your place until springtime, which also means that I can't stay there any longer as a single lady."

He frowned, but said, "All right. What's the second?"

"When time comes for me to herd Sweetpea into town so I can convince a banker to invest in my ranch, I'll have a lot better chance of getting the money if he thinks he's bankrolling me and my husband, not a woman alone."

"Makes sense, I suppose—at least for you." Daniel hooked his thumbs in the waistband of his trousers. "I still don't see why in hell you had to drag me into your fancy plans for the future. It wasn't my fault that Long Belly kidnapped you."

"I don't care whose fault it is. The point is that I got dragged into your life against my will. Besides," she added defensively, "I couldn't think of anything else to do but marry you."

"Damn, woman, you might have at least asked me for suggestions."

"Oh, what are you so worried about? It's not as if we'll have a real marriage. It'll just look that way until I get the loan."

He raised one eyebrow. "Father van der Velden is going to marry us tonight. How do you figure that isn't real?"

Josie rolled her eyes. "You just said that you don't ever want to get married again, right?"

"Now you're talking my language."

"Well, if you marry me but I don't live with you except on a temporary basis until I get my ranch, then you'll be married without actually having to put up with a wife. Best of all, no one else can trap you because you'll legally be married. It's perfect for you, can't you see that?"

Looking back out at the river, Daniel puzzled on this a minute, then shook his head. "All I know is that I can't think of anything worse than having you for a wife. Not only are you ornery as a mule with a burr in its blanket, you aren't worth your salt when it comes to wifely duties."

"But that's my part of the bargain," she quickly assured him. "I get my buffalo and a husband's name, and until spring, you get the best cook west of the Mississippi, a seamstress without equal, and the finest housekeeper in all the Territories."

"I do?" Daniel looked over his shoulder. "Where the hell is she?"

Josie slugged his shoulder. "I'm talking about me, you fool. I lied to you when I said that I couldn't cook or anything. I even had to force myself to keep from making our Thanksgiving supper any better than it was. I can also sew and keep house with the best of them."

Daniel glanced at her, a little too long and a little too speculatively. "If all you wanted out of this is Sweetpea, I don't see why you couldn't simply have made a deal with me for her before we came to the mission."

"I told you—I want my own ranch, and to do that, I have to get money from the bank. To do that—"

"I know, I know, but you're such a damn good liar, why couldn't you just lie to a banker about having a husband?"

It wasn't that Josie hadn't thought of that—she had. She also knew that if she'd played that card before showing her hand to the priest, Daniel would have found a way to ruin everything.

"Are you saying," she asked cheekily, "that you would have agreed to let me go back to your ranch to stake my claim on Sweetpea if I'd asked?"

Daniel's hesitation was good enough answer for Josie. "I didn't think so. And that's why you and I are getting married come six o'clock tonight."

"Just one more thing," he said, looking grim. "I have to know—that story you told me about catching a pox. Is it true?"

Josie burst out laughing. "Of course it's not true. I overhead some of the girls at Lola's talking about how worried they were about such things, but I don't even know what a pox is."

Daniel smiled then, really smiled for the first time since she'd sprung her scheme.

Then he brought up a subject she'd given little, almost no, thought to.

"In that case, I guess I'm trapped, no matter what," he said, still smiling. "Since you're so gee-whizzley smart, you must have figured out by now that means you are, too."

Chapter Fifteen

Marriage.

The full implication of what she was about to do didn't actually hit Josie until Caleb walked her down the chapel's short aisle and she found herself standing before her husband-to-be and a priest. In fact, she didn't think about much of anything as the sisters draped her body in a pair of bedsheets they'd tacked together to form a reasonable substitute for a wedding gown, then topped her off with a veil made out of a lace altar cloth. Now all she could do was think—and fret about whether she was making the right decision.

Josie stole a glance at her groom, noting that he was the model of composure, his expression as solid and impenetrable as a pair of new barn doors. In profile, Daniel's strong, straight nose and serious brow gave his Indian heritage the dominant edge over his features, making him look the part of a full-blooded Cheyenne warrior. He'd tied his shoulder-length hair at the nape of his neck with a leather thong sporting stone arrowheads and a single eagle feather, a hurried bit of grooming that did nothing to lessen the image.

Someone—the priest, Josie assumed—had lent Daniel a

clean white shirt and a long black coat that reached to mid-thigh. In keeping with his Cheyenne name, Daniel Two Skins, he wore his buckskin trousers and beaded moccasin boots beneath the jacket. No longer an invalid, he stood straight and tall, his two feet planted firmly on the floor, the picture of potent masculinity. Never before had Daniel struck her so profoundly as the product of two nations—or as a man. The very thought that soon she would call him "husband" made Josie go weak in the knees.

Marriage.

She heard Father van der Velden say the words, "Dearly beloved," then caution that the vows of marriage were sacred, not to be taken lightly or frivolously. Josie immediately saw in that statement the opportunity to back out of this idiotic plan and take her chances in Miles City, without benefit of Sweetpea. She hadn't forgotten Daniel's insinuation that she was as trapped as he by this marriage.

"Do you, Josephine Baum, take Daniel McCord as your lawfully wedded husband?"

"Josephine?" Daniel whispered, laughing under his breath. *"Josephine?"*

His amusement over her given name rattled Josie so that she completely forgot that she was having doubts about going through with the wedding. Before she realized what she'd done, she'd promised to love, honor, and obey Daniel McCord until death did them part. Surprisingly enough, he made those same vows to her in return, all without so much as a whispered protest.

It didn't seem real, this long religious ceremony with constant references to God and blessings and children, and yet when it finally drew to a close and Daniel was invited to kiss his bride, Josie's were the lips he brushed with his own. A moment later, when the priest christened her Mrs. Daniel McCord, she damn near fell over in a dead faint. What the hell had she gotten herself into?

Josie did manage to recover well enough from the shock of hearing herself addressed as the wife of a half-breed to enjoy a wedding supper of roasted antelope and squash. She even took a perverse pleasure in Daniel's sour expression when Father van der Velden explained that the mission did not have facilities for married couples—which meant they would have to spend their first night as man and wife in separate quarters. It wasn't until she and Daniel took a private stroll around the mission grounds that the reality of what she'd let herself in for kicked her in the gut, good and hard.

Hips swaggering with a hard-muscled cockiness she hadn't noticed in him before, Daniel slipped his arm around Josie's waist as he guided her around the windmill and toward a copse of trees between the mission and the White House. The night was still and quiet, made for lovers without so much as a wispy cloud overhead. Clusters of sparkling stars filled the inky sky and the moon was bright, casting giant elongated shadows of Josie and Daniel as a couple in the path ahead. Mesmerized by the way their phantom selves blended together so smoothly, his hard edges melting into her rounded curves until they seemed one, Josie's mind wandered to mergings of another kind.

"I want to head back to the cabin at first light," said Daniel, disrupting her indecent thoughts. "Make sure the nuns wake you in plenty of time."

"What's the hurry?" she asked, glad for the distraction. "I was kinda looking forward to a nice leisurely breakfast tomorrow morning, and maybe a nap afterward. I haven't gotten a whole lot of rest lately."

"You can rest when the next storm hits. Before that happens, I've got to deliver supplies at the reservation. I live smack between the mission and Lame Deer, so we can easily make the ride in one day."

"We?"

"I want you to ride along with me."

Pausing near a barren cottonwood tree, Josie considered the request. She had no interest in visiting the home of a bunch of no-account savages, or of making sure that a group of murdering

Indians had their bellies full when her own father and brother lay dead in their graves, never to feel hunger again.

"I'd just as soon you drop me off at the cabin," she said, sure that Daniel's invitation was simply a courtesy. "I want to check on Sweetpea, then I've got a lot of cleaning to do in that house."

Daniel braced himself against the tree just above her head. He was so close, she could smell their wedding wine on his lips and the lingering scent of the alkaline soap the nuns had given them for their baths. She felt rather than saw his eyes on her, hot and inquisitive.

"I'll help you with the buffalo," Daniel said, still urging her for no reason Josie could think of, to join him. "And the cabin can wait. You'll probably enjoy the ride out to Lame Deer. The deeper you get into reservation land, the thicker the forest. We might even scare up some game. You'd like that, wouldn't you?"

He lowered his head and leaned into her then, confusing Josie so, she wasn't sure what the question referred to. She only knew that she wanted Daniel to kiss her, to hold her in his arms and kiss her until she couldn't think at all anymore.

She said, "Yes," giving him permission for just about anything he had in mind.

As if sensing her hunger, apparently sharing it too, Daniel raised Josie's chin with the tip of his finger, bringing her mouth within inches of his. He looked at her for a long moment, brooding and reflective, then slowly ran his tongue along his bottom lip. Sure her torment was about to end, Josie closed her eyes and let her head fall back.

"Then it's settled," Daniel said in a whisper. "I haven't gotten around to training The Black for dragging a travois yet, and I doubt he'd take too kindly to it, so we'll haul most of the load behind your mount. Think you can handle it?"

Disappointed, feeling robbed and embarrassed, Josie opened her eyes again. "I can handle about anything, I guess, but what about that poor mare? How's she going to feel about having a big load like that strapped to her hips?"

Daniel grinned, blue eyes glittering. "About the same way you're going to feel with me strapped to your hips, I expect—thrilled to be of some use for a change."

Josie felt her cheeks grow hot. Never had he spoken to her so blatantly, not even when he thought she was a whore.

"Bedding you is not a part of our bargain," she said, her tummy doing a slow, sensuous roll at the memory of the pleasures his touch could ignite. "I said I'd cook, sew, and clean. Nothing else."

"Bedding me became an unspoken part of our bargain the minute you took your vows." Still grinning, he ran a finger down the front of her dress, lingering there at the sensitive juncture of her thighs. "Why are you so worried about that part of our deal? You already know that you won't be the least bit disappointed."

Daniel had the audacity to wink at her then, irritating Josie even as he turned her insides into a kettle of hot mush. She tried to think of something equally glib in reply, but before she could, he pulled her close and lightly kissed her forehead.

"See you at first light, Missus McCord." Then he turned her around and gave her a shove toward the White House, adding, "Don't be late."

The following morning, as Josie finished saddling the mare, Caleb strolled out to the barn to say good-bye. Gone were the nervous gestures and darting glances he'd developed since riding away from his father's home. He almost seemed at peace.

"The nuns wanted you to have this," he said, handing Josie the altar cloth she'd worn as a veil. "They thought every gal would want to have some kind of memento from her wedding. Maybe you ought to put it on now. At least then you'll look a little more like the white girl you used to be."

She whirled on him. "What's that supposed to mean?"

Caleb pointed out her apparel. "Criminy, ain't you had a look at yourself lately?"

While she knew she wasn't exactly a female model of decorum in buckskin trousers, Josie hadn't thought of herself as looking particularly different. She just knew that she'd never before known such freedom of movement—a commodity for a future cattle rancher worth all the snickers and stares of polite society.

She gave Caleb a shrug. "You try riding herd or mending fences wearing a skirt and petticoats. See how much you like being trapped in yards of lace and calico."

He dragged his toe in the dirt. "It ain't just your clothes, Josie, it's them braids and geegaws you got hanging off them and your neck. You look like a damned Injun squaw. I thought you hated redskins even more than the rest of us."

She impulsively touched the stone arrowheads in her hair and the tiny medicine bag at her throat. She did hate Indians and what they'd done to her family—she did. And yet for some reason, Josie hadn't been able to remove the artifacts Long Belly had given to her. It was ridiculous and superstitious, she supposed, but as long as Sweetpea remained on the Cheyenne reservation, it seemed wisest to keep the charms in place.

"These are only temporary, Caleb," she assured him. "Just like the marriage."

"Yeah, well," he complained. "That's another thing. I still don't see how come you had to tie yourself to a no-account half-breed. What if he treats you mean once he gets you back to his cabin?"

Of all the things that could go wrong with the scheme, that was the one thing that didn't concern Josie in the slightest. "He'll treat me just fine, Caleb. Don't you worry your head about that. Daniel McCord may be a lot of things—bull-headed and set in his ways among them—but I know he'll treat me right."

"Well . . . if you say so." He didn't look or sound convinced. "But just in case you get any trouble out of him, I want you to know that I'm gonna be right here at the mission."

Josie had assumed that Caleb would be heading for Miles City about the time she took off for Daniel's cabin. "How long do you figure on sticking around? The next storm could be sitting on tomorrow's horizon.''

"Don't matter. I'm staying as long as you're up in them hills. I already talked to Father van der Velden, and he said I could stay on if I helped out with the cooking and such to pay for my room and board.''

Since Caleb really had no place else to go at the moment, hiring on at the mission suddenly didn't sound like such a bad idea. He wouldn't be earning much money toward the ranch that way, but she doubted he'd do much better in Miles City over the winter, especially given his lack of experience in working with anything except cattle. No point in arguing with him about it anyway. Caleb seemed to be as determined to carry out his plan as she was hers. Her bed was made, so to speak, and now she had to lie in it. So to speak.

As they rode back to the cabin, Daniel insisted that Josie take the lead so that he could follow along behind to make sure that the mare could handle the large job he'd assigned her. The travois she dragged bowed in the middle under the weight of the supplies Daniel had piled onto its hammock, but over halfway into the ride home, the little brown horse still seemed equal to the task with energy to spare. Following the mare instead of leading the way also gave Daniel an unequalled view of Josie's backside as she bounced along in the saddle.

His wife. Mercy.

Although the thought of getting trapped into yet another marriage didn't set right with him at first, it didn't take long for Daniel to see the advantage in simply going along with Josie's plans to hornswoggle him down the aisle. She'd freely admitted that she was using him to get what she wanted, but damned if he wasn't using her, too.

Not only was Josie an uncommonly handsome female and apparently chaste to boot, she knew her way around household chores a whole lot better than he'd been led to believe at first. Having a woman around the house who possessed such wifely skills would be a great benefit to Daniel's two young sons, a rambunctious pair who desperately needed the discipline and nurturing of a good mother. In that light, he hadn't walked blindly into Josie's trap. Daniel had practically sprung it himself.

There could be, of course, a small problem with just up and surprising his new bride with the boys. He probably should have mentioned them to her by now, but before today, there really hadn't been a reason to bring up the subject. He hated the fact that the twins had to stay with their mother's family on the reservation, but a man alone wasn't enough of a family to raise two small boys. Having Josie at the cabin might just turn the place into a home, which meant that Long Belly actually did have a damn fine idea when he first set out for Miles City.

At any rate, now that Daniel thought about it, it seemed foolish to worry about Josie's reaction to his sons. Any woman would be thrilled to take over as the boys' mother, at least for a little while. How could she help but fall in love with a pair of adorable four-year-old twins, even if they were little hellions at times?

Convinced he'd handled the situation correctly, Daniel leaned back in the saddle, warmed as he thought ahead to the next few weeks and having his sons back home in time for the holidays. Home with a brand new mother to tend them— Josephine Baum, the woman who'd shot their father, lied to him, and kept him up nights from the want of her.

Mercy.

Surprisingly enough, and even though they were loaded down with supplies, the return trip to the cabin took less time than the journey to the mission had the day before. The little caravan arrived back at Daniel's place well before noon.

While her new husband separated and unloaded their supplies from those that belonged to the reservation, Josie watered the horses, then assured herself that her prized buffalo was still there and doing quite well. Long Belly's horse was missing from the barn, which meant he was off somewhere, probably looking for a bull bison to mate with Sweetpea. This left Daniel to finish his task alone, while Josie headed to the cabin to look for Sissy.

"Guess who?" she called as she crossed the threshold and saw her friend bent over the stove.

From over her shoulder, Sissy replied, "I knew who a good long while ago. I seen you in the yard when you rode in."

"Then why didn't you come on out and welcome us home?"

Sissy gave a stiff shrug. "Too busy cleaning the grease off this stove, I guess. How come you ain't on your way to Miles City no more? Weather turn bad?"

"Nope. Guess again."

Sissy shrugged and continued working on the stove.

"Oh, you're no fun," complained Josie as she fell into a chair at the table. "I came back here because I went and got married—to Daniel."

The scraper Sissy had been using clattered to the floor. She spun around in surprise. "Huh?"

"I am now Missus Daniel McCord, queen of this"—she waved her arm around the room and grimaced—"palace."

"B-but . . . I thought you was all worked up about getting back to Miles City."

"I was, and I am. Come sit down and I'll tell you all about it."

After Sissy poured a couple of cups of coffee and took a chair across from her at the table, Josie quickly revealed her plans for the buffalo and how it tied in with her future as a cattle rancher. Then she explained why marrying Daniel had been essential to make the plan work.

"And so you see?" she said, finishing. "Now I don't have to worry about Sweetpea and what those no-account Indians might to do her in my absence. As Missus Daniel McCord, I'll also stand a very good chance of getting the financial backing I need to get my ranch going."

"Makes sense, I reckon." Sissy frowned deeply. "What I

don't understand is why Daniel went along with your plan. What does he get out of it?''

"Simple. I'll be the housekeeper he and this cabin have been wanting for a long, long time."

Josie glanced the room, startled to see that Sissy had already taken charge of the place as if it were her own home. The floor was swept and cleared of male debris, the dishes were cleaned and stacked along the counter, and her clothing now occupied the rack where Josie's yellow dress had been hanging.

Following her gaze, Sissy surmised, "I reckon you're gonna want me outta here pretty quick, huh?''

"Oh, no. Stay, please? I can use all the help I can get.''

"I wasn't talking about housework.''

Josie studied her expression, noting the raised eyebrow and knowing gleam in her dark eyes. "Believe me, you won't be in the way.''

"A newlywed couple don't need no whore sitting around staring at them every minute of the day. Guess maybe it's time I headed back to Miles City.''

"But I thought you were happy here with Long Belly, and that you didn't want to go back to whoring for a living.''

"I don't, but things is gonna change around here now that you two went and got married.'' She hung her head and stared down at the scarred table top. "It's best for everyone—even me, I expect—if I go back to Lola's.''

Josie moved the coffee cups aside and reached for Sissy's hands. "Nothing's going to change. We're friends, and I want you to stay as long as you like. Who knows? Maybe you and Long Belly will be the next to get married.''

Sissy jerked her hands away. "We were friends at Lola's because you didn't have no one else. Now that you're a respectable married woman, you can't go around having friends like me. T'aint fitting.''

"Why not?'' Josie leapt to her feet. "You're the first real friend I've ever had in my life. Who's going care up here, anyway?''

Sissy glanced up at her, dark eyes slick. "Me, I expect. You get me to thinking about things I got no right to think about—things like getting married and having stupid birthday parties.''

"Stupid?" Josie paced in front of the table. "You think the birthday cake I baked for you was stupid?"

"I didn't mean that exactly. The cake was nice," Sissy amended, softening the blow a little. "And I know you meant well baking it for me, but truth is, Josie, before then I never had a birthday or wanted one. A gal can't yearn for something she never had or even feel sad for the lack of it. Now, thanks to you, I do.''

Josie wasn't entirely sure she understood what Sissy was trying to say, but she could feel her sincerity and a little of her pain. "Sorry if I got you to feeling that way. I only meant to do something nice for you.''

Staring down at the table again, Sissy nodded slowly. "I reckon you did. It's just that I can't stand thinking how no one else has ever cared if I live to see another birthday and that no man will ever want me for his wife. I was better off not thinking about those things at all. Understand?''

Josie shrugged. "Not really. Birthdays aren't so blasted important, but I don't see why you and Long Belly can't get married—if he's the one you want, that is.''

Sissy looked up, startled, and then burst out laughing. "Honey, don't you know that men, even savages, don't marry women like me? I was born in a whorehouse, raised in a whorehouse, and I expect I'll die in a whorehouse. You saying otherwise ain't gonna change that a smidgen.''

Although she sorely wanted to, Josie couldn't argue the point. She even felt a certain kinship there, realizing that Sissy was also trapped, her cage being her own dark skin and the circumstances of her birth. Still, there had to be something she could say, anything to lighten what had to be a terrible burden. Before she could think of the right words, the door opened and in came Daniel. He was limping more than he had been at the mission, making Josie think that the trip had been a little too much for his still-healing leg.

"Morning, Sissy," he said. "Where's Long Belly gone off to?"

She wiped what might have been a tear from her cheek as she looked up and said, "He was gonna try and herd them cattle closer to the cabin. He's wanting to get them penned before the next storm hits."

"Hmm, good idea." He thought on that a minute. "No sense waiting around for him to show up. Long Belly's so good at herding cattle, he could be out there looking for strays until next winter." He paused to laugh at his own joke. "Tell him that we've gone on ahead to Lame Deer to drop off supplies. We'll be back sometime tomorrow."

"Tomorrow?" This came as a surprise to Josie. "I thought the reservation wasn't but ten miles from here."

"It's not, but that's going to be about all the riding this leg of mine can take for one day. Besides"—he paused to smile and wink—"when my friends at Lame Deer find out I've got a new wife, they're going to want to congratulate us somehow, maybe even offer a little wedding feast."

Josie backed toward the table. "In that case, I think I'll just stay right here with Sissy."

Daniel reached out and caught her hand. "Relax, darling. This'll be a good experience for you. You might even have a good time."

Then, with a backward glance and a silent plea to Sissy, who was sitting at the table laughing, she let him pull her through the door and out to where the horses waited.

The ride to Lame Deer was everything Daniel had promised and more. The forest got thicker as they rode deeper into reservation land, with pines and oaks in equal abundance. Picturesque streams and ponds seemed to be everywhere, fed by recent snows. They didn't scare up any game, as Daniel had suggested they might, but squirrels were everywhere, racing madly about during the lull in the weather to gather extra supplies for the coming winter. Overhead, magpies chattered on, warning any who cared that there were strangers riding through the forest, approaching from the east. A few concerned Cheyenne were listening.

As she and Daniel crested the last rise before coming to the encampment, Josie spotted a small group of savages standing before a clearing dotted with tipis and horses. Some of the Indians were wrapped in blankets and others were draped in what looked like ceremonial robes adorned with feathers and beads. For all she knew, they were a war party.

"Daniel!" Josie shouted in a whisper, twisting around in the saddle. "There's Indians up ahead. What if they don't recognize you and attack us?"

"Holy Christ, Josie." He coaxed The Black up beside the mare. "This is a reservation. The Cheyenne are no longer at war. They're just curious about their visitors."

Although she trusted that Daniel knew these people as well as he knew himself, Josie remained wary as they drew closer to the knot of savages awaiting them. Then one of the Indians wrapped in a colorful blanket startled her by breaking rank and running toward them.

"Daniel Two Skins, my friend!" he shouted, still on the run. "Are you well again?"

Daniel slid down off The Black, then braced himself for the exuberant welcome coming his way.

"Hello, Big Ribs," he said, after a brief, back-slapping embrace with the young man. "I'm pretty well healed. In good enough shape to bring you a few extra supplies to distribute among your families, anyway."

Daniel pointed out the travois behind the mare, but Big Ribs had eyes only for the horse's rider. "And the woman? Is she to be distributed evenly among our men?"

Josie shrank inside her buckskin jacket, terrified by the thought, but Daniel just laughed. "I'm afraid not. This is my new wife. Josie, meet Big Ribs. He's one of Long Belly's many cousins."

As the Indian started for her, she thought of turning the mare and running like hell, but Daniel caught the horse's halter in his hand and led her toward the crowd gathering to welcome them.

As if aware of her fears, he looked up and said, "Remember that no one here means to harm you. Trust me, all right? You'll be just fine."

After that, everything happened so fast, Josie didn't have a chance to be frightened. The crowd swarmed them, everyone talking at once in a language she didn't understand, and then Daniel swept her off the back of the mare. He kept her close to his side, thank God, but was so busy answering the many questions hurled his way, he never had a moment to explain what they were talking about or where they were taking them. Like a big human tumbleweed with Josie and Daniel at the core, the group of braves just kept rolling toward the tipis where the women and children had gathered to stare at the visitors.

A pair of naked young boys suddenly broke out of the pack of children, their bare feet kicking up the snow that remained on the ground, and bounded toward Daniel. Surprising Josie, he not only welcomed them with open arms, but picked them up and crushed them to his chest.

"My God," she said, appalled to see how thoroughly the youngsters were exposed to the elements. "Are these children orphans?"

"Orphans?" Daniel gave her a cockeyed glance from over the shiny black head of one boy. "Why the hell would you say that?"

"Well, look at them." She pointed out the obvious. "It's freezing out here, but they don't have any clothes or shoes. Doesn't anyone care what happens to them?"

"Hell, yes, someone cares—I do." Daniel turned to face her directly, swinging an identical pair of small round faces around with him. "The boys are naked because that's the way Cheyenne children play, even when it's cold."

One of the twin boys shot her a withering look and said something in Cheyenne.

Daniel answered the child in the same language, but Josie did manage to pick out mention of her when he said, "Josephine."

Both boys wrinkled their noses and giggled. But when their father began to speak again, this time in English, the amusement quickly left their faces and they glared at her with something akin to hatred.

"This is Two Moons and Bang, Josie," said Daniel, unaware of their hostile expressions. "They're my sons."

"*Sons?*" The word alone was enough to gag her. Josie grabbed her throat, unable to breath for a moment. "You never mentioned that you had children. Why the hell didn't you tell me?"

He shrugged. "It never came up, I guess. Aren't they just about the cutest little pups you've ever set eyes on?"

Chapter Sixteen

It was a good thing that Daniel didn't get a chance to ask Josie what she thought of his adorable pups. If he had, he'd have gotten an earful about how much she hated children, *male* children in particular, and that she thought it was downright rude of him to populate the world with not one, but two little pisspots at a throw. Of course he didn't question her then and not even later, when the twins ran off to resume playing with the other children, all of them as bare-assed naked as they were. Not that her thoughts on the matter could be shared with him here in the presence of all his heathen friends. And maybe not even later, in privacy. If they ever found any.

She and Daniel were still enveloped in that tumbleweed of savages, although as they strolled through the campsite, more and more men seemed to break off and go in other directions. The chatter continued, however, most of it female and all of it in the Cheyenne language, which made Josie feel alien and isolated.

The biggest surprise was the conduct of the Indians themselves. While she hadn't known exactly what to expect when she rode into the camp of a band of heathens, Josie had imagined that she'd be the subject of malevolent glares and salacious leers. Quite the opposite. The few warriors she did see treated her with respect and dignity; and several of them were too shy to even look her directly in the eye.

When the group had dwindled down to four Cheyenne women, who led Daniel and Josie to a large tipi decorated with paintings of stick figures and horses, he finally spoke to her privately.

Waiting until after the squaws had opened the flap and ducked inside the tipi, he said, "As I suspected they might, my friends here want to honor us with a wedding feast."

"But how can I take part in that when I don't even know what any of you are saying?"

"I'll translate where necessary. For now all you have to do is sit quietly and let the women inside the tipi get you ready for the ceremony."

She glanced nervously through the flap. "What are they going to do to me?"

Daniel laughed. "Nothing you won't like, I promise. They'll dress you, groom your hair, and maybe paint your face a little. That's all."

That's all? "Where will you be while they're covering me in war paint?"

Again he laughed. "Conducting agency business with the tribal council. When you're ready, someone will take you to the feast, and I'll join you there."

Josie snuck another peek inside the tipi. Four pairs of eyes glittered back at her from the semidarkness. "I don't know about this. I'm not sure I want to stay here without you. I'd be lying if I didn't say that I'm more than just a little nervous about the idea."

Daniel touched her cheek, his fingertips warm and smooth again her skin, and then he leaned in close and kissed the spot he'd touched. "I know you're afraid, and I have a pretty good idea why. After you learn a little about our customs and our people, I think you'll find we're not so different from your own family back in Miles City."

This did not reassure Josie in the least. In fact, the thought made her want to turn and run as fast as she could back to the cabin. Instead, she sighed heavily and said, "Oh, I guess it won't kill me, at that. Will you at least be in shouting distance?"

"Until it's time to meet you at the feast, I'll be as close as that tipi over there the whole time." Daniel turned and pointed out a lodge situated in the middle of the camp, one with even more elaborate figures and symbols than the others. "Anything else?"

Josie glanced around, noting that the women and young girls were bustling about the other tipis, some carrying sticks to the large fire ring at the center of camp, some toting cooking supplies. Most of the men had disappeared, and several young boys were playing games with miniature bows or kicking around a leather ball. She almost laughed when she realized that Daniel had been right—the reservation did remind her of home, in far too many ways. Females worked; males played.

"Oh, and another thing," Daniel said, bringing her attention back to him. "When you enter the tipi, be sure to go to your left before you pick a spot to sit down."

"Why?"

He shrugged. "It's just good manners. That, and when you do sit, don't do it cross-legged the way the men do. Women are supposed to sit on their heels or with their legs to one side. Got it?"

Josie had never considered that savages might have rules of conduct to follow, much less a proper sitting etiquette for their women. The idea amused as much as fascinated her.

"Got it," she said, suddenly eager to find out what was in store for her. "See you at the feast—be sure to save me the biggest piece of beaver tail, or whatever it is they're cooking up for us."

Daniel frowned and wagged a finger in Josie's face, then swatted her backside as she turned and ducked inside the tipi.

He chuckled at the little yelp she made, then waited for her to settle in with the others before turning on his heel and heading to where the tribal council had gathered. Damned if he didn't want to do a hell of a lot more than just swat that cute little bottom, he thought, eager for the night. He didn't doubt that there would be a few rough spots living with a consarned female like Josie over the next few months, but Daniel suddenly realized that he was actually looking forward to their life together. And hoping it would continue beyond the few months she had sentenced herself to be his wife.

When Daniel reached the tipi that belong to White Bull, the religious leader of the tribe, he stepped inside the open flap, and then closed it when he realized he was the last to arrive. All the others members of the council were already sitting on beds positioned along the circular wall. Working his way to the right, he eased down on the empty bed between He Dog, Long Belly's younger brother, and their father, High Backed Wolf.

"Your leg has healed?" asked White Bull in his native tongue as Daniel settled himself.

He nodded. "It's a little sore yet, but good enough to hunt."

The theologian, a man thick of jowl and neck who rarely smiled, passed his favorite ceremonial pipe, the bowl of which was an intricately crafted buffalo carved of steatite. Daniel inhaled several lungfuls of kinnekinick smoke, a mixture of agency tobacco, larb leaves, and willow bark, then passed the pipe onto He Dog. After everyone had their ceremonial puffs of smoke, White Bull got down to business.

"I see you have brought us flour, sugar, and a small amount of bacon, but no other meat."

Daniel sighed. "There was none to spare at the mission. The drought has hurt us all, even the whites."

"Bah, the whites, they are bad. They have deprived us of game, conquered our lands, and stolen everything of value to us." The elder warrior, whose hatred of whites ran deep, shook his fist, rattling beads, arrowheads, and the other decorations befitting his standing in the tribe. "They will not be happy until they exterminate the Cheyenne and all others like them."

There wasn't a hell of a lot Daniel could say to dispute White

Bull's accusations. The best he could manage was, "Not all whites feel that way. Many are trying to help our people."

"Humph. The way your officials helped last winter when four of our women died of hunger?"

"I told them about those losses, but by then it was too late to do anything about it." Christ, but he had a hard time defending a system that clearly was not working as well as it should have.

White Bull persisted. "Will you tell them now that we shall all die before spring if we do not receive more rations? The few antelope left in these hills were killed last year, and now the ranchers come and steal what is left of our horses. We also need food and blankets if we are to survive this winter. What will the white government do about these problems?"

"I don't know. I'll write Washington again and make sure they understand how difficult life has become here." This was the part of being an agent for his people that Daniel hated the most. Lying to them. "I'm sure when they understand the situation, they'll immediately send the rations we need so desperately. In the meantime, we'll just have to eat the cattle Long Belly and I are raising."

White Bull snorted, sounding very much like a live bison. "The whites expect us to become farmers and ranchers, but do not give us the proper tools or training. They tell us to water our crops, but allow other whites to live in the best areas where the water runs free and the meadows grow high. Now we are to eat the few cattle we own? If we do that, we will have none left to sell or breed. Already we are forced to eat our seed potatoes. Soon we will have nothing."

Daniel didn't know what to say to that. He certainly couldn't argue the point. Nothing he said would make a damn bit of difference to the old man, anyway. The best he could do was offer the one thing the Cheyenne had precious little of these days—hope.

"We do have one thing of value that not even the whites know about," he said with a smile. "I have in my possession one of the last living buffalos in these parts."

White Bull sat forward so quickly, he almost fell into the fire at the center of the meeting. "This is true?"

Daniel smiled, gratified to see a gleam in the old man's eyes again. "Long Belly's woman found the place where it had been sleeping, and my woman found the beast. She talked to this buffalo and convinced it to follow her to my cabin. It rests there now in my corral."

The men began to jabber among themselves, and White Bull closed his eyes in prayer. When he opened them again, he flashed a rare smile as he said, "This buffalo will be a good thing for our people and good for Nature too, as long as we can keep it for ourselves and away from the whites. But we still need rations. You will tell them again?"

Looking over the head of the religious leader, since he couldn't look him in the eye, Daniel repeated, "I'll be sure to explain exactly what we need when I write my letter."

He didn't bother to mention that rather than mailing it when he finished, he might as well put that letter in the fire for all the good it would do.

In the tipi with the women who were fussing and giggling over her, Josie finally began to relax and enjoy herself a little. After they'd discarded her buckskin shirt and trousers and washed her, they covered her in a splendid dress of the softest elkskin imaginable. The fringed bodice was decorated with white, black, red, and yellow beads, the four sacred Cheyenne colors that Daniel had sewed onto her boots. Those were exchanged for another pair of high winter moccasins with fringed flaps that were also made of elkskin and decorated with beads in a pattern that matched the dress. When she sat down again, careful to rock back on her heels the way Daniel had instructed, an older woman began to drag a porcupine-tail brush through Josie's hair, and another got busy painting red dots on her cheeks.

The third, a young girl who seemed utterly fascinated by Josie's pale skin and freckles, approached her with a parfleche full of trinkets and jewelry after the painter had finished. Motioning for Josie to hold out her hands, the girl began to push a series of brass rings and bracelets onto her fingers and wrists. When her hands and arms were sufficiently weighed down with glittering baubles, the girl crawled around back to where the old woman continued to brush her hair, and then helped her to plait it into two braids that hung down the front of the dress. They left her hair unadorned and completed the wedding costume by adding a three-tiered necklace made of porcupine quills and colorful beads.

After they'd finished with her, the women shooed Josie out of the tipi and into the waning afternoon sunlight. Chattering among themselves, they linked hands and ran up behind her, bumping against her bottom.

"What?" she said, trying to push them away. Again they bumped her bottom. "You want me to sit on your arms?"

She squatted slightly, pretending to sit, and they nodded enthusiastically. Shaking her head, Josie backed away from the tangle of women. "Appreciate the offer, but no thanks. I'd just as soon walk as be paraded in front of a bunch of heathens like some kind of prize."

Despite her refusal, the armchair continued to follow her, some of the human links babbling excitedly, others giving orders. Then suddenly the older woman broke away from the human chair and came at Josie, muttering sharp, harsh words that transcended the language barrier.

"And the same to you, you old bitch," she snapped back without thinking.

The old woman responded by slapping her across the face.

Josie's first instinct was to punch the weathered squaw in return, but common sense prevailed. Any form of retaliation would undoubtedly be taken as an invitation for the others to pounce on her. With four against one, it wouldn't take them long to pummel her into the ground. Or worse. There was only one thing to do—find Daniel.

Turning on her heel, Josie hurried toward the lodge he'd

pointed out. As she bent over to open the flap, the old woman grabbed her from behind and pulled her away from the tipi.

This time instinct did take over.

"Dammit all, take your hands off of me and leave me the hell alone."

As the squaw barked hateful words in her ear, Josie whirled around, locked heels with her, and then gave a mighty shove, tripping the woman into falling backward. While her victim sat stunned on the ground, Josie returned to the tipi, tore back the flap, and stepped inside the large lodge.

A small fire burned at the center of the room, and the air was bitter with the flavor of tobacco. The smoke made it difficult to see, but she recognized the shadowy figures of no less than ten Cheyenne warriors sitting cross-legged in a circle. She couldn't make out any of their features, but all eyes were on her as she stood there, knees knocking. Remembering Daniel's advice, she moved to the left.

"Ah—afternoon, gentlemen," she said, wondering if she hadn't made a mistake in coming here. "Don't bother to get up on my account. I was just wondering if I might have a word with my husband. Is he here?"

In the midst of a sudden profusion of male chatter she couldn't understand, Josie heard Daniel's voice coming from somewhere in the shadows. "Yes, unfortunately, your husband is here. What the hell do you think you're doing?"

Following the sound of his voice, Josie picked him out of the darkness. "I'm having a little trouble with these fool women outside. You said you'd be here if I needed you. What did I do to get these fellahs so riled up? I went left like you said."

"I didn't say you could come inside this particular tipi, and you are never to just waltz into any lodge unannounced if the flap is closed. Never."

As her eyes grew used to the darkness, Josie realized that the malevolent stares she'd been expecting had finally descended upon her. "Sorry. I didn't know."

"You sure as hell know now." Daniel sighed heavily, then said something in Cheyenne to big-bellied Indian seated directly across from him. After he got to his feet and picked his way through the men to where Josie stood, he took her by the arm and escorted her out of the tipi.

The minute they were outside, the group of women converged on Daniel, each of them firing a steady stream of complaints as they pointed accusing fingers at Josie. The old woman got in the most licks, and finally finished her tirade with arms folded tightly across her breasts.

"What did she say about me?" Josie asked. "All I did was refuse to be carried around by them. The old woman even hit me, trying to make me sit on their arms."

"You really got them mad," Daniel said, glancing from the women to Josie. "They were just trying to carry the bride to the feast, as is the custom."

"If that's a custom, then you should have told me about it."

"Yes, I should have," he conceded, furrowing his brow anyway. "Did you knock the old lady to the ground?"

She hesitated as long as she could. "Sorta."

He nodded. "She's pretty pissed about that."

"She had it coming. She's the one who slapped my face."

"Doesn't matter," Daniel said, still stern. "You'll have to make amends somehow. They like your pretty red hair—a *lot*."

"You—you mean they want to s-scalp me?"

"I don't think so, but then again, I'm afraid you picked a mighty ornery female to piss off. Maybe if you let me cut a length of your hair as a present for her, she'll calm down a little."

Josie glanced at the old woman. Her arms were still crossed over her chest, her nose was tilted up, and her mouth was set in a firm, hard line. There was no way that woman was going to get so much as a strand of her hair. "Over my dead body."

"I'm sure that She Bear would consider that amends enough." Daniel turned to the old woman and began to speak in that funny, choppy way.

"Wait a minute," Josie said. "I didn't mean that. Go ahead, cut off whatever you think she wants."

"Now you're learning. Excellent decision, sweetheart."

"Just get on with it," she snapped in a whisper. "Before that bitch takes it in her head to come get the hair herself."

Daniel took a knife from the scabbard he wore at his hip and quickly shorted each of her braids by a couple of inches. He then dropped the severed sections into her palm, removed the thongs from each, and used the bits of leather to tie the now-reduced plaits in place.

"I suggest," he said, sheathing his knife, "that you make the offering yourself. Just be careful about the name-calling. I think she has a very good idea what a bitch is. I've used that term on her a time or two myself."

Josie had taken a step toward the woman, but paused to look back at Daniel. "Why would you have used that name on her?"

"Because she's my mother-in-law," he explained. "And believe me, they don't call her She Bear for nothing."

Josie turned back toward the old woman with new respect, to find that She Bear was glaring at her though narrow eyes as black and hard as coal. Keeping her distance, she held out the severed tails of her braids. "These are a gift. I'm sorry if I offended you."

The old woman lunged toward her, snatched the hair out of her hand, then retreated with her prize. As she flaunted her new possession to the other women, Josie said to Daniel, "Don't you think you might have mentioned She Bear's relationship to you before you left me at her mercy?"

He shrugged. "I didn't think she'd be so jealous of you or your hair."

Behind him the women began to grumble, old She Bear the bitch in particular. Daniel glanced at them, said something in rapid-fire Cheyenne, then turned back to Josie.

"You'd better wipe that scowl off your face," he warned. "My Cheyenne family and friends will forgive you for the mistakes you've made here today, but I don't think they're that all-fired fond of you just yet."

Josie didn't have to be told twice. She immediately lowered her head and assumed a more humble demeanor. She even managed to stay that way for the rest of the afternoon and all through supper, a surprisingly tasty, if meager meal that included a portion of fish, a small chunk of beef, a turnip, and some unleavened bread made of cornmeal that was smeared with a paste of wild berries. When the wedding feast was over, she and Daniel were escorted to a tipi on the fringes of camp, and then left to themselves.

After they'd ducked inside the dwelling, Josie immediately noticed that someone had been there before them to build and light a fire in a ring at the center of the room. Instead of the dirt floor she expected, the ground was covered with a raised mat carpeted with buffalo hide. A pair of grass-covered sod benches sat to each side of the entrance, accommodations for visitors, she assumed. A single bed made of buffalo fur and blankets occupied the back wall of the tipi. All in all, the dwelling was, like the other tipis, surprisingly civilized.

"What do you think?" asked Daniel, guessing the direction of her thoughts.

"It's . . . nice. Very nice."

"It belongs to Long Belly, who usually lives here when he's not out chasing buffalo or taking care of me." He began to undress as he spoke, removing his jacket and shirt, then folding them carefully and setting them on one of the sod benches. "One day he'll share this home with a wife, I suppose, if he ever makes up his mind to marry."

He tugged off his boots, dropped them near the door flap, and crossed over to where Josie stood. Firelight flickered over his naked chest, defining the hard ridges of muscle beneath the otherwise smooth, slick skin of his hard belly and shoulders. He was magnificent and, it suddenly occurred to Josie, he was also hers to do with as she pleased—and if she didn't know another thing, she had learned much about pleasing this man. She swallowed hard and began to fiddle with her brass rings.

Daniel took her hands into his. "Let me help you with those."

Then, every touch a tender caress, he slowly slipped the bracelets from her wrists, never taking his eyes from hers, and brought her hands to his lips when he finished. Instead of simply removing her rings, Daniel took each of her fingers into his

mouth and worked the brass baubles loose with his tongue as
he sucked them off, one at a time. Before he was half finished,
Josie's knees had turned to jelly and an earthquake had begun
somewhere deep inside her belly.

"Daniel," she said, breathless with need. "Let's go to bed."

"Soon." Smiling crookedly, he pulled the thongs from her
braids, then unplaited and smoothed her hair with his fingers.
"I hated having to cut your hair today, but I see that it's still
as beautiful as ever. So are you."

Josie raised her chin, looked him in the eye, and slowly ran
her tongue over her upper lip. "Now?"

Daniel leaned into her, enveloping her with his heat and his
scent, robbing her of the ability to think. Lowering his head,
he nuzzled the side of her neck and drew in great breathfuls
of her skin, as if he couldn't get enough of her scent. When
he brought his lips back to her mouth, kissing her with a passion
that rocked her soul, Josie felt as if every bone in her body
had melted away.

All through their previous experiments in pleasure, she'd
never let Daniel see her naked body. The thought alone made
her feel too vulnerable and submissive, as if stripping herself
were tantamount to handing him the reins of her life. Still, as
Daniel pulled away from her, then began to lift her dress over
her head, Josie forced herself to allow him this much, and
didn't even object when he opened her chemise, exposing her
breasts to his gaze and his hands.

"You really are a beauty, Josie," he said, admiration shining
in his eyes. "Absolutely splendid."

She fell into his arms, rubbing her naked breasts against his
smooth, warm chest, and Daniel responded by slipping one of
his hands between their bodies.

His palm cupping her breast, thumb circling and teasing the
nipple, he whispered, "God you feel good, so soft, so . . ."

He finished the sentence with his head buried between her
breasts, but Josie couldn't make out the words. By then Daniel's
mouth had gone to the hard little nub his fingers had made of
her nipple, and his tongue began to circle it in place of his

thumb. A bolt of sheer, unbridled desire shot through her, arching Josie's spine and sending spasms of pure pleasure throughout her lower belly. Caught up in the sensations, alternately wishing that Daniel would end this torment and hoping that he never would, it occurred to her that he might not have been kidding about his end of the bargain. Was it possible that he really did expect more than the usual from her this night?

Daniel wanted her as much as ever, that much was certain. And it wasn't just the heat of his rigid sex pushed against her belly that told her he was highly aroused, more so than he'd ever been before. She felt it in his voice, in the electricity of the air around him, and in the hot puffs of his breath against her skin. Surely he hadn't deluded himself into believing that she planned to submit completely to his desires.

Pushing away from him with the last of her strength, Josie drew her arms to her breasts and said, "Just what do you expect from me tonight?"

Reeling from the want of her, at first Daniel didn't understand what she was trying to say. Desire for this woman, hotter than anything he'd ever known, had him fully in its grip. He felt drugged, hot blood pooling heavily in his groin. The tantalizing glimpses she'd allowed of her breasts did nothing to cool his ardor.

"I want to see all of you naked," he murmured, reaching for the scrap of cotton. "And then I want to make love to you."

Josie backed even further away. "No, Daniel. I won't get undressed in front of you and I can't allow you to do—you know, the hurdy-gurdy."

He hadn't thought it possible, but she finally said something that cooled him down a little. "The hurdy-gurdy? What the hell is that?"

"You know." She made an obscene gesture with her fingers. "Mating. That wasn't part of our bargain."

Daniel nodded sagely. "Then I'd be happy to meet you halfway and amend our bargain a little. You can keep your clothes on until we're in bed—then I intend to hurdy-gurdy with you until dawn.''

Josie shook her head. "Oh, no, you won't."

"Sweetheart, be reasonable." Daniel went to her and took her face between his hands. "What are you so worried about? I'm going to make love to you, not force you into anything or hurt you. I know how much pleasure you've gotten out of our few nights together, and believe me, that's just the beginning. Trust me on this, will you? Just trust me."

She still had that look in her dark eyes, defiance mingled with a certain fear, a terror that went somewhere he couldn't follow. Then she cleared the road for him.

"It's not that I don't trust you or that I'm not mighty curious about how the hurdy-gurdy works and all, but I can't take the chance that you might put a baby in me." Panic had replaced the lust he'd seen glowing in her eyes. "I swear I'll kill myself before I let that happen."

Daniel hadn't planned on becoming a father again after Tangle Hair died, and children hadn't exactly been on his mind here tonight—not that he hadn't thought to bring a little preventative along to make sure a baby wouldn't come of their first night together. Josie's vow did give him pause, though, and made him think of the children the two of them might have created together—tough, clever, stubborn little shits who wouldn't exactly be prime candidates for President of the United States, but the kind who would most definitely survive.

It was with an odd sense of loss that he said, "If getting pregnant is all that's worrying you, I can ease your mind some. There are a couple of ways we can—er, do the hurdy-gurdy without risking a baby."

The fear in Josie's eyes ebbed. In fact they fairly gleamed as she asked, "Guaranteed positive, no babies?"

Daniel shrugged, choosing his words carefully. "I'm afraid that abstinence is the only guaranteed positive way I know of to make sure you stay barren, but we can get close."

Although wary yet, her eyes lit up. "How close?"

Daniel grinned as he reached into his pocket, withdrew the

condom he'd waved under her nose two nights before, and held it up. "These things aren't just good for the prevention of disease. If I use this, I think we're about ninety-eight, maybe ninety-nine percent sure that you won't catch."

Josie's gaze went immediately to his trousers and the powerful erection Daniel was beginning to think he'd never lose. She licked her lips, took a deep breath, and asked, "It goes . . . there?"

Daniel nodded, feeling that part of his body turn to stone.

"I don't see how it will ever fit." She blushed and averted her gaze as something else occurred to her. " 'Course, I don't see how you and I will ever fit together either."

"Come to bed," Daniel murmured, taking her by the hand. "I'll be glad to show you on both counts. In fact, I'll even let you help."

Chapter Seventeen

"Josie—ouch! Jesus, let me do that before you snatch me bald."

Lying beside him on the bed, she looked up from her task. "I wasn't aware that I'd touched your head."

"You didn't, but it feels like you're pulling out every hair in my body from that one spot. Besides," he said, grabbing her wrists before she could do any more damage, "if you keep hurting me with that thing, there won't be any point in wearing it. Now come here."

Although she was still slightly concerned about the one or two percent gamble she'd be taking, Josie crawled into Daniel's arms and allowed him to make the final adjustments to the rubber sheath. After that, all she could think about was her new husband and the way he made her feel.

In a way he'd done many times before, Daniel lavished Josie with kisses from her forehead to her belly while his hands and fingers worked the delicious tortures she'd come to crave. Unlike before, he left her burning for fulfillment just before she reached that highest crest.

"Daniel," she complained in a breathless whisper. "Don't stop now. Please don't stop."

"Hang on, sweetheart," he murmured, positioning himself between her parted legs. "This is where things start to get a little different."

He took his time, although she sensed it wasn't easy for him, and slowly pushed his way inside her. Josie felt a slight resistance at first, a moment's pain, and then suddenly he'd filled her, fully and completely.

"How are you doing, sweetheart?" Daniel asked, his breathing labored. "Am I hurting you?"

Josie adjusted her hips, making herself more comfortable. "No. Just go on. Show me what's next."

With the exception of a grin tugging at the corner of his mouth, Daniel didn't move a muscle. "You're sure this isn't a bit more than you bargained for?"

"I'm going to be a bit more than you bargained for if you don't get busy, and soon."

To illustrate her threat, Josie clenched her feminine muscles around the part Daniel had buried inside her, then ground her hips, writhing shamelessly beneath him. She heard his tortured gasp, and then suddenly the grin was gone. He began to pump against her, slowly at first, then increased his strokes until he was setting off lightning strikes each time their hips rubbed together. Josie began to tremble and shiver, her legs twitching from the vibrations that were erupting in her belly, and just when she thought she might collapse from the tremendous pressure building inside her, she suddenly tumbled over the edge, dissolving in a liquid fire that was unlike anything he'd unleashed in her before.

Josie had barely recovered from the powerful force of her climax before Daniel convulsed against her, crying out her name, and then collapsed on the blanket beside her. As he lay there panting and murmuring mindless words against the damp skin of her shoulder, Josie lost herself in the luxurious lap of her own lingering pleasure, savoring each delicious spark as the tremors slowly burned themselves out.

"I feel like a thief," Daniel whispered when his breathing finally slowed. "I don't care how good a cook and housekeeper you are, I know I got the best end of this bargain."

Josie chuckled from deep in her throat. "You cheated me pretty good, all right."

"How good?" he asked, brushing the hair from her brow. "I was afraid the first time wouldn't be much fun for you."

"Oh, Daniel, quite the opposite." To think she'd once vowed never to let a man gain entrance to her body. She laughed as she said, "You were wonderful."

"So were you." Daniel kissed her swollen mouth. "Stay right where you are. I've, ah—got to take care of something."

Turning away from her, he removed the condom and pulled back the covers in order to place it somewhere out of sight. Through the dim flicker of firelight, he noticed that the rubber sheath had cracked open.

"Shit," he muttered under his breath, unable to understand how it could have disintegrated so rapidly. The instructions said to wash the condom after intercourse and to reuse it until it cracked or tore. They said nothing about the thing cracking and tearing *before* it had ever been used. He hoped for Josie's sake that the old wives tale claiming that a woman couldn't become pregnant from her first encounter was true.

She tapped his shoulder. "What's wrong?"

"Nothing," Daniel lied, sparing her the worry. "I just pulled out a few more hairs getting this damned thing off, is all." He tossed the useless rubber into a darkened corner, then rolled over and took her back into his arms.

"Where were we?" he asked. "Oh, I know—you were telling me what a wonderful Indian agent I must be since I'm so good at bargaining."

Josie ran her hand across his stomach, stirring the butterflies, then slid it lower. "Mmmm, yes, you were quite good. So good, in fact, I think I ought to cheat you a little myself. How would you like that?"

Daniel laughed, wondering if he'd have the stamina to match

his suddenly arduous bride. "Maybe later, sweetheart, but right now I'm kinda tired."

"Really?" She then proceeded to run the tip of her finger up and down and all around the surprising erection she'd managed to extort from him. Daniel sucked in a breath. "Take it easy on me, would you?"

"You don't like this?" she asked.

"Well, y-yes," he said with difficulty. "But we can't use the rubber again."

"That's all right. I have other ways of cheating you out of what's yours. I promise you won't have to do a thing except hold up your end of the bargain."

The next morning just before dawn, Josie was still immersed in the pleasures of the night, still dreaming of Daniel's touch and all the wonders of their intimate joining, when he shook her out of that sleepy bliss with a firm hand to the shoulder.

"Josie," he said, waking her completely. "Morning, sweetheart. Get up and quickly slip into your dress. There's something I want you to see outside."

Rubbing the sleep from her eyes, she did as he asked without question, and in minutes joined him a few feet from the tipi.

"Look up in the sky," he said as she came up beside him. "See that star, how it lights the morning sky and shines more brightly than the other stars?"

She looked up and immediately saw what he was talking about. The sky was the shade of a ripe blueberry, and a quarter moon still hung above the horizon. The star Daniel pointed out glowed as if kissed by the sun and seemed in command of both heaven and earth.

"Oh, my Lord," she whispered. "It's beautiful. I've never a star like that before."

"The Cheyenne call it *wohehiv,* and often pray when it appears in the sky." He slipped an arm across her shoulders and squeezed. "When I saw it this morning, I figured there was a chance it came out just for us and our marriage. I didn't think you'd want to miss out on it.''

Daniel kept his gaze on the sky, leaving Josie to wonder how she ought to take his comments. He surely couldn't be hinting that he thought their marriage would last beyond the spring, the date they had both agreed to go their separate ways— or could he? Last night had been wonderful, but it was only a small part of their bargain—in fact, the only part on which they seemed in total agreement.

Concerned that Daniel might be making more of their union that he should have, Josie slipped out from beneath his embrace. ''Thanks for waking me. It's been lovely, but I suppose I ought to go get packed up for the journey home.''

He turned to her with a smile. ''Home, Josie?''

The word home meant nothing to her anymore. She no longer had a home. ''I meant to say the cabin.''

''You can call it home, if you like.'' He took her shoulders between his hands and kissed her forehead. ''It's going to be exactly that for at least the next few months.''

Increasingly uncomfortable with the conversation, with Daniel's hands on her, and with just about everything she could think of, Josie said, ''I'd better get myself cleaned up now. How soon before you'll be ready to go?''

He studied her a moment, wondering what in hell he'd said or done to make her turn so cold so quickly. When he'd awakened and glimpsed Josie lying beside him this morning, Daniel's heart had actually skipped a beat. Her freckled cheeks were rosy, her swollen lips even rosier, and a little smile played at the corners of her mouth. She'd never looked more beautiful, or seemed more real. And she was his. It was then it struck him that he really did want this marriage to work. In fact, he was beginning to hope that it would last forever.

Maybe Josie had sensed that, and for some reason it scared her. Maybe he was expecting too much from her too soon. Tired and a little too worn down to puzzle out anything remotely difficult, much less something as complicated as a woman,

Daniel decided to give her a chance to wake up before he caught her with his next surprise.

"Go ahead and get ready to go," he said. "I ought to be back with the horses in about an hour."

"I'll be ready."

Waiting until she'd ducked into the tipi, Daniel wandered through camp and finally found his sons playing down by the creek. Each of them was wet, probably because of the early morning bath their grandmother had given them rather than the fact they were throwing sticks into the icy water.

"Gather your things," he said to them in Cheyenne. "I'm taking you boys back to the ranch to live with me."

Bang, the youngest by several minutes, beat his brother to his father's outstretched arms.

"Papa! For how long?" he said, his husky voice high-pitched and excited. His twin asked the exact same thing at the exact same time.

"I'm hoping this will work out permanently. Would you two like that?"

"Oh, yes, Papa, yes!" they cried in unison, hugging Daniel until he thought they'd break his neck.

"All right then, let's get busy. We have to go to your grandma's tipi and gather up your things."

Two Moons tugged on his trouser leg, bringing up the next subject before Daniel could. "Is that white woman coming home with us?"

"Yes, she is," he answered in English. "She is my wife now, and I want you to start practicing your English again so you can speak it whenever she is around." He looked from Bang to Two Moons, making sure they still understood the language even though they rarely used it. "Do you both know what I just said?"

"That we must learn to speak the white man's language again," said Two Moons in deliberate, calculated Cheyenne. "But we don't want her to live with us. She is ugly."

"Ugly?" Daniel figured the boys might have some objections to Josie, especially to some of her decidedly un-Cheyenne ways, but he assumed they'd find her as attractive as he did. "How can you say that? She's a very pretty lady."

Again Bang tugged on Daniel's pant leg. Speaking Cheyenne as his brother did, he explained, "She has sickness spots on her face and she was ugly when she looked upon us and did this."

He squeezed up his mouth until it resembled the ass end of a hog, then made a stern expression, drawing a perfectly clear picture for his father.

Daniel laughed. "Well, the spots on her face are called freckles, something white folks are born with, not from sickness. As for her expression, I reckon she'll pretty up some once the three of you get to know each other. Josie is probably just worried that the two of you won't like her. I'm counting on you boys to show her she's wrong by treating her as right as you know how."

Bang, easily the most agreeable of the two, nodded solemnly. "I will make quiet with her and never cry."

Two Moons let his round features fall into a hard pout. "I will not call this ugly woman Ma."

Daniel nodded, easily able to understand this problem. "We'll just have to think of an appropriate name for you to call her. How about Ma Josephine? That's a respectful version of her name."

The twins tested this suggestion, in English at Daniel's request, but both of them tripped over the long, difficult name, time and time again. Finally in frustration, he decided to let them use the shorter version they came up with. Then came the difficult chore of packing their belongings on a travois and watching while their brokenhearted grandmother cried over them as she bade them farewell. No matter that she'd be seeing them as frequently as he could arrange it, Daniel knew he'd be hearing She Bear's sobs until they were deep into the forest.

By the time he had the boys mounted on the back of the horse he'd gotten them for their second birthday—an old sorrel they called Broomtail because that's all there was left of his tail—Daniel figured his troubles were all behind him. Of course,

that was before he rode up to Long Belly's tipi and found Josie
waiting for him outside.

"I'm ready," she announced, climbing to her feet with a
small bundle in her arms. Squinting into the sunlight, she looked
beyond Daniel to the horse carrying the twins. "Why are they
following you?"

"Those are my boys, remember? They're coming home with
us."

Josie's rosy cheeks blanched. *"What?* I thought they lived
here on the reservation with that mean old bitch."

He winced, wondering if the boys remembered that word
and what it meant. "They stayed with She Bear after their
mother died because I couldn't raise them alone and run the
agency at the same time," he explained. "Now that I have a
wife, I'm expected to take them home with me. I also want to,
very much."

Daniel didn't know what he expected from Josie, but it was
not the disgusted look in her eyes or the heavy sigh as she
said, "This was not a part of the bargain. I signed on as your
wife and housekeeper, not as anyone's mother. I hope you'll
understand that when I leave the care and feeding of them up
to you."

He didn't understand and he wouldn't just let it go at that,
but now wasn't the time for a discussion on the matter, especially with the twins listening in.

Tempering his voice until it matched the chill in Josie's,
Daniel said, "I'm sure we can work all that out when we get
back home."

She returned a curt nod, then approached The Black and
tried to give Daniel the wedding dress she'd worn yesterday.
"I don't know who this belongs to, but I figure you ought to
make sure it gets back to its rightful owner."

"It's yours," he said irritably, still smarting over her attitude
toward his sons.

"Mine? Why?"

"My mother-in-law wants you to have it. It belonged to
Tangle Hair."

"Was she your wife?"

Daniel was not going to allow her to draw him into a discussion of Tangle Hair in front of her sons. "Yes, but the dress was something she wore at ceremonies, not the one she had on at our wedding before we moved to the reservation. Give it to me if you don't want it." He reached out to snatch the garment from her hand, but Josie withdrew, clutching the elk-skin tightly against her breast.

"I'd like to keep it, if you don't mind. And I'd also like to go thank your mother-in-law for giving it to me. Do we have time?"

This wasn't simply unexpected, but such a surprise that Daniel wasn't at all sure how to respond. "Well, yes, if you're sure that's what you want to do."

"It is." Nothing but sincerity shone in her dark eyes. "Where will I find her?"

Daniel stuck his thumb over his shoulder. "In the tipi where they dressed you for our feast. I'll walk you there if you like."

"No, thanks. I'm sure I can find it myself. I'll be right back."

Suddenly it was very important to Josie not only to do this, but to do it on her own. Dress in hand, she set off for the heart of the camp, winding her way through tipis and squaws performing their morning cooking chores. Nowhere did she see any warriors, who were presumably still snuggled in their beds. Men lounging around while women did all the chores—as Daniel had said, not so unlike the family she had left behind. Of course, thinking of the Baums made her think of the twins and the nasty surprise of learning that she would be living under the same roof with them.

Mulling this over, wondering how she would ever survive until spring, Josie came across the tipi in which she'd been dressed for her wedding feast. She paused before the closed flap. Thanking She Bear for her generosity had seemed like a really good idea at the time, but now she wasn't so sure of the plan. What if the old biddy was still in a cranky mood, and she came flying out of that tipi, going after her tooth and nail?

Josie glanced down at the dress, giving a fleeting thought to just dropping it and running away, but couldn't make herself leave without at least trying to express her gratitude. After all, the poor woman had not only lost her daughter, but thought she was losing her grandchildren to a replacement who hailed from another world. A successor, she had no way of knowing, who didn't want to have a thing to do with raising her daughter's precious little pisspots.

Swallowing hard, Josie called to the woman, knowing better now than to disturb the closed flap. "She Bear? I've come to say good-bye. Are you there?"

After a few groans and a little rustling, the flap parted and out came the old woman. Her eyes were bloodshot and swollen, and her back was stooped in defeat. When she looked at Josie, her expression sagged even more than her shoulders, but there was no hatred there. Just a weathered face that looked as if it had been carved from an ancient pine.

Her heart going out to She Bear, Josie said, "Good morning."

She Bear waved her arms in reply and uttered something sharp in Cheyenne. Josie had an idea it wasn't, "How'd you do?"

Forcing a big smile, she held up the dress, then clutched the garment to her breast. "Thank you so much for sharing your daughter with me this way. I'll treasure this always."

She Bear's expression immediately lost some of its deep grooves, and her eyes took on a fresh shine. She understood, if not the words, the intent.

Josie impulsively slipped her free arm around the woman's shoulders and gave her a hug. She Bear responded by throwing her arms around Josie in a fierce embrace, then held onto her while she chanted a few Cheyenne words, soft pleas, probably in regard to her grandsons.

When She Bear released her, she quickly broke away and ducked back inside her tipi. Josie figured the abrupt departure was meant to hide the flood of tears on the old woman's cheeks and the sudden sorrow in her eyes. A good thing, too, considering that Josie's vision was also blurred with her own tangled emotions. Turning away from the tipi, she ran blindly through the camp to where her husband and his sons awaited her return.

Daniel was sullen all during the ride back to the cabin. No matter how hard he tried to rationalize Josie's surly attitude toward tending his children, he simply couldn't come up with an excuse good enough to have any effect on his sour mood. Hell, she'd mentioned having a lot of brothers, which meant she undoubtedly understood little boys and their ways. Why did the thought of having his two sons around seem to disturb her so?

No matter how hard he worked on it, Daniel simply couldn't figure it out. Understanding why Josie didn't want her own babies with him was a hell of a lot easier to grasp. Either she was dead set on ending their marriage come spring and didn't want to get stuck raising a child alone, or she couldn't abide the idea of giving birth to a baby with Cheyenne blood in its veins. Neither of these excuses set well with him, especially the latter, but at least he could understand her feeling that way. What he couldn't fathom, no matter how hard he tried, was her obvious aversion to mothering Bang and Two Moons a little. How hard could it be?

Daniel was still in that grumpy frame of mind when he rode into his yard and saw that Long Belly was pounding nails into a new brace he'd attached to the barn door. When his Cheyenne brother heard the approaching horses, he dropped the hammer and ran to greet them.

"You have returned, my brother," he said as The Black came to a halt just inches from his feet.

"I can't keep anything from you, can I?" Daniel replied sarcastically.

Grinning up at Daniel, Long Belly had the gall to say, "At least I think my brother has returned. You look like him and smell like him, and yet I am told that my brother has made a bride of a very bad gift. Can this be true of the wise man I once called brother?"

"Get out of my way, you obnoxious fool, or I'll let The Black run you down."

Daniel half meant the threat, but he did climb down off the stallion and drop his reins to the ground. By then the twins had hopped off Broomtail and had come running at their uncle, each of them claiming one of his legs as a way of gaining his attention.

After greeting the boys in Cheyenne, he rubbed their little heads as he said to Daniel in English, "I thought we agreed this woman was a bad gift. What craziness crawled into your brain and made you take her as your wife?"

From the corner of his eye, Daniel saw that Josie had dismounted and gathered her belongings, and was headed their way. "I'd change the subject if I were you, brother," he said under his breath. "You know how riled up that woman gets when your tongue gets to flapping about her."

Long Belly glanced over his shoulder as Josie strolled by. "Welcome home, Missus Daniel. I congratulate you on your fine marriage."

She frowned. "Thanks, I guess. Is Sissy in the cabin?"

He nodded. "Buffalo Hair is busy with her chores, and very good at them, too. As a woman should be."

Josie rolled her eyes. "For God's sake, you heathen. Is that all you ever think about, women's chores?"

She didn't stick around to hear his answer, but marched straight to the cabin instead.

Long Belly smiled at Daniel. "I see Broken Dishes has not changed now that she is a married woman. Again I wonder—what craziness made you do this?"

"I married her, and that's all there is to it." Daniel was not about to admit to this man, especially in front of his children, that he'd been trapped into marrying Josie or that he'd stepped willingly into the snare.

"But Broken Dishes is a bad choice as a wife," Long Belly persisted. "She can do nothing required of her, and have you forgotten? She is diseased."

Glancing at his sons, Daniel said, "I was wrong about that—

she's as healthy as I am. She can also cook and tend to my sons. They're reason enough for me to marry, aren't they?''

Long Belly nodded thoughtfully. ''In this, you are correct. Perhaps Broken Dishes will be a good mother for these two.''

In Cheyenne, Two Moons said, ''Papa's wife is ugly and we do not want her to be our mother. We do not like her.''

Bang tugged on his uncle's leggings. ''I do not like her either.''

Long Belly glanced up from the boys to their father. ''I hope if she can do nothing else right, my gift can learn to be the mother your sons deserve.''

Daniel heaved a weary sigh. ''Me, too, brother. Me, too. In fact, I'm counting on it.''

Inside the cabin, the woman in question was sitting at the table across from Sissy, but she was looking out the window, staring at the identical four-year-old boys raising hell with their uncle.

Her gaze suddenly shot to Sissy. ''Did you know that Daniel had those twins?''

''Nope,'' she claimed, glancing out the window. ''I didn't even know he'd been married before. Them boys are kinda cute, though, ain't they?''

''*Cute?*''

Josie took another look at them, conceding that she'd seen uglier children in her day, but that was as far as she'd go. ''They're all right, I guess, if you just have to look at a kid, but I wish to hell that they'd stayed on the reservation with their grandma.''

''You don't want Daniel's boys?'' Sissy sounded shocked.

It wasn't that Josie didn't understand such a reaction to her ''unwomanly'' attitude toward children, and she recognized full well Daniel's need to keep his sons with him, but something ugly rolled over inside her at the thought of caring for those two pisspots, and nothing she could think of would make it go away. She also knew that explaining those feelings to anyone, even a prostitute, would be next to impossible.

''It's not Daniel's boys so much as it is me.'' Josie paused, making sure that she chose her words with care. "I got stuck raising up twelve or so of my brothers from the time I was old enough to reach the stove. My entire life so far has been tending snot-nosed boys, and I'm sick to death of it. Maybe if they were girls I'd feel differently, but I doubt it. Does that make any sense to you?"

"A little, I guess." Sissy chuckled, her gaze lingering on the twins as they played in the yard. "You might think you hate kids now, but I bet you won't when your own little fellahs come along."

Josie bit her tongue, forcing herself to slow down and think her answer through. "Maybe," she said, lying. "But I know I'm not ready to be a mother yet. Think you can give me some hints on how to keep that from happening too soon?"

Sissy brightened. "Now that's something I know about. Trouble is, out here with no store, you ain't got the luxury of deciding if you want a rubber ring, a sponge, or a syringe for douching. Ain't but one thing you can do to keep from getting knocked up, and that's pulling out."

"What on earth is that?"

Sissy eyed her suspiciously. "You been with Daniel as a full wife yet?"

A sudden heat warmed Josie's cheeks. She had to look away as she said "Yes, but just the one time last night."

"Well? What'd you do then?"

"I didn't do anything. Daniel had . . ." She looked around, making sure they were still alone, then whispered the foul word. "A rubber. He said it was only good for the one time, so we need to think of something else."

Sissy laughed and sat back in her chair. "Overcoats is good for that, I guess, and they're supposed to last a lot more than one time, but even them newfangled rubber ones can get old or leak a little. Sometimes they just plain fall off."

Josie's face was growing hotter by the minute. "Daniel didn't have but the one . . . overcoat. What else can we do?"

"Pulling out, like I said."

"How do you do that?"

Again Sissy eyed her, this time with amusement. "I'll tell it as proper as I can, princess, so's I don't flusterize you no more than I have to. Let's say pulling out is like you inviting Daniel in for supper, but he don't stick around for the main course. See what I mean?"

Josie thought about that for a minute. By the time she'd figured it out, her entire face felt as if it were on fire. "Oh, my—yes. I think I understand perfectly. How often does that work?"

Shrugging, Sissy admitted, "Hard to say. Trouble comes, even if he don't, when a fellah don't know how hungry he is and he just has to have a little nibble on the way out the door."

She paused, making sure that Josie was still following along. She was, even though her face had to have been purple by then.

"Anyway," Sissy went on to say, "that little bit there can make you catch a baby, and it ain't something men are too happy about either. Sometimes when they leave before the main course, it fouls everything up so bad, a fellah can't even get his gun off afterwards."

Josie buried her face in her hands, too embarrassed to look Sissy in the eye any longer. Even if there were more options, she couldn't bring herself to ask about them. "Thanks, Sissy. You've been very . . . helpful." Then, forgetting herself, she asked, "What about you? Is pulling out what you and Long Belly are doing to keep you from getting in a family way?"

The amusement left Sissy's eyes, replaced by a deep sadness. "No, princess. I don't got to do nothing cause I'm barren."

"You can never have children?"

She shook her bushy head. "I almost did once, though. I got knocked up my first time out as one of Lola's gals. I was almost thirteen at the time and scared to tell anyone about it, so it wasn't until my belly tattled on me that Lola knew. She got rid of it that same day."

"Got rid of it?" Josie couldn't imagine what she meant. "How did she do that?"

Sissy took a long time answering, and when she did, her

gaze never left the table. "She poked a silver probe into my privates and then shot a lot of water up inside me. I don't know what all she done after that. I passed out from the pain."

Josie shuddered. "Lord almighty, I didn't know people did such things. Is that why you can't have babies?"

Nodding, Sissy explained. "Lola messed me up pretty good—so good, I almost bled to death. I ain't caught a child since."

Josie definitely did want to become a mother, but not at such a high price. Glancing out into the yard, she drew a deep breath and let it out slowly, giving herself a chance to think about how to respond to Sissy's sad story. She noticed that the men and the children had disappeared into the barn with the mounts. The wind had come up and the trees were swaying, yet oddly enough, everything seemed very still.

All she could think to say was, "Oh, Sissy. I'm so sorry."

This seemed to drag the poor woman out of the past and back to the present. Sissy looked up at Josie, her eyes clear again, and said, "Don't be sorry. I'm told my baby was a girl. At least this way I don't got to see her grow up a whore like her ma, and my ma before me."

Why was it that every time Sissy had something profound to say, Josie didn't have the first idea how to respond? She didn't even come close to finding the right words on this one before Sissy spoke up again.

"I guess it's time," she said in a strangely hollow voice. "Looks like I got to be going back to Lola's now."

Josie glanced into the yard and saw that Long Belly was standing at the hitching rail in front of the cabin, tying his paint alongside the mule. Both animals were saddled.

She turned to Sissy, grabbed her hands, and said, "But I don't want you to go. We're really and truly friends now, and I'll miss you terribly if you go."

Smiling, at least as close to a smile as she ever got, Sissy gently eased her way out of Josie's grip. "Maybe I'll come back and see you some time next summer, if you're still here. Right now, I got to go."

"I don't see why. All you've got to go to is a whorehouse. You don't really want to go back there, do you?"

"Wouldn't a been my choosing if anyone had asked, that's for sure." Sissy pushed out of her chair. "But that's what I do, and it's all I know."

Out the corner of her eye, Josie saw that Long Belly was headed up the steps. Making one last effort to keep her friend close by, she said, "There must be lots of things you can do, anything but whoring."

"Look at me, girl." Sissy stood tall and proud, a neat trick considering that the top of her head barely reached the five-foot notch on a door frame. "How many white men or women are going to hire someone like me as anything but a laundress or a maid? I couldn't even get one of them jobs if what I used to do came known, and it would. Thanks for trying, but I know where I belong."

The door opened before Josie could renew her efforts, and in came Long Belly. He glanced at her briefly, then directed his comments to Sissy. "Come outside with me, Buffalo Hair. I must speak to you, alone."

Sissy started toward him, but Josie hopped out of her chair and blocked the path. "No, you stay. I'll go. That way you two can have a little more privacy."

With one last look at her friend, Josie impulsively threw herself into her arms for a quick hug. Then she turned and ran out the door.

Chapter Eighteen

Trying not to think of Sissy or how much she was going to miss her, Josie decided to lift her spirits by checking on Sweetpea. Completely avoiding the barn—she was in no mood to face Daniel or his little goblins—she walked down to the privy, then made her way around back to the pen. She found the buffalo lying in a small wallow she'd dug in the snow, happily chewing her cud. Three heifers had joined her in the enclosure during Josie's absence, apparently the doings of Long Belly. As she approached the bison, it cocked its head and sniffed the air, then went back to chewing.

"Hi, Sweetpea," Josie called, bending over to reach through the pine rails and scratch the hide beneath the buffalo's thick matt of long, dark hair. "I see some of your old companions have moved in with you. Were you lonely?"

The animal grunted in ecstasy as Josie continued to scratch her shoulders, her small beady eyes languid and sleepy. Shifting positions so she could reach a little farther down the animal's back, Josie straightened her spine at the same moment something slapped against the back of her legs. Leaping away from the fence, she glanced down to see a slender pine branch lying in the snow at her feet. It was stripped of bark and sharpened at the tip into a little spear.

She glanced behind her, alerted by the sounds of muffled giggles, then caught a glimpse of Daniel's heathen twins hiding behind a tree. Josie considered ignoring them and simply walking away, but she knew from experience with her own brothers that they'd just keep after her until a few rules were established. Spear in hand, she marched over to the pine tree.

"All right, you two," she said, catching sight of their bobbing heads. "Come out of there this instant."

The boys remained huddled behind the tree. Josie ducked first to the right as if chasing them down, then veered around to the left of the tree at the last second, trapping them as they tried to run away. They wore little buckskin shirts and trousers, but were barefoot in the snow.

"Stop right there," she said, cutting off their escape. "Which one of you threw this at me?"

Two pairs of the biggest, blackest eyes she'd ever seen looked up at her, round and innocent. They muttered something to each other in Cheyenne, then shrugged their small shoulders.

"Don't you speak English?" she asked, watching as their eyes grew even rounder and more guileless. "Well, hell."

Getting down to their level, Josie dropped to her knees. She held the branch up in front of their faces, then shifted the spear from hand to hand, looking from one boy to the other. "Who . . . threw . . . this?"

The twins shot furtive glimpses at each other, but gave no indication that they understood her.

Josie touched the branch to the shoulder of the child on the left and asked, "Are you Bang?"

No response. "Two Moons?"

The child continued to stare at her, as adorable and silent as a porcelain doll. "Your father hasn't even taught you kids what your names sound like in English?"

They smiled in unison, still blissfully ignorant of Josie's careful interrogation of them. It was then she decided that it was just as well they couldn't understand her, especially considering that she'd decided to rename them Hell and Damnation.

"All right," she said, her tone less friendly. "Pay attention, you little pisspots, even if you don't know exactly what I'm saying. Since you can't understand me, I'm just going to have find another way to teach you some manners."

Josie climbed to her feet to regain her height advantage and waved the spear. "First of all, never, ever throw something like this at me again, or this is what you'll get in return."

She snapped the branch in half over her knee, then brought the two switches down hard on the palm of her hand. The boys flinched and stepped away from her.

Josie smiled. "Finally, a language you understand. In that case maybe you've also figured out that I'll be blistering your worthless backsides with a switch, not my own hand, next time you try something this stupid." Punctuating the threat, she whacked the branch against her palm again.

The boys cried out in unison, then took off running for the barn.

"Hey, wait up, you two," Josie called, afraid she may have demonstrated her point a little too forcefully. "I'm just trying to teach you a lesson."

It occurred to her then that it might not be a bad idea to catch up to them and calm them down a little before they went running to their father. She ran as fast as she could, but was no match for the boys' fleet little feet. By the time she got to the barn and stepped inside, the twins were huddled behind their father's legs, big-eyed and innocent.

"What the hell did you do to my boys?" Daniel demanded. "You scared them half to death."

They didn't look that all-fired scared to Josie. In fact, the one on the right wore a smirk.

"They shot me with an arrow, or whatever this thing is." She held up the sections of pine. Broken in half, the children's weapon suddenly looked no more lethal than two sorry pieces of kindling.

"How terrifying for you." Daniel's gaze, already narrow,

became murderous. He barked something at the twins in Cheyenne, apparently ordering them out of the barn. The little piss-pots crawled out from the hiding spot behind their daddy and made for the door, each of them flashing Josie a smug grin that Daniel couldn't possibly see.

Suddenly, it promised to be a long, hard winter, and not necessarily because of the early snows.

In the cabin, Long Belly surprised Sissy by reaching out and gently touching her cheek. She backed away from him, rubbing the spot, and said, "Don't do that. I don't like it."

Long Belly advanced on her again, strangely persistent. "Why is this? Why will you never let me touch your face or put these hungry lips on your mouth?"

Sissy didn't know the answer to that herself. Nor could she explain why a simple gesture like touching her cheek seemed somehow more intimate than what he did between her legs.

At a loss, she simply said, "I just don't like it, that's all. We leaving now?"

He nodded, wriggling his long, enviably shiny braids. She started for the loft. "I'll just go get changed into my own clothes."

"There is no need for that. What you wear is yours to keep."

Since Sissy figured she'd earned the buckskins, she didn't try to decline the gift. "I'll just go pack up my things, then."

"Later," he said, following her, then taking her by the shoulders. "First we have business."

Assuming he wanted to get off with her one more time, Sissy began to unbutton her shirt. Long Belly slid his hand atop hers. "Our business today is between our heads, not our legs."

Long Belly was so tall, towering at least a foot above her, that Sissy rarely tried to look him in the eye. At that strange statement, she arched her neck back and gawked up at him.

"What kind of business could you possibly have with this thick head?"

He laughed, then bounced his hands off the sides of her hair.

"You are a very funny woman, Buffalo Hair, one of the many reasons, I think, that I have grown these strange feelings for you."

Puzzled, she asked, "And what kinda feelings might they be, red man?"

He laughed, then repeated the second of the special names they called each other. "They are these, brown woman. I have a great warmth here for you." He put his hand over his heart. "A feeling that burns until it hurts when I think of sending you to live with the white man again. Do you have this strange burning for me?"

The feelings Long Belly spoke of were as foreign to Sissy as his Cheyenne language. She wasn't even sure what he was trying to say, or what those feelings meant.

Exasperated, she shook her head and said, "Maybe you got hold of some bad stew or something if you got a burning in your chest. Me, I'm the same's always. I don't feel nothing."

All the sparkle faded from Long Belly's eyes, but then it suddenly came back, even brighter than before. "You must feel something inside, even if it is hatred. I have thought of a way for you to discover what it is you feel for me. Will you let me try?"

Since he'd never done anything to hurt her before, and she couldn't imagine that he'd find whatever the hell it was he was looking for anyway, Sissy reluctantly agreed.

"What do you have in mind?"

Without warning, Long Belly picked her up and carried her over to the counter, where he made a great ceremony of clearing a nice spot on which to deposit her. Then he spread her legs and moved up between them so the two of them were just inches apart. Sitting there at eye level with him, Sissy couldn't stop herself from smiling.

"There, see?" he said softly. "I think you are having a good feeling for me. Tell me what you feel when I do this."

He leaned into her, his mouth heading straight for hers, and Sissy brought her elbows up against his chest. "No kissing. How many times do I have to tell you? No kissing."

Long Belly smiled as if he hadn't heard. "Just once. Allow me to kiss you once. Then tell me you have no feelings for this red man."

Sissy would not admit to a certain curiosity over what it would be like to taste what others accepted as part of their daily lives. And she sure as hell didn't want to examine why the thought of a harmless kiss frightened her so. In light of all that, it seemed that giving in would be the fastest and easiest thing to do.

"All right, go ahead, but be quick about it."

That said, she closed her eyes and offered her lips.

Long Belly was quick to take them, but that was all he did in a hurry. Once his mouth had claimed hers, he gently parted her lips with his tongue, and then somehow coaxed her into opening up for him. Images swirled in Sissy's mind the way his tongue twined around hers, brilliant reds and blues with shooting stars of yellow and white. She suddenly felt as if she were breaking up inside, losing little pieces of herself, and then her heart began to race, freezing her with fear. In a panic, Sissy began to fight against Long Belly's embrace.

He took his mouth from hers, but continued to hold her close as he whispered against her skin, "I have want of you as my woman, Buffalo Hair. I have no wish to take you back to Miles City. What do you want?"

She didn't know. No one had ever asked or cared what Sissy wanted, and now that someone did, the thought was terrifying, like offering freedom to a bird that had never known any life but the cage. She *didn't* know what she wanted.

Waiting patiently for her answer, Long Belly helped himself to another kiss, this one even deeper and more tender than the last. Something new stirred in Sissy as his mouth made love to hers, a feeling completely unrelated to the fear that any hint of intimacy usually spawned. She thought it might even be desire.

Pushing away from Long Belly's sensual lips, Sissy said, "Let me get this straight. Did you say you wanted me to go live with you on the reservation?"

He pursed his lips as if deeply troubled. "This is what I asked of you, yes, even though I know that it will be a hard and simple life for you. Difficulties will come, too, because I ask you to live among people who do not speak your language. None of this is good or fair to you, but I need to have you by my side. Will you join me?"

Sissy's throat swelled, almost closing up on her, but she managed to eke out, "Will I? Oh, red man, that sounds like heaven."

"This means you will go with me?"

"Kiss me again first, would you, just like before?"

This time, when he took her mouth, there was a new urgency, a deeper thrusting of his tongue, a tighter embrace. Unmistakable desire quickened in Sissy's loins as the kiss wore on, and suddenly she knew exactly what she wanted.

Tearing away from Long Belly, she said, "I'll go with you, and stay as long as you want me to. But first, would you take me up to the loft? And, red man—hurry."

In the barn, Josie sat on a grain barrel while Daniel went on and on about his wonderful boys and how much she would enjoy tending to them if only she'd give herself half a chance.

"It seems to me," he said, "that since you have all those brothers, you should probably know a lot about children."

She nodded grimly. "I do. In fact, I know a hell of a lot more about them than I ever wanted to know."

He paused to glare, making damn sure she realized how testy he was getting. "Why don't you just try a little harder to get along with the twins? There isn't a woman alive who can keep from falling in love with those boys after you get to know them."

Josie seriously considered telling Daniel that yes, there was such a woman, and she was sitting right in front of him. She refrained, knowing such an admission would only hurt his feelings—and probably make him madder as well.

"I'm not making any promises," she finally said. "But I'll try a little harder if they will."

"Josie." He spoke to her as if she were a child. "They're four years old. What do you expect them to do? Behave like short little adults?"

She expected them to behave, period, but Josie said, "I'm just asking for a little respect. I don't think they like me very much."

"You're new to them, is all. Maybe if you do something special for them, they'll warm to you a little faster."

"Special? Like what?"

He shrugged. "I don't know. Maybe bake something for them, like that cake you made for Sissy."

Josie sighed, feeling as if she were taking a backward step into the past, but agreed to give it a try anyway. "I guess it wouldn't kill me to bake some cookies for the little fellahs."

"Now there you go." Daniel leaned over and kissed her lips. "Your mothering instincts just needed a little nudge to wake them up."

"Mothering instincts," Josie muttered. "Right."

Having deluded himself into believing that she would actually enjoy baking for his little pisspots, Daniel then dragged Josie out into the yard and called his heathens in from their play.

Grumbling under her breath, she pulled away from him and said, "Send the boys on in when you get them rounded up. I'd better go get started on that batter."

When she stepped inside the cabin, Josie saw that Long Belly was just coming down the ladder from his loft. He carried a small bundle in his arms along with his parfleche.

As he passed by her, he flashed a rare smile and said, "I will say good-bye now, but hope to see you and my brother at the reservation soon."

Surprised to find that she actually had some friendly feelings toward him, Josie returned his smile. "Good-bye, Long Belly. It's been real . . . different knowing you. Where's Sissy?"

"She gathers her belongings." He inclined his head toward the loft. "Do not keep her long."

That sense of camaraderie rapidly fading, she muttered, "Don't worry. I'll see that she doesn't dawdle too much."

Josie resisted the urge to bury her foot in his backside as he strolled out of the cabin and contented herself instead by kicking the door shut behind him. She wondered if he'd been as abrupt with Sissy when he explained that he'd be taking her back to her life as a whore and got mad all over again as she dug through Daniel's meager pantry for cooking supplies.

Josie managed to find molasses, sugar, eggs, vinegar, flour, and even cinnamon, which meant that she only lacked one ingredient in order to make her usually delicious molasses cookies—ginger. Figuring the twins already had so much of that particular spice that they wouldn't notice if it was missing from the cookies, she cleaned up the only bowl in the house and began measuring flour.

She'd just dumped the third cup of "dumpling dust," as Daniel referred to it, into the bowl when Sissy came down from the loft and joined her at the counter.

"What are you cooking up now?" she asked, peeking into the bowl.

"Cookies for Daniel's little pisspots." Josie wiped her hands on the scrap of linen she used for a towel. "Not that it was my idea."

"It's right nice of you no matter whose idea it was."

Turning to her, Josie decided she might as well let Sissy believe that if she wanted to, and then noticed that there were several changes in her friend's appearance. For one thing, Sissy's cheeks were kind of flushed, not precisely rosy they way her own got, but shiny, as if glowing from within. Her dark eyes, usually so flat and dull, were sparkling with something that hinted at contentment, maybe even fulfillment. Strangest of all, she was smiling. Not simply smiling, but grinning like a big ole jack-o'-lantern.

"Sissy?" Josie said, unable to fathom this sudden transformation. "What's come over you? You're positively radiant."

Sissy averted her gaze with a coy little smile that made Josie think of innocence, debutantes and balls, and all the things that had never been a part of either of their lives. What the hell had happened between her and that crazy Cheyenne?

"Sissy?" Her tone deeper, demanding, Josie finally got her attention. "Are you all right?"

"I'm better than all right." Again the big grin. "Long Belly wants me to stay on with him. I said I would."

"You're gonna stay here, on the reservation?" Josie threw her arms around her and squeezed. "Then we'll for sure be seeing each other from time to time."

"For sure," Sissy agreed, hugging her back. "And as often as the weather permits, I guess."

Josie had more questions, a full string of them, but those pesky twins rolled through the doorway then, cutting the conversation short.

Sissy went right to them, her eyes even more brilliant than before, and said, "Hi, fellahs. What's your names?"

The boys just stared at her, in particular that great tumbleweed of dark brown hair, taking in her unusual skin color and features as if she were some kind of aberration. In these parts, Josie figured that maybe she was. But that didn't make the twins' reaction any less rude.

"Don't mind them," she said. "They're just gawking at you because they don't know what you said."

"They cain't speak English?"

"No," Josie muttered. "And they're not much on manners either."

Her covetous eyes all over the two young boys, Sissy sighed wistfully. "They look so much alike, I don't know how poor Daniel tells them apart. What are their names?"

"That one is Hell," Josie said, picking one at random. "And the other's Damnation."

Sissy turned to her in horror. "Really?"

"No," Josie said with a laugh. "But those names fit them better than Bang and Two Moons, which don't make a hell of a lot of sense either."

Although she was laughing along with Josie, Sissy scolded her. "Hell and Damnation aren't very nice names for their new mother to be calling a sweet little pair like this."

"I'm *not* their mother, and that's about as nice as I can be considering these *sweet* little pisspots tried to kill me."

Sissy cocked her head. "Kill you, princess?"

"Okay, maim me. They snuck up behind me and threw a spear that could have put out my eye." She looked down at the boys. "That is what you two had in mind, isn't it?"

When they grinned back at her in that irritatingly smug way, Josie pointed to her eyes, then crossed them and stuck out her tongue. The twins shrieked and ran screaming from the cabin.

"Oh, hell. Here we go again." Josie rolled up her sleeves, preparing for round two.

"Daniel?" Sissy guessed.

Josie nodded. "Daniel. He thinks those two are little angels that could never do wrong. If he only had eyes in the back of his head, he'd soon see that what he sired is a couple of ill-bred brats."

Sissy shook her great head of hair and laughed. "I don't think them boys grate on you nearly as much as you let on, princess. Why cain't you just enjoy 'em a little? They could be a real comfort to you over the winter."

Josie would have laughed out loud had Daniel not come through the door about then.

He paused there at the threshold, his skin looking sallow beneath its usual nutmeg hue. His fists were clenched and the muscles of his neck continually flexed as he clenched and unclenched his teeth. His eyes were on fire and bluer than they'd ever been, as startling as periwinkles in the snow. Bad to worse, the little pisspots were clinging to his pant legs as if they were frightened, but their expressions were pure rascal.

"Sissy," Daniel said tightly. "It's been nice having you as a guest, but I guess you'll be heading out with Long Belly now, right?"

"Uh, right, Daniel." Like a wooden statue, Sissy turned to

Josie, offered a quick hug, and said, "I'll be back to see you soon as I can. Go easy on 'em."

Looking at her friend in a new light, Josie whispered, "Turncoat. Just wait until you need me to stick up for you someday."

"You'll be there," Sissy said, kissing her cheek. "And you'll be there for them boys. I just know it." Then she thanked Daniel for his hospitality and walked out the door.

The cabin grew deathly silent after Sissy's departure and stayed that way until the sound of hoofbeats could no longer be heard. Then Daniel lit into her, his voice eerily quiet.

"I wonder if you might tell me the meaning of the word 'pisspot'?"

A little bell went off inside Josie's brain, a vague but ominous warning. She cleared her throat. "Ah, pisspot? I believe that's pretty much the same as a chamber pot or slop jar, isn't it?"

"You tell me." Daniel smiled, the expression more of a grimace. "I'm especially interested in learning how a pair of innocent young children could possibly be referred to as clay pots that hold urine."

Josie gulped. "I—ah, wouldn't know."

"You wouldn't? Then perhaps you'd like to know how I came by this word in the first place."

She shrugged and averted her gaze. "Not particularly."

Daniel told her anyway. "My sons here asked me what it meant. They said that's what you liked to call them when you weren't referring to them by their given names, Hell and Damnation."

The look Daniel gave her after that shot clean through her the way no spear ever could. It not only hurt, but somewhere deep inside, Josie knew she had it coming. She hadn't tried in the least to be decent to the young boys, even if they were a pair of goblins who sorely needed a good swift kick in the rear.

With a heartfelt sigh, she said, "I'm sorry, Daniel. Honest. I guess I got off to the wrong foot with your sons, and I'd like to make it up to them. And to you."

His expression looked forced now, as if he wanted desperately to stay mad at her, but couldn't deny the apology. With a resolute nod, he said, "All right. We'll start over. These are my sons, Two Moons and Bang."

Josie's hands went to her cheeks. "Oh, Daniel, they're absolutely adorable! How did you ever come up with such unusual names for them?"

He cocked one eyebrow, an expression she took as a warning, and then went on to explain. "The day they were born, their mother got up for her usual morning walk at sunrise and thought she saw two moons, one in the east and one in the west. She went into labor shortly after that and was taken to the birthing tipi, where Two Moons was born and named because of what she'd seen."

Josie laughed. "And here I thought it had something to do with his being a twin."

"We didn't even know there were two babies until I celebrated the birth of Two Moons in the usual Cheyenne way." Daniel smiled at the memory. "I fired my rifle to announce his arrival at about the same time a second son put in his surprise appearance."

"Don't tell me." Josie held up her hands. "I think I understand now. Your gun went *bang* as the second baby was born?"

"My gun went bang," he echoed, rubbing the head of the child on the left.

Josie dropped down on her haunches and studied the boys. To her eye they were as alike as blades of grass. "How do you ever tell them apart?"

"Just looking, it's easy to get confused, but Bang, oddly enough, is a lot more quiet than his brother."

That little bell in her mind rang again as Josie studied the boys. Ignoring it, she asked, "How am I supposed to communicate with them? I don't know a word of Cheyenne."

"I'm not expecting you to learn a new language." Daniel gave the twins a little shove in her direction. "They're quite capable of making their needs known. Go ahead, boys, let your new ma know that you appreciate her."

Together they said, "We are happy to meet you, Ma Jofess."

The "Ma Jofess" threw Josie for a minute, but something else eclipsed even that.

She looked up at Daniel, incredulous. "They speak English?"

"Sure. They understand it very well, but their verbal skills are a little rusty. Didn't you know?"

"No, I sure as hell didn't."

Two Moons and Bang flashed evil little grins her way; then the little pisspots turned angelic smiles on their father.

Cold, hard winter, my ass, thought Josie. It was beginning to look as though she was going to have to survive the next four months in the fires of hell.

Chapter Nineteen

They hadn't been but an hour on the trail leading to the reservation camp before the weather turned treacherous for Sissy and Long Belly. When they'd left the cabin, a single cloud rode high in the sky. Now storm clouds stampeded in from the north, surging over the lower ridges and obliterating the higher summits. Cold air settled around Sissy, numbing her fingers and even her toes through the buckskin boots. She burrowed deeper into her buffalo-hide jacket, and urged the mule forward.

"We gonna make it to the reservation before this storm hits?" she shouted to Long Belly, just ahead on the trail.

"It is my hope," he called over his shoulder. "I have no wish to sleep in the snow tonight."

As if prompted by his remarks, a light snow began to fall, swirling around the mule's legs and settling on the ground like wispy clouds. Two hours later, when they should already have reached the camp, they were still plodding through powdery drifts as storm clouds churned above them. Snow began to spiral all around them, sweeping the ground in great, powerful gusts until Sissy could barely make out the spotted rump of the horse in front of her.

When the paint suddenly came to a halt, the mule crashed into its backside and then shuddered to a stop. Long Belly shouted something as he dismounted, but Sissy couldn't make out the words over the howling wind.

"What?" she screamed into the blizzard.

"We are here," he said, coming alongside the mule.

It wasn't until he'd lifted her off the animal and set her on her feet that Sissy realized that they'd stopped in front of a tipi, an enormous structure almost completely veiled from her eyes by blinding snow. Long Belly hurried her inside the ghostly structure, then gathered a few scraps of wood by the opening and made a small fire.

"I must see to the horses now," he said. "And then I will find you a place to sleep tonight. Warm yourself until my return."

Sissy stopped him as he headed back outside. "Wait—why do you have to find a place for me? Aren't we staying here tonight?"

His cinnamon skin glistening with melted snow, Long Belly smiled in a most peculiar way as he said, "This is my tipi, the place where I sleep. You will have to stay with my mother or another female relative until we can arrange for the ceremony."

Explanation enough for him, he started for the flap again. Sissy beat him to the opening. "What ceremony are you talking about, and why cain't I stay with you like before?"

Long Belly kept that strange smile as he pulled her into his arms and said, "Forgive me, brown woman. I forget you know nothing of my tribe. We honor our women and keep them pure until they are brides. It would not be respectful of you, and my tribesmen would look upon us with contempt, if I stayed with you before our wedding ceremony."

Sissy dismissed everything he said except the words "wedding ceremony." Even then, she wasn't sure she heard him right. "Did you just say that we're getting hitched?"

"Hitched?" He cocked his head.

"Hitched," she repeated, almost afraid to use the other term. "Uh, married."

"That is what the wedding ceremony is for."

The look Long Belly gave her was new as he paused to make sure she understood, a gaze so intimate and reverent, Sissy simply couldn't imagine that it had anything to do with her.

"After the ceremony," he went on to say, "we will be given a great wedding feast. I cannot share your bed until this is arranged and done. Do you understand?"

Sissy understood what he was saying, but not why. When Long Belly had first asked her to come to the reservation with him, she'd assumed they would live together as they had at Daniel's cabin. Never had it occurred to her that he would want her as his wife—or that anyone else would, for that matter. Feeling numb all over, as if she were standing naked in the blizzard, Sissy marveled over the thought, unable to speak.

Tired of waiting for her to reply, Long Belly put his hands on either side of her head, crushing the springy curls there. "Why do you look so surprised, brown woman? Did I not tell you back at my brother's cabin that I have a big need to hold you for the rest of my nights?"

Something bubbled inside her, threatening to boil over. "Sure, it's just that I didn't understand how permanent you was figuring on making it."

"It is the Cheyenne way," he said with a shrug. "It is my way."

Sissy swallowed hard, holding the eruption at bay. "I'm gonna have to think on this some, red man," she said, choosing her words with great care. "And it ain't because I'm worried you won't make me a good husband."

He reared back as if she'd struck him. "You will *not* marry me?"

"I ain't said no, but I ain't saying yes until I can think on this some." He still looked so crushed, Sissy did the best she could to explain something she didn't entirely understand herself. "I ain't never had a choice before. I sure never had a chance to decide something big, like what I might want to do

with my life. Hell, I never even got to choose what I wanted
for supper. Marrying you seems like a mighty big decision—
the first one I've ever had to make. I don't want to make a
mistake my first time out."

Long Belly nodded, deep in thought. "You will be happy
with me, Buffalo Hair. We will be happy together."

The eruption imminent, Sissy whispered, "I know. Now go
on, do what you gotta do, but please don't make me go stay
with anyone else tonight—like your ma. I gotta be alone a
while so's I can think."

"You may have my tipi. I will find other lodging." With a
brief kiss, Long Belly ducked out through the flap, then carefully
closed it behind him.

When Sissy was very sure that he was gone and couldn't
hear, for the first time since she could remember, she gave
herself over to tears. She cried and cried. When she figured
she must be about cried out, she cried some more.

Ten days later the weather hadn't changed appreciably. When
it wasn't snowing, it was too cold outside to do much of anything except quickly take care of whatever business took a
body out of the cabin, and then rush back inside for the warmth
of the stove. Daniel's little pisspots even took to wearing moccasins, keeping them on whether they were inside or out.

Josie stared through the frost on the window, wondering how
much longer she could stand to be cooped up inside with the
little heathens. It seemed like all Bang and Two Moons did
was run around the cabin like wild Indians, demand to be fed,
or just generally find ways to make Josie's life miserable. The
only thing she was grateful for was the fact that her monthlies
had arrived this morning, a double-edged sword if ever there
was one. She was cramping something awful, her breasts were
so swollen and tender that she couldn't even stand the weight
of her chemise rubbing against her nipples, and if the twins
had looked at her cross-eyed, she probably would have ripped

their heads off. But at least she wasn't baking one or, God forbid, two of Daniel's heathen buns in her oven.

Josie breathed deeply, more sickened than soothed by the usually comforting aroma of spiced molasses. She generally liked the way the house smelled when she was baking up a batch of cookies, but not for days on end. The twins had never had cookies before and were so fond of them, she'd whipped up a batch almost every day for a week now just to shut them up and give them something to do. Like now, she thought, as they came scrambling down the loft from their nap.

The first twin to reach her slapped a pudgy little hand against her arm. "More cooks, Ma Jofess?"

She turned toward the child and grabbed his wrist, preventing a second assault on her person. His expression bordered on charming and he'd asked for the cookies, not demanded them.

Certain she had this child's identity figured out, Josie said, "The word is cookies, Bang. Cooks are the people who make cookies."

He grinned, not the devilish I-got-you grin the two usually threw her way, but an honest expression of delight.

"Me am Two Moons," he said, proud to have confused her.

"You are Two Moons," she corrected, an automatic response from her years of surrogate parenthood.

"You are Two Moons," he parroted.

"No, I am . . . oh, hell. Never mind. It doesn't matter what your name is, kid. They're still cookies, and no, it's not time to take them out of the oven yet."

His round face fell into a pout, a sure sign that he'd be thinking up ways to scare the hell out of her or just plain piss her off after he'd had his fill of cookies. Since she was in no mood to put up with any more of the boy's shenanigans, Josie decided to distract him. She'd noticed that both twins wore identical little bags around their neck, each of them made of blue and red beads fashioned into some kind of animal complete with round bellies, heads, and short little arms and legs made of strips of stiff rawhide. They vaguely resembled turtles.

After touching the bag that Long Belly had given to her,

Josie pointed to the one tied around Two Moons' neck and asked, "What is that? Good luck medicine like mine?"

The boy shook his head and glared. "Ma gives me. Is bad medicine for evil like *you*."

He poked Josie's belly as he finished the sentence, scaring a shudder out of her that ran the length of her body. Then he ran over by the stove to wait for the miracle of the "cooks."

"Why you miserable, no-account . . ." Josie let the sentence and the thought hang, knowing that if she finished it the way she wanted to, the little pisspot would run tattling to his father, which would in turn make her life even more miserable than it already was.

Adding to her misery, Bang approached her after his brother fled, pulled open the neck of his shirt and pointed to his own bag.

"Me, too," he said in his husky voice. "Bad medicine for you."

"Yes," Josie agreed. "The both of you are plenty bad medicine, but I have some of my own for you."

She got up from the table then, went to the stove, and removed the pan of cookies. Smiling as she lifted them out of the pan, she said, "Have you boys ever heard the word 'poison'?"

They looked at each other, big-eyed and wary, but said nothing.

"Poison is what makes my cookies so sweet." Josie held out the plate, offering them their pick. "Go ahead, eat up if you dare, you little goblins."

They eyed the cookies hungrily, but then ran away and scrambled up the ladder to their loft. About the time they disappeared over the top, Daniel blew in through the door. He was so cold, he didn't bother to remove his jacket, but immediately came to stand in front of the hot stove. Clumps of snow fell from the coat, melting into puddles all over Josie's clean floor.

"Give me that," she said, peeling the garment off of his shoulders and taking it to hang on its proper antler. As she returned to the stove, Josie glanced up to see the twins cowering at the lip of the loft. She smiled at them, showing way too many teeth, and sent them scurrying out of sight.

"Any signs of the storm letting up yet?" she asked.

Daniel chafed his hands above the burner. "Not yet, and it was at least twenty-five below out there before the wind came up again. The gusts are enough to slice a man in half."

Josie was familiar with winter storms and knew that twenty-five below could easily feel like fifty below when the wind was blowing. "Did you check on Sweetpea? And how are the cattle doing in all this?"

"The buffalo is fine, the cattle not so good." He shook his head in frustration. "That little warm spell we had crusted the snow already on the ground and now the cattle can't push their noses through it to reach the grass beneath. I stocked up enough hay to help them through the worst spells, but if this keeps up, it'll never last all winter."

Josie recalled how scrawny they'd been before the first blizzard. "There must be something we can we do to save them."

"Nothing I know of." Daniel turned to her, warming his backside. Exhaustion was etched in his features. "I wish to hell I'd been smart enough to have sent more than two head along with Long Belly and Sissy. All of our cattle might as well be butchered to help feed the tribe instead of leaving them to starve to death on my own land."

She couldn't imagine that so few cattle could be in such jeopardy. "They'll be all right. All we need is another break in the weather."

"I hope you're right." Grumbling to himself, Daniel pulled out the chair nearest the stove and fell into it. "I'm starved. What do you have to eat around here besides cookies?"

"I'll have to look," she said, suddenly irritable.

She didn't complain or put up an argument because at that point, Josie wasn't sure why she felt so agitated. She sure as hell didn't like the way Daniel had asked her to fix his food, but it was more than that. As she fried up a thick ham steak, warmed up a few biscuits left from breakfast, and added some fresh grounds to the coffee pot, she finally realized what was bothering her so—she'd bargained her way right back into her former role as housekeeper and cook to a bunch of ungrateful males. She might as well have never left the Baum ranch.

By the time the meal was ready, Josie was so steamed, she slammed the plate down in front of Daniel rather than serving it, then threw herself into the seat across from him.

He looked up, astounded. "What the hell was that all about?"

Since she couldn't exactly explain herself—she had, after all, agreed to cook for the man—Josie folded her arms across her chest and kept her thoughts to herself.

"Aren't you going to say anything?"

There was absolutely nothing she could say in her own defense.

Daniel's fist hit the table. "After I've spent all morning freezing my ass tending stock while you're in here warming your fanny at a hot stove, is this as nice as you can be?"

If the words hadn't been so close to the ones her stepfather and brothers had used on her all her life, Josie might have apologized then and there and been done with it. Instead, something inside her snapped, freeing her cantankerous tongue.

"What do you expect me to do?" she asked. "Get down on my hands and knees and kiss your feet each time you come through the door? I said I'd cook and clean. Being nice doesn't have a damn thing to do with our bargain."

Daniel's mouth dropped open.

"And neither do your brats, by the way. Do you think I actually enjoy being penned up in here with those two little pisspots running me ragged from morning to night? Is this supposed to be my idea of *heaven?*"

"Now hold on a minute."

"No, you hold on, and while you're at it, think about this— maybe if you stayed in here looking after your own damn kids and let me take care of the cattle, all the animals on this hellhole you call a ranch would be doing one hell of a lot better than they are now. I know I would."

Her face hot, the blood pulsing at her temples like hammers, Josie fell back against her chair.

Daniel just sat there and stared at her for a full minute before he finally commented on her outburst. "Oh, Christ, Josie. Are you pregnant?"

Her anger had been real, red-hot and bubbling over with so much righteous indignation, she thought her head might explode. Daniel's statement was like a bucket of ice water in the face and a chicken feather at the bottom of her foot. She burst out in uncontrollable laughter.

"Does that mean you're not pregnant and that you're going to let us live, after all?"

"Yes, on both counts." Still chuckling, she added, "I didn't mean to bite your head off, but I'm feeling kinda poorly this morning. I guess that makes me a little irritable."

"You're sick?"

"Not exactly." Josie explained as delicately as she could. "I'm, ah, doubled up with the female complaint."

"Well, thank the Lord for that." He wiped his brow. "I was more than just a little worried after our first night together."

Finally able to get to his meal, Daniel wedged a thick chunk of ham between the halves of his biscuit, then stuffed the entire thing into his mouth. Josie waited until he'd finished eating before she asked for clarification.

"Why would you be worried? I thought we were particularly safe that night."

"The damn rubber fell apart," he explained sheepishly. "I don't know why it broke, but that made it completely useless. In other words, you might easily have gotten pregnant."

Josie clutched her throat in horror. "Don't you think you might have told me there was a problem?"

Daniel shrugged. "I couldn't see the point in worrying you. After all, the—ah, horses were already out of the barn, so to speak, and there wasn't any way to put them back where they belonged."

Feeling flushed, hot all over, Josie collapsed against her chair and fanned herself.

"Are you all right, sweetheart? Your face is really red."

"I think I could use some air."

"Well, I suppose a walk to the barn might do you some good, especially if you meant any of what you said about switching jobs with me."

The smile Daniel gave her after that suggestion was impossible for Josie to interpret. Either he understood her frustration at being trapped in the cabin, or he was making what he considered to be a joke.

Josie glanced out the window. "I'd love to go have a look at Sweetpea, but I can't even see the barn through the snow."

"I had a little trouble finding it myself, so I strung a rope between the barn door and the front porch. Just hang onto it all the way, and Josie—don't dawdle out there. If you close your eyes, they might just freeze that way until spring."

"I'll go straight to the barn, take a fast peek at Sweetpea, then I'll come right back." She pushed away from the table. "Who knows? Maybe by then, I'll feel like being a little nicer."

"One can hope."

The smile he gave her after that was unmistakable and impossible to misread. It was the expression of a contented, satisfied, and truly exhausted man, one who'd probably be sleeping by the time she got back from her airing.

Josie slipped into Daniel's jacket and headed out into the storm. Welcoming the bite of freezing winds and even the blowing snow that spiked her cheeks, she easily found the barn, thanks to Daniel's rope, and quickly slipped inside. The cavernous building was dark except for a crack of light at the back door, which was ajar. That made it relatively easy to pick out the outline of two figures who were huddled near the crack.

Giving herself a moment to recover from the shock of finding someone else in the barn, Josie realized that the intruders were peeking out the door and into Sweetpea's pen. Recognizing the buffalo robe of the man on the right, Josie stormed down the center aisle.

"Long Belly!" she shouted, alerting him to her presence. "Damn your no-account hide. What the hell do you—"

The Indians turned at the sound of her voice, spears raised. When they pointed their weapons directly at her and then started her way, Josie noticed two sudden and terrifying details. The men were savages all right, their long hair in braids and faces painted, but Long Belly was not one of them. And neither of the heathens looked the least bit pleased to see her.

Chapter Twenty

At the Cheyenne reservation camp, Sissy curled up in front of the extravagant fire Long Belly had built for her a couple of hours before. She could hardly believe how warm and comfortable she was inside the crude structure, or that the bed could be even softer than the one she'd shared with Long Belly at the cabin. Even more surprising, given her treatment by whites, his tribesmen seemed to accept her without prejudice.

Astounded by the changes in her life since the night Long Belly had spirited her away from the whorehouse, Sissy fussed with the latest in a series of gifts he'd given to her. Today's presents included a pretty gold bracelet and a pair of fancy moccasins made with bright yellow beads and porcupine quills dyed red. They would be a nice addition, she thought, to the even fancier footgear he'd brought her yesterday, a pair of thigh-high boots done up with colorful beads and big silver buttons that jingled when she walked.

She slipped into those soft deerskin boots now, tugging them tightly over her feet, and caught herself marveling over this new, remarkably attentive Long Belly. Not a day had gone by in the week or so since he'd brought her here that he hadn't come to the tipi with gifts ranging from jewelry to baskets to clothing. If that wasn't miracle enough, he hadn't once pressed her for sex, insisting that he would never degrade her again by so much as touching her before their marriage. That gave Sissy more than just a little pause, especially as she considered their nightly assignations in the weeks leading up to their departure from Daniel's cabin.

Now, ironically enough, all Sissy could think about were the times when she'd begged the Lord to please give her a few days of peace with no man touching or invading any part of her body. After tasting this luxury for several days, she was surprised to find that her newly awakened desire pestered her as unrelentingly and persistently as any whoremonger ever had. The resulting frustration alone was almost enough temptation for Sissy to give in to Long Belly's pleas for an immediate wedding. But not quite.

She was still determined to make her decision based on what she wanted, a bewildering but thrilling dilemma she was facing for the first time in her life. It wasn't an easy thing to decide, especially in the face of the reception she'd received when the weather cleared long enough for Long Belly to present her to his family and friends.

Other tribal members, especially the children, seemed positively awestruck whenever they happened upon her. Long Belly said they were fascinated by her skin color, unusually curly ''buffalo'' hair, and all the wild tales he'd told them about the great buffalo spirit that lurked within her. Sissy knew she'd done nothing for anyone to hold her in such high esteem, but she couldn't honestly say that she didn't enjoy her elevated status or the warm and tingly sensations that came with it.

''Buffalo Hair?'' came Long Belly's voice above the crackling fire. ''May I enter?''

''Come on in,'' she called back, amused by the overly polite suitor he'd become.

After Long Belly stepped inside, careful to leave the flap open, he offered Sissy the small bowl he carried. ''I bring you soup to warm and fill your belly. The snow no longer falls, but the air is like a frozen pond."

"Sit down," she invited him, taking the bowl and setting it aside. "Are you saying that everyone else is outside having supper while I'm sitting here getting waited on like a queen?"

"Many have gathered around the cooking fire," he admitted, easing into a cross-legged position by the opening. "Not all have ventured outside."

His glance fell on a feathered crucifix featuring what Sissy thought might be the Cheyenne version of Jesus, and her polite suitor suddenly became a jealous child.

"Where did this come from?" he asked, grabbing the cross.

"A fellah come by and gave it to me. I couldn't understand a word he said, but he insisted that I keep it."

"Was the man His Bad Horse?"

She shrugged. "He didn't mention nothing about no horses."

Long Belly glared at the figure on the cross. "*Hesowxemehne* would do this. He has studied at the mission."

"What'd you say his name was?"

"Slippery Monster, a man who once was my friend. I think he carved this dog soldier to make himself proud with Blackrobe at the mission. Now he uses it to court my woman."

Court his woman? Sissy could hardly believe that she had one suitor. How was it possible that she had two?

The crucifix clutched firmly in his hand, Long Belly got to his feet. "*Hesowxemehne* will be very sorry he came to you after I stake him out beneath the Big Hard Face Moon tonight."

"Hey," she said, climbing to her feet. "I don't want no one getting staked or hurt over me. Your monster friend didn't do nothing wrong or treat me bad. You leave him be."

Long Belly scowled, but said, "I must speak to him then, only speak. And then I will return with a better gift—a fine young horse just for you."

Then he tore out of the tipi so fast, Sissy didn't even get a chance to thank him for the soup. She supposed that she really ought to have at least told Long Belly that she'd finally come to a decision regarding his proposal. She didn't know much about the proper behavior when it came to accepting or declining a man, but it struck her that informing him the minute she'd made her decision would probably be the kind thing to do.

Sissy glanced around the tipi at all her lovely gifts, thinking what a shame it would be when all of this ended—not just the presents, but the adoration and attention that came with them, everything she'd never had before and would never have again.

She would have to tell Long Belly about her decision, no doubt about it. But maybe it could wait until tomorrow.

In the cabin, Daniel was not sleeping, but wondering what could be taking Josie so long. She'd said that she was just going to have a quick look at her stinky friend, not spend the night with the damn thing. He wandered over to the counter and helped himself to a handful of cookies. As he stuffed one of them into his mouth, Two Moons cried out from the loft above.

"No, no, Papa, do not eat," he said in Cheyenne. "Ma Jofess makes these with poison, and you will die."

"Poison?"

Daniel looked up to see that both boys were peering down at him in horror. What in the hell had Josie done to them this time? And why, oh why, couldn't she make a little more effort to get along with the twins?

"What makes you think the cookies are poisoned?" he asked.

"Ma Jofess is evil," he said.

"And says she has bad medicine for us," added Bang.

"She wishes us dead," Two Moons finished. "And even told us of the poison."

Daniel knew that Josie wasn't particularly fond of the boys just yet, and that they hadn't completely accepted her, but he also knew this poison theory had to have stemmed from a big misunderstanding.

"Ma Josephine likes to make jokes," he explained with a chuckle. "But I think they might be a little difficult for you boys to understand. She's been feeding you these cookies for a week now and no one got poisoned." He sniffed a cookie, then took a bite of it. "They taste and smell exactly the same as they did before—delicious."

With that, he stuffed the rest of the cookie into his mouth, but even that wasn't enough to convince the boys they were safe. They stayed put, whispering to each other in their own unique version of Cheyenne.

Daniel wandered over to the window and glanced outside. Snow was still falling, but in gentle flurries now, making it possible to see the barn. There was no sign of Josie, who should have returned by now. Daniel thought about how nervous the buffalo had been when he tossed some hay to it and the cattle, and a certain uneasiness came over him. What if her damned pet had turned on her, goring a big hole in her chest and leaving her to bleed to death in the snow? It was too real a possibility to ignore.

Daniel swept the buffalo spread from his bed to use as a shield against the cold wind. "You boys stay right where you are," he cautioned. "I'm going to go outside to see what's keeping your ma."

Struggling to wrap his body in the heavy hide, Daniel started for the door about the time it suddenly burst open. Two Cheyenne braves bulldozed their way into the cabin with one of them holding Josie tightly against his chest. He had a big hunting knife creasing the skin at her throat.

The other brave pointed to Daniel and said in his native language, "Put your hands where we can see them."

Daniel let the hide fall to the floor and then spread his arms out at his sides. Also speaking Cheyenne, Daniel said, "As you can see, I am unarmed. Turn the woman loose."

The brave ignored him and directed his next words to his companion. "Daniel Two Skins does not remember us, yet he claims his work is to better the lives of the Cheyenne. He is no different from the white Indian agents who cheated us."

"That's not true," Daniel said. "Remove your coats so I can see who is speaking. And please, release my woman so we can talk as friends."

"Bah, friends."

Still, the brave peeled off his heavy coat and tossed it on the floor. As he helped his companion out of his jacket, Daniel recognized the speaker as Wolf Lies Down, a warrior who'd been banished from the tribe after killing two men during a camp quarrel. He'd left the reservation with his wife, Walking Strange, and a few other relatives, including his children.

Once the second warrior's jacket was removed, Daniel immediately remembered him as Stump Horn, cousin to Wolf Lies Down. Again trying to get him to lay the weapon aside, he said, "I know you both, and have no argument with either of you. Release my wife and the three of us can have a smoke and discuss your problems."

"We did not come here to smoke." Wolf Lies Down advanced on him, brandishing his knife. "Our children heard much talk at the mission about a great buffalo you keep penned. We have come to claim this beast as our own."

That stinking buffalo. Daniel almost wished he'd never laid eyes on the goddamned thing. "Take it if you must," he snapped irritably. "But be warned that the buffalo belongs to all of your brothers. They know it is here and that I am keeping it safe for them until the spring. When they come for it and it is gone, they will hunt you down and kill you."

Wolf Lies Down raised a fist and shook it at Daniel. "We are starving! Is it more noble to die with our bellies flat against our spines than at the hands of my brothers? My family will not last this terrible winter if we do not have that buffalo."

Daniel could see how scrawny they were without their coats to hide their slender bodies, and that they were half frozen. He wondered how they had ever found his place or even gone in search of it during the storm that had just passed through. He shifted his gaze to Josie and gave thanks that she couldn't understand the conversation. God knew what she'd do if she realized her captors intended to slaughter her precious pet. He was going to have a hard enough time convincing the renegades that they were wasting time holding her hostage without Josie attacking them.

"Release my wife," he repeated, this time with more authority. "Then we will discuss ways of feeding your family."

"Stump Horn will keep his knife at your woman's throat until we find a way to make this great buffalo follow me to our camp."

Daniel didn't care for the intensity in the warrior's manner or the crazed look in his companion's eyes. He remembered hearing a couple a weeks back that a band of renegades, probably these two here along with their women, had been surprised by a rancher and his cowhands while in the midst of stealing the man's cattle. In the ensuing confrontation, the renegades were run off empty-handed, but not before they killed the rancher. In addition to being shunned by the members of their own tribe, they were now hunted by white lawmen, a fact that would make them utterly ruthless.

If that weren't enough to complicate matters, Daniel realized that Josie's skin had gone pale beneath her freckles and that her eyes were glazed over with fear, a condition that put her in a helpless and dangerous daze. He'd been working hard to help make her understand that the Cheyenne were not so unlike her own family, but now he could see that all his efforts were for naught. If he didn't do something soon to secure Josie's release, she might just up and faint, and thereby invite her own accidental death.

"All right," Daniel said to Wolf Lies Down. "I'll help you get the buffalo, but not until you release my wife."

"You do not make the rules!" Wolf Lies Down jabbed his knife at Josie's ribs. She flinched and opened her mouth as if to scream, but didn't cry out. Then the renegade said, "Your woman will stay here with Stump Horn and you will come with me to help secure the buffalo for our journey back to camp."

As he recognized the desperation in both men's eyes and the despair in Josie's, Daniel realized that up until this moment, he'd lulled himself into believing that he was playing a game with her, that their relationship was little more than make-believe husband and wife. Standing here helplessly watching as a knife pressed deep into the skin he loved to kiss, he could almost feel the blade cutting into her, severing the pulse that had thrummed so passionately against his lips last night. Suddenly he knew what it would mean to lose her—and not as a wife or mother to his sons. As the woman he loved.

"I'll do whatever I can to help you," he promised. In an effort to hide the intense hatred he suddenly felt for this man, Daniel struggled to keep his voice level and reasonably friendly. "But I will not leave my wife here with a knife against her throat."

The renegade's eyes glittered with malice. "Then perhaps you would prefer to leave her behind with a knife *in* her throat." Wolf Lies Down turned to Stump Horn and shouted, *"Kill her!"*

Up in the loft, as quiet and still as a pair of newborn fawns in tall grass, Bang and Two Moons silently watched the argument between their father and the two angry warriors. In the way of all Cheyenne children, they had learned as infants that crying or speaking out in times of fear or anger was a danger to the entire tribe, and that the sound of their voices might alert an enemy to their presence. The early lessons were not forgotten.

The boys had seen enough wailing infants taken away from the camp and left alone to cry themselves out to know that they had also received the same treatment. As unruly two-year-old boys, they remembered their grandmother pouring ice-cold water over their heads until they quit fighting and their rage was quenched. Bang and Two Moons knew full well that this was a time for quiet observation. Their instincts were keen.

With just the tops of their heads and watchful eyes above the lip of the loft, they continued to listen to the conversation below. Although Bang didn't understand everything that was said, he sensed that his father and Ma Jofess were in danger. Bang was frightened for himself, but terrified that some harm would come to his father. He was even a little bit worried about the woman. She sometimes made with the mean face when she looked upon him and Two Moons, but then sometimes she smiled at them, too, and she always made good food.

When the hateful warrior, the one who called himself Wolf Lies Down, ordered his friend to kill Ma Jofess, Bang's father lunged toward the warrior, and the two fell to the ground. At almost the same time, the one called Stump Horn drew blood with his knife, and then Ma Jofess crumpled onto the floor.

Knowing instinctively that they were all in grave danger, Bang whispered to his twin, "What can we do?"

Two Moons did not speak or move. He was so paralyzed with fear, he didn't even blink when the question was repeated. Left alone with the big decision, Bang crawled silently to the back corner of the room and grabbed hold of the only weapon he could carry in one chubby hand—Long Belly's spiked club.

Creeping back to the lip of the loft, he peered down to see that Ma Jofess was still lying on the floor. His father continued to grapple with Wolf Lies Down. Behind the two wrestlers, Stump Horn approached, raising his knife as he prepared to drive it into the unsuspecting back of Bang's father. His tiny heart pounding with fear, Bang prayed that he would remember the lessons learned at play when he'd tossed toy hatchets as if they were real. He then rose to his knees and flung the old club at Stump Horn as hard as his little four-year-old arm could throw it.

The weapon clattered to the floor a few yards short of its target, but the noise distracted the warrior before he had a chance to stab Bang's father. Stump Horn whirled around in place, then glanced up at the loft.

Laughing evilly when he saw Bang, who'd forgotten to take cover, the warrior muttered something about ridding the cabin of vermin. Then he headed for the ladder.

As Bang prostrated himself beside his brother again, the last thing he saw was a bright twinkle bouncing off the tip of Stump Horn's knife. It reminded him of *Wohehiv,* the Morning Star, and of the Hanging Road above, known to the whites as the Milky Way. It was said that when a Cheyenne died, his spirit traveled up this Hanging Road to the bode of the Wise One Above.

Bang wondered if he would enjoy living among his long-lost loved ones as much as he'd enjoyed his life here on earth.

Chapter Twenty-One

Just as he thought he had Wolf Lies Down in his grasp, the warrior rolled, taking Daniel with him, and pinned him flat against the floor. Raising his knife high above his head, the Cheyenne swung it downward in a vicious, slashing motion. Daniel caught the man's wrist at the last minute, then bent it forward, forcing him to continue the arc he'd begun. The blade glanced off the warrior's ribs, then buried itself in his guts.

At almost the same moment, a terrific explosion rattled Daniel's eardrums. He pushed the wounded Indian away from his body, then rolled to his feet and saw that Josie was facing the ladder, her back to him. Halfway up to the loft, Stump Horn dangled from the steps, a look of surprise on his face. Then he suddenly fell away from the ladder and hit the floor with a soft thud.

"Josie?" Daniel said, trying to piece the events together. "Did you just fire my gun?"

"I pulled back the hammer." Sounding dazed, she turned with the Peacemaker still clutched between both hands. Blood ringed one side of her throat, half of a macabre necklace. "I pulled back the hammer."

"Josie—Christ! Don't move."

She pitched forward despite his instructions, and Daniel had all he could do to reach her before she hit the floor. After he'd gathered her into his arms and carried her to the bed, he sat down beside her to examine the wound more closely.

On the floor a few feet away, Wolf Lies Down groaned in agony.

"Papa," a small voice from above suddenly whispered. "Can we come down now?"

"No," Daniel said sharply. "I'll let you know when it's safe to move."

Josie, who was semiconscious, fluttered her lashes, but didn't open her eyes. "A knife," she murmured. "That savage has a knife."

"Shush." Daniel pressed the edge of his pillow against her throat, checking the flow of blood. "Don't talk and don't move."

"But he's going after the twins."

"The twins are fine." Christ, had she saved the lives of his boys? Daniel's throat tightened with unfamiliar emotions, and he had to swallow hard just to breath easily again.

"Am I hurt?" Josie whispered.

"Just a little," he lied, embellishing the tale so she wouldn't realize how close she'd come to meeting her maker. She was in shock now, but the pain would come soon enough, and along with it, the memory of Stump Horn's knife at her throat. "You hurt your shoulder when you fell."

"Silly me." Incredulously enough, she smiled. "I guess I must have fainted or something."

The fact that Josie had passed out was nothing short of a miracle, the one thing, near as Daniel could figure, that had saved her life. Wiping the wound clean, he took the pillow away from her throat. Blood was oozing now, not pulsing out of the cut, which meant that Stump Horn's knife had slipped as she fainted, costing him the angle on her jugular as well as the opportunity for a quick kill.

Daniel parted the cut with his fingers, gauging its depth and severity, and finally got a reaction out of Josie.

"Ow, that hurts," she cried. "What did you do to my neck?"

"You have a little cut there, but it's nothing. I'll just get something to clean it out. Don't move."

He rose, grateful that she'd closed her eyes and showed no signs of arguing with him, then paused to take a look at the fallen warrior. Wolf Lies Down was barely hanging on to his life. With another glance at Josie, who was resting comfortably, Daniel hurried to where the Indian lay.

"Wake up, man," he said in rapid Cheyenne as he hunkered down beside him. "Where is your family, your women and children?"

The warrior cracked his eyelids. Then he stupidly used most of what was left of his strength to hurl a wad of spit.

Daniel wiped his cheek, then took Wolf Lies Down roughly by the shoulders. "Don't be a damn fool. It's too late to save your miserable hide, but your family still has a chance. Where are they? Tell me so I can save them from certain starvation."

Daniel could feel the warrior's life ebbing beneath his fingertips, and worried that the same thing might be happening to Josie. He raised his voice in frustration. "They don't have to die, dammit. I promise if you tell me where your family is, they won't have to live on the run anymore. Now where the hell are they?"

The light in his eyes dimming with each breath that he took, Wolf Lies Down finally whispered directions to an area at the southeast fringes of the reservation. The spot was about five or six miles from Daniel's cabin, but in this weather, he figured it might as well have been a hundred.

"You will save them?" Wolf Lies Down eked out.

"I promise that I'll find them and make sure that they are returned safely to the tribe." Then, with a feeble nod, the formerly great warrior died in Daniel's arms.

"Now, Papa?" asked Bang.

"No!"

Since he rarely shouted at the boys, the rebuke startled Daniel almost as much as it did his younger son. But with two dead warriors and Josie bleeding all over his bed, he figured the twins would be better off viewing the carnage from above than from close up. Leaving the problem of what to do with the bodies for later, Daniel grabbed a few clean cloths, a needle and thread, and a bottle of whiskey before returning to Josie.

By then she was moaning and clutching her throat. "It hurts," she whimpered. "Why does it hurt so much?"

"Here," he said, filling a capful of whisky and bringing it to her lips. "Drink this and you'll feel better in no time."

Josie wrinkled her nose at the smell, then shuddered slightly as the alcohol bathed her tongue. Daniel refilled the cap and brought it to her lips again, repeating the process until she lay there grinning at him in a drunken stupor. Then he poured a thin river of whisky along the wound, and got busy with the disagreeable task of sewing her neck back together again.

As he worked, flinching each time his needle pierced her delicate skin, Daniel thought about the odd way they'd come together and how much she'd come to mean to him over the past few weeks. He'd been so certain that he didn't want another woman in his life, so damned determined to send Josie back to where she'd come from, that he could hardly believe how possessive he felt toward her now. She was his, and not simply because Father van der Velden had said so. His because Daniel wanted her, now and forever.

It was with a little stab of guilt that he glanced up to where his sons lay peering down as he worked on Josie's neck. He'd never felt so strongly about their mother. Never had he been so utterly solicitous of her either, or so damned frustrated when he couldn't get her to see eye to eye with him. With Tangle Hair, Daniel had simply walked away whenever an argument came to a stalemate. With Josie, he felt compelled to fight to the bitter end. Surprisingly enough, he got almost as much satisfaction when she emerged the victor as when he did.

Daniel wasn't quite sure why things were so, but it sure as hell wasn't because Josie was the perfect wife. He'd drawn many comparisons between her and Tangle Hair since the day they first met, and until recently Josie had always been eclipsed by her Cheyenne counterpart when it came to matters of hearth and home. Why should it be that this inferior wife had such a strong hold on him, a bond that made him feel as if he'd been mated for life?

Just asking himself that question finally clarified the main difference between the two women. Daniel had felt affection for Tangle Hair, and a definite sense of duty. But before Josie, he'd never known what it was to love.

It was dark in the cabin when Josie came around again, even though the flame from a single candle flickered at the table. Her head felt fuzzy, as did her tongue, and a dull ache bumped against the back of her skull. A sharper pain, more of a sting or a burn, bubbled at the side of her neck. She gently eased her fingers across the area, feeling a series of odd little bumps that felt as if she were petting the back of a very long centipede. Then suddenly she remembered the knife at her throat and realized what those tiny knolls represented—stitches.

Josie's eyes flew open in horror. Indians surrounded her bed as she'd feared, but the big round eyes staring at her belonged to Bang and Two Moons. One at each side of the mattress, they appeared to be standing guard over her, a sneaky little pair of pisspots disguised as miniature sentries.

Surprised to hear her own voice sounding so weak, she asked, "Where's your pa?"

One of them, Josie was too disoriented to figure out which, said, "In the barn. Food to animals."

She closed her eyes, relieved to know for sure that Daniel was all right. "Have you fellahs had your supper yet?"

A long silence, save for the slight rustle of their buckskin shirts, told Josie that the boys were either nodding or shaking their heads. She was suddenly too tired to open her eyes, so she said, "Yes or no?"

"Yes, Ma Jofess." More rustling of buckskins. Then a husky

voice again, but closer, at her ear. "Stump Horn and his knife meant to kill us. You put the big bullet in his heart."

Josie had to think about that for a minute before it made sense. Then she remembered taking Daniel's gun from the shelf and firing it at one of the savages. Her eyes flew open again.

"Are you two all right?" she asked, looking from one to the other.

They nodded in unison. Then the boy at her ear—Bang, she thought—lifted the animal-shaped bag at his neck, gave her a shy smile, and said, "Is not bad medicine. Is from my belly."

Again, it took her a minute, but Josie finally decided that he must be referring to his umbilical cord, and that his mother had sewn it inside the bag as part of a Cheyenne ritual.

"Thank you for telling me," she said, pleased by the child's small offering of friendship. "I guess in that case it's only fair to let you know that my cookies aren't poisoned, and never were."

"Pa said so to us!" Two Moons, who'd been silent but curious until then, slipped back into his usual belligerent attitude. "You lie."

Josie's weary gaze flickered over the boy, noting that his large dark eyes still burned with something akin to hatred whenever he looked at her. Bang muttered something to him in Cheyenne, and Two Moons responded with a series of quick, biting words that sounded as if they were curses or the like. Josie didn't need to understand the language to know that the twins were arguing over her, and that the hatred Two Moons felt carried far more clout than his brother's tiny show of sympathy. Bang struggled against his twin's arguments for a moment, but then dissolved into tears about the same time his father came back into the cabin.

"Oh, Christ," Daniel said, shrugging out of his jacket. "Now what?"

Two Moons quickly ran to him, babbling in his native language and pointing to Josie. Daniel glanced at her and frowned. By then Bang was at his side telling his version of the trouble. When the second twin finished, Daniel said something to both boys in Cheyenne that sent them scurrying up the ladder, leaving him alone with her.

"You saved my boys," he said, sitting down beside her. "I'll never be able to thank you enough. Never."

She wanted to shrug, but thought better of it. Her cheeks were warm with embarrassment. "Anyone would have shot that no-account heathen, going after helpless children with a knife."

"It wasn't just anyone. It was you."

There was something too intimate in Daniel's voice, too profound for Josie to face or accept. She closed her eyes.

"Try to stay awake a little longer," he said. "How are you feeling? Throat hurt?"

Her eyes popped open. "It stings a little, but it doesn't hurt near as much as the inside of my head does. What did you give me to drink?"

"Whiskey." His mouth twisted into a sideways grin. "Want some more?"

Josie's stomach rolled. "No, thank you. I could use a little tea. I don't suppose you have any?"

Daniel shook his head. "Sorry, fresh out. How about some ham and fried potatoes? I cooked some up for supper earlier. There's plenty left for you."

At the very thought of food, Josie's belly clenched in painful spasms. "No," she said. "Dear God, no. All I want is to rest a while." Then she closed her eyes again, this time intending to keep them that way, and settled deeper into the pillow.

"Don't go to sleep on me, Josie. Not yet." He gently patted her cheek. "I have to talk to you."

With a carefully controlled yawn, one that didn't pull her stitches too much, she rubbed the weariness from her eyes and said, "Can't it wait until morning?"

"Morning is what I want to talk about." He rose and began to remove his clothing. "I know you're in a certain amount of pain, but that cut isn't very deep. It seems to me that you should be able to tend the animals by tomorrow night. What do you think?"

"I suppose I could if I had to, but why would I have to? You've hardly let me near the barn since we got back from the mission."

Stripped down to his woolen drawers, Daniel blew out the lamp and slipped beneath the blankets beside her before he answered. "I have to head out first thing in the morning to try and find the women and children those two renegades left behind. I may not make it back before nightfall."

Panic gripped her at the thought. "But Daniel—you can't leave me here alone in the dead of winter. What if something happens to you?"

"I'll be fine," he assured her in the darkness. "And you won't be alone. Bang and Two Moons are here. They could really be a big help to you if you'd just give them a chance."

Josie wanted to laugh, but restrained herself. "I'd rather take my chances alone, thank you, than with that pair."

"Why the hell do you have so much trouble getting along with my boys?" Daniel's voice was sharp with impatience. "I can't leave you alone with the twins for two minutes without your upsetting them or making them cry. Is it asking too much for you to try and be nice to them?"

Josie paused for a deep breath, long enough anyway to keep from saying something she'd probably regret. Besides, nothing she said would convince him that his little pisspots were anything but precious angels who craved her approval. He would never believe that at least one of them would loved to have seen her dead.

"I do try to be nice to those boys," she finally said. "We don't seem to be able to communicate too well, I guess, but I really am trying with them. I saved their hides from that crazy savage, didn't I?"

"Yes, you did, and I already told you how grateful I am for that." Daniel slipped his arm around her shoulder, then nuzzled the back of her ear as he said, "The boys are grateful, too, believe me, and want to learn to get along with you. Will you give them another chance while I'm gone?"

Tears stung her eyes and an unreasonable rage rent the walls of her chest. "No, because I don't want you to leave at all. Why must you go?"

"For one thing, as the Cheyenne's agent, it's my job." Daniel pulled her more fully into his arms and kissed her softly on the mouth. "For another, even if it wasn't my job, I'd have to go. Surely you understand that."

"No, I don't." Josie didn't want to understand and she didn't want to be reasonable. She just wanted Daniel. "It's too risky for you. You said yourself that even the cattle couldn't survive another blizzard like the last. What makes you think you can?"

"I can because I have to. Do you want me to leave those helpless women and children out there to starve or freeze to death?"

She could hardly say "yes" to that. In fact, she wouldn't have wanted him in the same bed if he turned out to be the kind of no-account bastard who could stay with her in favor of rescuing those poor unfortunates. But she was damned if she had to like it. Josie knew Daniel was right on all counts, knew that of course he had to go, but God, how she hated him and their circumstances at that moment. She hated Daniel McCord almost as much as she hated his sense of honor and the fact that he was compelled to do the right thing. Somewhere deep inside, Josie had to admit that her reaction probably meant that she loved him a little bit, too.

The next morning before dawn, Daniel woke up with a start. He'd dreamed that the two renegades had awakened from death, crept away from the temporary and frozen tomb he'd prepared for them in his wellhouse, and were stalking him inside his own cabin. He listened intently, hearing nothing but the wind and the sound of his own heartbeat thundering through his ears. He laughed out loud at his own far too realistic imagination.

"Daniel?" Josie whispered. "What is it?"

He rolled toward her. "Sorry. I didn't mean to disturb you. I woke up in the middle of a dream."

"You didn't wake me. I've been lying here for some time

now trying to figure out a way to keep us all together. I was thinking that maybe the boys and I should go with you this morning.''

"Absolutely not. Not only does it sound like another storm might be on the way, who would feed the animals if we all leave? We even have an extra horse now, thanks to our uninvited guests, and it's going to need a lot of care over the next few days. If that isn't enough to convince you, think of your poor Sweetpea—she'd never forgive you if you left her alone.''

She grumbled a little, irritated by all the sound arguments he'd thrown her way, but snuggled closer to Daniel anyway. "What if I think of a way to make you stay here with me?''

Before he knew what she was up to, Josie had slipped her hand inside his drawers and found what he was quite unable to hide. Although Daniel rippled with a rush of pleasure at her touch, his Cheyenne education in the ways of women during their monthly bleeding was enough to dampen his ardor.

"Keep that thought,'' he said, removing her hand from his drawers. "Maybe by the time I get back, you'll be able to show me what you had in mind.''

"I can show you now,'' she insisted, draping one of her legs across his hip in open invitation. Again her hand went to his crotch, this time fondling him through the woolen material. "Believe me, I doubt this will delay your trip much.''

The last thing Daniel was worried about was losing time on the trail. "It's not that I don't want you, sweetheart—you know that I do and how much—but don't we have to wait until your—ah, you know, monthlies are over?''

"Oh, that.'' She laughed softly. "Those Indian friends of yours must have scared all that right out of me yesterday morning. Near as I can figure, my monthly stopped the minute that savage put his knife on my throat.''

Tangle Hair's female concerns had always kept her at the women's special lodge for upwards of a week, never less. A single day was unheard of.

"You're sure it's all right?''

"I'm sure.''

Josie increased her efforts on his behalf, making it difficult for Daniel to remember why he'd resisted in the first place.

Then she said, "Are you going to waste what little time we have before those heathen twins of yours wake up, or are you going to give me a good and proper farewell?"

There was plenty of good in what Daniel did next, but not one hell of a lot that could be thought of as proper. He also discovered that the memory of their lusty farewell was kindling enough to help warm him when he finally set out that morning, and a good thing, too. According to Daniel's personal thermometer—a method of spitting, then watching carefully to see whether the wad froze in the air or when it hit the snow—the temperature was around twenty below zero, and still dropping. If he didn't get to the renegade families soon, there would be no point in going after them.

At the Cheyenne encampment, Sissy was running out of excuses for delaying her response to Long Belly's proposal.

"It is true," he said, "that in the Cheyenne way, I would not be in so much a hurry for us to marry, nor would I embarrass you by asking you to be my wife. I would send a sister or perhaps a cousin to ask your permission. I would do these things and wait as long as I had to for you, but this is different between us. We should marry now."

Although she had a pretty good idea where he was going, Sissy said, "How so?"

"You are not Cheyenne, for one thing." Long Belly sighed, then raised his hands in frustration and rolled his eyes. "For another, I have touched your womanly parts. Because of this, you are mine. Why can you not say that you will marry me?"

It was time. Past time. Sissy knew that she'd been a little selfish in keeping her reply to herself for so long, but she'd hated the thought of her fantasy world coming to an end. Now she had to forget about herself, close this unexpected and lovely chapter of her life, and get back to what she really was.

"Sorry I took so long thinking about it," she said, her gaze fixed and staring at the fire. "I guess I took my time 'cause I didn't rightly know how to tell you that I cain't marry you."

He didn't respond at first. When he finally did, the direction Long Belly's thoughts took surprised Sissy so, she nearly fell over.

There was murder in his eyes, but his voice was strangely calm as he said, "You have chosen Slippery Monster as your mate?" The name was just another odd and particularly hilarious label to her at first, but then Sissy remembered that Slippery Monster was the warrior who'd brought her the little crucifix. Despite her sad heart, she found herself laughing.

"I don't know how you Cheyenne folks come up with such crazy names." She paused to catch her breath, then looked up at him. "How do you keep a straight face when you introduce each other?"

"Straight face? What does this mean?"

Sissy sobered. "This is a straight face," she said without moving her lips. "And it just means that you don't laugh when you meet someone named Not Quite a Bear, or Sticks Everything Under His Belt, or Afraid of Beavers."

Long Belly reflected a perfectly straight face as he said logically, "Why would I laugh at Afraid of Beavers? She is my cousin."

"Because her name sounds funny. Don't you think so?"

A serious suitor who wouldn't be dissuaded from his purpose, Long Belly said, "No, Afraid of Beavers is not funny. Nothing will make me laugh until you agree to be my wife."

Sissy sighed. "Well, then, that's just one more reason why we ain't suited enough to get married."

"I am wrong," he quickly said. "If it pleases you, I will laugh when I hear that you are asking for my cousin." He threw his head back and forced a round of belly laughs. "Now please, let me tell my mother that she and the others can begin our wedding feast."

"Oh, red man, you crazy fool." Sissy slowly climbed to her feet, her heavy heart weighing her down. "I'd marry you if I could, but it ain't right. I ain't good enough for any man cause of my whoring past."

"This is no concern of mine."

The sentiment touched her, even though Sissy wasn't quite sure she believed it, but there was another, more troubling reason why she could never hold him to his proposal.

"This might concern you," she said. "My insides is messed up. I cain't never have your babies."

His cinnamon skin, a shade or two lighter than her own, flushed to the color of a ripe berry. Then, surprising her, Long Belly's wide mouth spread into an even bigger grin. "You thought this was reason enough to keep me waiting for your answer these many days?"

"Well, yeah." Embarrassed by having her selfishness pointed out, Sissy hung her head. "Sorry I didn't tell you sooner. I just figured I'd enjoy myself a little before you sent me away."

"Oh, brown woman," he said, crushing her to his chest. "Perhaps Buffalo Hair is the wrong Cheyenne name for you. I think you should be called Woman Who Thinks Too Much and Speaks Too Little."

Letting her head fall back, Sissy looked up into his dark eyes. "Speak English, red man. I cain't follow you."

Long Belly released her, then brought the tip of his index finger to his own nose. "I say this is your child, the only one we need, and I confess, a very naughty child who must have many lessons on how to be a good husband."

"You mean that?" Sissy didn't dare believe that she'd heard him right. She couldn't, and continue to go on living, if she'd heard wrong. "You don't care if you never get no sons of your own?"

His gaze never leaving hers, Long Belly slowly shook his head.

"Yes" was perched on the tip of Sissy's tongue, and yet she heard herself say, "Why? I gotta know why you'd want to tie yourself to a used-up whore that cain't have your babies."

The back of Long Belly's hand grazed her nipples, more

contact than he'd allowed since bringing her to the encampment. "I would be very jealous if other lips suckled your breasts," he whispered fervently. "But I would very much like to do this myself tonight."

"You can and have done that and a whole lot more without getting hitched to me." Sissy knew the likelihood of Long Belly saying the words she'd never heard before were remote, but she couldn't stop herself from asking for them. "What's the real reason?"

He looked away from her as if ashamed. "It is the burning I told you about."

A sudden pressure swelled at the back of Sissy's eyes. "What burning is that, red man?"

Long Belly thumped his own chest, still unable to look her in the eye. "It is the burning I feel in here when I look upon you. It is like a great prairie fire that burns so far and so deep, even the rains from the All Father cannot put out the flames."

"You . . ." She swallowed hard against them, but the tears fell anyway, spilling down her cheeks and into her mouth as she said, "You love me?"

Finally looking at her again, Long Belly took Sissy's damp face between his big hands and said, "I love you."

Chapter Twenty-Two

As Daniel feared it might, it took him most of the day to find the lone tipi hidden amongst the snow-shrouded oaks and junipers at the lower-elevation hidey-hole. If that wasn't enough, the weather had turned nasty again, showering him with snow and slowing The Black's progress through deep powder that reached the stallion's chest in places.

After Daniel announced himself and stepped inside the tipi, he half expected to be attacked by the women the renegades had left behind. To his surprise and dismay, they barely stirred in their beds. He hadn't gotten to them any too soon.

"I am Daniel Two Skins," he said in Cheyenne. "I have come to take you with me. Wolf Lies Down told me I would find you here and that you would follow me back to my cabin. Are you well enough to travel?"

One of the women rose slightly from where she lay, and Daniel immediately recognized her as Walking Strange, wife of Wolf Lies Down. She opened the buffalo hide she'd wrapped around her body to reveal that her belly was terribly swollen.

"I cannot walk far," she said, her voice frail. "The child

of Wolf Lies Down lies heavy in my body. He waits for me at your cabin?''

Daniel nodded, intent on gaining her trust before informing her that her husband was dead. His glance went to the lump beneath yet another buffalo robe. ''Is your friend well enough to travel?''

''She is called Little Skunk and is very weak. She nurses the daughter of Stump Horn.''

Daniel remembered that one of the men had mentioned a family as if there were more than just the one infant. ''Where are the other children?''

''Wolf Lies Down took them to the mission to learn their lessons. He thought that if we did not come back for them, the Blackrobe would keep them safe and well during the winter. Is this true?''

Daniel nodded, assuming those children were the sickly boys he'd seen in Father van der Velden's kitchen. In any case, Walking Strange had nothing to fear. Her sons would be fed and no harm would come to them as long as they were on mission property. With himself and The Black as their only means of survival, Daniel wasn't so sure he could say the same about two starving women and a helpless infant.

When morning came two days after Daniel's departure and he still hadn't returned, Josie had half a mind to saddle up the mare and go after him. He'd mentioned the possibility that he might have to spend one night on the trail, but never had he suggested that he would be gone as many as two. Or, God forbid, three. She was already crazy with worry, not to mention slightly deranged after spending two days and nights trying to be both mother and father to Daniel's little pisspots.

Josie regarded the twins, quiet for a change as they gobbled up the pancakes and eggs she'd fixed for their breakfast. When he wasn't huddled with Two Moons, Bang was turning out to be a nice, thoughtful young man, a boy who reminded her in some ways of Caleb. Every chance he got, he'd sneak up beside

her, tap on her leg, and whisper, "I got tell you sumpting."
Usually the big secret was nothing more than a compliment
about her cooking, her pretty auburn hair, or yet another request
to try and wash the magical dots off of her face. Josie made a
mental note to ask Daniel to explain that freckles could never
be washed away from a person's skin, although God knew
she'd tried.

Two Moons, on the other hand, had to be the devil incarnate.
Josie could certainly understand that he might harbor a little
resentment over the thought of her taking his mother's place
in his father's life, and to some extent in his own. She had
tried to explain that she would only intrude in their lives until
spring, and that she had no aspirations of becoming his full-
time mother, but he either couldn't or wouldn't understand. In
fact, the little heathen laughed in her face. He didn't, Josie
noticed, glancing his way again, mind eating the food she
cooked. Maybe if she declared a truce using Two Moon's belly
as bait, she'd have better luck with the little pisspot.

By the time the twins finished their breakfast, the wind had
come up and gusts stirred the air. Visibility outside the cabin
was low as blowing snow smudged the landscape, making it
difficult to even pick out the shape of the barn. With each pulse
of wind came a temporary canvas of nothing but pure white,
a painting of a world that had completely disappeared. The
stovepipe groaned under the steadily blowing wind, and the
windows rattled in their frames, allowing puffs of freezing air
to invade the cabin. Time to close and lock the shutters again.

After wrapping herself up tight in the buffalo spread—all
she had by way of a jacket since Daniel had been forced to
wear their only coat out into the storm—Josie cautioned the
boys to sit quietly at the table; then she stepped outside into
the freezing winds. She'd managed to wrestle the shutters closed
on one window, and was heading into the wind to tend to the
window at the kitchen table when a flash of something dark
caught the corner of her eye. Turning, she could make out the
outline of The Black heading toward the barn. Strangely
enough, the shape atop the horse looked nothing like Daniel.

Clutching the buffalo spread tightly to her throat, Josie hurried down the stairs and into the blinding storm. "Daniel?" she called, chasing after the animal. "Is that you?"

By the time she caught up with them, Josie could see that Daniel was leading The Black into the barn, and that the odd-looking rider was in fact two Cheyenne women. She also noticed that the stallion, who'd been untrained before, was now dragging a large travois behind him.

Running past the animal and its burden after they'd entered the barn and closed the door, Josie threw herself into her husband's arms. "Oh, Daniel, I was so worried when you didn't come right back."

He squeezed her tightly, then held her long enough for a thorough kiss. "Sorry," he finally said. "It took me a little longer to get them out of there than I expected. I figured they would at least have a horse, but they didn't. Then we had to take down their tipi and pack it up. Come and meet them."

Taking her by the hand, Daniel led her to The Black. After helping both the women off of the horse, he drew one of them forward and said, "This is Walking Strange. She's going to have a baby any day now."

She peered out at Josie through the hood of her blanket, her eyes both wary and curious, and then let the blanket fall to her shoulders. The woman was filthy, her hair was matted, and there was a large gash on her forehead that hadn't begun to scab over yet. Walking Strange said something in Cheyenne, and Daniel relayed the message to Josie in English.

"She says she is happy to meet you and thanks you for taking pity on her during her time of sorrow." He turned to the other woman, drawing her forward, and said something to her in Cheyenne. When she lowered the hood of her own blanket, Josie saw that she was also in need of a bath and had a fresh gash gouged into her forehead, too.

"This is Little Skunk," Daniel went on to to say in English. "She has a baby daughter to care for, but she's been sick and is in need of a little nursing herself."

"Nice to meet the both of you," Josie said, feeling awkward.

"They look like they could use a nice hot bath. Shall I go put on some water?"

Daniel didn't bother to translate. "They're starving, Josie. They need food, not baths."

"I didn't know that." She couldn't help but grimace. "Can't they bathe and eat? Just look at them. They're filthy and their heads are cut up. What happened? Did you run into trouble on the way back?"

"No." He glanced at the Cheyenne women, smiled, and then said to Josie, "It's part of the grieving process now that they're widows. They are expected to be dirty and ragged, unattractive, and their wounds are self-inflicted."

Josie shuddered over the barbaric rituals these women put themselves through, but did her best to keep a pleasant expression. She opened her arms in invitation, and said, "Follow me to the cabin and we'll get something hot in your bellies."

Daniel passed the message to the women, but they wouldn't budge. After arguing with them for several moments, he finally gave up.

"They really do need some good nourishing food," he said. "But they won't come into our house. As widows, they're also expected to isolate themselves from the rest of the tribe, and I guess that includes us. I'm going to have to help them set up their tipi before we can eat."

Josie hadn't seen the baby yet, but it if was half as frail as its mother, she didn't see how it would ever live through the coming storm. She couldn't even think about the one woman, Walking Strange, giving birth under such conditions.

"Don't they know they'll die if they don't come in from this storm? It's working up to a blizzard out there, or haven't they noticed?"

"They've noticed." Daniel smiled and touched her cheek. "Once we get the tipi set up and I get a good fire going for them, they'll be just as warm and safe from the blizzard as we are in the cabin. All they'll need then is food."

"I'll go get started on a big pot of stew. You look like you could use a good meal yourself—that and a good rest.'' In fact, he looked as if he'd fallen asleep standing up.

The blizzard raged on for a full day, dropping an inch of snow for sixteen of those twenty-four hours. Daniel helped to erect the women's tipi on the south side of the barn, protecting it from as much wind as possible. He also tied a guide rope to one of the stakes, then attached the other end to the main barn door. That way, even in the worst of conditions, either of them could follow one rope from the cabin to the barn, and another from the barn to the tipi.

A couple of mornings after the storm finally let up, Josie made a big pot of soup filled with chunks of beef and dumplings, then directed Daniel to take a large portion of it out to the women in the tipi. As he'd warned, they'd proved to be totally reclusive, accepting nothing from their hosts except food. Josie felt sorry for the widows, especially when Daniel explained that they would isolate themselves this way for at least one year and up to seven, and continued to try coaxing them into the house. All of her overtures were politely turned down.

She was thinking of making a cake for the grieving widows when Daniel suddenly returned to the cabin, his face ashen. He stuttered around a minute, looking positively uncomfortable, and finally said, ''Uh—do you know anything about childbirth?''

Since she'd delivered twelve of her brothers, Josie figured she had some pretty extensive knowledge in that area. Still she hedged, afraid of what might be coming. ''A little. Why? Is Walking Strange in labor?''

''Ah—yes, and from what I could understand, she's having a pretty rough time of it. Little Skunk is still too weak to be of much use. I was hoping you'd know what to do.''

Josie's heart sank. The last difficult birth she'd attended had turned out so badly, she'd cost her own mother her life. Never again did she want to observe or take part in what most folks thought of as the miracle of birth.

''I'm afraid I wouldn't be much help.''

"Can't you at least go look at her and comfort her a little? I don't know what to do."

Josie sighed, knowing she'd never be able to forgive herself if she didn't do that much. "I'll go see her, but that's all. Do they have a pot of hot water going?"

Daniel shrugged, useless as only a man could be at such a time. "I didn't notice."

"In that case you'd better get some water on the stove. Bring it to me as soon as it starts boiling."

Taking the coat right off his shoulders, Josie slipped it on, grabbed the few clean rags she could find, and started for the tipi. She expected to hear at least a couple of yowls coming from inside the thin walls of the buffalo hide abode, but all was quiet, even when she opened the flap and ducked inside. To her surprise, Walking Strange was not lying on her bed, but kneeling on a pile of hay near the fire and hanging onto a stake that had been driven into the ground. She looked up when Josie arrived, her face slick with sweat, then groaned softly and increased her grip on the stake until her knuckles turned white.

"Lie down," Josie suggested, kneeling beside her. She gestured for the woman to recline, but Walking Strange stubbornly shook her head. Seeking an ally, she glanced at Little Skunk, who was nursing her infant in the corner. "Can you make her lie down? I've got to examine her."

Little Skunk just stared back, fear and exhaustion etched in her delicate features. Josie reached for the hem of Walking Strange's dress, and lifted it slightly.

"May I have a look?" she asked.

The mother-to-be nodded, apparently understanding what Josie wanted, and so she raised the dress higher and gauged her progress. The baby's head hadn't begun to emerge, and yet the woman looked as if she'd been straining in the final stages of labor for some time now.

"Lie down, please?" she begged, again using hand gestures to let Walking Strange know what she wanted her to do. The woman still refused to release the stake.

Left with nothing else to do, Josie sat there murmuring words of encouragement and waited for Daniel to arrive with the hot water.

"Is it safe to come in?" he asked from outside the tipi.

"Yes, and hurry," Josie said, desperate for a little help. Walking Strange was sweating profusely by then and straining with no visible results. When Daniel stepped through the flap, she gave him time to hang the water above the fire, then enlisted his aid.

"You've got to talk some sense into this woman. She won't listen to me."

He faced the outer wall, looking away from Josie and her patient. "I shouldn't be in here at all. Can't you just show her what you want her to do?"

He bent over as if to exit. Josie stopped him cold. "Don't you dare walk out on me. If you go, I'm going with you."

"But Josie—"

"But Josie nothing. I try to respect your Cheyenne rituals when I can understand them, but this woman needs help and doesn't seem to want mine. You've got to translate for me."

His back rigid, Daniel gave a short nod. "All right. What do I say?"

"Ask her if she's had a baby before."

"She has. Can I go now?"

"No. Ask her if this is different from the last time."

He spoke rapid-fire Cheyenne, then listened to the woman's weak reply. "She says something is wrong."

This was no surprise to Josie. "Tell her she must lie back so I can examine her. I can't help her if I can't see what's wrong."

Again he spoke in Cheyenne and again the woman offered a feeble reply. This time, when she finished speaking, she rolled away from the stake and curled up in a fetal position.

"That's perfect." Josie crawled over beside her, then continued Daniel's instructions. "Tell her to stay just the way she is, and let her know that what I'm about to do will probably hurt a little."

"Oh, Christ, Josie. I can't——"

"Tell her."

He nodded and slumped his shoulders. After explaining things in Cheyenne, he said to Josie, "I told Walking Strange that you were a midwife with great powers. She promised to do whatever you want from here on out. Can I go now?"

"You're not going anywhere, you miserable no-account coward. I'll probably need you to translate again."

Never, in all his memory, had Daniel ever wanted out of a situation as badly as he wanted out of this tipi. Even worse, he couldn't help but recall the day an extremely huge Tangle Hair went into labor with the twins. Guilt-ridden for having impregnated her in the first place, he'd gone a good long distance away from the birthing tipi and spent the better part of the day absolutely horrified by thoughts of what she must be going through. The experience so disturbed him, Daniel hadn't been the slightest bit disappointed about Josie's reluctance to have children, even if the underlying reason was the fact that she couldn't stand the idea of having a baby that was part Cheyenne. The last thing he wanted was for her to have to bear a child. The second to last thing was to have to stand around listening while another man's wife pushed a baby into the world.

"Oh, shit," Josie said, bringing him back to the present.

"You want me to translate that?"

"No, dammit." She got to her feet and came to him. That was when Daniel noticed that there were tears in her eyes. "The baby is coming feet first, and I think it's stuck."

Daniel squeezed his eyes shut against the sudden mental image of the upside down child. He'd pulled a turned calf once, killing it in the bargain, and couldn't stand the thought of a woman and baby having to suffer the same experience. He suppressed a shudder.

"Can you turn it?" he asked.

"Oh, Daniel, I'm afraid to even try." She threw herself into his arms, muffling her sobs against his chest.

"Take it easy, sweetheart, and don't be afraid. If you don't at least try, Walking Strange will die. You don't want that, do you?''

"Of course not." She pulled back, wiping her tears with the back of her hand. "It's just that the last time I tried to turn a baby, I killed them both, the child and my own mother."

At first Daniel didn't know what to say. He touched Josie's cheek, brushing away a few stray tears, then lightly kissed her forehead. "You didn't kill them, sweetheart. Sometimes these things happen even when we try our best."

"My stepfather didn't see it that way. He—oh, never mind." She glanced over her shoulder to where Walking Strange lay twisting on the bed. "Tell her what's wrong, Daniel. Then tell her that I'm going to try and turn the baby. Tell her to be brave and that I'll do my best not to hurt her too much."

His heart full with something that went beyond the boundaries of love as he knew them, Daniel swallowed his emotions and relayed the message to Walking Strange. When he'd finished and waited for her reply, he translated for Josie.

"She says she understands what you're going to do, and that she wants you to save the child if it comes down to a choice." Daniel hesitated a minute, then added his own thoughts. "I think you ought to do what you can to save the mother."

"That sounds familiar," she said sarcastically as she kneeled down beside her patient. "I think those are the exact words my stepfather said to me just before my mother died."

"Josie—Christ, I'm sorry. I didn't mean—"

"Never mind. I've got work to do."

Intent on Josie, on her courage and the big heart she tried so hard to hide, Daniel buttoned up his lip as she'd asked, but forgot to turn his back to the procedure. Too late to close his eyes against the sight, he saw Josie position herself between Walking Strange's legs and then slip her hand inside the woman. A buzz, something that sounded a lot like a great swarm of bees, suddenly filled the inside of his head. The tipi began to spin, rotating in crazy directions. The next thing Daniel knew, he was falling, falling, and still falling. And then he knew nothing at all.

When he came around again, Daniel wasn't sure where he was or what had happened. For a moment he thought he might even have died. An angel was singing a Christmas carol, of all things, the one about the silent, holy night and virgins and mothers and children. A baby suddenly cried. *Jesus?*

Daniel abruptly sat up, recognizing immediately that he was in the widows' tipi. Josie was singing the Christmas carol, and Walking Strange was lying beneath her buffalo spread, an infant at her breast.

"It's over?" he stupidly said.

Josie turned to him in midsong. "How nice of you to join us again. Yes, it's over. Walking Strange had a boy, and they're both in fine shape."

"Thank God for that."

"You can thank me, too. It wasn't easy."

The memory of what he'd seen just before he passed out suddenly came clear in Daniel's mind. His gut rolled even as he marveled over Josie's strength.

"Thank you," he said, picking himself up off the floor. "You did a wonderful job. Sorry I wasn't more help."

She laughed, easing his conscience. "You were help enough until you got all weak-kneed and passed out. Did you hurt yourself when you fell?"

Embarrassed, he dusted off his trousers. "No, but I might have hit my head a little too hard. I thought I heard you singing Christmas carols when I woke up."

"You did. I was singing 'Silent Night' because near as I can figure, it must be about Christmas, give or take a few days. Once the baby was here and healthy, I felt like singing."

"You're probably not too far off on the date. I'll tell Walking Strange she has a Christmas baby. The way those nuns have been shoving Christianity down the Cheyenne's throats, she might even understand the significance."

After he finished his discussion with the new mother, Daniel laughed as he said, "She understands all right. She's trying to decide between two names for her new son. *Vokeme* is her idea of a proper Christian name. It means Santa Claus."

"We can't let her call the poor thing Santa," she said, laughing. "What's the other choice?"

Daniel smiled. "Spotted Face Sings Nice. After you."

Christmas, as they defined it, came and went, and the snow continued to fall off and on during the first two weeks of January. Temperatures remained at better than twenty below zero, but Daniel was still able to ride out and check on what was left of his herd. Then suddenly, three weeks into the month, a chinook pushed the cold air from the mountains, bringing with it warm, dry winds that began to melt the snow.

Jacketless for the first time since September, Daniel trudged through the slush that filled the path he'd carved between the barn and the cabin, then went about the business of tending to the livestock. When he parted the back door to toss some hay to the buffalo and her bovine companions, he was startled to see that no less than a dozen Cheyenne braves were surrounding the corral.

Each of the men had donned a feathered headpiece and his finest quilled shirt, and their leader, White Bull, wore a quilled robe along with a headdress made of buffalo horns and wolfskins. At the moment, the center of their attention, good old Sweetpea, seemed more curious than alarmed over her surprise visitors. Daniel had worked around the mercurial beast long enough to know that she could go wild at any minute. He tossed the hay in the animal's general direction, then hurried outside to join the tribesman.

"Greetings," he said as he approached. "Our fine warm weather makes for a good visiting day."

"We come to see this buffalo for ourselves," said White Bull. "She is a very impressive beast."

"Impressive," Daniel agreed. "But also very dangerous. She gets pretty upset when strangers are around. Maybe we should go talk somewhere else."

White Bull didn't move. He just kept staring at the buffalo

as if he'd never seen one before. "We will talk and smoke, and when we leave, we will take this great beast with us."

Daniel had worked long and hard to gain the Cheyenne's trust, an especially difficult task considering how badly they'd been treated by some of the other agents they'd been forced to work with. While he felt comfortable around this group, and trusted them as much as he wanted them to trust him, he wasn't quite sure how White Bull and his council would react if he refused their request—which was definitely a declaration, not a petition.

Then, of course, there was Josie's reaction to consider. Could any form of punishment White Bull came up with be worse than what his red-haired wife would do if he let this group ride off with her precious pet? She hadn't been herself for the past few days as it was, crying one minute, grumpy the next. Daniel had pretty much been walking on feathers around her, assuming the monthlies were almost upon her again. If he so much as asked her to allow White Bull to ride off with Sweetpea, it would at least cost him a few incredibly lusty nights spent with her writhing in his arms—and not just because of the monthlies.

Testing what he was beginning to think of as the lesser of two evils, Daniel said, "You fellahs are going to have to leave that buffalo here for the time being. I'll figure out a way to get her down to the encampment by summer."

"The buffalo comes with us now," insisted White Bull. "My people need the joy the sight of this beast will bring to them. It is done."

It would be pointless to argue with the man any longer. He was taking Sweetpea, assuming he could get her to move, and no one could stop him. Daniel was simply going to have to find a way to explain it all to Josie, a chore he intended to put off for as long as humanly possible.

As it turned out, he didn't have nearly as long as he'd hoped. As two of White Bull's companions climbed over the fence and slowly approached the buffalo, the echo of a door slamming against its jamb filled the air, followed shortly by what could only be described as the screech of an enraged woman.

"Stop!" Josie cried as she raced toward the corral. "Stop those sons of bitches right this minute, Daniel. I swear, if anyone so much as lays a finger on Sweetpea, I'll shoot him where he stands!"

Incredulously enough, Daniel saw that she intended to carry out her threat. Josie was waving his Peacemaker toward the two braves in the corral. Instinct guiding him, he stepped between her and the target.

"Get out of my way," she screamed, utterly out of control. "I'd just as soon shoot you as them."

"Josie, for Christ's sake. Shut up and put that gun down before you get us in the kind of trouble I can't explain away."

"Shut up?" Her dark eyes seemed huge and she was breathing hard, just this side of snorting like a mad bull. "Shut up?"

She raised the Peacemaker, pulled back the hammer, and fired. The bullet went whizzing past Daniel's ear, close enough to give him one hell of a fright. He reached for the gun, wresting it away from her before she could cock the damn thing again.

"What the *hell* is wrong with you, woman? You damn near blew my head off."

"Give me back the gun. I promise I won't miss this time." She twisted in his grasp. "Turn me loose."

"Not until you tell me why you're acting so crazy."

"B-because, because . . ." She looked up at him with tears glistening in her eyes, a condition he couldn't reconcile with anger.

"Josie, what's wrong with you?"

"Can't you figure it out?" Tears were streaming down her face by now. "You've gone and knocked me up, you miserable no-account bastard!"

Chapter Twenty-Three

Josie remembered looking out the window and seeing a whole flock of savages done up in warbonnets and other fighting regalia. She even recalled thinking that if she didn't get outside and do something quick, the warriors would harm Sweetpea, or even kill her. What she couldn't remember, even after Daniel had carried her back to the cabin and laid her down on the bed, was threatening to murder him and everyone in sight.

True, she had been a little testy of late, and why the hell not? Last month when the miseries quit on her after just one day, she'd been about half sure that she had a bun in the oven. This month she'd skipped the mess entirely, a sure sign that a baby was under way. This morning when she got out of bed, any doubts she might still have entertained vanished. Not only had she suffered a dizzy spell on her way to the stove, but after one sip of coffee, her stomach lurched and she spat it back up. Now this, taking potshots at her husband. Complete lunacy.

Daniel, who was fussing near the stove, suddenly hurried back to the bed carrying a damp rag and a cup. He placed the cool cloth on her forehead, then sat down beside her.

"Here," he said, offering the cup. "Maybe if you drink some water, you'll feel better."

The thought made her tummy do a somersault. "Not right now, thank you."

Daniel set the cup on the floor. Then he looked at her the way a parent prepares to scold a child—with censure, but a fair amount of compassion. "What happened to you out there?"

Josie shrugged, still angry and too full of conflicting emotions to sort through them. "I don't know."

"You said you were—ah, that we might have had some kind of accident and that you, ah—"

"I'm pregnant, Daniel."

Surprising the hell out of her, his expression reflected the same disappointment she felt.

"You're absolutely sure about that?" he asked.

"If there's one thing in this world I know about, it's when a woman is going to have a baby. My mother had seventeen of them. I'm as sure as I can be."

Daniel brought both hands to his forehead and rubbed furiously for a minute. Then he muttered, "I don't know what to say."

"Shit seems appropriate."

From above them in the loft came a couple of small echoes. "Shit?"

"Shit, shit."

"That's enough," Daniel hollered, following up the reprimand with a few Cheyenne rebukes. Then he glanced down at Josie, his eyebrows drawn together.

"Sorry, I thought they were still asleep," she muttered. "I was raised in a houseful of boys who never minded a thing they said. I guess it kinda rubbed off on me. I'll try not to cuss in front of the twins again."

"I'd appreciate it." He drew in a deep breath and let it out in a long sigh. "Shit," he whispered under his breath.

"My thoughts exactly."

Daniel looked up, the scolding parent again. "Speaking of

your thoughts, you still haven't told me why you took a shot at me.''

Josie sighed, a little unsure of the answer herself. "I wasn't really aiming at you. I just wanted to let those savages know that I meant business." She bolted upright. "My God! Where are they? They haven't taken Sweetpea, have they?''

"No." He tried to remain stern, but Josie could see that Daniel was struggling to keep from laughing. "You scared the blue hell out of them, screeching and shooting off the gun the way you did. Cheyenne men take enraged wives very seriously. They ran out of here so fast, they're probably halfway back to the camp by now.''

Josie could not make herself feel the slightest bit of guilt. "They had no business coming around here in the first place. They're lucky I didn't accidentally shoot one of them.''

"You're lucky you're married to me. God knows what they'd have done if you weren't my wife.''

"Lucky?'' The tears fell then, blinding her. "If I wasn't your wife, I wouldn't be in this condition. You've ruined my life, Daniel McCord, ruined it beyond repair.''

"Is that so?'' Not surprisingly, this remark offended him deeply. He leapt off the bed. "As I recall, you're the one who wanted to get married in the first place. All I've done is give you a roof over your head, a place to keep that stinking buffalo, and a nice big target so you can practice shooting my gun. How the hell did any of that ruin your life?''

"You talked me into doing the hurdy-gurdy, that's how.'' Josie tossed one of the pillows at him, hitting him square in the belly. "All I wanted was my freedom and the chance to build a ranch of my own, but look at me. I'm right back to doing what I swore I'd never do for any man—cooking, cleaning, and God help me, making babies!''

She threw herself face-first into the other pillow then, sobbing against the soft flannel cover, and stayed that way until she felt Daniel's weight on the bed again.

He patted her back as if she were a child. "I can understand why you're upset about the baby, I guess, but I thought you enjoyed the rest. You're such a good cook, and the cabin has never looked this good before. I didn't know you hated it so."

Sitting up, Josie dabbed her tears with the sleeve of her buckskin shirt. "Oh, Daniel. It's not that I hate the cabin. What I hate is being a housewife and the thought of becoming a mother. I just want my freedom and my own ranch."

He looked deflated, like bread that hadn't quite risen to the occasion. "I guess I didn't realize how serious you were about that."

"I was, and I am, but how can I make that dream come true now? I'll be lucky if I can even get Sweetpea to Miles City come spring when my belly is out to here." She circled her arms in front of her stomach. "Even if I manage that, no banker in his right mind is going to give a pregnant woman and her kid brother money to start a ranch."

"Maybe you don't have to do that." Now his expression was full of hope. "What's wrong with ranching here? We're already raising cattle, and as you've mentioned before, you could be quite a lot of help."

Josie wouldn't let herself consider the possibility. "It's your ranch, that's what's wrong. I want my own."

"I wish I could think of a way to help you," Daniel said with a heavy sigh. "I'm afraid that sharing this place with you is about the best I have to offer."

Josie laughed bitterly, thinking how much easier these things were for men. "You could help by going to the bank yourself and asking for the loan. Of course, then my dream ranch would be in your name, not mine."

"I wouldn't waste your time worrying about that," he snapped. "Bankers won't give their money to a half-breed any faster than they will to a pregnant woman."

In all her scheming and planning, Josie had never even considered this, but Daniel was right, wrong as it seemed. He was painfully right.

"I'm sorry," she said softly, feeling the sting of something that went beyond guilt. "I never thought of that."

"Maybe you should have before you married me."

Daniel pushed away from the bed in such a rigid, cold way that Josie knew he wouldn't be coming back to it for a good long time. Maybe not even tonight.

"Cheer up," he continued tonelessly. "The name, if not the man you borrowed, should still be worth something to you. It might take a little longer than you had in mind, but Missus Daniel McCord ought to be able to get that loan once the baby is born. And don't worry—I'll be damn sure to stay away from town so no one catches sight of the man behind the name."

With that, he turned and strode out the door, slamming it harder than Josie had when she went chasing after the Indians.

As she feared, Daniel didn't come to their bed that evening, choosing instead to sleep up in the loft with his sons. Josie supposed she couldn't blame him for having hurt feelings, but she missed his warmth and the sense of security it gave her to lie there in his arms. She snuggled in his pillow, breathing deeply of his scent, and found some measure of comfort. Still, she spent most of the night tossing and turning with very little sleep.

The following morning, Daniel got up before the sun, managed to sneak past her as she dozed fitfully, and fired up the stove. It was the smell of coffee that finally awakened her, not the opening and closing of the door or the sudden lack of his presence. The smell. Josie's stomach got her moving before she was ready to face the cold room, and it got her moving fast. She barely made it to the garbage bucket before she heaved up the remnants of last night's supper.

Afterward, as she lay there panting on the frigid floor, a small voice whispered, "Are you sick, Ma Jofess?"

She turned her head to the side and saw a small worried face. "Just a little bit, Bang. Nothing for you to get upset about."

"I Two Moons. I can save you."

Josie forced herself to sit up. "Save me from what?"

"From sick."

"There's no need," she said, struggling to her feet. "I feel better already."

"I want *save* you," he insisted.

Although she didn't understand what drove him, Josie did see the urgency in his fiercely tense little features. She feigned a swoon.

"Oh, no," she cried. "I think I'm going to faint. Quick, Two Moons, pull out the chair for me."

He scrambled around behind her, did as she instructed, and then Josie let herself fall into the chair. "Oh, thank you, kid. If you weren't so quick, I might have fallen on the floor and hurt myself."

"Bang saves Pa." He grinned, showing off an uneven row of front teeth. "I save Ma Jofess."

It suddenly made sense. Daniel had told her that one of the boys had flung a war club at the renegades and probably saved his hide. Because he was the more aggressive of the two, she'd mistakenly assumed that boy was Two Moons. She supposed that now he either felt a lot of guilt over not having helped his father, or he was just plain jealous of his brother. In either case, the child had decided to make her the target of his good deeds. Seeing a way to smooth things between herself and the usually ornery twin, Josie lightly ruffled the top of his head.

"Thank you, kid. You're a really big help."

"What is kid?"

Josie thought about that a minute, wondering if Daniel would think the nickname any better than hell or damnation. She thought he'd find it acceptable, even if it wasn't quite as respectful as he would have liked.

"It just means child," she said, making light of the name. "Kinda like when your pa calls you mooksush, or whatever it is."

"Moksois," he said, correcting her.

"Right, *moksois.* What does that mean?"

He screwed up his round features, then pushed out his belly and wrapped his arms around it. "Big like pot."

"Potbelly?"

Two Moons laughed, his dark eyes twinkling. "Potbelly."

Josie laughed along with him, but not for long. Thinking of potbellies only made her remember what her own tummy would look like in a few short months. Feeling her stomach churn at the thought, she said, "Can you reach the biscuits, Two Moons? I'd think I'd feel better if I get part of one down."

Still glad to be of service, he scampered over to the counter and pulled himself up. It was then she noticed how much he resembled Daniel in profile. That made her wonder what her own baby would look like. And if it would fit in with the world of the whites, the Indians—or neither.

Later that morning, sometime around noon, Josie found that she was suddenly so tired that it was all she could do to keep her eyes open. The twins had gone outside to help their father gather wood, the dirty dishes could wait, and she hadn't gotten around to making the bed up yet. Dragging herself across the room, she flopped onto the inviting sheets and fell asleep before she'd even tucked a pillow under her head.

As she dozed, Josie dreamed of babies and soiled diapers, of miniature Indians chasing after her wearing huge warbonnets with feathers that trailed the ground. Somewhere in the middle of that dream she heard birds singing and The Black's high-pitched whinnies as he kicked against his stall. Vague scratching sounds met her ears after that, and then suddenly she had the sense that someone was nearby. Josie's eyes flew open to see that Sissy was standing next to the bed.

"Oh, my God," she said, sitting up. "You scared me half to death."

"Didn't mean to. I knocked on the door, then slammed it hard enough to wake the dead."

"I guess I was more tired than I thought." Josie climbed off the bed and gave her a quick hug. "I'm so glad you came. You look wonderful."

And she did. Not only did Sissy have a new dress with beautiful, intricate beading, something about her entire face had changed. She looked younger, for one thing, and her features no longer seemed to droop. Her hair was still bushy, but she wore it in braids, in the way of the Cheyenne. In fact, she could almost have passed as a full-blooded member of the tribe.

"It looks to me like you're starting to like living on an Indian reservation."

"Where I live don't matter much to me. I'm happy s'all." With a shy little smile, Sissy headed for the stove. "Mind if I help myself to the coffee?"

"Please do." Josie took a seat at the table, eager for a little female banter. "So how are you and Long Belly getting along?"

"Pretty good." Sissy slipped into the chair across from Josie. "We went and got hitched."

"Married?"

"That's right," she said, blowing on the rim of her cup. "At least we're hitched as far as the Cheyenne are concerned. Don't know how legal it is anywheres else."

The legalities weren't exactly what Josie was after. Living with Long Belly instead of going back to a whorehouse was one thing, but actually marrying him, even under the temporary terms she and Daniel had agreed to, was quite another.

"Tell me about all about it. Did he propose? Why did you say yes?"

"Ain't that much to tell," Sissy explained. "He wanted to get hitched and so did I. Then his family dressed me all up, painted my face, and stuffed me with a whole lot of strange eats. After that I was officially known as Buffalo Hair, woman of Long Belly. Something like that."

She frowned then, looking a little like the Sissy of old. "That's enough babbling about me. I came to find out if it's true that you took a shot at White Bull."

"White Bull?" Josie batted innocent eyelashes. "Who's that?"

"He's the big chief know-it-all in charge of the tribe. He come up here yesterday with some of the elders. Now do you remember him?"

Josie casually looked out the window, feeling anything but

indifferent as she admitted, "Oh, yes. Now that I think of it, I do recall a few Indians circling the corral yesterday and upsetting Sweetpea."

"Do you also recall going after them with a gun?"

"Vaguely." At least that was the truth. "And so what if I did? They were trying to steal my buffalo."

"Oh, princess, you cain't mean to keep that animal for yourself. The Cheyenne people worship that buffalo like it's some kinda God."

She'd figured out by now that a certain spiritualism was involved with Long Belly's quest to have Sweetpea presented to his tribe, but Josie refused to accept the idea that she had to give up her own dreams in favor of theirs.

"Why doesn't anyone care how I feel about Sweetpea or how she figures in *my* future?" she asked, wounded to think that her only friend in the world had turned on her too. "That buffalo is my only chance for freedom. Does she mean that much to the Cheyenne? What if they decide to sacrifice her or something?"

Sissy shrugged. "I don't know what-all they got in mind for her. I just know that Long Belly said I had to talk you into giving her up. I don't think he'd-a asked me to do it, if it weren't real important."

"And I wouldn't be trying so hard to hang on to her if I didn't think it was real important, too." Josie had a few more thoughts on the subject, but before she could express them, the crazies caught up with her again. She suddenly burst out crying.

"Hey, princess." Sissy reached across the table and patted her hand. "I was just wanting to talk. No need to get all drip-nosed over a stinking buffalo."

"Oh, Sissy," she said, still sobbing. "It's not just Sweetpea that has me so upset. You don't know the half of my troubles. I—I'm in a family way."

"You're knocked up?"

Josie nodded, then burst into a fresh round of tears.

"Well, isn't that something." Sissy's voice was soft with both wonder and longing.

"It's something all right." Josie couldn't have kept the sarcasm out of her tone if she'd tried.

"You ain't happy about the baby?"

"Hell, no." Grabbing the edge of the tablecloth she'd made out of her chemise, Josie blotted her tears. "How am I supposed to start up a ranch with a belly that stretches from here to Miles City? And what about after it comes? I can't see me rounding up strays with a coil of rope in one hand and a baby in the other."

"I guess maybe pulling out didn't work so good, huh?"

Still sniffling, she said, "Daniel says it was that stupid rubber, that it broke or something. It doesn't matter how it happened—what matters is that my life is ruined."

"Ruined, princess? I can think of lots worse things to ruin a gal's life than a little baby."

Both Sissy's tone and her expression as she stared down at the unusual tablecloth gave Josie pause. She realized in that moment that Sissy was probably thinking of her own lost child and the fact that she could never have another. They were at polar extremes when it came to thoughts of having their own children, but not so different in the area of regret.

"Too bad," Josie said carefully, "that we can't switch our bodies about now."

"That would be the answer to both our prayers." Sissy looked up with a smile. "Since we cain't do that, what are you figuring on doing?"

"About the baby?" At Sissy's nod, Josie shrugged. "Not much I can do but have it, is there? I sure wouldn't want to go through what you did."

"You wouldn't have to this early. Lola's got some French female pills and powders you can swallow that's supposed to rid a gal of what she don't want."

"Without messing up her insides?"

Sissy nodded solemnly.

Josie glanced out the window, noting there wasn't a cloud in the sky, and idly said, "I wonder how much longer this weather is going to hold up."

* * *

When Daniel and Long Belly had finished moving their cattle closer to the ranch, they headed back to the cabin. Feeling hot and sweaty in his buckskin shirt, Daniel peeled the garment off and soaked up the warmth of the sun for the first time in months. Long Belly, who'd arrived shirtless, said, "Will our cattle survive now that the snow is melting so fast?"

"I guess so, as long as they're able to get at what's left of the grass. If we get another cold spell and they move away from the barn again, I'll never be able to get enough food to them to help them through the winter."

"We need fences," Long Belly surmised.

Daniel laughed. "First we need the money to build the fences."

"We, our people, also need that buffalo."

"Oh, not that goddamned buffalo again." Sure he knew what was next, Daniel reined up The Black, then turned in his saddle until he could face his brother-in-law head on. "Did White Bull send you to me?"

Long Belly nodded and quickly looked away. "I am sorry, brother, but yes. My job is to bring the beast back to camp."

"Well, good luck, brother." Daniel turned his back on the man and urged The Black forward again. "Unless you can get Josie to herd the damn thing for you, and near as I can figure, she'll shoot you before she'll give up that animal, I don't see how you're going to get it to go anywhere."

"Broken Dishes will bring it to us if you speak to her on our behalf. She is your woman."

"She won't do a damn thing unless it's her idea." Daniel might have laughed, but right then he couldn't think of anything funny about his marriage. "If you want her to give up that buffalo, you're going to have to talk some sense into her yourself. She's not even speaking to me right now."

Since Long Belly had to already have known that his chances were zero when it came to swaying Josie, he didn't let up on Daniel all the rest of the way home. He jabbered on and on, trying to convince him that his duty as agent to the Cheyenne nation took precedence over a white woman who obviously was not thinking clearly. When Daniel explained why Josie wasn't particularly reasonable at the time, that she was pregnant and none too happy about it, Long Belly became even more determined to claim the buffalo for his people.

By the time the two men walked into the cabin, Daniel was more than ready to sic Josie on Long Belly, but then he discovered that she wasn't even there.

"What do you mean, she's gone?" he said to Sissy.

"Just that. She asked me to keep an eye on your young'uns until you got back, then she saddled up the mare and rode off."

Daniel threw his shirt across the back of the empty chair. "Where the hell could she be going?"

Avoiding him, not the question, Sissy looked down at her hands and began to pick at her fingernails. "Miles City, I reckon."

"Why would she even think about going there?"

Sissy shrugged, her gaze still pinned to her hands. "I mighta give her a little bad advice."

Chapter Twenty-Four

She saw Daniel before he saw her.

Actually, Josie spotted The Black first as the animal trudged up the sloppy trail. She continued to watch as Daniel drew near, liking what she saw, the way his hips rolled easy in the saddle and his nude chest glistened in the sun. His black hair was shiny and unbound, free to skim the tops of his shoulders, but she couldn't see his bright blue eyes. Daniel was staring down at the ground, tracking her, the intensity in his expression suggesting worry or even anger. She never meant to cause him either.

Josie hadn't known exactly where she was going when she left the cabin, or even why. She only knew that she had to get away. When she came across a sun-drenched knoll about a mile from the ranch, it occurred to her that what she'd needed the most was simply to be alone with her thoughts for a while. After spreading the mare's saddle blanket over a nice flat boulder still warm from the sun, Josie stretched out on it and let her mind go to work on her problems. Never had she planned to go all the way to Miles City. At least, she tried to convince herself of that.

As Daniel reached the spot where she'd turned the mare up the side of the hill, he reined in The Black, then suddenly looked up. Obviously startled to see Josie sitting just a few feet away, he threw himself off the horse and headed for the boulder. As he approached, Josie rolled to the ground and ran toward him.

"Daniel," she said, flinging herself into his arms.

He held her tightly, squeezing the breath from her lungs. "Christ, Josie. What are you doing?"

"I don't know," she cried, suddenly awash in tears. "I honestly don't know."

Daniel kissed her face, the tips of her ears—everywhere, it seemed, but her mouth—as he murmured, "Sissy told me that you were on your way back to Miles City."

Ashamed of herself, even though there had been no censure in his tone or suggestion that he knew why she'd considered making the trip, Josie admitted this much. "I had some thinking to do."

"And?"

"And nothing. I'm still thinking."

Daniel pushed her away and held her at arm's length. "You promised to stay on until spring. I thought you'd gone . . . for good."

Josie didn't miss the raw emotion in his voice or the erection stretching his tight buckskin trousers to the limit. Following her suddenly fascinated gaze, Daniel looked down at himself, then up at Josie again.

"I can't help it," he whispered. "I see you, I touch you . . . and I have to have you."

"Oh, God, Daniel. If only everything could be that simple." Josie was shaking uncontrollably, and yet she wasn't the least bit cold. "I want you, too."

"For now, maybe that's enough. It is for me." There was challenge in his tone as he added, "How about you?"

He released her then, no longer keeping her from him, but not moving to take her back into his arms either. They stood there staring at each other a while, a mere foot or so apart, both afraid to step into the flames that enticed as well as threatened to incinerate them. Josie burned for Daniel, feared she might go crazy if he didn't take her there and then, but knew if she went to him first, she'd be surrendering something that went beyond the physical. He was asking much too much of her. In an effort to lure him into doing what she couldn't, she parted her lips and ran her tongue over them, first the top and then the bottom. Her breasts were heaving and her legs were trembling with unholy desire, but she remained firm where she stood.

Daniel's eyes were drugged with lust, his hands balled at his hips in frustration. For a wild, torturous moment Josie thought he was going to step into the flames, then drag her down to the ground with him and take what they both obviously wanted so badly. But then, suddenly, a new resolve seemed to harden the rest of him.

"I'd have followed you all the way to Miles City, Josie, but don't ask me come the rest of the way now." His voice was hoarse with both need and emotion. "Give me at least this much of you. I won't ask for anything more."

Lord, how she wanted to go to him then, to surrender herself wholly and fully to this husband of hers and not think about tomorrow, her dreams, or the despair that washed over her whenever she thought of giving birth to the child in her womb. Something made Josie hold back, made her hang on to her control as if it were the deed to paradise.

Nirvana on earth, the man in the tight buckskin trousers, gave a very curt nod. Then he turned on his heel and headed back down the slope to where he'd left The Black.

They'd barely gotten back to the ranch before the weather started to turn. Though it wasn't much past noon, the sun disappeared behind rolling dark clouds, and the winds began to kick up. After a hurried supper, Long Belly and Sissy headed back for the reservation, leaving the uneasy family of four alone to nurse their private wounds.

Daniel, irritable and sullen, kept pretty much to himself,

excluding even his sons. Two Moons, while more resigned to having Josie around than before, had gotten over the urge to help her with the chores. Bang, sensing the general foul moods of those around him, sought out a corner of the cabin where he sat content to play with a small collection of stone arrowheads.

Once Josie finished cleaning up the supper mess, she slipped into Daniel's coat and headed for the door.

"Where are you going?" he asked, not looking up from the scraps of rawhide he was sewing together.

"Don't worry," she snapped. "I'm not going to steal another horse and run away from home. I just thought I'd go see how the ladies are getting along in the tipi. Is that all right with you?"

"Don't be gone too long," he grumbled. "I don't want to have to go chasing you down in a blizzard."

A cheeky reply was that close to falling off her tongue, but instead Josie decided to let the door speak on her behalf. She rattled the hinges she slammed it so hard, then took off for the forlorn tipi.

Announcing herself as she stepped inside, Josie said, "Hello? It's just me come to pay a visit."

One of the women shouted something in Cheyenne that Josie took as welcome. Pulling the flap closed behind her to keep the brisk wind out, she headed toward the warmth of the fire.

"Brrrr, it sure turned cold in a hurry, didn't it?"

Walking Strange looked up from the pile of buffalo hide on her lap. She smiled, as if that were enough to keep up her end of the conversation, then went back to her needlework.

"I hope you two don't mind me barging in on you like this, but it's tons warmer in here than it is in that cabin with Daniel."

Her needle suddenly still, Walking Strange gave off a feminine glow as she softly repeated, "Daniel." Then she quickly went back to her work.

Widows in mourning or not, it seemed that Daniel's brand of sensuality was capable of reaching even these two. Little Skunk, who was nursing her baby, wore the same fleeting

expression as her friend, then favored Josie with a slightly
amused expression.

"My husband is kinda irresistible," she said, again reminded
of her condition. "Lord knows I couldn't resist him. I don't
mind you two hankering after him, as long as you don't mind
visiting with me a little."

Josie of course got no argument from either woman.

"Good. I'm about to go crazy trying to figure out what I'm
going to do and how I'm going to go about doing it. Think
you ladies would mind helping me out some?"

They exchanged a glance, a few whispered words, and looked
at Josie and smiled.

"Thank you," she said, translating their conversation into
the words she wanted to hear. Warm now, Josie slipped out of
Daniel's jacket and hung it on a stake driven into the ground
near the flap. Then she dropped onto the buffalo rug, careful
to sit with her legs sideways, and went on with the one-sided
conversation.

"You're probably wondering why I'm feeling so low that I
had to come talk to a couple of women who don't have any
idea what I'm saying, right?"

Walking Strange smiled, and then did the most curious thing.
She bit off the thread she'd been working into the buffalo hide,
shook out the garment until it fell into its natural shape, then
draped it across Josie's knees. It was a jacket similar in style
to Daniel's, but about half the size and twice as ornate.

"For me?" Josie asked, bringing her hands to her breasts
in amazement.

Walking Strange nodded, then pointed to the child asleep in
the cradleboard beside her.

"Because I delivered your baby?" She shook her head.
"That isn't necessary. You keep this for yourself."

When she tried to return the coat, Walking Strange crawled
over to where Josie sat, took the jacket from her, and forcefully
slipped it over her shoulders, making damn sure she understood
that the gift was meant for her.

Josie figured that arguing at this point would probably get

both of her arms broken. She smiled and said, "Thank you. I don't know when's the last time I got a present—well, yes I do. Daniel made me this nice pair of boots, and Long Belly gave me some clothes and trinkets. Other than that, I haven't been on the receiving end of too many gifts during my lifetime. I really appreciate this. It's not often I get anything new."

She laughed as she thought of her last new item. "I did make a couple of fancy aprons out of my yellow dress. Do you think they count as new? The dress got ruined by soot from Daniel's damn stove, so I figured the material might as well be good for something. How about if I give one of those aprons to you? Would you like that?"

Little Skunk keep looking at her as if she were crazy, but Walking Strange was trying to get into the rhythm of Josie's conversation. She nodded wildly.

"I'll bring it to you on my next visit."

The baby stirred then, making the funny little choking cry of a newborn, and Walking Strange lifted her son from his nest of beads and animal hides. As she drew out her breast and adjusted the child's mouth to her nipple, tears welled up in Josie's throat, threatening to spill out of her eyes.

"That's another thing," she said, her voice cracking. "Seems like all I do lately is cry, me who probably hasn't filled a thimble of tears in all the years since my pa got murdered. Guess it's because I'm going to be having one of those babies in a few months, and I don't want it. What do you think of that?"

Walking Strange looked up from her nursing infant and smiled.

Josie returned the expression. "It's nice to meet someone who feels the same way I do. I can tell you understand that every woman isn't born to be a mother. I sure do. I've seen some downright terrible mothers that ought to be horsewhipped for even thinking about bringing a baby into this world, my own dear mother among them. Does it make me some kind of beastly, hateful woman because I don't want to be like her?"

Again Walking Strange smiled, this time with a little nod.

Ignoring the gesture, but accepting the smile, Josie said, "Why can't I get anyone else to understand that? I know if I tried to explain it to Daniel, he'd think I was the most dreadful, spoilt woman he ever met. Of course, I couldn't tell him anyway. He already thinks I'm a miserable excuse for a female because I don't fawn all over those little pisspots of his."

She laughed, thinking of them in terms of Hell and Damnation, then said, "It's not that they're such rotten little brats. Now that they've decided to let me live, they're no worse than any other four-year-old boys I've been stuck with. It's just that there's two of them, which gets me to tearing out my hair twice as fast."

The wind howled against the side of the tipi then, and a flurry of what sounded like little cat feet skittered along the buckskin wall. It was snowing.

"Well, I guess I'd better get going before I get snowed in here and Daniel has to come looking for me again."

Slipping fully into her new jacket, Josie hugged it tightly against her body and said, "Thanks again for the beautiful coat and the conversation. I'll be back, maybe tomorrow, to pick up where we left off."

As it turned out, Josie's next visit to the tipi was slow in coming. Another blizzard hit that night, dropping the temperature to fifty below zero and sometimes worse. It snowed for seven days straight in flurries so thick, visibility was less than forty feet. During that time Daniel had all he could do just to make it to the barn and back twice a day, checking during one of those trips to make sure the Cheyenne women had enough wood and provisions to get them through the worst of the storm. When it finally stopped snowing long enough for him to go check on the herd, the news he brought back to the cabin wasn't good.

"C-christ," he muttered, heading straight for the stove. "It's still at least f-fifty below out there."

As he warmed his hands, Josie removed his fur-lined hood and cupped his frozen ears in her palms. When his body had finally heated enough for him to stop shaking, she helped Daniel out of his coat and sat him down at the table with a cup of steaming hot coffee.

"How are the cattle?" she asked, easing into the chair across from him.

"They'd be better off dead." He took a few eager sips of coffee. "That warm spell we had left about a foot of water on top of the old snow, and now it's frozen solid. There's no way for the cattle or anything else to break through to what's left of the grass beneath. Those that are still alive are moving to lower elevations."

"Couldn't you take them some hay?"

Looking defeated, he shook his head. "I tried, but there are so many hidden ice shards under the snow drifts, The Black kept cutting up his hocks, and I had to turn back. I've got to get back out to the barn to doctor and wrap his legs so he doesn't turn lame on me."

Josie leapt out of her chair. "I'll do it."

"Sit down." Daniel pointed to her chair. "You're in no condition to be messing around with the feet of a stallion who's in a lot of pain."

"Dammit, then what can I do?" The outburst surprised even Josie, but not enough to slow her down. "If I don't get out of this house and do something besides bake cookies, I think I'm going to go out of what's left of my mind."

Daniel stared at her for a long moment. "I don't know what you're complaining about. You're safe and warm; you've got the boys to—"

"The boys are your problem," she said, grabbing her jacket off the rack. "You entertain their sorry little hides. Make them some cookies and tell them the same story over and over. I'm going out for a taste of freedom, so don't bother to come looking for me!"

With that, she slammed out the door.

Josie hadn't gotten down the stairs before she remembered the women in the tipi. Retracing her steps, she walked back inside the cabin to see that Daniel was sitting in the exact same spot wearing the exact same expression—abject shock. Without a word, she snatched up one of the aprons she'd made, then headed out the door again.

She'd cooled off by the time she reached the tipi, thanks in large part to the frigid weather, but still had enough fire left to launch into an immediate tirade once the women welcomed her inside.

"What the hell is wrong with that man?" she asked, knowing of course that she wouldn't be getting an answer. "One minute he treats me as if I'm fragile as spun sugar, and the next, as if I don't have a brain in my head. Does he think I'm so stupid that I'd march up to that idiot horse of his and let it kick me to hell and back?"

Her eyes wide with alarm, Walking Strange nodded.

"And does he think that I'd up and faint over the sight of a little blood?"

This time, both women nodded.

"Hah! I've sewed up more wounds and set more bones than most doctors, and never once have I so much as felt queasy. But what did our brave-hearted Daniel do when your baby was born?"

Looking very afraid, Little Skunk retreated to her corner. Walking Strange gave a tentative nod.

"That's right," Josie went on. "The big coward *fainted*. What's he going to do when I have mine?"

To make sure the women understood this much, she stuck out her tummy and stood sideways.

Walking Strange stirred the pot of soup she was tending over the fire, then glanced at Little Skunk with a knowing smile. She muttered something in Cheyenne, drawing the other widow out of her corner; then they both looked at Josie, pointed to her slightly swollen belly, and giggled.

"I'm afraid I haven't found the humor in the situation yet," she said, calm at last. "I believe I mentioned my mother while I was here about a week ago. Did I tell you that she was so sickly from having all those baby boys that I was the lucky one who got to deliver and raise them up for her?"

Both women seemed particularly interested in her tale. Josie was happy to oblige them. "That's why I'm so pissed about this baby. I've been a mother to one little pisspot after another since I was five years old, always a mother, never a child. I'm done raising up kids, especially the kind that come with the equipment capable of getting me into this fix. You hear? Done."

The widows exchanged a hushed conversation, then turned to her with sad faces.

Josie softened her tone, taking pity on the poor women. "Sorry if I yelled, but I had to talk to someone about my problem. If that isn't enough, Daniel seems to think that because I'm going to have a baby, I'm useless everywhere except in that stifling cabin, cooking and cleaning. I kinda wish that I'd had the guts to go on to Miles City while I had the chance."

She frowned, thinking about what she might have done had she made the trip, then found herself gripped with an urge to return to the cabin and Daniel. After all, it was about time to get their own supper on the stove.

"Well, thanks for listening again." Josie reached into the pocket of her jacket and pulled out the apron. "Here's that little gift I promised. You two are going to have to share it."

Walking Strange took the scrap of gingham from her hands and examined it, making quite a commotion over the ruffled edge Josie had added to dress the apron up a bit. First she tied it to her head, thinking it was a hat. After Josie fit it around her waist and tied with a big fluffy bow, she left it there, undoubtedly thinking it was the strangest, most scandalous skirt she'd ever seen.

While the two Cheyenne women fussed over her handiwork, Josie slipped out of the tipi and dragged herself back to the cabin. To her surprise, she found Daniel working at the counter. His hands and the floor were covered with flour and splotches of something brown. He was also, she couldn't help but notice, wearing the ruffled yellow apron she'd left behind. The twins were sitting on the counter, one on either side of their father. Both of their little brown faces were dusted with flour, and they were grinning like thieves, happy to be "working" with

Daniel even if they were making an even bigger mess out of the chore.

After hanging up her jacket, Josie moved a little closer to what could only be described as utter chaos, and asked, "What's going on in here?"

"We're making cookies like you suggested." Daniel turned around to face her. His cheeks, chin, and shirt were blotched with flour, and her pretty apron was smudged with molasses.

"It looks to me like you're wearing more dough than you have in the bowl."

"Actually," he admitted with a crooked grin, "I've cleaned up a lot of the mess. The boys got started on the dough while I was out in the barn wrapping The Black's legs. They were having a little trouble trying to figure out how much molasses to put in with the flour."

Almost afraid to look, Josie tiptoed across the filthy floor to the counter and peeked inside the bowl. It looked as if the trio of chefs had scraped the mud and slush off the steps, then glued it all together with a glaze of raw eggs.

"We made cooks," said Bang. At least she thought it was Bang.

Josie chuckled. "It looks to me like you boys and your pa are making some mighty sticky cooks. How many eggs do you have in there?"

Daniel shrugged. "About a half dozen, I guess. The boys said that's how many they saw you use."

"I used two eggs per batch, Daniel. We'll have cookies coming out of our ears for a month. You might as well get out of my way so I can try to turn this mess into something edible."

"I appreciate the offer, but we'd rather you didn't help out except for maybe giving us a few instructions."

Josie had a hard time reconciling Daniel's determination to continue the job with his appearance. The comical sight of such a virile-looking man wearing a frilly yellow apron, added to the splashes of flour and molasses he wore from head to toe, made him look as if he'd just survived a bakery explosion.

She tried hard not to laugh as she said, "I'm sorry about

storming out of here and being so testy and all, but I really don't mind cleaning up this mess and starting over.''

Daniel remained firm in his refusal, stinging her a little. ''Thanks, but if I don't learn how to do this now, who's going to fix our botched cookies when you're gone?''

Josie cocked her head. ''Gone?''

''You're still planning to leave come spring, aren't you?''

Something uncomfortable washed over her at the thought, a splash of both hot and cold. ''Thereabouts,'' she said, swallowing hard. ''I figured I'd probably better wait until after the baby comes.''

''Spring or late summer, doesn't much matter, does it?'' He leaned against the counter, then wiped his messy hands across the front of her apron. ''You've got my boys addicted to those damn cookies. Who's going to bake them up for the twins when you aren't bunking with us anymore—or have you decided to stay?''

Caught by surprise, Josie just stood there looking from Daniel to the boys, and back to Daniel again. He whispered something to Bang out the corner of his mouth, and then did the same to his twin. As the boys jumped down from the counter, Daniel suddenly took Josie's face between his hands.

''We want you to stay,'' he said softly, traces of molasses sticking his palms to her cheeks. ''In fact, we're prepared to do just about anything you want in order to make sure that you'll stay. Aren't we, boys?''

A twin hugging each of her knees, she heard one of their husky little voices say, ''Don't go, Ma Jofess. Don't go.''

The other—Two Moons, she assumed—tossed in his two cents. ''Ma Jofess-*seen*. Pa said.''

A roar that sounded like a great rush of water filled Josie's head. More tears, she assumed. ''Oh, Daniel,'' she whispered, her throat tight. ''You don't know what you're asking of me.''

''I think we do.'' He winked and smiled. ''The walls of a tipi are very thin.''

Had he overheard her one-sided conversation? Assuming that he had, she explained, ''Then you know that I can never be the kind of wife and mother you and the boys deserve. There's no way I could replace Tangle Hair in your lives. Ever.''

Daniel nodded thoughtfully. "No, I doubt that you could. She was a good and eager cook and very willing housewife. She was also a wonderful mother to the twins and would never have referred to them as little pisspots.''

Biting her lip as much to keep from laughing as crying, Josie glanced down at their dark little heads. "You and the boys must miss her terribly.''

"I'm sure the twins will always miss their mother in some ways. As for me . . .''

Daniel took her into his arms then, a child still dangling from each of her legs like a pair of baby possums, and whispered, "She wasn't half the woman you are, Ma Jofessine. Please don't go. We love you.''

Chapter Twenty-Five

The temperature stayed better than forty below zero for three weeks whether it snowed or not. During that time Daniel lost track of most of his cattle. The few he did locate on his rare treks outside were frozen dead in their tracks. Winter hung on through March with a tenacity he'd never seen before—and hoped never to see again.

During the long periods they were trapped inside the cabin, Daniel continued urging Josie to teach him how to cook several of his and the twins' favorite things. He didn't do this in anticipation of her leaving, but as part of his campaign to win her love. Since he already knew how to make fairly decent biscuits, it didn't take long for her to instruct him on methods of making them lighter and fluffier. She even complimented his cooking, claiming that his soups and stews didn't need any improvements, and moved on to the proper way of seasoning and roasting large clods of beef. Getting the hang of molasses cookies, however, looked as if it might just take a few more months. Or even years.

Romancing Josie was turning out to be even tougher than learning how to make those damned cookies. As a man raised in the wild, a hunter and a trapper, Daniel had absorbed a couple of hard, fast lessons through the years about all living creatures. Foremost was the rule that sometimes a wild thing could be tamed, and sometimes it couldn't. Those that wouldn't be tamed couldn't be trapped or they'd soon die. Daniel felt as if he were walking a fine line between taming and trapping Josie on an almost daily basis.

As it was, he'd nearly waited too long to recognize her wild side for what it was, and had come perilously close to pushing her right out of his life. If he hadn't accidentally overheard part of the conversation she'd had with herself in the widows' lodge, he figured she might even be back in Miles City by now, blizzards and all. Daniel now knew the only chance he had of keeping Josie with him was to love her exactly the way she was when he'd found her—unconquered and untamed.

There wasn't a lot he could do about their baby except try and be both mother and father after it was born, but there was plenty to do around the house. To help ensure the success of his plan, Daniel took the lessons he'd learned to the boys, teaching them to clean up after themselves, to make up their bed, and even to keep the floor of the cabin clean with a pair of little brooms he'd fashioned for them out of pine boughs. Josie still insisted on washing the dishes, although Daniel doubted she enjoyed it much, but now that the weather had cleared, she was spending more and more time outdoors or in the barn. Now that the sun was shining again, that could be a problem. Soon he would have to go in search of what was left of his herd, which meant that Josie would have to care for the twins and pretty much be confined to the cabin again.

Daniel glanced out the window at the new beginnings of spring. Although there were slushy puddles everywhere, higher sections of ground were covered with tufts of grass that seemed to have grown overnight. Some of these lush green mounds were splashed with clumps of bright yellow bells and lavender crocuses. Into this welcome change of scenery, Josie suddenly burst around the corner of the barn and dashed toward the cabin. As colorful of any of spring's bounty, her sun-kissed hair streamed out behind her, as free and untamed as the woman it adorned.

Afraid Josie might slip and fall on the snow melting on the stairs, Daniel hurried out the door to meet her. "Hey, what's the big hurry?"

"Walking Strange and Little Skunk are taking their tipi apart." Her cheeks were as colorful as cherry blossoms as she paused to catch a breath. "Do you think they're leaving us?"

"Could be." Daniel stepped out from under the porch and into the warm chinook winds. "We've got a real snow-eater blowing out here. We put their tipi up in the best spot to protect it from ice and wind, but now that the snow is melting so quickly, it'll soon be sitting in a big puddle of slush."

"Then maybe we ought to help them move it to a drier spot."

"First let me talk to them to see what they're up to." Daniel glanced over his shoulder. "The twins are napping and ought to be out for a while. Why don't you lie down and rest, too?"

Josie hesitated, clearly attracted by the idea, but said, "I will, but first I have to find out what my Indian friends are up to. Mind if I go with you?"

Daniel didn't mind Josie's company a bit, especially after they reached the side of the barn and discovered that the tipi was already down and transformed into a large travois. Both of their guests also had their babies tucked into cradleboards strapped to their backs.

"Going somewhere, ladies?" asked Daniel in Cheyenne. After they answered, he translated for Josie. "They're leaving the ranch. The weather is warming up so quickly, they want to return to the encampment now and send some family members back to collect the bodies of their dead husbands."

"Oh, my God." Josie grimaced and clutched her stomach. "I forgot about the men in the wellhouse. Are you going to ride along with the women to make sure they make it to Lame Deer?"

Daniel had considered the possibility, and even suggested it, but his offer was turned down. "They said they'll be fine, and that they know this area better than I do. I'm going to the barn to get the horse Wolf Lies Down left behind, so maybe this would be a good time for you to say your good-byes.''

"Oh, do I have to?" Again a grimace. "I know I'll cry."

"These days you cry just because the sun comes up. I'm sure they're used to it by now." With that little reminder of her condition and a quick smile, Daniel turned and headed for the barn.

Girding herself and thinking of her husband as a coward for leaving her to face the chore of making her farewells alone, Josie approached Walking Strange, who was still dressed in dirty, torn clothing.

"I wasn't figuring on you two leaving us so soon," she said, twisting the rawhide fringe on her bodice. "In fact, I was kinda hoping you'd be here when the baby came."

She patted her swollen abdomen, and immediately Walking Strange seemed to understand. The Cheyenne widow began murmuring soothing phrases and even gave Josie's tummy a comforting pat.

"If you're telling me that everything's going to be fine, I hope you're right. I have to admit that I've never been so scared in my life as I am when I think about having this baby, and not just the birthing part of it. How good a mother can I be when I don't even want to be a mother?"

Walking Strange smiled, looking as if she knew exactly what Josie had said, and threw her arms around her for an unexpected hug. Again murmuring Cheyenne phrases, she patted her shoulder, then released her and backed away. Josie thought she might have been crying.

Little Skunk approached next, wary as usual, and muttered something under her breath.

"Same to you, I guess."

Little Skunk didn't respond or even meet her gaze. Josie put a touch of amusement in her tone. "I expect you probably think I'm crazy doing all this talking when no one can understand a word I'm saying, but it sure has been good conversation for me. I thank you for putting up with me, even though you must think I'm nuts."

"I doubt she thinks you're nuts," Daniel said from behind as he returned with the widow's horse in tow. "You might be a little peculiar from time to time, of course, but never crazy."

Josie flashed him a grin. "You do have exceptionally good hearing, don't you?"

"Yes, ma'am, I most certainly do. In case you haven't noticed, I'm exceptionally good at most everything I do."

The look he gave her after that suggestive remark was intimate, to say the least. A little embarrassed, even though she knew the Cheyenne women couldn't understand what Daniel had said, Josie turned her back to them and faced her husband.

"I've already said my good-byes." Her eyes prickling with those confounded tears, Josie blinked them back. "I think I'd better go to the barn now before I start crying. Would you meet me there after the women have gone? I think something's wrong with Sweetpea."

"I'll be along in a minute."

Daniel watched Josie as she walked away, far more interested in her than that damned buffalo. He always wanted her, but something about watching her bloom with his child, as if she were another flower of spring, really woke up his libido and set his blood to boiling. Their lovemaking had taken on a new wildness now that Daniel no longer had to withdraw at crucial moments, but Josie still held something back from him, a part of herself she refused to release. As she had the night after they wed, she still refused to undress in front of him, claiming a modesty she sure as hell didn't show once she got him beneath the covers. Today Daniel intended to see every beautiful inch of his wife, to feast his eyes as well as his body as she writhed beneath his touch.

His thoughts going more and more to the moment he could hold Josie in his arms, Daniel hurried the Cheyenne widows off of his ranch, then headed straight for the barn. He found her standing near the feed bucket, an overturned can of precious grain at her feet. She was braced with one hand against the backside of a stall, and holding her belly with the other. She was also staring off into the distance, her features rigid with shock.

"Josie?" Daniel asked quietly. "Is something wrong?"

Her eyes went to him, then cleared, but her voice sounded dazed. "No. I just had a little bubble of gas, or something."

Thinking he knew what that bubble might have been, he made a guess as he drew near. "Did the baby move?"

"Baby?" She released her tummy. "No, nothing like that."

As always, Josie grew remote when talk turned to discussion of their child. It was as if speaking out loud about the miracle growing inside her body made it too real for her, and that by ignoring the subject altogether, it wouldn't be true. Daniel hated that Josie felt that way, but loved her so much he was willing to accept her attitude. Her pregnancy was such a forbidden subject that even Daniel tried not to think too much about the coming baby, refusing to let himself wonder if it would be a boy or a girl, a single baby or twins. Or which of them the child might favor.

"Daniel," she said, cutting off his musings. "I want you to have a look at Sweetpea. I think she—"

"Let's have a look at you first." Before she could stop him, Daniel took her by the waist and pulled her to him, caressing her hips and following the contours of her bottom. He hiked up the hem of her dress, feeling the nude woman beneath the buckskin. "Oh, my," he murmured huskily. "This is a nice surprise."

"It's wash day," she said, her voice catching. "S-stop that."

"Stop?" He cupped the mound of her sex, then caressed her there in a teasing, circling motion. "Are you sure that's what you want?"

"Y-yes," she hissed, leaning into his fingers. "For now, anyway. Tonight we can—"

"Now would be even better." Daniel not only left his hand where it was, but worked his fingers through the mat of burnished hair there until he felt nothing but moist, lusty woman. "Your Cheyenne friends are gone, the twins are asleep, and spring seems to have sprung up on me in the damndest place. Want to see?"

Josie's eyes rolled and her lashes fluttered. Her breath came out in a shaky sigh as she said, "Daniel, for heaven's sake. Why can't we wait until tonight?"

"Because, my love, *I* can't wait that long."

With very little resistance from Josie, Daniel lifted her up onto the apple crate directly behind them, bringing her hips level with his. Then in one swift movement he raised the dress over her head. She immediately snatched it out of his hands and tried to cover herself with it.

"Daniel! Have you gone crazy?"

"Why is it crazy to want to have a look at you? How can you still be so shy?"

Josie chewed on her bottom lip, her expression filled with concern, not modesty, as if she were puzzling out a great problem.

"All I want is the pleasure of looking at you," he whispered. "I love you too much to ask for more than that."

"Oh, Daniel, I wish—"

He placed a finger across her lips. "I swear, this will be enough."

Her eyes suddenly swam with something Daniel didn't dare believe was love, and then Josie released the dress and stood there naked before him, her gently rounded tummy somehow adding to her magnificent allure.

"Jesus, you're beautiful," he said, filling his eyes and heart with the woman he loved. "More beautiful than I even dared to dream you were."

Her breath was coming in little puffs by then, a sign Daniel knew well. His trousers were down around his ankles before she could even finish a surprised gasp. Then he went to her, kissing, fondling, and then finally filling each delicious inch of his wife's very responsive body. She came fast and she came hard, arching her back so rigidly, she nearly fell off the apple crate. Daniel had meant to prolong her pleasure and his, to luxuriate in the sensations and the intensity of the moment, but he convulsed on the heels of her climax in a mind-shuddering release, an explosion that almost took his feet right out from underneath him. His last lucid thought as he went over the edge was of heaven. And that he would never, for any reason, let go of the angel in his arms.

Later, after they'd cooled down a little, Josie lingered in Daniel's embrace, trading kisses and mindless words that were for him expressions of love. When he got around to pulling her dress down over her head and adjusting his own clothing, again he spotted the overturned can on the floor.

"What were you doing with the grain?" he asked, noting the bright red flush on Josie's cheeks as she smoothed her dress. "We're about out, you know."

"Oh, sorry. That was an accident." She dropped to her knees and began scraping the grain back into the container. "I was about to go check on Sweetpea and give her a treat, but I dropped the can when the baby—I dropped the can. Will you come have a look and see what you think of her?"

Daniel didn't miss how close she'd come to acknowledging their child, or the fact that even that special moment didn't take precedence over her damned buffalo. It seemed almost sacrilegious.

"How am I going to do that?" he snapped. "She pitches a fit if she so much as catches my scent."

"Hide behind the barn door, but please, have a look." Not even his sudden irritability could detract her from the beast. "She's acting really strange. Not only did she refuse to eat her hay this morning, but she started bullying the cattle as if she were trying to push them right out of the corral."

The three cows penned up with Sweetpea were due to calve soon. From what Daniel had seen so far, they and his shorthorn bull pretty much represented the last of his herd. Unwilling to take chances with those calves no matter how much Josie adored her stinky pet, Daniel not only accompanied her, but beat her to the back of the barn.

"If that buffalo is attacking my cattle," he warned, pushing the door open a crack. "We're going to have to get rid of her. Those cows are probably all I've got left of my herd."

Josie squeezed by him and looked out into the corral. The buffalo was grunting loudly and walking in circles at the far end of the pen. The cows were huddled together under the lean-to near the door.

"Sweetpea isn't attacking them," she said. "I'm going to go have a look at her. See what you think, okay?"

The moment Josie stepped into the corral, the buffalo stopped its aimless circling and raised its tail in anger. Then it charged.

"Josie—Christ!" Daniel stepped into the corral and made a grab for her, but she ducked under his grasp.

"Get back out of sight," she shouted. "I'm all right, but you're making her nervous."

"Goddammit, she'll kill you."

"No, she won't. Trust me."

True to the confidence her mistress had in her, Sweetpea stopped several feet short of Josie, but stood there sniffing the air, pawing the ground, and grunting. The beast couldn't see Daniel by then because he was hiding in the shadows just inside the barn, but she sure as hell knew he was there.

Josie slowly looked over her shoulder and whispered out the side of her mouth, "See what I mean?"

Daniel grumbled to himself, hating the idea of his pregnant wife trapped in a corral with a half-crazed buffalo, but he studied the enraged beast anyway, looking for clues to her odd behavior. If, however, for one moment it looked as if Josie might be in danger, Daniel intended to keep her from harm if it meant he had to wrestle the beast with his bare hands.

As usual, Josie's presence had a calming influence on the buffalo. She walked right up to the animal, shaking the can of feed, then petted its nose before offering a handful of grain. Sweetpea refused the offering, but allowed Josie to continue petting her and murmuring words of comfort.

Talking to Daniel now, she said, "I can't understand what's wrong. She won't even take the grain." Still talking, Josie slowly circled the beast, running her hands along its shaggy body as she went. "Maybe she's got a splinter or hurt herself somewhere. Do you see any signs of blood?"

Daniel knew better than to alert the buffalo by answering or questioning Josie unless he had some concrete facts, so he continued to watch quietly as she examined the beast. When she disappeared behind Sweetpea's slender rump, Josie suddenly popped right back out again.

"My God!" she said, her eyes huge. "She's dilated. She looks as if she's about to calve."

In his surprise, Daniel forgot himself and stepped into the corral. "That's impossible," was all he got out before the buffalo charged.

Ducking back inside the barn, Daniel managed to get the door closed a split second before a very lethal head crashed against it.

When he heard the animal moving away from the barn, he opened the door a crack and whispered to Josie, "See if you can get Sweetpea backed into a corner, then use that can of grain to lure my cows into the barn. If it's privacy she wants, it's privacy she'll get."

Again surprising Daniel with the ease with which she handled the situation, Josie herded her unusual pet to the far corner, where it immediately began to circle again. Then she quickly and quietly led the cows to the door, where Daniel stood at the ready. "Come on, girls," he urged, slapping their rumps to keep them moving. "You never know when your ugly friend out there will turn on you again."

"Be quiet, Daniel. She'll hear you." Josie clutched her throat and took several deep breaths. "I can hardly believe this is happening. I had no idea Sweetpea was pregnant beneath all that hair."

"I'm not so sure you're right, Josie. How would she have gotten pregnant? We didn't see any signs of a bull buffalo before or after winter."

She hesitated, thinking about that, then suggested, "Maybe the bull got killed or something shortly after he bred her. How long is a buffalo pregnant anyway?"

Daniel shrugged. "I don't know, maybe like cows, around nine months. What difference does that make? Sweetpea doesn't look any different than she did when she got here."

"But she does," Josie insisted. "Her fur is at least twice as thick as it was, and it hangs down to the ground. There's no way to tell what's been going on under there."

As if tired of listening to the argument over her condition, the great beast chose that moment to stop circling. Then she dropped to the ground. Without another word, Josie dashed out to where her precious pet lay. Moments later, Sweetpea gave birth.

From his vantage point so far away, Daniel couldn't quite see the new baby, but he did spot the glistening birth sack as it emerged. Stunned by the unexpected event, he got an even bigger shock when Josie exclaimed, "It's a girl, and she's almost as white as the snow!"

While he'd never actually witnessed the birth of a buffalo, Daniel had seen enough bison calves to know that they usually had red or rusty tan fur that darkened as they aged. Thinking that Josie had confused the birth sack with the animal's fur, he sneaked out the front door, circled the barn on the upwind side of the corral, and quietly approached from Sweetpea's blind side. By then the new mother had risen and licked her calf clean. Clean enough, anyway, for him to see that the impossible had occurred—Sweetpea had given birth to a white buffalo.

Daniel fell to his knees in both wonder and utter disbelief, then whispered as if praying, "Dear God in heaven."

Within hours of the calf's birth, it was scampering around the corral on spindly legs and greedily sucking the rich milk Sweetpea was producing on its behalf. Two Moons and Bang had awakened and now stood outside the corral with their father, as awed as anyone. Josie barely had a chance to get over the surprise herself, much less the opportunity to relish the sheer miracle of owning a rare white buffalo, before Daniel had to go and spoil the celebration.

"You can't keep this to yourself, you know."

Misunderstanding at first, she said, "Oh, I suppose we'll have a few unexpected visitors. I don't mind as long as they behave themselves."

He shook his head. "I mean, I hope you aren't planning to keep both buffaloes all to yourself."

"Why not? Since I own the mother, I also own the offspring, don't I?"

"Legally, I suppose you do, but I'm talking about something a lot more important—the spiritual significance this will have for the Cheyenne nation."

Josie looked from Daniel to his boys, who were staring up at her in undisguised worship. She hadn't actually thought about what she would eventually do with the white buffalo, but she did know that it was already worth its weight in gold, especially when it came time to secure a loan for her ranch.

Gazing out on the ungainly calf, she said, "Just how important is a thing like this to the Cheyenne?"

Daniel paused to collect his thoughts. "They'll see this calf as an omen, something that will signify healing and a chance for their dreams and visions to return."

"You mean they'll worship her or something like that?"

He shrugged. "Something like that."

Josie returned her gaze to the white miracle staggering toward her mother's teats and suddenly became determined to keep the rare prize for herself. "In that case, I don't see why the Cheyenne would expect me to turn her over to them. Can't the chiefs just come and visit her when they want to go into a trance? I won't mind."

Sighing heavily, Daniel said, "Let me put it another way, one you might understand better. This white buffalo isn't just some rare object that will make them hallucinate. To them, this will be like the second coming of Christ."

Chapter Twenty-Six

The news traveled fast.

Within days, tribal elders from both the Cheyenne and the Crow nations showed up, many of them bearing gifts. A few tried to use their offerings as barter in securing the animal for their own tribe. All of them looked on the calf as nothing short of a miracle. Josie was quickly renamed *Voestae*, White Buffalo Calf Woman, and the ranch and its treasure became the scene of utter chaos.

Indians were all over the place, most of them chanting and praying, and tipis dotted the meadow where Daniel had hoped to be fattening up his cattle for market—a herd, thanks to the terrible winter, that numbered only three cows, two calves, and one bull. The cows and their young had rejoined Sweetpea and her baby in the corral. The third cow, due to have her young any day, had taken up temporary residence in the barn.

Josie was down at the swollen creek with Daniel and the twins washing all the bedding in the house when another surprise visitor approached on horseback, this one coming in from the east.

"Doing a little spring cleaning, are you?" he asked, climbing down from his mount.

"Caleb!" Josie cried, dropping a soggy blanket in the creek and running to him. Hugging her brother close to her breast, she said, "I've missed you so much—what took you so long to come see me?"

"Been digging out from under that god-awful winter, I guess." He broke out of his sister's embrace and shook hands with Daniel, who'd approached. "We took a real beating down at the mission. How'd you folks do up here on the hill?"

Daniel blew out an exasperated sigh. "Like to froze to death a couple of times, and I lost most of my cattle, but we're doing all right."

Caleb nodded sagely, looking as if he'd aged several years since Josie had last seen him. "There's dead cattle carcasses everywhere. Word is that ranchers in our area lost sixty percent or even more of their herds. A lot of them went out of business."

"Jesus," said Daniel. "I knew other cattlemen must have suffered some, too, but I didn't know things were that bad."

"How bad can it be for you two?" asked Caleb, grinning like the young man she remembered. "I heard you went and got yourselves a white buffalo. Is it true?"

"It sure is," said Josie, linking arms with her brother. "Mind if we go to the corral so I can show him, Daniel?"

"Of course not." He shooed them away. "Go on and visit with each other for a while. The twins and I have this laundry situation under control, don't we, boys?"

Josie could hear the twins chipping away at their father in Cheyenne as she and Caleb walked away, undoubtedly scolding him for lining them up with even more "women's work" when they should be out playing in the sun instead.

When she and Caleb reached the corral, Josie gave him a full minute to gawk at the baby bison before she offered any commentary. Across the way, several chiefs decked out in feathered headdresses lurked near the tree line, straining to get a better view of the animal without upsetting its mother.

"I named her Miracle," Josie said at last, casting a loving gaze on the calf. "Isn't she beautiful?"

"Dang," said Caleb, as awestruck as anyone else who saw Miracle for the first time. "She's something all right."

"She's more than just something, Caleb. A white buffalo is sacred to the Indian tribes in these parts, more important even than the scripture the nuns are teaching the children at the mission. She's so special to them, in fact, that I've given Miracle to the Cheyenne. They'll take her to their encampment when she's weaned."

It hadn't been an easy decision to make, but Josie was proud of it and the fact that she'd made it for what she saw as all the right reasons. There had been no sense of guilt or further pressure from Daniel, or any selfish motives behind the decision. While Josie had never been particularly religious, she did recognize an all-being, someone who filled a far more significant slot in the universe than mere mortals ever could. If she played a vital role in what had occurred here on Daniel's ranch, it was simply the fact that she'd been chosen by Sweetpea to guard over her so that her spiritual offspring could be born into relative safety.

Josie suddenly realized that Caleb was looking at her with the same awe he'd reserved for the calf. "Well, ain't you something," he said.

Still uncomfortable with the decision, or rather the reaction of those who'd learned of her decision—Daniel and Long Belly had been fawning over her as if she were some kind of saint—Josie lost her temper.

"I'm not a greedy, selfish little hog, you know." She lifted her chin indignantly. "I can do the right thing by others when I figure out what the right thing is."

"I wasn't calling you greedy. I just know how much you used to hate Indians, s'all, and so it kinda surprised me that you'd do something so special for them."

Josie had to look away, her new best friend "tears" sneaking up on her again. "Yeah, well," she muttered, "I guess that's because I didn't used to know that Indians are simply folks like us—and that they're just doing the best they can to survive."

Caleb threw a surprisingly muscular arm across her shoulders and gave her a squeeze. "I'm proud of you, Josie. I come to pretty much that same conclusion after spending the winter working with them Cheyenne kids."

She had to tell him sooner or later. Now seemed the perfect opening. "Speaking of kids," Josie muttered. "It seems that I'm going to be having one of my own around the end of August."

Caleb released her as if she'd suddenly grown spikes. Then he hopped back a few steps, looked her up and down, and said, "You mean you're—ah, gonna be somebody's ma?"

She nodded, dislodging a single tear.

"B-but I thought marrying this fellah was a temporary thing so you could get a ranch. I never knew you was really gonna be his wife."

She shrugged, embarrassed. "Me neither. It just sorta happened."

Caleb propped one of his gangly legs on the bottom rung of the corral and draped his long arms across the top rail. Then he burst out laughing.

"What the hell is so funny?" Josie asked, hands on hips.

"I shoulda come to see you a couple of weeks back," he said, still chuckling. "But I was too afraid to stop by until I heard about the white buffalo."

"Afraid of what?"

Wiping the grin off his face, Caleb turned to her and said, "I was afraid to tell you that I ain't gonna be your partner no more. Silly, huh?"

Josie doubled up her fist and gave him a quick rap on the forehead. "What do you mean you aren't going to be my partner? I need you, Caleb."

In a hurry to put a safe distance between them, he tripped and nearly fell as he untangled himself from the fence. "You don't need me now that you're gonna be a ma."

"What's a baby got to do with our ranch? We're just a little delayed is all.'' She pointed to Miracle. ''Take another look at what we've got to entice a banker now. Not only do we have the last living buffalo, she is the mother of a rare white buffalo. With any luck, Long Belly will find the bull that sired the calf, and then maybe she'll have another. Bankers will be throwing money at us, Caleb. You can't quit now.''

He had the decency to look a little guilty, but surprising her, he stuck to his guns. ''Sorry, Josie, but I never wanted to be a rancher. I only agreed to be your partner because you wanted it so much.''

Even though something inside her wasn't as fully committed to the idea as it once was, Josie wouldn't let her brother off so easily. ''And now I don't matter?''

'' 'Course you matter, but now you're a wife, almost a ma—''

''Will you leave that blasted baby out of this discussion?''

Caleb looked at her cockeyed, but nodded. ''All right, but all's I was saying is that you got everything you need right here if you want to go into ranching. Me, I found another calling.''

Part of her wanted to continue arguing with him, but another, bigger part of Josie was more interested in this new side of her brother. ''What calling is that, Caleb?'' she asked softly.

Looking down at the toes of his boots, he shuffled his feet as he said, ''I'm gonna stay on at the mission with Father van der Velden. Maybe even become a priest like him.''

Since religion had never been a part of the Baum family life, this declaration came as quite a shock to Josie. She stood there staring at her brother for a long moment, wondering whether it would be appropriate to congratulate him or if she ought to just rap him alongside the head again.

Finally she said, ''What's got you so fascinated about church all of a sudden? Is it the Latin, the pot of smelly smoke, or do you fancy the long black robe and funny hats that priest wears?''

Caleb looked away from her and back out to the small miracle in the corral. ''None of that, Josie,'' he murmured serenely. ''What I fancy is peace, and love, and the chance to learn the reason for our existence. I'm happy helping others, and I want you to be happy for me.''

Feeling like a piece of cow dung stuck to the bottom of her own moccasin, Josie patted Caleb's back about the same time that Miracle, who'd been butting heads with the other calves, called to her mother.

"I'm sorry I didn't understand at first,'' Josie said, preparing to let her brother out of his promise entirely. "I was just—''

"Wait!'' Caleb said, staring intently at the white buffalo. He continued to study Miracle for a few minutes, then suddenly turned to Josie and said, "Did you hear that?''

She listened a moment. "What?''

"Your white *miracle* out there just bawled to get her ma's attention.''

Josie looked at him, wondering if too much smelly smoke could fog up a fellah's brain. "So?''

"Bawled, Josie, as in mooed.''

Her opinion didn't change and neither did the reply. "And so?''

"So I don't know much about buffaloes, but I do know that they grunt or maybe snort from the time they're born. They don't moo. Cows moo.''

Josie's gaze shot to the corral. "What are you trying to say?''

"That your miracle ain't nothing but what a rancher friend of Pa's from up north calls a *cattalo*.''

Josie swore her brother to secrecy, then kept the information to herself until later that evening. After Caleb had headed back to the mission and the twins were asleep in the loft, she finally made herself approach Daniel with the news.

"Feel like taking a little walk outside?'' The nights were still chilly, so she took her jacket off the rack. "I've got something I need to talk to you about.''

Daniel had been running himself ragged trying to put the ranch in order as well as keep the constant stream of visitors under control. For a minute she thought he was going to decline the invitation and turn in early, but he grabbed his own jacket and followed her out onto the porch.

"What is it, Josie? You're not having second thoughts about turning Miracle over to the tribe, are you?"

"No, of course not." The fact that he thought she might do such a thing grated on Josie, but the slight paled in comparison to the subject she had to bring up. Broaching it as gently as possible, she asked, "Has Long Belly found any fresh buffalo tracks yet?"

Daniel shook his head. "He started near the wallow that Sissy spotted a while back and has been circling it along with the area where you found Sweetpea, but nothing has turned up so far—not even tracks."

"Well," she said, eager to get it out in the open. "I believe all he has to do to trail the sire of that baby buffalo is follow your shorthorn bull around the pasture."

They'd almost reached the corral. Daniel stopped dead in the middle of the yard. "What did you say?"

"Caleb thinks your white bull fathered Miracle."

Daniel laughed. "I wouldn't normally put the words 'Caleb' and 'think' together. This is a joke, right?"

"No, Daniel. I wish it were a joke, but I'm afraid it's true."

He shot her a particularly suspicious look, then continued his journey to the corral. Although it was so dark that it was difficult to see, Daniel moved right up to the fence and studied the calf. Sweetpea, for once, seemed completely oblivious of his presence.

After a while, Daniel finally said in a very quiet voice, "Why does Caleb think my bull sired Miracle? She looks just like any other buffalo calf I've ever seen, except she's white."

Josie joined him by the fence. "Have you ever listened to her? She moos."

Daniel glanced back into the corral, then buried his face in his hands and groaned. "Holy Christ. She does, doesn't she."

"Caleb says that buffalo calves don't make the noises Miracle has been making. They grunt or snort."

"I never thought I'd hear myself say this, but Caleb's right.

I've been around buffalo of all ages most of my life. I don't know why I didn't notice that something wasn't right with her myself. Shit.''

Josie gave him a few minutes to absorb the shock, then addressed the more pressing issue. "What are we going to do? Our Cheyenne friends have so many hopes and dreams pinned on Miracle, I shudder to think what they'll do when they find out she's not quite what they thought she was."

He pondered this a long moment, head hung low, shoulders slumped, and finally straightened up with a weary sigh. "We aren't going to do anything. I can't tell them she's not really a buffalo. I simply cannot take the only scrap of hope those people have had in years and throw it back in their faces."

"But won't they figure it out sooner or later?"

"Undoubtedly. What's the harm if it turns out to be later?"

Josie considered this, knowing that Daniel was right even if it did feel a little wrong. It wasn't as if they'd sold the tribe a pig in a poke. They'd given the Cheyenne a spiritual gift, bestowing it with nothing but the best of intentions.

"I'm not telling—ever," she said, forging a pact.

"Neither am I." Daniel turned to Josie and pulled her into his arms. "What about Caleb?"

"I made him swear on a Bible that he'd keep our secret safe. He wants to be a priest, so I figure we don't have any worries there."

"A priest? Caleb?" Daniel laughed, but then quieted almost immediately. "Actually, that's not a bad idea. Working at the mission ought to cut the odds to zero of him carrying a gun and accidentally shooting some poor fool's head off. Neither one of you should be allowed to handle weapons."

Josie slapped at his chest. "Don't pick on me or my brother. He's my favorite, remember?"

Daniel kissed her forehead. "I remember. I also recall that Caleb was going to be your ranching partner. How can he do that and be a priest at the same time?"

"He can't." Josie sighed. "I guess I'll just have to go it alone."

"You don't have to, you know. Seems to me like you and I would make pretty good partners, and we already know that our livestock gets along."

Somewhere in the back of her mind, Josie knew that she'd been thinking the same thing herself. It would cost her the precious freedom she'd worked so hard to claim, but then, what was freedom if not the right to choose her own circumstances? She no longer felt trapped or dependent, stifled or caged. She was as free as she'd ever been in her entire life.

Snuggling against Daniel's chest, Josie whispered, "You mean you want to breed your bull to Sweetpea again?"

He shrugged. "Why not? If it worked once, it can work again. We might even get another white buffalo, one that we'll have to market as a—a—"

"Cattalo, according to Caleb."

"A cattalo, huh?" With a husky chuckle, Daniel took Josie's face between his gentle hands. "What about your ranch, sweetheart? I know how important it is for you to own your own ranch."

She shrugged, but didn't feel the slightest bit indifferent. "I'm willing to wait a couple more years before looking into that. You know, until we get your herd built up enough for the Cheyenne to take over."

"We?" he said, his voice faint with hope. "You mean you'd help me here for as long as it takes?"

"Sure. I know a whole lot more about cattle raising than you do, and might even get it done quicker than you think." She glanced at him with a conciliatory smile. "Besides, now that I know a few members of the tribe, I want to help them out. After all—the only bad Indians I know of are the ones who killed my family."

"Josie." Daniel reached for her, tucking her into his embrace. "What about after, when the Cheyenne can manage on their own? Will you still want your own place?"

"The Buffalo Queen Ranch? You bet I will."

She felt him stiffen as he said, "Then you haven't changed your plans about leaving us."

"Leaving you?" Those damnable tears sprang into Josie's eyes, but before she dissolved into sobs, she managed to say, "If I have my way, you're the ones who are going to have to do the leaving."

Daniel looked so confused by then that Josie quickly put him out of his misery.

"I never said you and the twins couldn't come live on my ranch, did I?"

PART THREE

No one can be perfectly free till all are free;
No one can be perfectly moral till all are moral;
No one can be perfectly happy till all are happy.
                                        —Herbert Spencer
                                        English philosopher

PART THREE

Chapter Twenty-Seven

Late August, 1887

Josie rolled off the bed and lumbered toward the door. "That's it," she said. "I'm not gonna do this."

Daniel beat her to the door, no big trick considering that Josie's belly was so huge, it took her an hour to cross the room.

He stood before her, blocking her path. "Where the hell do you think you're going?"

"Anywhere but here, so get out of my way. I am *not* doing this."

Daniel folded his arms across his chest and stood his ground. "You don't have any choice, sweetheart. That baby is coming whether you like it or not."

"Well, I don't like it and I'm not having it."

About that time another pain rolled across her belly and tightened the muscles there into a fist. She leaned against the wall, grunting involuntarily, like a damned buffalo in heat, and waited for the worst of it to pass. She glanced out the window and saw the twins playing in the yard. They were riding little stick horses and carrying toy bows and arrows, each doing his best to try and murder the other one first. Boys being boys. *Please God,* she thought, trying desperately to believe in Him. *If I have to have a baby, let it be a girl.*

"Josie, sweetheart." Daniel reached out to her as if thinking of drawing her into his embrace.

"Don't touch me, you no-account bastard. Leave me be a minute."

He leapt back as if scalded, then stood there waiting for her next signal. Unfortunately for Josie, it was a long time in coming. Not only were the pains hitting her so frequently now that it was all she could do to catch her breath between them, but once they grabbed hold of her belly, they hung on with the tenacity of a mink on a mouse.

When at last she could draw an easy breath again, Josie straightened her spine and said, "Get out of my way."

"No, goddammit. There's no place for you to go where you'll feel any better, and nothing you say or do is going to keep that baby from coming." He softened his voice. "You can't ignore it any longer, sweetheart. You're going to have a baby, and soon."

She knew he was right and that made Josie even madder. "What I should have done was ignore you. If not for you and that stupid rubber thingamajig, I wouldn't be in this mess."

"I said I was sorry about that. How was I to know the damn thing would break?"

"You just should have, that's all. You just should have."

The tears came then, although Josie wasn't even sure why she was crying, and she turned away from the door and dragged herself back to the bed. If the next pain was as bad as the last, she'd never be able to remain standing.

Daniel, as useless as tits on a boar, followed her and stood by as she rolled onto the mattress.

"That's better, isn't it?" he said, looking wounded the way the twins had when he sent them outside to play.

"Nothing is ever going to be better again," she cried, hating the sound of her own wails as they filled her ears. "It hurts, and I'm afraid."

Daniel had taken a seat in the chair he'd pulled up alongside the bed, but when she admitted that, he leapt to his feet again. "Let me go down to the encampment to get Sissy or one of the women who know about these things. I swear I won't be long."

He'd wanted to leave the moment he knew she was in labor, the no-account bastard. She probably should have let him go, but at the time, she'd been too scared to face any part of the ordeal alone. Josie wasn't scared anymore—she was terrified.

Reaching out to Daniel, she filled her palm with the hem of his buckskin shirt. Then she gave the material a vicious jerk. "You're not going anywhere," she said, her voice guttural, as if coming from somewhere deep in her chest. "If I have to suffer through this, so do you."

She might have said more had another pain not come along about then, squeezing the breath from her lungs and all thought from her brain. Still clinging to Daniel's shirt, she twisted and pulled on the material until she brought him to his knees at the edge of the mattress.

"If things don't go right," she said, gasping in the throes of the worst agony. "Promise you'll shoot me."

"Josie, for Christ's sake. How can you talk like that?"

"Promise, you no-account bastard. And Daniel—" She paused to catch her breath. "If it's not a girl, go ahead and shoot me anyway."

"Aw, Jesus." He reared back and peeled her rigid fingers off his shirt. "I've got to go get you some help. How about I send the boys in to keep you company while I'm gone?"

Josie heard herself snarl, or it might even have been a growl, but she managed somehow to control her temper. Something new was happening to her battered body, making the pains feel even more intense and the urge to push nearly unbearable. She couldn't be alone now. Not now.

"Don't leave me," she begged, meaning it. "It's time. Now is when I need you the most. Please, don't leave me."

Daniel came back to the edge of the bed, tentative and white-faced. "Are you sure?"

"Yes. We can do this together. Bring the pot of water we boiled earlier and set it on the floor at the foot of the bed." When that was done, she hiked up her thin nightgown. "Now I want you to take a look and tell me if the baby's head is showing."

He grimaced like a child with its first slice of lemon, and his face turned the color of sleet.

"Don't you dare faint on me, you no-account bastard. Not after what you've put me through."

Daniel drew a couple of deep breaths, then hunkered down at the foot of the bed.

"Well?" Josie said. "Can you see her head yet?"

He nodded and gulped.

"Is it out?"

He shook his head.

"Oh, God." Another pain rippled in a not-too-distant warning. "Quick, Daniel, wash your hands with a rag dipped in the boiled water, then get ready to help the baby out when I start to push. You got that?"

He rose up to meet her gaze. "You want me to pull it out when you push?"

Pain roared down on her, an avalanche of convulsing muscles that threatened to squeeze the very life from her, but Josie managed to say, "Don't pull on her, just help ease her way."

And then there was no time for talking, at least nothing that made any sense. Josie heard her own voice well enough to know that she kept on jabbering, but near as she could figure, most of what came out was a string of curses mingled with a few vague promises to God and a phantom buffalo.

At last the pain eased, leaving behind in her womb a peace and quiet that could only mean one thing. "Is she here?" Josie asked, suddenly too weak to lift her head.

"Yes! I've got the baby." Then, in a much quieter voice, "Mercy—I'm holding our baby."

"Why isn't she crying?"

"Is it supposed to?"

"Yes! Make her cry so she can start breathing. Take one of

the rags and clean her mouth and nose, then give her a little slap on the bottom. And Daniel—hurry!''

A moment later, the infant's enraged cries filled the cabin.

Josie closed her eyes, wondering when in hell those damnable tears would ever stop running. When she felt she could control her voice and emotions again, she asked, ''Did you cut the cord?''

''And tied it, just like you said.'' Daniel was sounding stronger by the minute.

''The afterbirth will come soon. You have to take care of it, too,'' she said, her own body reminding her of that last little detail.

''I know. I'm just getting the baby cleaned up and wrapped in the blanket.'' A moment later he got to his feet and came to the side of the bed. He was still pale, and a row of perspiration stood out just above his eyebrows, but his eyes were shining with pride and what she already knew was love.

''We did it,'' he whispered with awe as he settled the baby in the crook of her arm. His eyes were slick blue raindrops. ''You were great, Josie, just great. I love you.''

''I love you, too.'' Tears splashed down her cheeks, and Daniel kissed them away. ''You've got to finish taking care of me now. Do you remember what to do?''

He nodded, then swallowed hard. ''Ah, Josie—there is one thing I should mention. It's, well . . . I'm sorry your little girl isn't all she should be. Maybe we ought to call her Miracle, too.''

Confused, Josie looked down at the infant. She half expected to find that something was dreadfully wrong, but quickly saw that her baby was beautiful, with a full head of thick black hair, long slender fingers, and an extraordinary cute nose. She instinctively dropped a kiss on the baby's head, inhaling a scent she would never forget, and then eased the blanket open to examine the rest of marvel that she and Daniel had created. Her daughter's shoulders were large and well-muscled for a newborn and her trunk was long—almost as long as her legs, which were joined at the top by a healthy little spigot and the rest of his manly equipment.

Josie's head snapped up and she glared down at the foot of the bed. "It's a little pisspot!"

Daniel looked up from his task and grinned. "I kinda noticed that myself. What do you think? Shall we keep him or throw him back?"

Josie groaned, again kissing the top of her baby's head. "I guess we'd better keep him. Do you have any *boy* names picked out? I'm afraid I haven't been thinking along those lines."

Daniel shrugged as he took his place on the chair at the edge of the bed. "How about Daniel McCord, Junior?"

Josie shook her head. "Too confusing. We've already got Hell and Damnation. Why don't we call this one Thunderation?"

Daniel raised one indignant eyebrow. "I've got a better idea. Why don't we call him Jofess?"

She laughed, promising to think about it, and then Daniel turned serious and took her by the hand. "I want you to know," he said, kissing each of her fingertips, "that I intend to do everything I can short of staying out of your bed to make sure that this never happens to you again."

Josie considered that, then surprised herself by saying, "Well, it wasn't quite as bad as I thought it would be—I sure as hell didn't die. And since you're such a good father, and a pretty good mother, too, I guess I wouldn't mind if we were to have another baby someday. Especially if you think there's any chance of us coming up with a girl."

Daniel crawled onto the mattress beside her and scooped both Josie and the baby into his embrace. "That means you're going to have to keep me and this little fellah around a lot longer than you figured on. You sure you want to do that?"

Josie nuzzled the baby's head, then leaned over and kissed her husband's lips. "Oh, yes," she said. "I think I'll be keeping the both of you with me for a good long time."

She lay back against her pillow and brought the infant to her breast for the first time, feeling the baby enrich her soul as she nourished his body. It made her think of the person she'd been less than a year ago, and all that she'd been through. Most of all, gazing on her husband at her side and the baby at her breast, it made her realize how truly fortunate she was.

And to think, but for the toss of God's coin, she'd have been born male . . . and missed out on being the happiest woman alive.

AUTHOR'S NOTE

With the exceptions of Father Aloysius van der Velden and Sister Ignatius McFarland, all the characters in this book are purely figments of my imagination. I set *Untamed* in the year 1886 because the winter of '86–87 has been documented as one of the worst on record in the Montana and Dakota Territories. That winter was particularly hard on cattle ranchers, most of whom lost fifty to seventy-five percent of their stock. The experience so devastated Theodore Roosevelt, who owned a ranch in the Dakotas, that he quit cattle ranching and went into politics.

The Cheyenne names you'll find scattered throughout the book are all authentic, culled from biographies and historical books on the Northern Cheyenne tribe. The only exception is "Daniel Two Skins," a name I made up myself. The Saint Labre Indian Mission is still going strong, and today includes a wonderful museum where many Cheyenne artifacts are available for viewing. Cheyenne traditions remain vital to tribal members today, including strong ties between members of the same family, band, and tribe, and a mutual sharing of goods. Theirs is a give-away lifestyle based on spiritual values. I hope, in keeping with Cheyenne traditions, that I've been able to give to you, dear reader, a glimpse of what it meant to be a part of this great tribe.

I'd love to hear from you. I can be reached at PO Box 1176, El Cajon, CA 92022; by E-mail at s.ihle@poboxes.com; or on the Internet at www.poboxes.com/s.ihle.

ABOUT THE AUTHOR

Sharon Ihle is the award-winning author of a dozen historical romances set in the American West. She swears that one of these days she's going to pen a novel set in Scotland, especially since she can write off the trip and visit her London-based daughter at the same time. Word has it, however, that she was last seen poking around in the dusty old gold mines of Arizona. Stay tuned. . . .

BOOK YOUR PLACE ON OUR WEBSITE AND MAKE THE READING CONNECTION!

We've created a customized website just for our very special readers, where you can get the inside scoop on everything that's going on with Zebra, Pinnacle and Kensington books.

When you come online, you'll have the exciting opportunity to:

- View covers of upcoming books
- Read sample chapters
- Learn about our future publishing schedule (listed by publication month *and author*)
- Find out when your favorite authors will be visiting a city near you
- Search for and order backlist books from our online catalog
- Check out author bios and background information
- Send e-mail to your favorite authors
- Meet the Kensington staff online
- Join us in weekly chats with authors, readers and other guests
- Get writing guidelines
- AND MUCH MORE!

**Visit our website at
http://www.zebrabooks.com**